THE SHADOW

OTHER BOOKS BY
KIMBERLY RAE

STOLEN WOMAN
STOLEN CHILD
STOLEN FUTURE

SHREDDED
SHATTERED
RESTORED

CAPTURING JASMINA
BUYING SAMIR
SEEKING MOTHER

ABNORMAL RESULTS
SOMEDAY DREAMS
THE STREET KING

NON-FICTION TITLES:
CAPTIVE NO MORE
OVERCOMER
SICK & TIRED
YOU'RE SICK, THEY'RE NOT
WHY DOESN'T GOD FIX IT?
LAUGHTER FOR THE SICK & TIRED

PRAISE FOR SHREDDED
BOOK ONE IN *THE BROKEN* SERIES

...this book really blew me away! So many nice little Christian novels out there, but so few that really attempt to be life-changing....It makes such a difference!... I was so taken away with the story. All the emotion, the drama, the romance and tenderness, the action, adventure. I couldn't wait to see what happened but I didn't want it to end either. I really can't say enough good things about it and how much I enjoyed it. WOW!... I was nervous with anticipation and crying and so caught up in it all. I had to put the book down to give myself an emotional break. :) ... I rarely cry over books, but I think that other than Karen Kingsbury, [Rae is] the only other author that has made me cry while reading a book. -Sue

Shredded was compelling, convicting, and compassionate at once...a deeply disturbing reality packaged with grace, humor, and a sweet love story. I couldn't put it down. –Joy

I think this is [Rae's] best book yet. It is so relative to today's church and how we treat people. It is a wonderful mix of relationships, interwoven with suspense and love. It is a must read for anyone who thinks their past defines them and gives them no hope, whether they are a victim of human trafficking, child abuse, or just bad decision making, because Jesus can wipe the slate clean. –Wanda

I love it!!!...[Rae's] best book yet I think! Can't put it down. –Mary

I couldn't put the book down... a compelling story of suspense and romance. -Jeanie

...incredible. –Michael

This is an intense book! Very well written, great character development....I don't know someone that couldn't identify with one or more characters in it, the heart, the heartbreak, the discomfort with someone they don't know/understand, the living in fear. I LOVE Candy's character....She is so raw and real....I literally cried. I cannot say enough about this book. I literally couldn't put it down. It was SO GOOD. -Amy

...hands down my favorite author. –Tiffany

Warning!! You won't want to put it down once you get started!! ...there's no stopping. Awesome, awesome book!!!! -Sue

Wow. Here's what I can say, years after my first encounter with Shredded: I didn't realize it at the time, but it changed me and gave me a new level of compassion for the hurting. It showed me my own pride and blindness. It made me a better Christian, better mother, better counselor--and I can't recommend it highly enough. – Joy

Rae brings to light difficult subject matter with empathy and restraint, gracefully exploring the pain of overcoming violation and trauma through the eyes of the victims. Rae's characters are realistic and endearing. This is an uplifting story about the courage it takes to reform a community and care for the marginalized and neglected.
– Publisher's Weekly

PRAISE FOR SHATTERED
BOOK TWO IN *THE BROKEN* SERIES

...absolutely amazing–very interesting characters and very suspenseful! – Sue

I was enthralled the whole time....I so desperately needed this balm for my soul. – Laura

I stayed up way too late two nights, because I could not stop reading....I can't wait to read Restored! [Rae has] taken a horrible, disturbing topic and presented it in a true, but appropriate, acceptable way.... – Betsy

I just couldn't put it down!... I know in my heart that Shattered will be a great success and touch the hearts of every reader.... I also feel compelled to share that perhaps Shattered could reach an even larger audience, a targeted audience with a vested interest focusing on prevention-Christian educators, counselors, parent teacher associations, etc... Imagine Shattered as part of an age appropriate required reading for specific classes within school curriculums, support groups for students, outreach programs, increased awareness for students leaving home for the first time and entering college or ministry, and most importantly, the number of potential victims saved from a life of slavery. – Chris

...enjoyable and expertly written. – Jeanie

This book is amazing...loving it...not ever wanting it to end....these books touch a place in my heart. – Laura

This book held my interest and hit a nerve at the same time.... I read the book straight through (staying up until 2 in the morning on a week night!) because I was riveted by the authenticity. – J.

...excellent and convicting! – Jacqueline

Kimberly does a good job putting a difficult topic into a form people can accept and digest. This book will hold your interest and expose a nerve that needs awakening at the same time. The different perspectives of the various characters to sexual abuse and the prostitutes is a great representation of how Christians struggle in dealing with this issue. Sexual abuse and trafficking are realities not just in large cities but also in small town America. Whether the topic is something you are familiar with or not, this book is a must read! Even better...join in the fight to putting an end to this evil. – Christie

...so full of suspense, it was hard to put down.... The book definitely left me hanging. I wanted to read the next one NOW! – Wanda

Riveting! – Carol

[Rae] is seriously my favorite author now! Her books keep me so engrossed that I have to force myself to go to bed....Even though it is fiction, the words hit me as hard as something I might read in a devotional. – Mary

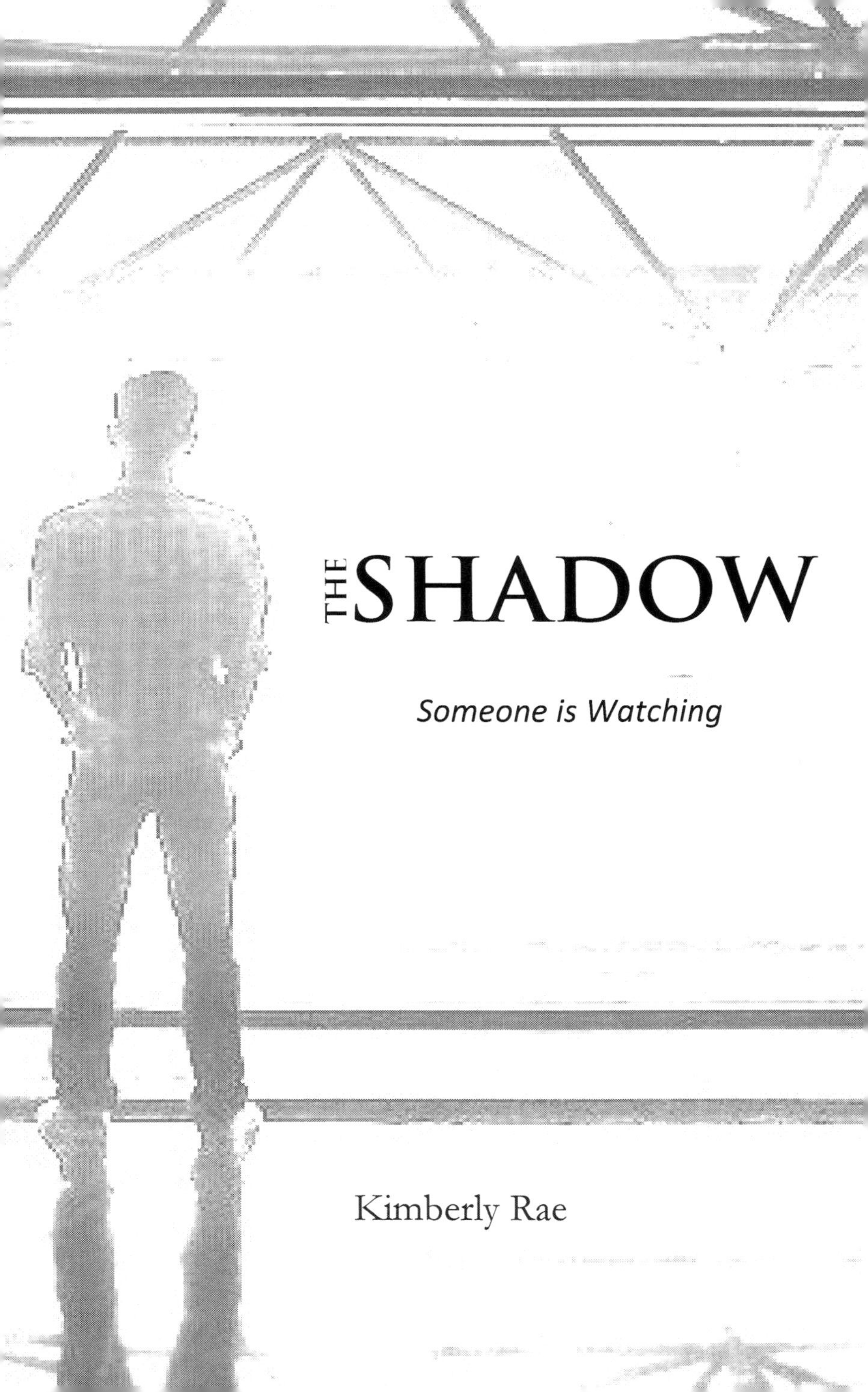
THE SHADOW
Someone is Watching
Kimberly Rae

THE SHADOW

Copyright © 2017 by Kimberly Rae

www.kimberlyrae.com

Cover Design: Narrow Way Design

All rights reserved. No part of this book may be reproduced or transmitted in any form or by any means, electronic or mechanical, including photocopying and recording, or by any information storage and retrieval system, without permission in writing from the author. Unless otherwise noted, all Scripture verses taken from the Holy Bible, New King James Version. Copyright © 1982 Thomas Nelson Inc. Used by permission.

Library of Congress Cataloging-in-Publication Data
Rae, Kimberly
The Shadow/Kimberly Rae - First edition.
Pages 355
Summary: "Meagan Winston is suspected of drug trafficking on her trips to India. As former Marine Cole Fleming searches for the truth, he discovers clues of a possible stalker, but is the stalker real, or has Meagan created the possibility to distract him? Meagan herself fears trusting Cole. Is he truly there to help her, or is he the enemy in disguise?"
-Provided by publisher.
Library of Congress Control Number: 2017906967

ISBN-13: 978-0-9993041-0-5
[1. Romantic Suspense-Fiction. 2. Romance-Fiction 3. Suspense-Fiction 4. Human Trafficking in USA-Fiction. 5. International Human Trafficking-Fiction. 6. Drug Trafficking-Fiction.] I. Title. II.
Title: SOMEONE IS WATCHING.

Printed in South Carolina, the United States of America

The full characters and events in this book are fiction. Aside from the grandfather, any resemblance to real people, living or dead, is coincidental.

DEDICATION

to the real-life
Rahab's Rope team,
especially Emily Cohen,
whose hair-coloring story
sparked the idea for this book!

You are all heroes.

1

Thursday, December 25
3:30 p.m.

Lucias Maddox Moore licked his thin lips and sighed. Meagan Winston was special. Extraordinary, really. She had to be tired from this last eleven-hour flight to Atlanta, as he was, but still she smiled at disembarking passengers near her and even helped an elderly woman with her bags before reaching for her own. Within the next twenty-four hours, her hair would be blond again. She always dyed it back after she returned from India. Lucias knew these things. He knew Meagan better than anyone. Perhaps better than she even knew herself.

"Need help?" Lucias edged around a woman holding a fussy baby, and with his free hand grasped the small red carry-on Meagan had used every trip for the past three years. He pulled it down from the overhead compartment and placed it into her outstretched hands.

"Thanks." Her eyes met his for a brief moment and she smiled.

The baby near him cried, and Meagan turned from him to pick up the pacifier the kid had thrown to the floor. She wiped it clean with her bright red scarf and handed it to the frazzled mother.

Look at me, Meagan. Smile at me again. Lucias clenched his briefcase, hating it when she gave her smile, the smile he lived for, to the baby instead. She cooed at the kid then pulled her carry-on down the narrow aisle toward the exit door of the plane. He watched from behind as he had all six trips, dreading their parting, scrambling for a way to delay it.

This last trip had been the most successful, his largest sale yet. He'd brought back something special this time, something that would be worth a lot to his connection. All because of Meagan. He had to find a way to thank her, to tell her how much she meant to him.

Lucias quickened his pace the moment he stepped from the tunneled jet bridge onto the carpeted airport terminal floor, but other passengers merged between them. The woman with the baby stopped right in front of him to dig a ratty stuffed animal out of her diaper bag. He moved to the side and ran to catch up. He almost called out Meagan's name.

Instead he came to a sudden halt in the center of the concourse passageway and watched her walk away. Again. Now was not the time, or the place. It had to be when no one else was around. He looked at the crowd rushing around him and felt his breathing quicken. Claustrophobia slid up his spine and clamped tight around his throat. Lucias counted his steps toward the shuttle that would lead him out of the world's busiest airport. There were too many people, too many strangers, all of them probably judgmental hypocrites like his old co-workers, so quick to claim he had an anger problem.

His co-workers didn't know him at all. He hadn't been angry when he did it, just hurt. Claudia had rejected his love, had been cruel, had laughed at him. The police had never found any evidence, they never even found a body, but he still lost his job. His co-workers were afraid of him, afraid he'd done it, but they didn't need to be. He was good to people as long as they treated him fair.

The shuttle doors closed him in. He tried to calm his heart rate and ignore the heavy, fish-tinged breaths puffing out of the pot-bellied businessman to his right. The shuttle shot to twenty miles an hour within seconds, and fish-breath man grabbed the metal pole with the hand he had just used to wipe sweat from his neck. Lucias positioned his feet in a stabilizing position, both hands clamped around his briefcase handle, safe from the billions of bacteria thriving unseen across the surface of the pole, the walls, the people. "Arriving at B Gates," the robotic voice announced above his head. He liked it better when they called them concourses. The doors opened, people exited, and he inhaled a lungful of clean air before a new batch of bodies crammed in around him. No, even if he caught up to Meagan, the six-million-square-foot Atlanta airport was not the place to tell her his feelings.

"Arriving at A Gates." He jostled his way through the open doors and headed for the escalator that led to baggage claim. If he hurried she might still be there, collecting her two charcoal grey suitcases that he knew bulged with jewelry.

He stepped off the escalator and strained for a glimpse of the baggage area. His foot caught on the wheel of a passing child stroller, and his briefcase flew as he tumbled to the ground.

The woman pushing the stroller halted. "Are you okay?"

He scrambled to his hands and knees. "Where is it?" He grabbed the edge of the stroller and pushed it out of the way. "Where is it?" he shouted.

The woman saw the briefcase just as he did. She picked it up but he rose to his feet and snatched it from her hands. "It's mine!" He backed a step away and clutched it to his chest. People around them stopped, looked. Some pointed fingers. He forced himself to hold the briefcase in one hand and drop it to his side. *Turn. Walk calmly. Act natural. Think about something pleasant.*

When Meagan was frustrated, she would find a place to sit down, then close her eyes and bow her head. He followed her example and chose a bench far from the staring people near the stroller. He dropped his chin and tried to think. This was not the day to bare his heart. January eighth was a possibility. Meagan's twenty-sixth birthday was circled in red on his pocket calendar, her name in bold. But to wait two weeks would be hard. He'd rather create the perfect moment before then, something special they could both remember forever.

He clenched the briefcase and battled inner fears. What if she laughed at him? Rejected him? He could not bear it.

He lifted his face and gazed across the baggage claim area. Just beyond the fourth carousel, she materialized into view, so beautiful, like a touchable ray of sunshine. She headed for one of the seven possible exit doors, pulling the two grey suitcases, her red carry-on slung over one shoulder. He watched until the crowd hid her from his vision, like clouds blocking the light.

His heart stilled. Meagan wasn't anything like Claudia. If he did everything just right, Meagan would care for him. She had to.

2

Friday, December 26
12:35 p.m.

The metallic blue SUV, sleek and brash, pulled onto the road from Lakeshore Mall's parking lot and barreled straight toward Meagan Winston's little VW bug.

In her lane.

Meagan's pulse skittered and her hands gripped the steering wheel to the point of pain. If this was a game of chicken, there was no chance she would win. That big vehicle would pulverize her beat-up jalopy, and at the speed it traveled, her car would not be the only thing broken.

"Get out of the way!" Meagan screamed. She swerved to the left, her bones jarring as the car lurched up onto the sidewalk. She swerved again to avoid the neighboring ditch. A telephone pole and fire hydrant filled her view next. Meagan slammed on the brakes and turned the wheel to maneuver away from the pole. The car fishtailed and stopped hard. Her forehead slammed against the steering wheel.

Had she hit the fire hydrant?

No water gushed from the red landmark. Not yet anyway. Meagan put the car in reverse. As she edged backward, she felt the car lower slightly and groaned. Her first day back in the country and she'd hit government-owned property. All because some crazed driver couldn't confine his joy ride to the right lane.

The right lane…

Meagan put the car in park and dropped her head against the steering wheel. "Oh no."

Minutes passed. She had not yet lifted her head when she heard a slight tap on the window. A look up revealed the flashing blue lights of a Gainesville Police Department car in the rearview mirror. With a long sigh, she used the handle to roll down the window. "I'm so sorry..." she began.

"Are you okay, miss?" An officer in uniform stood next to her car. His breaths formed tiny clouds before they faded into the cold air. "We got a call saying another car tried to run you down."

"A call?" Meagan squinted at the policeman. The midday sunlight blinded her every time he shifted from one foot to another. "I didn't call anyone."

"No." He looked over the pad of paper in his gloved hand. "The call came from an anonymous source. A male. Said you were driven off the road and might need assistance."

The only assistance I need is to have my head examined, and not because I have a new lump on it. "I'm not hurt." She might as well get it over with. "And it wasn't the other car's fault. It was mine. I was driving in the left lane." The officer looked out at the road. His gaze took in the skid marks that ran up the sidewalk to the edge of her back tires. What a humiliating day. "You see I just got back from India yesterday, and—"

"Ma'am, I need to ask you to step outside the vehicle for a moment."

Meagan obeyed. "They drive on the left side over there, and I got used to it. I drove to several places this morning, and got it right all the other times, but there weren't any other cars on this road—well, not till that car, and I—"

"See this line along the edge of the sidewalk, ma'am? Would you mind walking down that line for me? One foot in front of the other up to the telephone pole."

He thought she was drunk? "No, you don't understand. I—"

The man in uniform, no taller than herself, but armed with a weapon and the law, gestured toward the line. "Go ahead."

Meagan glanced at the mall parking lot. She hoped none of the women in her Bible study were out shopping for after-Christmas sales today. If he did a breathalyzer test on her and someone saw, she'd never hear the end of it.

"You said you were in India?" the man asked. He jotted something on his notepad.

"For two months." Meagan shivered, holding her arms out as she walked the line. She never did have good balance. She glanced back and saw disbelief all over the man's face. No doubt he heard plenty of creative stories by people trying to get out of tickets. Hers was going to sound like a whopper. "I work with a group that rescues women in brothels, trafficked victims who've been sold against their will."

"Oh, really?"

Meagan thought of looking back but knew it would knock her balance off. "I go out twice a year to help with the children's program."

"You said it was with women in brothels."

"Yes, but many of them have children, and the kids grow up in horrible conditions, stigmatized and rejected by their society." There. She'd thrown in enough big words that he should know she wasn't drunk at least.

"So you work with Mother Theresa or something?"

Mother Theresa died in 1997, but that wasn't a pertinent fact at the moment. "My group is called Rahab's Rope. We're a Christian ministry that—wait, I have a card." Glad for the opportunity to make it look like she hadn't just fallen off the line, Meagan returned to her car and reached through the open window for her purse. The officer took the card she offered, looked it over and then wrote a few things on his pad.

"Well, miss..." He looked at the card again. "Miss Winston, I had already decided you must be telling the truth, because nobody would make up something so elaborate." He held up the card and smiled. "But thanks for the proof just the same. Since you didn't seem to do any damage to public property, I'll let you go today." He grinned. "But do us all a favor and stay home next time until you're sure which side to drive on, okay?"

Cheeks burning, Meagan assured the officer she would pay more attention, then climbed back into her little bug and rolled up the window to block the sound of his amused chuckle. He'd enjoy telling this one back at the precinct.

That thought triggered a memory. Meagan turned the handle the other direction and the window lowered again. "Officer, can I ask you a question?"

He had bent over for a closer look at the fire hydrant, but stood at her call. "Sure."

"Do you work with someone named Cole Fleming?"

"Cole Fleming?" He looked at his notepad and shook his head. "No, I've never heard of a Cole Fleming. Why do you ask?"

Meagan bit her lip. "I got a call this morning from a guy by that name. He told me he was coming into the store this afternoon to ask me some questions."

"About what?"

She shielded her eyes with her hand. "He didn't say."

"And you think he's a policeman?"

"He said he was with the law."

The officer frowned. "Hmm. Sounds a little suspicious to me, since he's not with our department. But he could be from an outlying area, or from Atlanta. When you get to a phone, you should call and run a check on his name."

"I'll do that. Thanks."

She turned the key and was about to put the window up again when he put a hand on the edge of the door. "But don't call while you're driving," he said, chuckling again. "You should focus on the road till you get to wherever you're going."

I deserved that. "Yeah, will do." With a wave, she backed up, then turned until the car perched at the edge of the sidewalk, ready to pull back onto the road. She looked left, then right, then in both directions again. Oh dear...

"The right side," he called out behind her.

Meagan drove out onto the road, on the right side, trying to ignore both the ache in her forehead and the laughter coming from the sidewalk behind her. What a day.

3

Friday, December 26
1:30 p.m.

"She just went in the store. You shouldn't have roped me into doing this, Steve. She seems like a nice person." The song on the CD ended in abrupt silence as Cole Fleming turned the key and shut off the ignition.

"We see nice people every day who are criminals. I'm guessing what you mean is, she's pretty."

Cole ignored that. "She got in an odd sort of accident on her way here." He balanced the phone between his shoulder and his ear so he could reach back for his tablet. "A policeman made her walk the line, and she wasn't all that steady."

"You were watching her?"

"Following her. I did a background check and found out she lives at the same address as her grandparents. I drove by to see if there were two buildings on the property or one."

"And?"

"Just one."

"She's probably mooching off them to save money for her habit."

"You don't know that."

"No, but I'm good at assuming."

Cole surveyed the stores, still decorated with lights and wreaths, most of them closed for the holidays. If Steve were there he'd snowball the woman before they knew all the facts. "Are you sure she's the one you're after?"

"She's on every single run, right there on the video. How can it be any clearer? Look, we're overlapping with the DEA on this one and they need something to tell their guy in India. An address, name, anything. He can find lower rung meth sellers on the streets easy enough, but that isn't going to help. We need her direct contacts—the one in India and the one here."

Cole stepped out of his car and pocketed the keys. He took another quick look around the quaint downtown square. No one had followed the woman into the store, and he didn't see any loiterers who looked too alert. The cars parked parallel to the store were all empty. Two cars on the opposite side of the street had occupants: one in the passenger seat, one in the driver's seat. The second car, a grey Oldsmobile, pulled out and left. Cole shoved his sunglasses back over his cropped black hair to rest on his neck like he had eyes in the back of his head, an old habit from military days. "You should be doing this yourself," he said into the phone. "Not me."

"Yeah, but I'm running three cases right now, not to mention I don't want to be recognized."

"By her?"

"By anyone. There could be others in on it with her."

"You're paranoid."

"That's why I never lose. I can sense all the possibilities."

Since Steve was not present, Cole allowed himself a small eye-roll. "Can you sense my desire for a large meat lover's pizza?"

"Ask her to dinner."

"Yeah, that'd be classy."

A truck drove past and backfired. Cole tripped and landed on one knee, helpless against the sudden flashback triggered by the sound and the impact:

She removed her headscarf to reveal glorious waves of long black hair and features that would inspire poetry. Delilah, he'd named her, the woman with haunted eyes, who asked for secrets.

"Don't do this," he pleaded.

Her hand wrapped tight around the grenade. "I have to," she said. "I warned you. I told you." They both heard the unmistakable roar of the lead tank of his battalion's envoy. She removed the safety clip. "There is no other hope for me."

"Please..." He reached out.

She pulled the ring. He had two seconds to assess the facts. Distance. Trajectory. Length of time before her grenade would detonate the eight other explosives strapped to her body.

The number of his men who would die...

"Cole, are you there? Can you hear me?"

Cole shook himself free of the memory and stood. "What did you say?"

"I said just get her to come here and I'll do the rest."

"And then I'm out of the picture, right?"

"Right."

Cole hesitated at the door. He swiped a hand across his chin. "And even though I live in Gainesville now, you're not going to call me up every time you need a side job done, right?"

"This was a one-time thing. I appreciate the help."

"I don't—" Cole realized Steve had hung up and didn't bother to finish his sentence. He surveyed his surroundings again, this time for quick exit routes, another skill he'd never expected to use as a civilian. A large amount of his experiential training, both in and out of combat, was proving useful in his new life. Too useful for his comfort.

He swiped his phone to record mode and slipped it into the inside pocket of his jacket. Comfort didn't matter. Neither did his personal feelings or impressions. "Time to get the job done," he muttered. He pushed open the door to Rahab's Rope and found himself in a heaven for women who loved jewelry and pretty things. He stood just inside the door, a bull afraid to step too far into the china shop.

Meagan Winston stood twenty feet away near the register. She was taller and more lithe than he'd expected from his study of online photos and surveillance from a distance, and her hair was a different color than the photos he'd examined, and shorter. She had flown in just yesterday. What twenty-five-year-old single woman chose to fly internationally on Christmas Day instead of spending time with family or friends? What kind of woman got tested for driving under the influence during lunch hour?

The facts all pointed in the same direction. She was the one.

Friday, December 26
1:30 p.m.

Lucias arrived moments after Meagan but parked across the street, noting his mileage counter had tripped ninety thousand one hundred miles exactly. He wanted to park next to her, get out and talk to her, but he couldn't today. He wasn't wearing the right clothing. Didn't have the right name. So he waited, watching, making sure she was safe. Her stride was purposeful—she always strode purposefully—as she walked from her little yellow car to the front entrance of the store.

His heart filled at the memory of the day he met her, at that very store, the first day of February, 2010, back when the sparkly jewelry had appealed to his eyes, before the terrible headaches. She had been kind to him. She gave him a tour of her store and told him about her trips to India. Lucias' contact had wanted him to cross over to South America to expand their drug trade internationally, but from that day on, for Lucias there was no option but India.

A car door slammed. Lucias looked back to make sure the police had not followed Meagan to the store. It was not a police car, not a marked one. The man who emerged was big. His broad shoulders stretched his open suit coat so much, Lucias doubted it would button. The wind nudged his jacket off his barrel chest and revealed a gun holster strapped over his left shoulder. It wasn't empty. Lucias watched through his rearview mirror, shaking, as the giant pushed his dark sunglasses off his eyes and looked at the sign that said, *Rahab's Rope, a Global Marketplace*. He walked toward the store, talking on his phone, looking around. He saw Lucias. Was he an undercover cop? Had Lucias somehow raised suspicion? Had someone discovered that the little vial of colored sand-art packaged in his trunk wasn't a cheap souvenir?

With trembling fingers, Lucias put his car in gear and merged into traffic. He had to get away, get home, right now. He could check on Meagan later.

That man had better not do anything to the woman he cared about, or he would pay. Lucias would do anything to protect Meagan.

4

Friday, December 26
1:30 p.m.

"Your hair! What happened?"

Meagan stepped back and angled her head to look in the mirror positioned behind the cashier counter. A stranger stared back. It wasn't just that ten inches of hair was gone and it was a different color; her loose Indian-style top flowed even more than usual. Indian curry and her stomach typically had a love-hate relationship, but this trip the love part had been missing entirely, sending her home minus a few pounds she had not needed to lose.

Then there was the bruise where her forehead had hit the steering wheel an hour ago. Nothing like a big black-and-blue mark to inspire people to ask what stupid thing she had done lately. She'd stick with the story about her hair.

"It turned orange," she told Brianna, the newest intern at the store, whose own chestnut hair cascaded in curls down to her waist. "The stylist said it had been dyed too many times and there was nothing she could do." Meagan shrugged. "So now I'm a pageboy."

"That's not a pageboy cut. You're a pixie," Brianna corrected. She reached to move Meagan's bangs aside. "Is that a bruise on your forehead?"

Meagan pushed the hand away with a laugh. "Don't worry about it. Whatever you want to call my hairstyle, the short length is great for showing off this latest batch of earrings I brought back from India." She glanced in the mirror again at the silver wire hoops their Indian partners had styled through and around jade beads, creating a design unique to Rahab's Rope. Her gaze drifted up to her forehead, and she arranged her bangs to cover the skin better.

"These are my new favorites. I'm so glad I didn't have the stock in my bag when I got mugged."

"You got mugged?" Brianna dropped the marketing postcards she'd labeled and bent to retrieve them from the floor, calling up from where she crouched, "What happened? I hadn't heard anything about that."

"It was the last day there, and I've had the creepiest feeling since that someone is following me. It was so strange, this—"

Their pleasant-sounding bell announced an arrival. Meagan swiveled on her cork-heeled sandals to tell the customer the store was closed until New Years. She should have locked the door. "Welcome to Rahab's Rope. We're doing inventory today, but—"

Her words faded to silence. Was this bulky, intimidating man Cole Fleming? She had given him the store address when he'd asked about meeting her, not willing to share home information, a precaution she felt doubly thankful for now that she knew he wasn't a policeman. Not a local one anyway. Maybe he was a reporter out to sneak a good story and just lied about being with the law, or he might be a lawyer for someone they'd been instrumental in prosecuting. Whatever he was, if he was a liar she wanted nothing to do with him.

Brianna put a hand on the counter and pulled herself up enough to peek toward the doorway. "Wow," she whispered, and added with a giggle, "Weren't you just saying this morning how hard it was to find a guy taller than you? What are the chances ..."

"Shh!" Meagan directed back toward the counter.

What would her perfect guy be like? Brianna had asked the question just that morning. She hadn't teased when Meagan said he had to be a guy she could look up to, both physically and spiritually, but she had joked about Meagan's stipulation that he not be too thin. Meagan didn't have anything against thin men, but if she got to create her dream man, she was particularly attracted to ones who had some meat on them.

This guy was downright beefy. His sport coat stretched around muscular shoulders and even the hands passing his tablet back and forth were huge. He stood standing just inside the door, surveying, a crease of concentration between his eyes. She followed his gaze around the room, encompassing jewelry, scarves, window-hangings and woodwork. When his eyes stopped on her, she wondered what he saw that made him frown. A glance down at her white broom skirt and turquoise silk top, embroidered in white and accented by one of their finest necklaces, told her all her clothing pieces were where they should be.

"I'm looking for Meagan Winston," the superman in a suit said, and Meagan blinked.

Brianna stood and her sudden appearance behind the counter seemed to startle him. "That's Meagan," she said brightly, pointing. "I'm sure she'll be happy to help you find what you're looking for."

She was too far away to jab with an elbow. Meagan hoped her smile looked unembarrassed. "I'm Meagan. What can I do for you?"

He assessed her with his eyes, rather boldly, but without any indication he was flirting. "I'm Cole Fleming. We talked on the phone this morning. I'd like to ask you a few questions."

"Um...are you a lawyer?" She decided he couldn't be with a newspaper. Journalists usually tried for charming. This guy was as charming as a brick.

He approached and she noted they were the same height. No, she wore heels, which meant flat-footed he'd be taller than her.

"FBI," he said.

What a chatterbox. He stood, feet spread, hands positioned at his sides but not relaxed. She brought her gaze up to his wide face with its prominent jawbone and chiseled features. His eyes were a dark green, almost emerald, the exact same shade of his shirt. "You're with the FBI?" she asked.

He quirked an eyebrow. "Today I am."

She crossed her arms. He had called her that morning *before* she ran off the road, so it couldn't be about that. "What do you want to know?"

"You should give him a tour," Brianna offered.

Meagan resisted the urge to throw one of their coffee-table books at her young, grinning friend. "He's not a customer, Brianna. He just wants—"

"A tour would be great."

She eyed him, and after a moment said, "Alright, Mr. Fleming. This way please." With some effort, she morphed into professional mode and ignored the man's unnerving silence as he followed her around the room. Pretending he was an average customer, she regaled him with stories of how their work began and different women whose lives had been changed for good. Tears gathered when she talked about the children she had hated to leave just days ago.

"It's difficult to get the women out of the brothels, for many reasons," she explained, pushing aside wooden doors attached to the wall via wheels that slid along a metal rail. They opened to reveal space where they stored materials and created new designs. "But we have had great success rescuing children who are growing up there. Brothel children are ostracized in their society, so giving them a place where they are treated with love and value can make a big difference for their future options."

"I'm sure it makes a difference to their present hope as well."

She noted with curiosity how his eyes had softened when she spoke of the children. "Yes, I find loving the children, and being loved in return, is the most rewarding part of what I do." She hadn't planned to say that, but when his eyes turned to her and some kind of connection passed between them, she did not regret her words. "And best of all, we get to offer them the unconditional love of God and the eternal freedom that only comes through Jesus Christ."

The corners of his mouth moved, as if he was trying to make them go upward into a smile, but then he frowned again and his next words surprised her.

"Would you be able to leave work for a couple of hours?"

Both her eyebrows shot up. "Excuse me?"

She had led him back into the main part of the store, close to the cashier counter. Brianna listened to their conversation with unveiled interest.

He did not seem embarrassed or even shy. "I'm sorry, Miss Winston, but I'm afraid I have to ask you to come in for questioning."

5

Friday, December 26
2:15 p.m.

Meagan reached out to steady herself on the cashier counter. "What?" she asked. "Wh—why?"

The black-suited man lifted his arm and rotated his shoulder counter-clockwise. His face remained impassive. "I'm afraid I can't give you that information. Your name has shown up in reference to an investigation I am helping with. I'll need you to come with me."

Meagan heard Brianna gasp behind her, followed by the sound of postcards fluttering to the floor. "I most certainly will not," Meagan announced.

The sliding doors between the shop and the back room slid open with a protesting squeal. Kelsey Sanders, owner of the store, peered through and motioned to Meagan, a question in her eyes. When Meagan shook her head, Brianna whispered, "I'll go," then said loudly, "Coming, Kels." She gathered the postcards into a clump and dropped them onto the counter. "Don't say anything interesting until I get back."

Meagan rubbed the tense spot on her forehead. Another squeak let her know the doors to the back room had either been opened wider, or slid shut. They needed to oil those runners. She dropped her hand to see Kelsey whispering to Brianna, gesturing Meagan into the work room. Something was not right.

"I think..." Meagan faced Cole. "Would you excuse me for a minute?"

He frowned. "Miss Winston, I—"

"I really don't have time right now to—" Meagan's own interruption was cut off by the appearance of a third person in the doorway. Alexia Rivera moved into the space just behind Kelsey's right shoulder, mascara running lines down her face; her outfit, as usual, woefully inadequate for the season. Nine months locked in a basement had caused her to forget things like the need to check the weather before dressing for the day.

Brianna left Kelsey and Alexia in the doorway and made her way back to Meagan. "She's in bad shape," Brianna said, not needing to gesture back to the girl now weeping against Kelsey's shoulder. "The guy who trafficked her is up for parole and she's terrified he's going to come after her."

"Meagan," Alexia called out. She motioned for her to come. "Meagan!"

Meagan turned to face Cole. "I need to go."

"But I need to—"

Would the guy not give up? Alexia whispered frantically in Kelsey's ear and Meagan saw Kelsey's face tighten. "Meagan," Kelsey said with a calm softness Meagan knew was her chosen tone for intense situations, "there's a code red for you."

She nodded. She could see that for herself.

Kelsey glanced at Cole and then locked eyes with Meagan. "And a code blue."

Meagan felt the blood drain from her face. Alexia was looking at Cole Fleming with unmasked terror. Brianna let the postcards she had retrieved fall back on the counter. She murmured, "I've been here all summer and no one's used code blue." She abruptly veered around the cashier counter and grasped Meagan's elbow. "We have to go."

Meagan was not about to leave this man in their store while they hid in the back room. She faced Cole Fleming and said with slow and measured words, "I want you to leave now."

The man looked from Meagan to Brianna, who took baby steps away from them both as she tugged on Meagan's arm, urging her to follow. "You have to come into the FBI office with me for questioning," he said.

Meagan clasped her hands in front of her. "Do you have ID that shows you're with the FBI?"

His forehead creased. "Not with me. Listen, I—"

"I will not go anywhere with you, and I am politely asking you to leave."

"But you haven't answered my questions yet."

"You haven't asked any." She released her arm from Brianna's painful grip and led the way toward the front door, her hand out in the way she might guide a lingering customer after closing hours. "The shop opens again on New Year's Day. If you return then with some ID, we can talk."

She opened the door. Brianna stood rooted to her spot, her hand still out, looking much like a mannequin someone had irresponsibly left in front of the cashier counter.

"But I—" he started to say.

Meagan didn't let him finish. "Thanks for stopping by, and Happy New Year." The moment he had both feet outside, she pushed the door closed and locked it. She smiled and waved through the glass then made her way back to the register. She grabbed Brianna by the arm and rushed her to the back room. Once behind the stockroom door, surrounded by organized drawers of beads and scarves and partially-made product, Meagan whispered to Kelsey, her voice shaky, "What happened? Why did you say there was danger to me personally?"

6

Friday, December 26
2:25 p.m.

Alexia curved around Kelsey to cling to Meagan. "Brianna said he wanted you to go in for questioning. Don't you remember?" She wiped at her cheeks, spreading a large black smear across her face and onto the back of her hand. "Don't you remember how I got trafficked? How my pimp got his girls?"

Kelsey's red curls bounced around her freckled cheeks as she patted their youngest rescued victim's shoulder and handed her a tissue from a nearby box. "He'd tell them he was a plainclothes policeman and that they needed to come in for questioning, and once he got them in his car, he'd drug them," Kelsey said, still using that deceptively calm voice that helped their young victims but always put Meagan's senses on edge.

"Yes, I remember." Meagan nodded. "But he's in jail."

Alexia dropped into a chair, trembling. "What if he got out already? What if he hired that guy in the store to come after you? Don't ever get in a car with a man you don't know!"

Meagan's ears started ringing. She told herself to be rational. It wouldn't make sense for Alexia's trafficker to target any of them. He went after pre-teens. She glanced at Kelsey and saw her own thoughts mirrored. Unless it was for revenge.

"Brianna," Meagan whispered, turning so Alexia could not see as she composed her face. "We need to distract Alexia. Get her thinking about something else. She's starting to panic."

"She's not the only one." Brianna stood twisting her scarf into multiple knots. "What if she's right? I became an intern here to help the people who were fighting trafficking, not to meet up with a real trafficker right here in the store!"

Kelsey covered over the fear radiating from Brianna's voice with her own calm statement of, "So, Meagan, on the chance that this man is really who he says he is, doesn't he fit all those things you described as your perfect guy?"

Meagan blushed. She knew they would have a hard time keeping Alexia hidden and safe if she was checked into the hospital with another panic attack, but still, could Kelsey not have come up with a better topic? "Well, I'm not sure," she responded, trying to mimic Kelsey's ability to look and sound casual when she felt anything but. "He was tall and muscular and really good looking, with short dark hair and amazing eyes. Did I mention all that? Oh, and he dresses well. I loved that suit."

Brianna and Alexia stared at Meagan for several beats. Meagan told herself the humiliation was for a good cause. "Well?"

Alexia stopped crying. She swiped the blackened back of her hand across her miniskirt. "My pimp was short and chunky, with a comb-over."

Kelsey cocked her head. "I thought you said he had dreadlocks."

"They're fake. He puts them on when he goes on the streets to try to look cool."

Meagan dropped into a chair, letting a real smile show through this time. She grabbed another tissue and wiped Alexia's cheeks as if she were still a child, which in many ways she still was.

"Do you think he truly is with the FBI?" Brianna asked. She looked down and seemed surprised to see her scarf in knots. She tugged at one, which tightened the knot rather than unraveling it.

"I doubt it." Meagan tossed the dirty tissue into the trash. "And this is a perfect example of why I don't want you, or anyone else, trying to find me a guy." She opened a stand-alone plastic drawer set next to the table and pulled out a worn photo album made with thick, handcrafted paper from India. She flipped through page after page of photos, each one labeled with a teen girl's name, age, and current situation. Most said "Freed" or "Back with parents," but the few that said "Missing" or "Returned to pimp" were still hard to view.

She pushed the album toward Brianna. "I've spent the past five years hearing girls tell me their traffickers were good to them, were handsome, clean-cut, or promised them the world. The traffickers gave them jewelry or a safe place to stay. They pursued the girls, offering whatever they wanted most, until it was payback time."

Alexia nodded vigorously. "Yeah, that's true. Except that mine wasn't good-looking. He looked like a skunk and smelled like one too most of the time. But his phone icon was really cute. And he sent me the nicest texts. I didn't know he was a skunk until it was too late."

"Not every guy is like that." Brianna closed the album and slid it back across the table, then pulled her scarf from around her neck and handed it across to Meagan.

"I know," Meagan said. She unwound the scarf and wrapped it around Alexia's exposed shoulders. "But I also know that emotions distort thinking and I don't want to make a mistake that has lifelong consequences. I can know all the signs, know the patterns, but if my heart gets involved, who's to say I won't give it to a guy who ends up being a liar or a fake?"

Alexia hugged the scarf tight around her and started rocking in her chair. Kelsey sent Meagan a look. Meagan winced and mouthed, "Sorry." She scrambled for something random to say.

Brianna rescued her by perching on the table and saying to Kelsey, "If I stay here five years, am I going to be as cynical about love as she is?"

"I'm not cynical," Meagan argued with forced lightness to her voice. She returned the book to its place and shut the drawer.

"Yes, you are. You avoid men whenever you can, like they're all untrustworthy or bad."

"I don't avoid all men." She held up fingers to count. "There's Kelsey's husband, and my grandfather, and...and my pastor, and..." She looked at her three fingers and Brianna shook her head at her. "Oh! And the guy at Chick-Fil-A who always gives me an extra cherry when I order a milkshake."

Brianna put her hands on her hips with a laugh. "You'd go out with the Chick-Fil-A guy?"

Meagan put a hand near her neck but grasped air. She used to twirl her hair in her fingers before it got cut off. "Well, no..."

"See? You *are* cynical."

Alexia's hint of a smile brought out a full one in Meagan. "Is it chilly back here today?" Meagan rose and peeked through the cracked door back into the storeroom. "I need one of those big scarves from the front window display."

"Shouldn't you be calling the FBI?" Alexia asked. "Or the police or something?"

Meagan returned to the table and put a reassuring hand on Alexia's shoulder. "Don't worry. I'll call the local FBI office and check on this Mr. Cole Fleming, but that can wait until later. Right now you're our most important priority. Let's get you something to eat, and then take you back to the safe house so you can rest."

Kelsey already had her phone to her ear. "I'm checking on that parole situation. We'll make sure that he, that your—"

"My skunk?"

Alexia's slight laugh was a good thing to hear. "Yes," Kelsey said. "We'll make sure your skunk, even if he's out of jail, can't get anywhere near you."

Brianna slid the door open to the store. "I guess I'll get back to work on the inventory."

Meagan nodded gratefully. "That'd be better than staying here dissecting my love life."

"Your lack of love life."

"True enough." Meagan shrugged and spoke almost as if to herself. "This has been the oddest week. I'm sure glad I didn't bust open the fire hydrant."

"What?" Brianna and Kelsey both asked.

She let out a sheepish laugh. "I'll tell you later. Maybe."

7

Thursday, January 1
12:45 p.m.

"You know this is a bad idea, right?"

Cole sat on one of the outdoor benches and grabbed a bite of meatball sub while Steve argued his case. "None of my ideas are bad. You said she told you to come back with ID on New Year's Day. Today is New Year's Day."

"And we're staking out her store."

"Do you want to go in and shop? Stephanie would love a new purse."

Cole's mouth tipped. "When was the last time you bought your wife something for no reason?"

"About six months ago." Steve unwrapped his cold-cut sub. "I was investigating a guy who owned a kiosk in the mall and needed an excuse to talk to the salesperson."

"Nice." A gust of wind passed through the Christmas trees set up in the middle of the square, rattling their ornaments and knocking off more of their needles. If the wind kept up, those trees would be bare by the end of the day. During the warm months, the square hosted a large farmer's market on the weekends, with vendors from all over the area, but today it was empty except for himself and Steve. Everyone else was smart enough to stay inside. "You said you wouldn't ask me anymore to do these side jobs." He relaxed against the back of the bench and spread his legs out in front of him. Despite the temperature, it was nice to get out of the office. Staring at the computer all day was bad enough on the eyes, but what he had to look at was hard on the soul. He had never wanted a job like this. If it wasn't for Sadie...

Steve pumped his legs in a semi-jog, huffing in the cold air. "After this one. You didn't even manage to get her in for questioning."

"She didn't trust me. You know, these people fight human trafficking. It'd be a bad thing if she was okay climbing in a car with a guy she'd just met."

Steve talked around a mouthful of bread and meat. "Whose side are you on? You're talking like she's a good guy."

"She'd never be mistaken for a guy, and good or not, she's headed this way."

Tan coat buttoned to the top, a red crocheted scarf hugging her neck, with a matching cap covering her short hair, Meagan Winston walked across the curved sidewalk on the opposite side of the square, then up past the twenty-eight-foot statue of a Civil War soldier in the middle, headed toward where they sat near the corner across from her store. She carried a brown paper bag flat in both hands. Cole fought a smile. She must have decided to walk to get lunch today rather than risk driving.

"Those surveillance cameras don't do her justice," Steve said. He wiped his mouth. "She's hot. You should have asked her out."

"Someone you suspect?"

"Well, you said you didn't think she was guilty. Besides, a date might have gotten me some info. You should have asked."

"Right before or right after she locked the door on me?"

Cole had a sinking feeling as she approached, and it sunk further when she saw him and stopped short. He had enjoyed the Christmas song she'd been humming, but knew he wouldn't enjoy whatever would come out of her mouth next. Her eyes narrowed. "What are you doing here?" she asked.

"Hi," Steve interjected before Cole could respond. "Steve Campbell here, with the FBI." He stopped jogging in place to set his sub on the bench and put his right hand out. With his left he flashed his ID, but not long enough for it to be useful. When Meagan didn't shake his hand, he waved it toward Cole. "He's with me."

Cole watched her look over at the store, then back at him. "I know you don't work for the FBI," she said, her chin up. "I called and checked. You aren't with any police force in Georgia either." He was glad when her glare moved to include Steve. "Would you like to leave now or should I call for help?"

Steve chuckled and the woman's eyes shot sparks. She held out her package. "Would you hold this for me a second?"

Steve took the bag and looked inside. "Two Styrofoam containers," he said. "Sharing today?"

By the time he looked up, she had reached into her purse and pulled out a phone and a can of mace.

"Whoa." Cole dropped his sandwich onto the bench and stood, hands out. "No need for that."

She dialed only three numbers and held the phone to her ear. "Hello? Yes. I'm on the square in downtown Gainesville. Two men are stalking me, claiming to be with the FBI."

"What?" Steve held the bag out, as if he expected her to take it back. "You've got to be kidding me!"

"Meagan," Cole said, his hands still up. "If you'd give us a minute—"

"Yes," Meagan said, but she was talking into the phone. "Meagan Winston. I'm at—oh, you did?"

She held the phone away from her ear and did a three-sixty turn. "Someone already called them about you."

"What?" Steve said again. He hunted around and eventually put the bag down on the bench. "Why would anybody do that? We weren't doing anything!"

Meagan stood in the ready position, her outstretched hand holding the can of mace that Cole noted was packaged in a perfect-sized pink carrier with black zebra stripes. Did they sell those at her store?

Police sirens neared and Cole dropped back onto the bench, almost sitting on Meagan's lunch. He picked up his sub and set it on top of her bag. "So, Steve, what was that you were saying about never having bad ideas?"

A grey car pulled away from the square just as the police cars arrived. Cole turned to watch it drive by. "Hey, I remember seeing that car here before, the day I came to the store."

"Don't move," Meagan warned. "I don't want to use this on you, but I will."

He shifted back to face her. "I believe you," he said wryly.

"This is so stupid." Steve waved his arms around. "You're the criminal here. Not us!"

"Excuse me?"

Cole stood and moved several feet away from Steve. "She's holding a can of mace. You may not want to antagonize her right now."

Two officers exited the police cars and ran across the brick walkway toward Meagan, who supplied them with information about the situation while Steve protested his innocence.

"This is ridiculous. I'm with the FBI. I'm here to take *her* in for questioning, not the other way around."

Meagan lowered her hand and with it the mace. She glanced at Cole. "But you're not with the FBI. I checked."

"Not officially. I was just helping out."

A police officer spoke into his radio and got a reply. "This guy checks out, ma'am," he told Meagan. "He is with the FBI, and apparently they do have reason to bring you in."

"But...but..." She directed her puzzled gaze at Cole. "Who are you?"

"Cole Fleming, ma'am, as I said. But I don't work for the FBI. Sorry for the confusion."

"Confusion?" She gazed, red-faced now, at the policemen, Steve, and then him. "I thought...but..." She put a hand to her head and let out a little moan. "What has happened to my well-ordered life?"

8

Thursday, January 1
1:10 p.m.

Lucias Moore slammed his car door shut, anger surging hot within him. He had called the police to come protect Meagan, but when he drove through the square a second time to check on her, the police had left and she was walking away with the very men who harassed her. The one guy, the big one, had been to Meagan's store before. Did he want Meagan to be his girlfriend?

Lucias had almost lost his temper. If Meagan developed feelings for him, it would be bad for her. Lucias had to protect her from that.

He opened the trunk and double-checked to see his briefcase was still there and intact, hidden under a well-positioned spare tire and blue metal jack. Those men messed up his plans. Meagan was supposed to work in the store her normal hours, giving him time to make it to the drop-off point and back before she drove home. They had taken Meagan away and Lucias planned to find out why, but first he had to set up another time to hand over the money and his little gift for the connection.

Lucias drew cold air into his lungs, exhaled loudly, and decided it wasn't such a bad thing to delay the drop-off a day or two. With a glance at the wooded area secluding his trailer from the outside world, he moved the numbers of the briefcase combination lock to 01-08-1988—Meagan's birth date. The briefcase popped open and Lucias hungered after the stacks of Indian rupees inside. He'd get his cut, but not until the connection saw the entire amount first. Lucias had sifted two stacks from the side, just a few hundred dollars' worth, and hidden them in the usual place. After all, he had to make room in the briefcase for the gift.

He lifted the small glass bottle from its secure bed between hundreds of rupee notes, removed the lid, and poured an insignificant amount, just the span of a dime, into his palm. The connection didn't know anything about this new acquisition, so Lucias could enjoy a hit or two while he waited to get his money. He returned the bottle to its safe hiding place, closed the briefcase and secured it under the tire, then shut the trunk. The grains of colored powder in his hand promised a good evening, a calming diversion from his rage at another man trying to take his place in Meagan's heart.

He lived to keep a close eye on Meagan, but for a while he might have to keep an eye on the man in the black suit instead.

9

Thursday, January 1
1:30 p.m.

Meagan reluctantly followed Steve Campbell and his partner for the day up the stairs and into the Federal Building on Spring Street. "You could have told me you were just three blocks away," she muttered at Cole.

"I didn't know." He shrugged. "I've never actually been to Steve's office before now."

"So you're just some hunk-for-hire that he calls up when he needs someone bigger than he is to intimidate people?" Oh, honestly, when was she going to learn to think before she spoke? Her cheeks would match her red hat now. This day was getting worse by the minute.

He grinned at her, then laughed when Steve looked back with a frown and said, "He's not that much bigger than I am. I just asked him to do it so I wouldn't have to go out in the cold."

"This may be funny to you," Meagan said as Steve held open the door for her to enter his office, "but I'm still trying to figure out why I'm being brought in for questioning in the first place." She sat in the chair he offered and set her multi-shades-of-red purse, recycled from sari dresses in India, on her lap. "For us normal people, getting in trouble with the FBI is kind of a big deal."

Cole Fleming, who was still there for some unknown reason, pulled a chair from the far wall of the office and set it next to Steve's desk across from her. He lowered himself into it and looked her in the eye. "Steve forgets sometimes that his position scares people. He just needs to ask you some questions."

"And you're here because...he needs a bodyguard?"

Steve clicked open a document on his computer. He grunted but Cole chuckled. "If you pull that mace on him again, I'm out of the room," Cole said. "Right now I'm only here for moral support."

"We don't call people in here who have a lot of morals to support," Steve said, pulling several papers out of the printer next to his computer.

Meagan sat up straighter and told herself to remain calm. "Why am I here?" she asked. Was not telling her anything part of some intimidation method? If it was, it was a good one.

The FBI officer put a hand-held recording device on the desk. At the push of a button, a red light came on, and he proceeded to ask her routine questions about her trips to India and her work with Rahab's Rope. When he got to her personal life, she balked.

"I'm not answering any more questions until you tell me why I'm here. Am I being accused of something?"

Thursday, January 1
2:15 p.m.

Steve Campbell looked the woman over. She was good, but he was better. He might have fallen short in Baghdad, his marriage might be a wash, but in the FBI he had found his place. In this building he would climb the ladder and he wouldn't stop until he had reached the top. His name would be on a plaque on the wall someday, for exemplary service. For making the world a better place. For being better at something than the man sitting next to him. Let Cole be all nice to the girl. He never wanted to play good cop anyway.

It was time to drop the first bomb. "Just when did you start using crystal meth, Miss Winston?" he asked, watching for her reaction. She didn't disappoint. Her eyes got all wide and round, like his wife's had when he'd returned from his tour and said they were moving to Georgia in less than a month. With Stephanie, it was questions, always questions. Why didn't you talk to me about it first? Why do you make decisions without me? Why don't you love me like you used to?

Here in his office, he was the one who got to ask the questions. The woman on the other side of his desk began to say something, but he dived in with his second bomb. "And how long have you been selling crystal meth on the international circuit?"

She gasped and pulled her bag to her chest. He wished she would make a run for it. He'd chase after her, catch her in the hallway. Everyone would see it.

"I haven't ever done drugs or sold drugs in my life," she said, her voice breathy and innocent. People were such fakers. Women especially. They painted their faces and added padding under their clothes. Stephanie had been brilliant at it. The morning after his wedding, he'd woken up to a stranger. He still wondered if her claim to be pregnant had just been a ploy to get him down the aisle. Now she sat around all day, crying about the baby they'd lost, moping about how he didn't love her anymore. What did she expect? Should he be happy to come home to a naggy wife who never changed out of her sweatpants anymore?

The girl across from him looked over at Cole, where she'd get more sympathy. "What is he talking about?"

"Steve believes you've been involved in selling drugs on your trips to India," Cole said. It was a good thing Steve was the one the FBI had hired. Cole was too nice for face-to-face work with criminals. Too gullible. The woman spy in Baghdad had proven that.

The girl in the red hat gasped again. "What? I'm with a ministry that helps people! How can you possibly—"

This conversation was useless. Steve had the proof right there on his desk and on his computer screen. "Miss Winston, I've got a signed statement here from a man we brought into custody—a real greasy character with connections to an Atlanta meth lab—who confessed to selling drugs for a commission from their sales to Indian buyers."

"What does that have to do with me?" She looked from him to Cole, as if Cole might save her. And Cole might be naive enough to try, even though he still had shrapnel in his shoulder from the last time he tried to save a beautiful woman. Steve hadn't trusted Delilah, and he didn't trust this girl either.

"The man gave us dates, one run every six months for the past three years."

"And?" she asked.

"We pulled up every flight pattern option from Atlanta to India within a twenty-four-hour period after each sale, and studied the passenger lists for those flights."

Her eyes were even bigger now. "And?" she whispered.

He'd found her out. "Yours is the only name that showed up all six times. You're guilty, Miss Winston. You might as well admit it."

10

Thursday, January 1
3:00 p.m.

This can't be happening. Meagan wanted to tell herself she was dreaming. Having a nightmare. Hallucinating. Anything that meant she wasn't actually sitting inside an FBI office with two men who thought she was a drug pusher. Steve Campbell moved his computer screen so she could see it. "We've got surveillance of the flights that connect with the drugs. And we have the list of ticket holders. You are the only one on every flight."

"Steve sent me the videos and I watched them myself," Cole Fleming added. He looked at her like he felt sorry for her, like he had a hard time believing she was a criminal. She knew how he felt. "I checked to see if there was a repeat person on each of the flights who might have used different names."

Her voice squeaked. "Did you find anyone?"

He shook his head and those deep green eyes never left her face. "I'm sorry to say I didn't. I saw the same old lady a couple of times, but no one every time but you."

Meagan rubbed her forehead with both hands. "I don't understand." She posed her next question toward Steve, who pulled up a video on his computer. "If you knew when the flights were, why not check everybody's luggage and find the drugs?"

"I wish we could have." Steve kept his eyes on the screen. He used his mouse to click one window down and pull up another. "But the guy got arrested after you were in India. We had to wait until you got back to find out more."

"So that's why I got double-searched this time," she murmured.

"Did you find anything on her?" Cole asked Steve.

"No."

"Wouldn't she have had the money with her?"

"Maybe she has a liaison."

"A liaison?" Meagan fought dizziness. "You can't be serious. Why don't we go see this guy who got arrested? He'll tell you he didn't sell me any drugs."

"Nice try," Steve said. He clicked more with his mouse. "The guy is a middle link in the chain. He never sees the person, just delivers the stash and then picks up the money later." He glanced her way. "But you already know that, don't you?"

"I don't know anything about this," Meagan said again. She took in a deep breath and tried not to give in to tears. "You can come search my house if you want. I don't have anything."

"We've got DEA personnel at the drop-off point. Whoever you have leaving the money, we'll get him the minute he shows. If you don't want your sweet little grandmother to know about your side job, you'll cooperate with us."

She stood. "That was rude and unnecessary. I will cooperate without you needing to threaten my family." She remained standing a moment, but then dropped back into the chair, suddenly drained. "And Nana died four months ago. May I see the surveillance tapes you mentioned?"

Cole had stood when she did. He was frowning, but at Steve. "I think we should be done for today."

"Here." Steve Campbell pulled the video window up again and pointed. "You're in 39C."

"I know where I sat." She looked over the other passengers as they filed onto the plane and took their seats, or stuffed various sized carry-ons into the small overhead bins. No one looked familiar until she saw herself arrive. Strange, the thought of people watching her when she was unaware. On the video, she thanked the man who put her carry-on up for her, then sat and took out her small journal and began to write, as she always did, a prayer for God's blessings on her trip and the work she hoped to accomplish while she was there. She had not thought to ask God to keep FBI agents from thinking she ran drugs across international borders.

"See anyone suspicious or familiar?" Cole asked beside her.

"No. This is just the most recent flight though. Do you have the others? I might spot something you didn't."

"This is a waste of time," Steve said, but he pulled up another window. "I'm going to get some coffee." He stood and motioned for Meagan to take his seat. "You can sit here. Cole, when she's done with this one, the others are all opened but minimized." He scooted around her and Cole. "Make sure she doesn't look at anything else on my computer."

The door shut and Meagan tilted her head. "Rather bossy, isn't he?"

Cole stood behind her. He leaned over the desk enough to see the computer screen well, making her pulse jump at his proximity. "Always," he said with a smile in her direction. His cheeks filled out and one dimpled, a compelling mixture of little boy and adult male. He smelled like soap and pine. He must have noticed how close his face was to hers, for he backed away several inches. "The first video is ready when you want to click it."

She moved the mouse and pushed play on the video. "This one is dated six months ago, the last trip I took." She watched with growing disappointment. "I don't see anyone I remember here either." She braved another glance in his direction. "What will he do if there aren't any trails other than the ones that lead to me?"

A muscle in his jaw shifted. "I'm not sure," he said.

"He can't arrest me, can he? Not without evidence."

That muscle worked again. He focused on the screen. "I'm afraid he has evidence."

"But I didn't do it!" She motioned toward the video. "Somebody else must fly out the same days I did. Maybe they're setting me up."

He looked at her then and didn't need to say it. She was the only person on each of the flights. "Do you know how bad it would be for Rahab's Rope if I get arrested for this, even though I didn't do it? People send money for our ministry. In the time it would take to clear my name all sorts of damage would be done. I'd probably have to leave the ministry just so people wouldn't assume this is all connected."

He kept silent and she turned back to the screen. She pressed her fingers tight against her temples and rubbed in small circles while another batch of people got on the plane, herself included. An older man in a plaid suit jacket helped her with her carry-on that time. She finished the video and sighed. "Nothing again. I don't suppose it's of any use to watch the others, but what am I supposed to do?"

He pulled up a third video. "Here's the one farthest back, three years ago."

She watched, emotionally numb, the same routine: passengers arrived, sat, put bags away. No one helped her with her carry-on that time. On the video, she simply sat down and began to write. Meagan remembered that day. "That was my first trip overseas. I was so excited. See the woman next to me with the thick curly hair? That's Kelsey. Usually she goes out a different time of the year, but she came with me that first time to train me. She founded the work with the children, and...I..."

She felt Cole shift near her but her eyes did not leave the screen. "What is it?" he asked.

"There." She put a fingernail against the screen. "Three rows behind me."

"The guy with the ball cap?"

"No." She moved her finger. "The old lady. Do you have this video in color? I think I remember that dress."

The door opened and Steve entered, two cups of coffee in hand. "I got one for you, Cole, but not for our suspect. Caffeine and drugs don't mix."

"Let up, Steve," Cole said behind her. His hand on the back of her chair felt somehow reassuring. "She's seen something."

"Yeah? Like what?"

Meagan scooted the chair as far forward as it would go and leaned close to the screen. "I think that's the lady who stopped my mugger."

11

Thursday, January 1
4:30 p.m.

Cole didn't need to ask what might make a woman so lovely and full of potential start down the wrong road. Meagan Winston didn't have the sunken cheeks of a meth user, and definitely didn't come across as someone who would use ministry as a cover to haul drugs overseas. He saw Sadie's face in his mind, her sweet, lovable face those days before he left for Iraq.

Looks could be deceiving.

He hated to think it, but wondered if Meagan was making up stories as she went along, trying to find some way to divert attention and get herself off the hook. If Steve let her go today, would she leave town and disappear, proving Steve right? Was she being blackmailed? This latest tale she spun at Steve, about getting mugged and some old lady running up and scaring the robber away with a briefcase was about as far-fetched as it got. And even if it was true, how would that clear her of any of the charges?

Steve asked the same thing out loud. "Don't you see?" Meagan pointed back at the computer screen again. She stood, right in front of him, close enough that had she been Sadie, he'd pull the little ball at the top of her cap just to inspire that playful face he had loved the most. "She was on the first flight, but not on the most recent one. But I saw her on my trip. Doesn't that seem suspicious to you?"

"No," Steve said bluntly. "If she was moving out to India that day, she'd still be there now."

"And what are the chances I'd see her on a trip three years later?" Meagan took off her gloves and shoved them into her purse, then removed her scarf and hat. She had to be toasted by now.

"What are the chances you're telling me a big fish story?"

She dropped her purse, hat and scarf on the desk and sat down in Steve's chair. "Where are the other videos?" Without waiting for his help, she clicked windows until she found one they hadn't watched, then pushed play. Steve complained about not being able to use his desk, but Meagan ignored him. Long minutes passed and Cole felt tension pull his stomach muscles tight. If this woman was guilty, he wanted to help her, find a place for her to get straightened out before it was too late.

"There!" She pointed again. He leaned forward and Steve came around the desk to look over her shoulder. "Three rows back. It's the same old lady! Look, she even has the briefcase!"

"This is that same video," Steve said, jostling to get in front of Cole.

"No, it's not," Meagan argued. "See the date at the bottom? But she has on the same outfit."

"She does? That's weird." Cole looked down and noticed static cling from the hat she'd removed had spiked Meagan's hair in all directions. It annoyed him that he thought it was cute and bothered him further that he had to fight the urge to smooth it down for her. "But why isn't she in all of the videos?"

Meagan stopped eyeballing the screen and sat back. "I don't know." She rubbed her forehead, but then winced and dropped her hands.

"It's not plausible to think some old lady is taking international trips to sell drugs in a briefcase." Steve picked up Meagan's scarf and, with his lack of spatial awareness, tried to stuff it into her purse, which was much too small to hold it.

"That's just it," Meagan said. She took the purse from him and pulled the stuffed-in parts of the scarf back out. "When I got mugged, I remember thinking it was amazing that someone so old could move so quickly. She waved her briefcase around like it was nothing. And then, when I tried to go thank her, she ran off. Literally. And not like an elderly person at all. I know; I live with one."

"So you think the person might be pretending to be an old lady?" Cole leaned over to look at the video again. "But why?" He touched the screen but then moved his hand to the mouse. "You need to get a touch-screen computer, Steve."

Meagan put the scarf around her neck, then looked at it and took it off again. "I don't know, but don't you think that's strange?"

"I do." He pulled up one of the other videos they hadn't watched.

"Of course you do." Steve sat in one of the extra chairs and crossed his arms. "You're always on the side of the needy underdog."

"I resent that," Meagan said. She reached for the mouse still in his hand. Her small palm covered his fingers. She jerked away. "Sorry."

He removed his hand and pushed the mouse toward her. "Go ahead, needy underdog."

She glared at him, but when he smiled, her scowl dropped and her bottom lip quivered in a way that did make her look needy. And appealing. He needed to get a grip of his thoughts. She was a potential drug runner, not a potential date.

Her gaze drifted back toward the computer and he heard her quick intake of breath. "I see her on this one, too!"

This time Steve stood and came around the desk. He pulled on the back of her chair. "Can I sit there?"

She got to her feet but Cole was in the way. They did an awkward dance to get around each other without touching while Steve put himself into his chair and mumbled about personal space. Once they'd settled, Steve in the chair, Meagan behind it leaning over Steve's left shoulder, Cole leaning over his right, he moved the mouse until the cursor hovered over the passenger with white curly hair and a large dress that billowed out over her knees.

"Why am I thinking that kind of dress is named after a cow?" Cole asked.

Meagan sent a small smile his direction. "It's a Muumuu."

"A moo-moo? Seriously? As is the cow goes moo?"

Her soft laugh was as pleasant to hear as the hint of vanilla he'd smelled when she brushed by him. She spelled the word. "My grandmother wore them all the time. I'm guessing yours must have, too."

He felt his own smile fade. "I wouldn't know."

Her look on him held curiosity, and a little sympathy. She opened her mouth, but he turned and faced the computer again. He wasn't there for someone to ask him questions. "We should start at the first tape and study them all again," he told Steve.

Steve agreed but not without grumbling.

"I want to watch them with you," Meagan said. "But I can't today. I need to be back home soon for..." She hesitated. "An appointment."

Steve shook his head. "I don't trust you to leave this building."

"I want to find out who is doing this as much as you do," Meagan said. "It's my reputation and testimony on the line. Here." She dug around in her purse and took out a camera. "This camera has all my pictures from my trip to India. These photos are priceless to me." She set the camera on his desk. "I'll leave it here with the promise to be back tomorrow at whatever time you choose."

"Nine a.m. And I'll need your phone, too." Steve held out his hand. "Wouldn't want your liaison with all those Indian rupees to mysteriously never show up."

She shook her head. "I need my phone."

"You wouldn't if you were in jail."

Biting her bottom lip, she fumbled in her purse and brought out a Smartphone in a custom-made case covered with photos of Indian children. "I'll be here in the morning. But for now I have to go. Okay?"

Cole picked up her scarf and held it out to her. "I'll drive you back."

"I'll walk." She reached for the scarf and followed her curt words with a hint of a smile, like she was throwing him a crumb.

He took it. "Then I'll walk you back."

She did a one-shoulder shrug. "If you want, but there's no need. I have mace, remember?"

He grinned. "I remember. It's pink with stripes."

"Well, the container is anyway." Her scarf was around her neck and she positioned the hat onto her head again. He noticed she looked into the glass partition between the office and the hallway and made sure her bangs were down over her forehead, though it did not fully cover the fading purple mark underneath.

"Did you hit your head when you ran off the road last week?" he asked.

Her gaze left the glass and shot to him. "How do you know about that?"

"Way to go, Cole," Steve leaned back in his desk chair and clasped his hands behind his head. It was the first time he had smiled all day. "You're a real smooth one."

She looked at him like an animal did a newly discovered predator. Cole wanted to kick himself.

12

Thursday, January 1
5:00 p.m.

Meagan pressed her bangs down and grimaced. The bruise was still tender. "How do you know I ran off the road that day?" She hadn't wanted to walk with Cole Fleming back to her car, still parked near the store, but having this conversation in the office with Steve's added comments would be worse.

"I'm sorry. I know that sounds creepy," he said.

"Sounds creepy? It is creepy. Were you following me?"

"Not for any weird reason." He stuffed his hands in his pockets. The wind picked up her scarf and she barely caught it before it blew away. He wasn't wearing anything over his suit coat, and it had to be less than forty degrees.

She refused to feel sympathetic toward him. "So you have a non-weird reason for following me? Did the FBI ask you to?"

"No." He looked even more chagrined. "Steve asked me to find you and bring you in for questioning, but I did the background check on my own." His shoulders went up, then down. "I found out where you live, a few other things about you, and...man, this does sound creepy."

She picked up her pace. "You're telling me." They had reached the parking spaces across from the store. Meagan grabbed her keys. "I don't want to know anymore. I'm going home." She got inside and peered up at him through the open door. "You aren't going to follow me, are you?"

"Look, I'm not the kind of guy who follows women around." He put his hand on the top of her car and leaned toward her. "Usually."

"Oh, so I'm just an exception?"

"Exactly."

She shook her head. He acted like what he said made sense. She shut the door and turned the key. The car gave a gurgle and a cough, then died. "You've got to be kidding."

Cole was still there. "Try it again," he said through the window.

She did. Same result. She let her head fall back against the headrest. "I don't believe this whole day."

He motioned for her to come out. She opened the car door. "Don't tell me you're a mechanic when you're not working for the FBI."

"I'm not," he said, smiling. "But I have owned a few old cars, and one of mine had trouble with the starter. It made that same sound, just like yours did."

"Were you able to fix it?" She didn't have money for expensive repairs. Everything had gone into her trip. No matter how much she planned not to, she never could keep from leaving all the money in her possession with the workers in India. They had so many children to feed. Their work was much more important than her getting a new outfit, or splurging on those winter boots she wanted. Then again, car repairs didn't fit under the unnecessary-luxury-item category.

"Yeah. A friend taught me how to hit the starter with a hammer whenever it died like this."

"Are you joking?"

"No. It worked every time. Do you have a hammer in the store? I'd get mine out of my car but it's parked a few blocks away."

She looked him over, from his large dress shoes up to his ears, red from the cold. Was he crazy? "You want me to go get you a hammer?"

He nodded. "And a screwdriver, in case your starter is hard to reach." He leaned down by her feet and found the lever to pop the hood. Once it was open, he rummaged around in the engine as if the car was his.

In no position to refuse free repairs, however unconventional, she tucked her keys into the pocket of her khaki pants and made her way across the two lanes to the store. She had to unlock the door; everyone had gone home for the day. Without the lights on, the store took on a haunted look. Or maybe she was just jittery. She wished she could tell her grandmother about the mess she was in and get her wisdom and insight. But Nana was in heaven. Meagan's days of asking her advice were over.

Crossing the store, using the fading light from outside rather than turning on the overhead lights, she made her way around jewelry displays and baskets of decorative carvings to the register. Brianna had put up new wall hangings recently, so she might have left the hammer in one of the cubbies under the register. Now where she'd find a screwdriver was a mystery.

Once around the counter holding the register, she put a hand on the wooden surface for balance and squatted to look in the cubbies. Down there, everything was dark. She should carry around a flashlight along with her mace. Not that it would help; she'd left her purse in the car, in plain sight of a man who admitted he'd followed her the other day but still hadn't explained why.

She imagined all sorts of spiders or bugs or even furry rodents as she reached into each of the small squares and felt around. She pulled out one pad of sticky notes, several pencils, tags for pricing items, and finally, a hammer.

"Good enough," she said and rose. He'd have to do without a screwdriver. She wasn't going in the back room to get one. Even turning the lights on would not curb her apprehension, and she needed to get back to her car and get her purse.

When she stood, the move of her hand brushed a paper off the counter. The yellow sheet floated to land a foot away where some of the outside light shined. She leaned down, picked it up, and glanced at it as she set it back on the counter.

The sticky note on top of the sheet was in Brianna's handwriting. Meagan would recognize it anywhere; they used the adhesive notes to leave messages for each other multiple times throughout the work day. She read it aloud. "Meagan, a guy came in and left this for you. I wasn't here and didn't see him. Are you dating somebody?" The last question had six question marks on it. Leave it to Brianna to be trying to set her up again. With the way Meagan's day had gone so far, it was probably the CIA.

She removed the sticky note and skimmed the words on the paper. *Dear Meagan, I'm glad the bruise on your head is healing. I was worried about you. You are a good person and VERY beautiful. I love to watch you. Soon I will tell you in person.*

Meagan's heart pounded. Who had left this? Her gaze darted around the room, now seeing shapes in every shadow. Was someone in there, watching her? She crushed the paper in her right hand and, too fearful to worry about looking foolish, rushed to the door. She threw the paper in the wrought-iron wastebasket on her way by, but then stopped and went back to retrieve it. Kelsey might recognize the handwriting.

Meagan locked the door and as she made her way across the street, she could not help but wonder about the man who stood in front of her car, wiping a dipstick with a napkin he must have gotten from her glove compartment.

He couldn't have left the note. He was with her all afternoon.

But what if he sent someone to drop it off? Or what if he left it there before he sat in the square to wait for her? She hadn't gone back into the store after that. The note could have been there all afternoon.

It didn't seem like the kind of wording she would expect from him, but what did she know about Cole Fleming really? Nothing except that he didn't work for the FBI, he admitted he'd followed her, and he was too good-looking. He was nice, nicer than Steve Campbell at least, but nice did not always mean trustworthy.

"Lord, I'm getting kind of scared." It was a meager prayer, but all she had time for before Cole saw her approach. He held out his hand and moved toward her. Was he going to grab her? Had he tampered with her car and that was the real reason it wouldn't start? Was he going to use it as an excuse to offer her a ride home, and then...and then what?

"The hammer?" he said, his hand still out.

She looked down, surprised to see the large tool gripped in her left hand. "Oh! Sorry." She handed it over, careful to maintain a safe distance as she did so. He gave her an odd look but then put his attention back under the hood.

"Did you find a screwdriver?"

She looked back at the store. Whoever wrote the note had been in there, inside her store. "No. I didn't."

"Hmm." He moved to consider various parts of the engine. "It's possible..."

She found herself drawing closer. If she got a good look at the engine, she might be able to tell if someone had messed with it.

"Here we go," Cole said. He leaned down and worked the hammer in between parts she could not name but were probably important. He lifted his hand and gave something a loud whack. The metallic sound twanged and reverberated through the air.

"That made the insides of my ears itch." She moved her jaw back and forth, then rubbed a finger in each ear.

He raised his head with a chuckle. "Better plug them, then. I'm going to hit it one more time."

After the second hit, he closed the hood. "If that doesn't do it, you'll have to call somebody. That's the extent of my car knowledge, unless you need a battery jumped or a tire changed."

She slipped back into the car and tried the key. The little Volkswagen sputtered to life again. "It worked!"

He wiped his hands on the one dirty napkin, and she lowered her window to offer him a handful. "Thank you."

With a smile, he said, "Do you want me to follow you home, to make sure it gets you all the way there?"

"No!" The note in her pocket crinkled as she put on her seatbelt. She lowered her voice. "No, thank you. I'm sure it will be fine."

"Okay. But keep that hammer handy. I should show you where to hit it if it acts up again."

She had to get away from this guy. "I think I know where the hammer goes. I watched you do it. Thanks." She shifted gears and rolled her window up, refusing to feel rude for driving off so abruptly. He wasn't her friend. He was barely an acquaintance. And if he followed her again, she would call the police. She didn't care if Steve Campbell checked out or not. The police hadn't checked on Mr. Cole Fleming.

When she got home, she was going to do some checking herself.

13

Thursday, January 1
5:30 p.m.

Cole had no intention of following Meagan Winston again. He was in enough trouble with her already. But when she drove around the corner, and a familiar grey Oldsmobile took the same road moments later, Cole's gut told him something wasn't right. He'd seen that grey car too many times for it to be coincidence.

Suspicion growing, he raced to his own black Sedan. By the time he got onto the road, both vehicles were out of sight, but if Cole's theory was correct, they'd be headed on Meagan's typical route home. Three minutes later, he spotted the grey car and in front of it, Meagan's VW bug. Was the grey car following her, or was the person in it connected to Meagan? She said she had to get home for an appointment. People went to appointments at doctor's offices, or at the dentist, not at home. Was it to meet someone and warn them about the investigation, or to get money, or more drugs?

He hit the fifth number on his speed dial. "Steve," he said when Steve's phone went to voice mail, "there's a grey Oldsmobile trailing Meagan Winston. I've seen it twice before." He listed the license plate number. "Check it out, would you? If you find the guy's phone number, you can see if Meagan's phone has any calls to it."

He hung up and tossed the phone onto the passenger seat. Cole didn't want to think of Meagan Winston as a drug-dealer, the kind of person who sold to buyers desperate for their next hit, the kind of person who knew they were part of lives being damaged forever, and they did it anyway. Never far away, Sadie's face came to mind. He had not even recognized her this last time, she was so changed from the girl he'd left behind. He'd thought she would be safe. Never dreamed...

He should stop thinking about her and focus. And he needed to start looking at Meagan Winston as a real suspect. It didn't matter that she was likable, smart, and had more than a handful of appealing qualities. Her story didn't hold water, and the evidence was there.

This grey car only added to it.

The Oldsmobile remained far enough behind Meagan to avoid detection, or perhaps far enough behind to make Cole think he wasn't collaborating with her. Cole slowed to keep a good distance back once the grey car veered off the main road onto a two-lane side road, and he put even more distance between them once they were within a mile of Meagan's home. Cole had the route memorized from when he'd looked it up online, another skill he'd developed in the service. His sense of direction rarely failed him; if only his discernment about people was as accurate.

Cole parked at a lone gas station and waited five minutes, then resumed his route. He turned off onto the gravel drive that led to Gerald and Alice Winston's home, where Meagan had lived since college. He skimmed the bordering woods as he jostled his way toward what a more romantic person might call a cozy cottage, with stone exterior across the front, an arched doorway, and a small stone front porch that extended from the front door to the circular drive. Meagan's little car was parked in front of a tottering wooden outbuilding that might collapse with a good gust of wind. It looked nearly as old as the house itself, and the whole place gave the impression no one had been in a condition to keep it up for some time. Steve would say it was more evidence. People hooked on drugs cared little for maintaining anything else.

He slowed to a crawl as he neared the house. Where was the grey Oldsmobile? Cole would have seen if it had returned to the road, for the drive circled around like the path of a boomerang. The grey car would have passed Cole on its way out. He didn't see any kind of garage. Was it hiding somewhere?

A quick survey then a deeper one did not reveal the missing car, but as Cole's gaze passed by the house, he saw a woman looking out through the front bay window. His car was just passing the house at that moment, so there was no way he could avoid being seen. Meagan Winston's eyes found him and widened. She took a step back and lowered the shade. He stopped the car and considered his options. He could go up to the door and explain about the grey car, watching for clues as to whether she knew the person in it or not. He could just leave and have her think he'd followed her again, but that would make things worse. Then again, if he waited to explain, she might be less angry than she would be if he rang her doorbell right now.

Stuck in the mire of indecision, Cole jumped when a blue van drove up beside his and then left the gravel drive to park next to Meagan's VW. Out came a woman in scrubs, snow white hair curled around her head. She carried a medical bag of sorts and walked with confidence up to the front door. Before she could knock, the door opened and Meagan ushered her inside with a hurried, fearful glance his way.

Meagan's actions and reactions seemed so innocent, but the facts continued to stack against her. Was this new person Meagan's appointment? Was she the old lady with white hair Meagan had seen on the video?

The middle man Steve had arrested told them the drug money was scheduled to be delivered today. DEA personnel were waiting at the drop-off point in downtown Atlanta. If Meagan was handing off money to this lady instead of at the drop-off point, those DEA guys in Atlanta were in for a long, boring stint.

He heard the sound of gravel shifting behind him and turned. The grey Oldsmobile shot out from the wooded area about a quarter mile down the drive. The car sped in the opposite direction and Cole did not get even catch a fleeting look at its driver. He turned the wheel and raced after the car, keeping up with it for several miles until losing the trail in traffic on the freeway.

He'd made the wrong choice. He should have stayed and tried to talk to Meagan, or waited to talk with the white-haired lady with the bag. Now with no answers, closer at this point to his apartment than Meagan Winston's home, he decided to call it a day. Maybe after the weekend he'd have a better idea how to approach this whole thing.

Thursday, January 1
6:00 p.m.

"How did you find my number?"

Meagan skipped Steve's question. "He followed me home. I told him if he followed me again, I'd call the police, and he did it anyway."

"Who?"

"Cole Fleming!" Meagan wanted to shout at the man. "Who else?"

"Did you call the police?"

"No, he drove away when I saw him, so calling the police wouldn't do any good. This has to stop or I'm getting a restraining order."

Steve sounded exasperated. "He's not a criminal."

"Yeah?" Meagan was surprised the phone didn't break in two from her grip. "Well, I'm not a criminal either, but me saying so doesn't seem to mean much, does it?" She yanked a newspaper up from where Pops had dropped it on the hallway floor and ripped it into shreds as she barked out, "I want to know who he is."

"Cole?" She could hear typing in the background. He wouldn't even get off his computer to talk with her? "We did a tour in Iraq together. He saved my life a few times. I saved his hide when it counted most. We both grew up in this area, but when I moved back here to get this job, he was out in California somewhere, recovering."

She wadded up the paper shreds and stuffed them into the trash. "Recovering from what?"

"Can't tell you that." The typing continued. "What else do you want to know? He orders a large meat lover's pizza every Friday night, and eats the leftovers cold for breakfast the next morning. He's never been married, or even engaged. He broke his ankle once playing soccer and is no good at card games. He likes old spy movies, which I refuse to watch with him."

Meagan's grandfather called to her from the living room. She put a hand over the phone. "Just a second, Pops. I'll be right there." Removing her hand, she said to Steve, "Why is he following me?"

"Maybe he has a crush on you."

She thought of the note. "That's not even close to funny."

His sigh was loud enough for her to hear. "Look, I'll take care of it, okay? You just be sure to be in my office at nine tomorrow."

"I will be." She finished with a parting shot. "Don't touch my camera." She slammed the phone down on a little side table in the hallway. Steve said he would take care of it, but what did that mean? As soon as she got Pops settled for the night, she would take her laptop up to her room and search everything she could find on Cole Fleming.

14

Friday, January 2
9:00 a.m.

Steve said he had work to do and refused to spend the morning studying tapes he'd already looked at, so Meagan found herself ushered to a cubicle down the hall with a computer on an otherwise empty desk. Sawdust covered the floor and much of the desk, tamped down on the carpet by footprints and smeared across the desk by a hand or an unsuccessful paper towel.

Meagan sneezed. "Classy place."

"This section of the building is being remodeled," Steve said. He set down a chair he'd carried in from the hallway. "I've uploaded the tapes to this computer, but nothing else, so you can be in here without supervision. Write down anything you find of interest."

She wanted to ask him how he had dealt with Cole yesterday, but decided to just be relieved the man was not there. Steve went back to his office without leaving paper or even a pen.

"Guess he's pretty sure I won't find anything," she muttered. She pulled out the small notepad she always carried in her purse, set it on the desk, and dug around for a pen. Once ready, she put the videos in order and watched them one by one, pausing at frequent intervals to study the passengers and their behavior. By the third tape, she had three pages of notes, and by the last tape, she had the beginnings of a theory. Going back to the beginning, she watched each tape again with a focus on the passengers three rows behind her seat. Yes, her theory was correct, except for that one change on the last trip.

Would it be enough to convince Steve to turn his investigation elsewhere, and not incarcerate her? She gathered her pad, pen and purse. Her coat and scarf were still back in his office. She began to make her way from the cubicle but stopped when she saw Steve just outside his office talking with Cole Fleming. She backed up and was about to retreat to the cubicle when their conversation caught her attention.

"Did you check out the plate numbers I gave you?" Cole asked. Had they run her plates? All they'd find was one speeding ticket she got when she was seventeen. She didn't think the officer would have reported the incident with the fire hydrant last week. She touched her forehead. Her bruise was healing, which was good; she was tired of people asking about it.

"I did, but you need to back off, Cole. I don't need you following people for me, or leaving instructions on my voicemail. Like I wouldn't know to check her phone record."

"Just trying to help."

"Like always." From Meagan's viewpoint, Steve did not look appreciative. "The plate runs to a woman named Darla Moore. She's got a record but it's out of state. A few drugs charges. One petty theft. I've got a man on it."

"Does Meagan have a record?"

Steve crossed his arms. "Squeaky clean, which makes her perfect for a big operation like this. You know they pick people like her. They're expendable. If they get caught, there are always more people looking for an easy way to get rich. No one would suspect a thing, not with that innocent face of hers."

Meagan touched her cheek. She had an innocent face?

"Or maybe she is innocent."

"Didn't you see her hold her purse in front of her when I asked her questions? That's a deliberate wall and a sign of dishonesty."

"Or of distress. Come on, Steve, what person wouldn't be under stress getting called in and questioned by the FBI?"

Meagan took two steps back and noticed her boots left imprints in the dust at her feet, just two among scores of shoe-shaped spaces, though hers were smaller and more feminine than most of the others. If Cole thought she might be innocent, why was he following her? She'd heard of girls being targeted by men who defended them just to keep other guys away. Alexia's pimp had bailed her out of jail twice, but of course the bail had not bought her freedom, only a transfer back into his brand of captivity.

The thought had her stomach churning. She decided to go back and hide in the cubicle until Cole left, but he saw her and immediately headed her direction, not stopping when Steve called him back.

"I need to talk to you," Cole said. His voice and gaze were equally intense. He loomed over her and she decided she didn't like men to be so tall after all. Or so bulky. If he chose to grab her with those muscled arms she'd never be able to get away, not even with her self-defense moves. She backed up but he moved forward. "I didn't mean to scare you yesterday. I was following a car."

"Yeah. Mine."

The shake of his head stopped her thoughts of flight. "No, a grey car. An Oldsmobile. It's been tracking you for several days. Do you know whose it is?"

She studied his face. "I haven't noticed anyone following me but you."

"Then you don't know the driver of the grey car?"

"I don't know anything about a grey car." She stepped to the side so she could see Steve, still down the hallway in front of his office. "You told me you'd stop him from accosting me."

"Accosting you?" Cole said the words as if they were poison he needed to spit out. "I've never accosted a woman in my life."

She thought of the newspaper article she had found late the night before with his name on it, about him being nearly blown to bits in Baghdad, with questions about why he was in a building alone with a local woman, known to be a spy, away from the other men in his battalion. "Hero Goes AWOL, Woman Dies in Terrorist Attempt" the headlines read. There had been no follow-up article attesting to his integrity. The reporter said the truth had died with the woman in the blast.

Meagan resisted the pull to apologize for the grief in his eyes that she seemed to have caused. He could be, after all, a dangerous man. A killer even. "Would you please go away and stop following me? I know it's not for the FBI. I'll get a restraining order if I have to."

He seemed to be on the verge of speech several times, but each time clamped his mouth shut again. She waited until words came. "I'm not trying to make things worse for you, Meagan," he said. "I want to help. If you're in trouble, I'll help you find a good place where you can get clean and stay clean, and get away from the people who want to use you."

"I told you I'm not part of any of this!" She marched around him to Steve and pushed her notebook up into his face, fed up with the entire situation. "I found things that you should have found if you hadn't wanted to pin the blame on me from the beginning."

People in the hallway looked their way and Meagan saw heads pop up from cubicles around the large open area. Steve's face reddened. "Get inside," he hissed, pulling her by the elbow into his office.

Cole joined them. "I don't want him here," Meagan said.

Steve yanked his chair back and it crashed to the ground. He picked it up and sat in it. "Show me what you *think* you found," he ordered.

Meagan tried to ignore Cole's large presence beside her as they sat in the two chairs opposite Steve's desk, set against the glass near the door. She set the notepad down as evidence, though neither man would be able to read her own personal version of shorthand. "I watched every tape twice. On two trips, the old lady is sitting three rows back in the aisle seat. She has the briefcase I remember from the mugging."

"Are you sure it's the exact same briefcase?" Cole asked.

She glared at him. "How many old ladies have you seen carrying a leather briefcase with gold trim and what looks like a combination lock?"

"Keep talking," Steve said.

"Two other trips, that seat is taken by an older gentleman wearing a plaid suit jacket. He has the briefcase, too."

"You think it might be different people taking the drugs out?"

"It makes sense. It's harder to trace, and easier to frame someone else that way."

Cole looked at Steve. "She has a good point."

He frowned at them both. "What about the last two trips?"

She picked up the notebook and looked it over. This was the one hole in her theory. "These last two trips were different. The one before this one, that seat had a younger guy with longer hair, dressed kind of hippie-casual. He had a bag instead of a briefcase, but he kept it in his lap or between his feet at all times, just like the others did with the briefcase."

"And this last trip?" Steve had his arms crossed.

Meagan shook her head. "This trip the hippie guy sat there on the way to India, but on the trip back, it was someone else. A guy in his twenties or thirties, with thin short hair, wearing dress pants and a collared shirt. No tie."

"So it's not consistent."

"Not the people, I admit." She leaned forward. "But this last trip, both the hippie and the new guy had the same briefcase. There's got to be a connection here."

Cole shifted to face her. "So these people—aside from the last guy—they always wore the same clothes on the flights over and back?"

"Yes, and normally people wouldn't do that."

"A disguise perhaps?"

She couldn't keep excitement from bubbling up inside. "That's what I'm thinking."

"So are these all different people using the same briefcase, or the same person in different disguises?" Cole looked at Steve. "That would be easy enough to find out, wouldn't it? We could do a trace of the names on the tickets for that seat. See if any of them are phony, or have criminal records."

Steve opened a drawer in the file cabinet next to his desk. "I don't need you to tell me how to do my job, Cole." He pulled a file out and slammed the drawer shut. "Get out of here, both of you."

Meagan shouldered her purse and stood. "You don't suspect me anymore?"

"Oh, I still suspect you," he said, not once looking at her or Cole. "Don't leave town until I've gotten this sorted out."

She grabbed her camera and put it with her notepad into her purse. "Thank you," she said, though she was not sure what she was thanking him for. Not putting her in jail, for one.

Cole stood to follow her out. "You should get back to your own job, Cole," Steve said, still engrossed in his file. "Stay out of this from here on out."

Meagan couldn't help but notice Cole seemed disturbed by Steve's words.

The office door opened and a man's head, covered in a mop of hair too blonde to not come from a bottle, popped in. "Hey, Steve, nice office," he said with a grin. "Bet you're going to be bummed when the construction workers are finished with your cubicle."

"Shut up, Jensen," Steve groused. "I've got work to do. Get out, all of you."

The light-haired man left, laughing, and Meagan followed Cole out the door. "What is your real job?" she asked once they were in the hallway.

Cole's lips turned downward and he looked back at the room they had just exited. "I wondered how he'd gotten such a nice office so quickly," he said almost to himself. "He's still the new guy on the team. Doesn't even have anyone under him yet." Shaking his head, he turned to Meagan. "I thought you didn't want to talk to me."

"Well, once Steve finds out who did this, he can investigate the criminal instead of me, and you'll have no reason to follow me anymore, right?"

"I wasn't following you for—" He shook his head. "Never mind."

This whole mess would be over soon and life would get back to normal. As he held the entrance door to the Federal Building open for her, she found herself smiling at him. "Now you can get back to your own job, whatever it is, and forget all about me."

He stared at her and she wished she could read his thoughts. At last he said, "Goodbye, Meagan Winston. Be safe."

"You, too." She walked down the steps, but then turned back to say, "And enjoy your meat lover's pizza tonight." She laughed at the stunned expression on his face, feeling lighter than she had in days.

15

Friday, January 2
8:00 p.m.

Cole turned the hot water knob on in the sink, removed his shirt, and stared at the scars reflected in the bathroom mirror. The pizza had not set well with him tonight. How had Meagan known about the pizza anyway? Steve must have told her. Cole wished he hadn't. He didn't like when people talked about him, thought they knew things about him.

He would go see Sadie in the morning, remember why he did what he did, and get the strength to go back to it for another week. When she was free, he would be too. Not until then.

Reaching up, his fingers traced the collection of bubbled scars that spread across the skin of his left shoulder and pectoral muscle in the pattern of a small fireworks explosion. The marks were like a moonlit night after a battle, calm and quiet, a mockery of the rage and blood that filled the daylight hours.

She removed her head covering and smiled, looking him straight in the eye before she swept by. "Let's go someplace quiet, where we can talk."

"Go for it." Steve nudged him from behind. "She's the first woman we've seen not wearing a big black tent in weeks. Every guy in the place is salivating over those curves, and the woman just invited you to follow her into a dark private corner. Why are you still here?"

"She's after something." Cole had seen her before, had noted how she worked a room of soldiers. "Her smile doesn't reach her eyes."

"You were looking at her eyes?" Steve downed a shot glass and ordered another. "If you don't go, I'll take your place. Who cares what she's after?"

He had sat with her that night, and the next. She had asked about his family, about his dreams, about his battalion...

Cole remembered the blood draining out across his uniform, his fellow soldiers dragging him to a vehicle, shouting at him to stay awake. Later, he feigned unconsciousness when the journalists and generals questioned his actions and his honor. The journalists had written whatever they pleased, whatever would cause the most sensation. The generals had found him again, asked again, and got the truth, as much as he knew it.

The honorable discharge he'd received carried weight with him, but not many others, who put more stock into words in a newspaper than an official document. Cole had never defended himself to them, never told his side of the story despite opportunities by *Time* magazine and *Newsweek*. He'd given enough pieces of himself for his country; he would not cut out another pound of flesh for an image. They said it would repair his reputation. Cole had no use for that. Why should it matter if he was hero or villain to people who cared nothing for him?

Cole leaned over the sink and cupped handfuls of hot water to wash his face and neck. He held a frayed washcloth under the spigot until it was soaked, then pressed it against the skin over his heart. Warmth seeped into his body and water dripped down his torso to land in puddles on and around his feet, soaking the towel he'd placed on the floor. The wound there had almost killed him, and the surviving scar tissue made his shoulder stiff, his mind extremely wary of anything that resembled a grenade, and his heart, well, his heart condition wasn't something he wanted to analyze. No one else prioritized it, so why should he? Sadie needed him, said she loved him, but it hadn't been enough to keep her from going back. Steve was supposed to be his best friend, but he'd turned cynical lately. He had it all—a nice wife, nice house, great job—but life didn't seem to be working out like he'd hoped. Or it could be that since Cole had given his life to Jesus, he'd changed, while Steve still insisted that he didn't need anybody to be in charge of making his life count.

Cole folded the washcloth and wrung it out over the sink, then soaked it in hot water again and placed it back against his chest. That was the one good thing that had come of his life being blown apart; he'd finally submitted to his need for a Savior. Giving his life back to Jesus had brought peace he hadn't been able to find even during those days he'd been hailed as a hero, before the condemnation. And having God as his Father had healed the deepest wounds inflicted by the person he should have been able to trust most.

But healed wounds left scars, like the ones he could see now, that each morning were stiff and sore. Life was a battle, the PTSD counselor told him once. Those who developed skills and exercised them fought better than those who didn't. That's why each morning he stretched physically with fifty pushups and a two-mile run, and spiritually with time in his Bible before the run and a talk with his God during it.

Some days Cole wondered if every day was meant to be this much of a battle, in a war with no end in sight. He thought of Meagan Winston, of the joy in her voice when she talked about rescuing children from some of the darkest places in the world. She battled, but did not seem defeated.

He turned off the water, wrung out the washcloth again, and hung it to dry. With sudden resolve, he dried off his chest and arms, changed into dry pants, put his shirt and shoes back on, and walked across his one-bedroom apartment to pull his jacket and keys off the hooks hanging near the front door. He had too many questions about Meagan Winston, too many conflicting feelings, and little patience for either.

Cole jogged down the outside stairs to his car, glad the sunny day earlier made for a mild winter night. He hated wearing a coat. The moon was over three-quarters full and the sky cloudless and serene. He cranked up his Sedan and put the car in drive, heading toward the road to Meagan's house. He wasn't sure how he would explain his appearance at her house at night, but he felt a need to talk with her. Ask questions. See if he could find out if she was on his side of the fight or Sadie's. Did she need his help as a victim of misinterpreted evidence, or was she a victim of her own wrong choices?

He couldn't ignore that he felt drawn to her. If nothing else, tonight he wanted to find out why.

Cole turned on the radio but after a few minutes switched to a CD. Even that could not penetrate through the fog of his thoughts, so he turned the music off and drove in silence. At some point, he told himself he should be paying more attention, keeping alert to the possibility of being followed, but that seemed unnecessary. The few cars on the back road had dwindled to just him and one other car, and no one had reason to follow him. If Meagan were in the car with him, that would be a different matter

Three miles from her house, he noticed the headlights behind him made a sudden wild shift to the left. "Not smart," Cole muttered at the passing car. "Can't you see we're nearing a bridge?"

The car pulled up alongside. A good ways ahead, Cole saw another set of headlights in the oncoming lane. He slowed, but the car beside him slowed as well, then jerked to the right, slamming into the side of his vehicle.

"What are you—" Cole tried to center the wheels and stabilize the vehicle. The car beside him swerved right again. Cole took a split second to look to the left at the driver. A horn honked. The oncoming vehicle was close now, on the bridge. Cole's Sedan was half off the road, speeding toward the guardrail. Cole had no choice. He swerved to the right, just missing the guardrail, and skidded off the road. The car flipped and dived down a steep embankment. He saw the river rush up to meet him, but had no time to react, only to think that now none of his questions would get answered.

16

Friday, January 2
8:30 p.m.

Lucias grabbed an empty pillowcase off his bed and wiped the makeup from his face. He smiled at Meagan's picture on the wall. What a rush. He yanked off the wig he'd found two years ago in a dumpster behind a costume store and threw it onto a pile of dirty clothes. When he wore it, he became Agatha. He'd never known his grandmother, but it felt nice using her name, like a connection. When he was Agatha, people were nice to him. They didn't judge Agatha like they judged Lucias. They didn't accuse her of crimes. Of murder.

But tonight, Agatha had shown a surprising violent side. It energized him. Agatha had banged up the side of his car, but she was a little eccentric. He understood that, and forgave her. The car already had a few dents it in anyway.

It was Agatha who had taken the drugs to the trade-off point in India this last trip, and Agatha was the one who'd seen Meagan in trouble that same day. Lucias liked to walk by the building where she worked, liked to see the light in her eyes when she hugged the children or taught them a new song. Meagan would be a wonderful mother someday. Not like his mother.

That day Meagan had left the building and was summoning a rickshaw when the attack came. A man held out a knife and yelled something. Meagan reached into her bag and gave him a handful of money, but Agatha saw that he was not satisfied. He was about to cut the bag from her shoulder. Or cut her.

Agatha had run toward them, screaming, swinging the briefcase that had just been emptied of drugs and filled with Indian rupees. The man had been surprised, and ran. Meagan had been surprised, too. She said thank you and started to walk toward him. He could not let her discover Lucias underneath Agatha, so he also had run away.

Later, three rows behind her on the plane, empowered enough by his act of heroism to ride as himself for the first time, Lucias realized the robbery had brought out his true feelings for Meagan. He didn't just admire her. He loved her. Needed her to love him.

He was still waiting for the perfect time to meet her face-to-face, to show her how he felt. She might not believe him at first, but he would tell her all the times he had watched over her. Protected her. Like the day after they'd returned, when she'd been run off the road. Then on New Year's Day when those men had bothered her in the square near her store. He knew the 9-1-1 operator had told her he'd called. Meagan had turned all the way around, looking for the hero who helped her. He had felt his chest swell with pride, with hope.

And he had protected her tonight. Getting rid of that man in the black suit had been the right thing to do. Meagan belonged with him. No one else.

He finished the double cheeseburger he'd picked up at a fast-food restaurant on the way home and threw the wrapper across the room. It landed in the corner near the trash can. He wasn't a messy person really; it was the trailer. If he lived in a nicer home, he would make the effort to keep it up better. This old dump was his mother's, or had been before she ran off for good with some drifter who offered her a ride and a new life, but didn't have room for a kid. Lucias had taught himself to drive the old grey Oldsmobile she'd left parked in the yard. The car was his now. So was the trailer, and everything else she had left behind. The heat in the trailer didn't work. The sink was full of plates and cups from back before he decided to switch to disposable dishes. Under the counter, behind the trash can where no one would want to look, he kept his cut of the tiny bags of powder that made the headaches go away for a while.

He hated the trailer. Hated the drugs. Hated his whole miserable life.

But things would soon change for good. Meagan wasn't like his mother or like Claudia. She didn't leave the people she loved. She wouldn't reject him.

She was the one and only woman for him. He would tell her with actions, then with words in person. He'd launched the actions with the note. It was time for the next step.

17

Friday, January 2
9:15 p.m.

Cole woke to find himself still alive and in pain. Glass from the windshield littered the front seat and his body. He brushed it off, grimacing as shards sliced across his skin. He unbuckled his seat belt and pulled the door handle. Mangled metal screeched but the door would not budge.

The trickling sound he had at first assumed was the ringing in his ears increased to the unmistakable rush of water. He fought through the pain to stretch upward and across the seat to reach his glove compartment, discovering as he tried to move that his right leg was pinned beneath the dashboard just below his knee. With a lunge and a moan, he opened the compartment and rummaged frantically for his flashlight.

Grasping it, he clicked it on and fought panic. The car had landed right side up, but was perched at a diagonal angle on the bank of a river. The front of the car was already submerged, and water pooled over the floorboards. That trickle he'd heard, now more like a faucet turned on, was water washing into the car through the open space where his driver's side window had been. The passenger side, tilted a foot or so up onto the embankment, was dry, but Cole could feel the car sinking.

Adrenaline surged. He had to get out. Now. Where was his phone? Pulling off his jacket, every movement bringing pain, he reached into his back pocket. With one hand wrapped in his jacket and beating at the dashboard that pinned his leg, he used his other hand to speed-dial Steve.

"Hey," Steve answered. "What are you—?"

"Get help out here now!" Cole shouted. His attempts to free his leg were futile. "I'm trapped in a car that's sinking into the river." He named the lonely back road, the river, and his position.

"How much time do we have?" Steve's voice took on the edge Cole knew his own had, that acute awareness that kicked in during every battle. This was a different kind of fight, against the enemy of death, and time was not on Cole's side.

"Five minutes, maybe less, before the water fills the car enough to pull it under."

The silence on the other end told Cole more than words could. He was too far out of town. Steve couldn't get anyone there in time. Cole hung up. He was on his own.

"God," he prayed, attacking the dashboard again, forcing his leg to pull against the pain. "I don't want to die tonight. I'm not finished. I think You still have work for me to do, but if You do, You'll have to show me—"

It came to him. The hammer! Lunging again for the glove compartment, he thanked God for the beat-up starter that had taught him to carry a hammer ever since. Once it was in hand, he banged on the dashboard area that held down his leg. Bit by bit he knocked off portions of plastic, feeling a slight release in the pressure on his leg each time a piece fell into the cold water rising up his calf.

The car groaned and tilted farther to his left, knocking him off balance. He fell against the door and dropped the hammer onto his knee. He let out a yell, then found the hammer and pounded again. Water rushed in his window and soaked his left arm and side.

With one final bang, the main section of the dashboard column broke apart and Cole pulled his leg free. He wrapped his right hand in his jacket again, now heavy with water, and climbed upward toward the passenger side, using the steering wheel, the seat, and the middle partition as leverage. The car fell to stand on its left side. Cole lost his footing. He grabbed at the window casing with his left hand and glass pierced into his palm. The car began to slide downward, into the river. Skipping the door handle, Cole used his jacket-covered hand to knock out the remaining pieces of broken glass lining the passenger window. As the river began to pour like a waterfall into the car, he pulled himself up and out of the vehicle.

The car sank to the point that only the right side of the back end was now above the water. Cole used his legs against the door to push away into the water and half-swam, half-trudged back to the embankment.

Red and blue lights neared as Cole waited for the dizziness to pass and then dragged himself up the incline to the bridge. He stood and saw Steve throw open his car door and race to the guardrail alongside the bridge.

"Cole!" Steve yelled, then shouted back at arriving emergency personnel, "The car is submerged. We've got to get a rescue team down there now!"

"I'm here," Cole tried to shout, but coughed up water instead. The sound alerted a fireman on the scene, who gestured and issued orders to his crew. Soon Cole found himself in the back of an ambulance, its heat on full blast. A stranger took his vitals, and Steve paced the pavement in front of the open back doors as Cole gave a report on what happened.

"It was the old lady," he said, rubbing his aching knee with his bandaged left hand. "I think."

"What were you doing heading for the girl's house in the first place?" Steve moved in closer and said through gritted teeth, "Do you have any idea how this makes me look to my team head? He questioned me on the way here and I didn't know anything about what was going on! This was supposed to be an easy case to crack. We had the evidence. I was assigned to get Meagan to testify and we could close the international part of the case and hand the rest to the DEA team. You've turned it into an attempted homicide investigation."

Cole's head felt like a watermelon split open. "Sorry my almost getting killed caused you embarrassment." He rose and stepped down onto the road. With a swipe, he removed the blood pressure cuff from his upper arm and tossed it back onto the gurney in the ambulance.

The woman who had checked him came to stand between the vehicle's open doors, bent at the waist to keep her head clear of the ambulance roof. "Where are you going?" she asked over the roar of the heater, pen poised in mid-air above her clipboard. "Your blood pressure is high and you have multiple abrasions. You could have bruised ribs!" He waved her off.

"You need to get checked out," Steve said, his tone a little less antagonistic.

"You want this in the newspapers?" Cole smirked at the war of emotions on Steve's face, but even the smirk hurt. He grabbed his jacket off the ambulance bumper and looked it over. Unless he was willing to go after it with a needle and thread, which he wasn't, it was time for a replacement. He hadn't gone into a clothing store in years and didn't want to now. He could get something online, but he'd have to remember he had twenty pounds more muscle than back when he'd bought the jacket in his hand. He tossed the wet material to Steve. "I'm going home," he said.

Steve balled up the jacket and set it on the hood of the nearest police car. "In what? Your car is underwater."

Cole groaned aloud. "I need a car for a week or so, until insurance gets me a new one."

"And I'm supposed to what? Buy you one?"

"Loan me something. You have to have resources for someone whose car got destroyed as part of your investigation."

"I didn't ask you to continue in this investigation."

"I didn't ask for the guy to send me into the river," Cole ground out.

"He wouldn't have wanted to if you hadn't been following that girl around." Steve pointed down the road. "She called me and told me you'd followed her to her house. She already called the police about us stalking her before. So this time she gets somebody to knock you off the road."

"Do you seriously think she's behind all this?"

"It's possible."

Cole looked over the rail to the river. "I liked that car."

Steve let out a heavy breath and handed Cole a set of keys. "You can use my car for now. I'll catch a ride home with one of the guys and borrow Stephanie's car until you can get a new one."

"Thanks." Cole accepted the keys and rounded Steve's car toward the driver's side.

"Why don't you let somebody drive you home, at least?"

He shook his head. "I've got a stop to make first."

Steve slammed his hand against the hood. "Cole, I told you—"

"I don't think she did this," Cole said, opening the car door. "But if she did, I want her to see that I'm still here and I'm seeing this through until we find the truth."

He was in the car, ignition turned on, when Steve knocked on the window. Cole lowered it and Steve said, "You aren't part of this investigation anymore, Cole. You're out."

"A guy just tried to kill me, Steve." Cole's jaw set. "I'm in this investigation till the end, whether you—or I—want me to be or not."

18

Friday, January 2
10:15 p.m.

"My momma done told me," Pops sang as he strummed the chords on his old guitar, making up his own version of the song as he always did. "That women...make you sing the bluuuues in the night."

Kelsey, curled up near the window on an old green couch that looked like a return to the seventies, laughed and asked him to sing it again. "Thank you so much for coming over," Meagan told her. "I feel badly taking you away from your house and your husband, but after what's happened these past few days, I'm just plain scared."

"Nathan's fine," Kelsey said of her husband. Meagan wasn't surprised Kelsey wore one of her many outfits from India, all of which had drawstring waists and flowing tops. Kelsey hated tight waistbands, or tight anything other than socks. Even her watch was clasped loosely on her wrist. "He recorded a couple of bowl games he missed while we were with Alexia the other day and has been itching to watch them. I'm happy to stay here as long as I'm needed, just as I'd stay with any girl being accosted."

Meagan carried her grandfather's blood sugar checking machine over to his recliner and got everything ready for his evening shot of insulin. She thought of the sadness in Cole's eyes when she'd said that word. "He hasn't really done anything bad. In fact, this last time he said he wanted to help me get clean and stay clean. He thinks I'm guilty."

"Do you think that's why he followed you, to try to find evidence or something?"

"Maybe. But then he said some grey car has been trailing me for days. I don't know what to make of that. Did you ever find out who was at the counter when that note for me came?"

Kelsey glanced out the window into the darkness. Meagan had wanted to pull the shades closed, or sit in a room without windows facing the road, but if she changed the routine, she'd have to explain why to Pops. At least the driveway was gravel. No one could come down it without making enough noise to alert them. "We had two volunteers manning the register that day," Kelsey said, "but neither of them remember anyone leaving a note. The second girl, Valerie, did mention she was over in the opposite corner for several minutes answering a customer's questions about the fair trade spices. She said there were several other people in the store, so someone might have left it then." Kelsey took the insulin syringe from Meagan's hands. "You're so distracted you hardly got the sugar reading. Let me do the shot."

"I can do it," Meagan's silver-haired grandfather offered. He set his guitar on the floor. "What's distracting you, Meagan? I heard you say something about a guy following you home. Sounds promising."

"Oh, Grandpa, stop teasing." Meagan felt ridiculous for blushing. "He's just a guy trying to dish up dirt on me, that's all."

"Well, why don't you dish up some of that peanut butter fudge you're so good at making, and change his mind?" He plunged the needle in without any signs of pain. After thirty years of daily shots, he said his skin was so thick he didn't even feel them anymore.

"This girl needs to get a husband, or at least a boyfriend, before I kick off," Pops said to Kelsey. Her eyes widened, but Meagan laughed. He'd talked like that since she was a kid. "Here I am, old as the hills. All my friends are sick or dead, but I can't die or even go senile until I know my little girl is taken care of. Seems kind of inconsiderate of her to make me hold out this long, don't you think?" He reached over and patted Meagan's hand. "Get yourself a guy who can fix things. That pipe under the kitchen sink is leaking again."

While Kelsey mumbled, "Good gracious," Meagan thought unaccountably of Cole's statement that he couldn't fix cars other than hitting them with a hammer. Maybe he could hit the pipe back into place.

What was she thinking?

"It's time I got you to bed," she told her grandfather, clearing the empty syringe and sugar-testing machine off the table, and placing his pills—two large, three small—on it within reach. She stood next to his chair, hands full, until he had taken all five pills with water. "It's late."

"You women love telling us men what to do," he grumbled, rocking back and forth until the momentum was enough to lift himself out of the chair. She was glad to not have to help him up tonight. He had a good fifty pounds on her, and she felt drained in every way.

"Do your legs feel tight?" she asked.

"The wrappings feel tight, if that's what you mean. Can't feel my legs much at all these days." He winked at Kelsey, mischief in his eyes. "I think about a third of me has already died and gone to heaven. The rest of me is just running late." The seventy-five-year-old man wobbled and fell back into the recliner.

"You did that on purpose," Meagan said, using his same teasing tone, "just so I'd have to check your legs again tonight."

"Well, it takes a lot for a guy to get any attention around here."

Meagan heard Kelsey's soft laugh from her stance near the window. When Meagan left the room to wash her hands before re-bandaging her grandfather's legs, Kelsey followed her. "You're blessed to live with someone with such a sense of humor," she said. "But how do you know when he's serious?"

"He's serious about me getting settled," Meagan said. She lathered her hands then rinsed off the soap. "After Nana died, my parents wanted him to go to a nursing home where he could get full-time care, but he wouldn't consider it. He says he has to stay in this house until I'm ready for him to give it to me."

"Who takes care of him when you're in India?"

"My parents pay for someone to stay with him during the day while I'm gone. I know I'm supposed to trust God and not be anxious about anything, but I struggle with worrying about him when I'm overseas. One time he fell during the night, and had to lie there until someone came the next day to help him up."

"So what, in his mind, means you're ready for this house?"

"Getting married." She smiled as she filled a glass with milk and carried it back into the living room, speaking loudly enough for both of them to hear. "He wants to leave this house to a future generation, not just a single girl, right, Pops?"

"Right-o," he said, accepting the milk as she propped up the recliner's footrest and pushed his brown polyester pant legs above his knees to look over the bandages. Diabetes had taken its toll on him. The skin on his lower legs was so thin that just pulling on his pants tore into it like it was tissue paper. A nurse had taught Meagan how to wrap his legs in protective layers of mesh and ace bandages, and Meagan had grown to enjoy the ritual. She got to hear stories from Pop's life she would have missed otherwise in her busy schedule. "This house needs to be full of kids, not just giggling females in their pajamas." He grinned at Kelsey. "No offense."

She smiled back. "My pajamas aren't nearly as worthy of offense as Meagan's."

He let out a hearty laugh. "Never saw anybody dress the way she does for bed."

"There's a reason for it," Meagan defended, glancing down at her big slippers, fleece pants covered with red-nosed reindeer, pastel purple flannel nightgown that came down to her thighs, and her silk flowered robe that wasn't as long as the nightgown. "I like to sleep in a nightgown, but Grandma used to sleepwalk sometimes, and I couldn't run around the house with bare legs, so I started wearing pants with it. The robe was a gift from her. And the slippers..." She grinned at the bunny heads on her feet. "It just cracks me up to wear bunny slippers."

"They don't match the reindeer," Kelsey said.

"But they go great with the flowers," Pops joked.

Meagan laughed with them. "I like them and I'm going to keep them."

Her grandfather chuckled as he sipped his milk. "And she wonders why she's not married yet."

"Hey, no guy has ever seen my slippers."

"Maybe you should keep it that way." Kelsey grinned like a child and Meagan smiled. It was good for her to have a night away from the store and the phone and the needs always coming in. Atlanta was one of the worst cities in the world for human trafficking. Their work in Gainesville encountered the spillover, and there was always more than they could handle, particularly when the bulk of their focus and time stayed allotted for their passion for rescuing victims in India. They should get together away from work more often.

Meagan tightened and secured the bandages before pulling her grandfather's pant legs back down to his own staid, practical set of slippers. "Well, I think that—" She heard the crunch of gravel outside. "What was that?"

Kelsey rose and looked out the window. "There's a car coming down the driveway." She turned to Meagan. "Are you expecting someone?"

Meagan shook her head. "Not at ten-thirty at night."

"Should I call Nathan?"

Meagan glanced at her grandfather, who sat straighter to look outside. The car stopped just in front of the house. "Someone's come to visit. How nice."

His words were pleasant, but they shot cold fear through Meagan's heart. She looked at Kelsey. "What should we do?"

19

Friday, January 2
10:30 p.m.

Stephanie Campbell used to hate nights like these, when Steve worked late and didn't bother to call. When they were first married, she would eat her fingernails to the quick, afraid he'd been shot, or was lying in some ditch, beaten half to death.

Now she just filled the holes with other things—the holes he made in her days and nights with his long absences, and the holes in her heart from their marriage fading into two annoyed strangers who shared the same house. She'd had such hopes for their life together, for the baby. Her miscarriage had been the turning point. Steve disappeared into his work. He never talked about it, acted like nothing had happened. Didn't he know her most beautiful dreams had died? Didn't he understand how much she needed his comfort and reassurance?

If he did, he didn't care. So she decided not to care either, about the food she ate or the clothes she wore or the spreading condition of her body. He never looked at her anymore, so what was the point? She turned to other things to fill the lonely hours. First it was romance novels, stories of first love, passion, desire, all the things Stephanie missed most. In the books she remembered and felt desirable again for a time. Once the book was closed, however, reality came in, harsh and stifling and dark. Nights were the worst. She told herself that she needed the videos to keep herself distracted from the fear and loneliness. Most of them weren't bad, after all. The best kissing scenes from movies—nobody could judge her for watching those. She'd slipped into heavier material, nothing anyone would call hard porn, but told herself if she had some attention from her husband, she wouldn't need to get the feelings her computer now provided. If she deleted the computer history before Steve came home, well, that was to avoid endless arguments about how she never met his needs. His needs? What about her needs?

The word divorce reared its ugly head, as it had more and more lately. Stephanie had never wanted to go through that kind of pain, but would it be any worse than the rejection she felt already? At least then she could move on with her life, find someone else who would appreciate her. She could admit her marriage to Steve had been a mistake and start over.

She picked up the romance novel on the top of the second pile beside her chair. Its cover showcased a muscular man without a shirt caressing a woman whose clothing seemed in danger of blowing off in the wind. It wasn't the steamy scenes she fed on most, Stephanie told herself, but the looks he would give her, the words he would say, the love she would feel, even if it was in a fantasy world.

After a skim through the book for the best parts, she tossed it aside. She had to find something more distracting than a book. She reached for the computer on the arm of the couch next to her chair, always set within reach now. It booted up too slowly, and Stephanie considered getting up to dish herself another bowl of ice cream. The little dings that meant the laptop was ready convinced her to stay put. She clicked on the internet icon and tapped her fingers on the keyboard while she waited for it to pull up. Just one video tonight. A romantic one, where the man wants the woman with desperate desire and pursues her until she can resist no longer. She just needed one. Then she'd go to bed.

The distinct sound of a key in the lock made Stephanie want to cry out in frustration. Why did he have to come home right at that moment? Couldn't he even let her have one enjoyable thing in her day? The door opened with a slow creak, like some horror movie before the wife alone at home gets murdered. Stephanie wanted to laugh. The door creaked because her husband was so busy hunting recognition he never got around to oiling it.

"Ran out of things to do at the office?" she said in greeting.

Steve stepped inside and looked over the room, at the books, the computer, at her in her aqua sweats and t-shirt. He sighed. "I thought you'd be in bed by now."

She shut down the internet connection and closed the computer lid with a snap. "Sorry to disappoint you."

"No, I just..." He frowned. "Is there anything for supper?"

"Supper?" She set the laptop back on the couch. "As in the food eaten in the early evening? It's going on eleven, Steve."

"I know. I had a long day."

"So did I."

"Yeah?" He dropped his coat onto the couch and tossed his keys on the side table. "Do anything interesting?"

"Like you care."

"Do we need to have this conversation right now?"

She lowered the footpad on the recliner but did not get up. "There are leftovers in the fridge."

He walked around where she sat, not stopping to give her a kiss or any kind of touch. Of course. On his way by the chair, his leg knocked over her two stacks of novels. "What are those doing here?" He kicked at them.

"Stop!" She reached over the armrest and tried to keep the stacks from falling further. "I'd just organized those into the ones I'd read and the ones I hadn't. Can't you be even a little considerate?"

"Me?" Steve threw out his hands. "You're home all day, but the house is a wreck. I never get a home-cooked meal. And you're still wearing the same thing you've slept in all week. Who's being inconsiderate?"

"All you do is complain! You don't ever try to understand." She let the tears go. They were always just below the surface. Let him see them and feel guilty. He should. "You never try to help, or be here at all. Why should I clean the house when you're always gone? Why should I bother to get dressed when you don't even look at me anymore? And—"

"I'm looking at you now."

He was, and it made the hurt cut deep. She knew what he saw. She had seen herself in the mirror that day, a sad, broken woman who had nothing left to live for. "Why weren't you there for me, Steve?" Her voice was hoarse. Her hands clutched at the front of her wrinkled shirt as she stood and faced him. "Why didn't you care when our baby died and my heart broke?"

For a moment, the skin on his forehead lined with compassion. He lifted a hand and rubbed the creases away. "Stephanie, please, not tonight. I'm tired. I'm on a case that's getting more complicated every day. Did you know the DEA investigated over ten thousand meth lab incidents in the U.S. last year? I'm just—"

"You're just so busy playing superhero you don't have time for your wife!"

"Do you want to say it louder so the policeman who dropped me off can hear you?"

She walked over to look through the one window out onto the street. "Why did someone else bring you home?"

"Can we talk about it tomorrow?"

He left the room but she followed him into the kitchen. "Where's your car?"

His head was down and his words muffled as he rummaged through the nearly bare refrigerator, but still she heard his irritation. "Cole's car ended up in the river tonight. I had to loan him mine for a while."

"A while? How long is a while?"

He pulled out a can of beer and popped the tab. "It's not a big deal. I'll just use yours. You don't go anywhere anyway."

"I would if there was somewhere to go. Now I'm stuck here!"

"You want somewhere to go?" He slammed the can down on the table and she jumped. He came close and said, "Then I've got a place for you to go. I dare you to go."

His anger always scared her. She could only whisper, "Where?"

"To church. Sunday morning."

It was hard to wrap her mind around the unexpected words. "What?"

He turned his back on her and took a swig of the drink. "I've got a job for you, if you'd get out of your sweats and off that chair and actually do it."

She searched for words with bite to volley back at him but he continued. "There's a girl, Meagan Winston, our main suspect in the drug trafficking I was telling you about. She goes to a church near here. I found out what Sunday school class she's in, and the lady I talked to said the lesson is interactive." He sent an unpleasant smile back her way. "Which means they like to talk. You could go to her class and scope her out, get her talking about India. I need to know where she goes. Who she sees."

"Why would a drug pusher be going to church?" The thought of going out in public, having to talk to other people, made her feel cold all over. Had it been that long? What was wrong with her? She used to love getting out and meeting new people.

"She's hiding behind this good girl persona." He crossed his arms and she heard the challenge in his voice. "What do you think? I stay home Sunday morning and you go find out about this girl?"

She sneered. "Why don't you come to church, too? You could use some religion."

"I brought her in for questioning already, so she knows me. You'll need to use your maiden name."

"No problem. I don't feel all that married these days anyway."

"What a nice thing to say." He downed the beer and crunched the can between his hands, tossing it on the table. "I'd throw it away, but I'll get to it some other time."

He always knew how to hit back. Why would anyone want to stay in a marriage like this?

"Fine." She'd take his challenge. "What time does Sunday school start? It'll be nice to have a reason to look good for a change."

He left the room without a word or a look back. She stood next to the cluttered kitchen table, seething. She'd show him. On Sunday he'd be watching her leave the house. She'd look like a million bucks and walk away from him just as he'd walked away from her a thousand times now.

Let him be the one sitting at home wishing her back.

20

Friday, January 2
10:30 p.m.

With calculated movements, Meagan patted Pop's knee and stood, speaking casually as she made her way to the window. "Who could be coming to see us so late at night, I wonder?"

Kelsey caught the caution in her tone and kept the conversation light. "Perhaps it's that handsome new suitor of yours." Her smile was wide but not quite genuine. She faced Meagan's grandfather. "Did Meagan tell you about the man who came into the store the other day for a tour? He's tall, and Meagan told me he's a soldier. He must look wonderful in his uniform."

"He's not a soldier anymore," Meagan commented. She positioned herself beside the window out of sight, and moved the curtains enough to see porch lights and headlights. Whoever was in the car had yet to step out. "And he's not a suitor. In truth, I think he doesn't like me much at all." She wasn't telling her grandfather that said man, handsome or not, thought she was some kind of drug lord.

The older man's eyes twinkled. "Oh, the look of love is so rarely seen at first by its recipient, though it is clear to others. You might be in love and not know it. You didn't eat much at supper."

Of all the nights for him to wax poetic. "My stomach still hasn't gotten over all that Indian food yet." Heart thudding, and not because of some assumption that Cole Fleming was anywhere near in love with her, Meagan brought her hand up and edged the curtain away from the window again. The car remained running, headlights shining toward the porch.

When the driver's door opened, Meagan dropped the curtain back in place. "I'll be right back," she said.

Kelsey moved to take her place next to the window. "I'll stay here. Let me know if you need anything." She pulled her phone from the pocket of her flannel pajama pants and held it up. "I'm ready to call Nathan if..." She looked at Pops. "...if our visitor is a friend of his or something."

Meagan nodded and tried to keep from running on her way to the front door to check the deadbolt. Locked. Next, now out of Pop's vision, she raced to the table in the hallway near the kitchen where she had stashed her purse earlier. She tore through it, mumbling at herself for not having sense to keep important items in one of the outside pockets. "There you are." She grabbed hold of her cell phone, then her can of mace.

She could hear the crunch of heavy steps on the gravel. Whoever it was had no qualms about being seen, or the person would not have left the headlights on. *Be calm. Stop shaking.* She snapped open the protective cover on her mace and positioned it to be ready if the need arose. The little defensive weapon seemed so insufficient all of a sudden. Should she get a gun? She hated guns. Didn't know how to use one. And if she got one, what if Pops found it on a day his blood sugar was off and some tragedy occurred? Meagan would never forgive herself.

"Meagan Winston!"

The masculine voice rang loud and clear. Meagan's stomach quivered and she clamped her jaw tight to keep her teeth from chattering. At the bolted front door now, mace in hand, cell phone in her other hand in case she needed to summon help, she called out, "Who are you? What do you want?"

"Meagan, it's Cole. Come outside."

"Is that the handsome soldier?" her grandfather asked from the next room. "He's here at a rather late hour. Kids these days," he muttered, then grinned at her. "Go on out! Maybe he'll serenade you."

That's about as likely as the man getting down on one knee to propose. Meagan unbolted the lock and turned the knob, determined to only crack the door enough to tell him to go home. She pulled the old wooden door back and the sight that met her made her gasp. Cole Fleming stood several yards away. The headlights and porch lights illuminated blood and dirt all over his torn clothing. She yanked open the door and moved out onto the porch before realizing it.

"What happened to you?" She tried to shove her mace and her phone each into her pockets, but remembered her fleece pants didn't have pockets. She rushed forward but stopped at the edge of the porch. "Are you all right?"

He swayed slightly and shivered where he stood. His jacket was nowhere to be seen and his white shirt was soaked on the left side, if not all over. His right pant leg was in shreds below his knee. Blood stains spattered the arms of his shirt, and several matted his face as well. The side of his face without blood was smeared with dirt. "I've been worse," he said. "I'm glad to see you're at home."

"You need medical attention." She came down the steps. "Who did this to you?"

"An old lady in a grey Oldsmobile." His eyes, reflecting the porch lights, penetrated deep into hers, never leaving her face. "Anyone you know?"

"What?" She had come close and reached a hand toward the largest cut on his cheek. "You think I had something to do with this?"

"You tell me, Meagan Winston."

She dropped her hand. "I've told you since the beginning. I'm not part of this at all! How could you even think I would—would—" She looked him over. "What on earth happened to you?"

"It's a long story, but I need to get home."

"You need to get to a doctor!"

He shook his head. "I can handle it." She was shocked speechless when he reached out a hand and cupped her jaw, pulling her chin up until she met his intense gaze. He looked at her for several moments before saying, "I won't tell you what job I do, Meagan Winston, but if you want to know, I can show you why I do it."

Breathless at his unexpected touch, the calluses of his fingers against her skin both comforting and disconcerting, she nodded once. "O-okay."

"I'll pick you up tomorrow morning at seven."

When she revised his statement with, "I'll follow you in my car," he dropped his hand and turned away. As he walked out of the beam of the headlights, she looked past and saw he'd come in an unfamiliar car. Had he wrecked his? If he'd been in an accident, why hadn't EMS workers on the scene taken him to the hospital? "Be careful on your way home," she said, once it was out of her mouth realizing what a silly statement that was.

At the door of the car, he turned and began to speak, but then, mouth still open, he stopped and stared. His gaze went from her flowered robe to her reindeer pants, all the way down to her fluffy bunny slippers. "Am I imagining things?" he asked.

She wrapped both arms around herself, though it did nothing to hide her atrocious outfit. "If I said yes, would you believe me? And not remember this in the morning?"

He shook his head and almost smiled, then got into the car and shut the door, soon making his way out of her driveway and onto the road again. Meagan took slow steps back inside, her mind swimming, questions overriding embarrassment. Who would want to hurt Cole? Why Cole instead of Steve? Even more pressing, why Cole instead of her?

"You should have invited him in."

Meagan imagined her grandfather's reaction had Cole come inside covered in blood and dirt. "I don't think he wanted to come in tonight."

"Well, he'd better know that he needs to ask your old grandpa before he starts up anything official. You be sure to let him know that."

"I don't think you need to worry, Pops." She helped him stand and stabilize his weight, then they hobbled together toward the first bedroom.

He chuckled as he dropped onto the bed. "I'm not so old I don't remember that it's more romantic outside, without having to make small talk with old folks. It's tough pretending you came to visit them, all the time knowing you really came to get a goodnight kiss in the moonlight."

Meagan smiled as he began the familiar story of how he met Nana. He talked as she helped him through the bedtime rituals, making sure he took his final supplements for the day. She removed his slippers and set them neatly on the floor next to his bed. Would Cole get home safely? She did not even know where he lived, or how to contact him to check and see if he was okay. He had been a soldier, she reminded herself, and was more than capable of dealing with violent situations. Unlike herself. Was the person who set her up to take the blame for the drugs the same person who had harmed Cole tonight? Why? She thought of Cole's assumption that she might be part of the attack. Just the thought that he would consider such a thing made her feel ill.

There was no use trying to figure it out. Wherever Cole took her tomorrow morning and whatever he shared might help some of this make more sense. At least now she was fairly certain Cole was a person she could trust. Someone else must have left the note and, according to Cole, followed her for days. But who? And why?

She pulled the covers up to Pop's chin. Hopefully he would sleep hard and she would get a good full night's sleep as well. She blushed with the hope that Cole would also sleep hard and not remember the bunny slippers or the rest of her getup in the morning, or at least have the grace to not mention them.

"Did he kiss you goodnight?" her grandfather asked on her way out of the room.

"No, Pops. He didn't."

"Could be he doesn't know how you really feel. You are good at hiding your feelings, you know." Her grandfather smiled from the bed. "I could always tell when your Nana wanted to be kissed. She'd take just one step closer and lift her chin just a hair, or she'd run a finger across her bottom lip. That used to drive me distracted. You should try it with your man."

"Pops, I—"

He coughed and Meagan reached for the glass of water on his bedside table. After she helped him drink, he sighed deeply. "I just want you to know the happiness we knew for forty-nine years. Next to God's love, married love is the best thing in the world."

She smiled at him. "Right now I just want to get some sleep."

His eyelids slid closed. "Sweet dreams."

Meagan left the room and found Kelsey watching the news back in the living room. "I don't see anything on here about an accident or any kind of attack or anything," Kelsey said. "But from what I could see, he looked pretty banged up. What do you think happened?"

She told Kelsey as much as she knew, and after Kelsey agreed to return in the morning to watch over Pops, Meagan said goodnight and retreated to her own room. Weary in too many ways, she climbed into bed, certain her dreams would be far from sweet that night.

21

Saturday, January 3
1:00 a.m.

"Show your love with flowers," the commercial said. Soft music played while the man on TV gave a vase of red roses to a woman. Her eyes shone. She kissed him.

Lucias rolled to his side on the one twin bed in the trailer, irritated as always at the squeak of the broken spring underneath. His mother should have fixed that before she left, or replaced the whole bed. It sagged, and had rips in the mattress from that one year he'd found a stray dog and kept it inside. He'd named the dog Snap. The ungrateful creature tore the place apart. Snap had been Lucias' first kill.

Feeling a small twinge of pain on his ankle, Lucias threw off the sheet and reached down to slap away the eight-legged creature and scratch a new bite. That made three that night. He would have to make some changes before Meagan came to live with him. She wouldn't want to sleep in a bed with spiders.

He found his phone under an empty milk carton on the chair next to his bed. He'd bought it brand new, his first Smartphone, with the money from the big sale six months ago. It took forever to figure out how to use the dumb thing—it didn't have any buttons, and the man who sold it to him said to swipe it but all that did was bring up more little square pictures of things. Four new holes got kicked into the wall before he figured out how to make a phone call. He dug around on the kitchen table for the phone book, looked up the nearest florist, and dialed the number, breathing hard as he waited, imagining Meagan's face when she saw a vase full of flowers. He'd order a bigger vase than the man on TV had. Would she want to kiss him?

"Hello?" he said when a voice reached his ear. "I want some flowers. Big ones. I—"

The voice on the other line droned on about leaving a message. Lucias looked at the clock. They would be closed now. Disappointment ran through him like heavy rain. The recording ended and he heard the beep. "I want some flowers," he said. "The best and biggest you have in your shop. I can pay. I have cash. Take them to Meagan Winston's house." He listed directions, but then decided he could not bear to miss seeing her face when the flowers arrived. He had to be there, and not watching from far away.

This was it, he realized. The perfect opportunity. He would deliver the flowers himself. He would start out in disguise, just in case, but if she invited him in, or if she cried because she was so happy about the flowers, it might be the perfect moment, the time when he could show himself and tell her how he felt about her.

"I'll deliver the flowers myself," he said. The rush was heady, and Lucias knew it wasn't just leftover buzz from a hit. He was in love. It was wonderful. "I will come in the morning to get them. Bye."

He'd never be able to sleep now. Lucias tore out the page in the phone book with the florist's address on it and set it on the kitchen counter near the door, placing his phone on top to keep it weighted down. Next he began to pick up trash and clear some of the dirty clothes piled high on the wall side of his bed. He emptied the sink of the dirty dishes, throwing them all into a trash bag and tossing the bag outside. He didn't need dishes anymore now that he used paper plates and plastic silverware. It might take all night to get the trailer looking nice, but it would be worth it. If Meagan came soon to be with him, he wanted things to be good for her.

Lucias could hardly wait for tomorrow morning. Three long years he'd watched and planned. It was finally time.

22

Saturday, January 3
6:30 a.m.

Cole's alarm went off at six-thirty and he rolled out of bed with a moan. His whole body ached. A near scalding hot shower eased his muscles but lathering up caused the multiples cuts on his arms and legs to scream pain. He dressed in a high-collared sweater over jeans, covering most of the bruises and cuts, but there was no hiding the ones on his face, or the large slice across his left hand that looked worse this morning than it had the night before. Cole didn't have time for an infection. He rummaged with his good hand through a drawer of forgotten first-aid supplies. Finding an expired tube of triple antibiotic ointment, he applied a liberal line of the goo over the cut, then wrapped his palm in gauze and taped it until it held. The makeshift result looked unsightly, but it was better than the flaring red cut.

Military training had never taught him the skill of getting toothpaste onto his toothbrush using only one hand, but it had taught him how to bear pain, so he used his cut hand as he got ready, putting the thudding into a separate part of his mind. But without the pain overtaking his conscious thoughts, memories flooded in to fill the space.

"You're different than the others." Her dark red lips curved and she leaned forward. "Or am I not attractive enough?"

The woman defined seduction. She was as beautiful in movement as firelight, and as potentially destructive. Cole sat back in his chair and forced his eyes to remain on her face. "What is it you're really after?"

Her false smile dropped to a pout. "Why don't you have a drink or two? You need to loosen up."

"Lose my sense of caution, you mean." Cole put his hands on his knees, wired tight, alert to her growing frustration.

Without transition, her eyes began to glisten and her tone dropped from a purr to a hurt and wounded sound. "You think I want to be like this?" she asked. "You think I want to be rejected by my family and my community, an object for men to desire but not to love?" She placed both palms on the table and leaned on them to stand. "They force me to be here, to act like a cheap whore. This isn't who I am."

He stood and used his body to shield her from curious eyes. "Who is forcing you?"

She had the eyes of a child in a woman's face. "I can't talk here, in public. They'll find out and punish me." Her whisper turned urgent. "Meet me in the old concrete building two blocks down, the one that got bombed out in the last raid. It's empty."

"I can't leave my barracks without—"

She grasped his shirt. "All I need is one piece of information. If I get it, I can go free. Please," she whispered. "Meet me at midnight and I will tell you everything."

Cole returned his toothbrush to its place with his injured hand, using the ache caused by the grip to force his thoughts into neutral territory again. Questions for the dead could not be answered. He turned his mind to a living woman, Meagan Winston. Why had he been willing to take her to see Sadie but not to tell her about his job? Wasn't taking her to Sadie the higher risk?

He analyzed himself as he awkwardly pulled his coat on—he needed to buy a new jacket as soon as possible—and found his keys. If Meagan wasn't guilty of Steve's accusations, then he wanted her to meet Sadie. If she was guilty, he'd be showing her the perfect spot to find future victims. But he could not stop thinking that, if she saw them, the victims, if she looked them in the eye and knew their names, it might make her pause the next time she made the choice to buy or sell.

Meagan was already on the porch when he arrived. She sat on a rocking chair, bundled up against the cold. Smoke billowed from her little VW parked just off the drive. Her message was clear: he was not welcome inside her home. She didn't trust him.

He didn't fully trust her either. They were quite a pair.

For a moment, as she rose and made her way toward his car, he determined that any woman who wore mismatched pajamas with bunny slippers couldn't be a hardened criminal. The memory made him smile as he rolled down the window of Steve's car. "Good morning. You look a lot different than you did last night."

She turned beet red and he wanted to laugh. "As do you," she commented. She looked over his face and then noticed his bandaged hand. "Are you okay?"

The fact that she asked, that she seemed to care, affected him more than was reasonable. "I'm fine. Ready to go?"

She nodded. "Where are we going?"

"Just follow me."

All along the twenty minute drive, Cole checked to make sure Meagan was behind him. He also made sure no grey Oldsmobile was behind her. The last thing he wanted was to lead the real drug seller to Shady Grove, Sadie's secret place of hope and restoration, a place he would fight to protect if necessary. He felt his fight did, in a small way, help Sadie and the others within its walls.

He pulled into the drive but veered off the path before they reached the security gate. Meagan mirrored his actions behind him and got out of the car. "You've definitely maintained your sense of mystery," she said as he exited the car and joined her outside. "What is this place?"

"It's a recovery location for teens who've been victimized into drug or alcohol addiction," he told her. "From here, would you ride with me? They don't let in a lot of visitors, so it will be easier to explain that you're with me if you are, literally, with me."

She glanced around, her face wary. Her gaze landed on the sign with the campus' name and purpose statement on it. "Okay." She locked her car and walked to Steve's vehicle, commenting on Cole's music once she was settled inside. "I wouldn't have guessed you to be a Southern Gospel fan." The guard waved them through the gate and she looked back. "Will my car be okay parked out there?"

"It'll be fine. Like I said, they have few visitors."

"It sounds like you know the place well."

He found himself increasingly aware of her presence beside him in the car. She smelled like vanilla and he kept catching himself wondering if her lips would taste like sugar cookies. "I've come here every weekend since I moved back to Gainesville." He turned to park in a space reserved for guests and shut the engine off. "She knows I'll come spend every Saturday morning with her."

"Who does?"

"When I was a kid, we had an old radio that only got two stations. One was rap. The other was Southern Gospel. You can guess which one stuck."

She looked over at him. "Question evasion noted. Who is your favorite singing group?"

"The Mylon Hayes family." Did she ask because she thought he was making things up to seem more approachable? "After the bombing in Iraq, I was hospitalized with a guy from North Carolina who got his leg blown off. He had all their CDs. When he got an infection and everyone said he wasn't going to make it, he gave them to me."

She winced. "Did he die?"

"He pulled through, but by then I'd been transferred to Emory in Atlanta. When I got better, I sent him a new set and kept these." He ejected his CD and handed it over. "Their newest one, and my favorite, is hymns and classics, but it was in my car and is now at the bottom of a river. I need to order a replacement."

She looked the CD over then slid it into the case he held. Their hands almost touched and he felt like a teenager on his first date. "Let's go," he said gruffly. He got out of the car and kept enough distance between them as they walked to avoid her vanilla smell. Into the building and through the security checkpoint, Meagan followed, looking bewildered. She submitted in silence as the guard hovered over her with his wand. "Clear," the guard said, and ushered them into the large main room furnished with a warm but hodge-podge collection of chairs and couches, with a baby grand piano in the corner. At the piano, a young woman with straight dark hair and multiple earrings in her left ear played chopsticks until she glanced up and saw them enter. "Cole!" She jumped to her feet and rushed to him, but halted midway. "You're hurt!" What began as a glad cry switched in an instant to one of despair. She pressed knuckled fists against her eyes. "You found him and he hurt you!" The girl dropped onto a couch and pulled her knees up to her chest, wrapping her arms around them.

"No, nothing like that," Cole said with quick steps closer. "It had nothing to do with him."

She lowered her hands enough to peek at him. "Promise?"

"I promise."

Her smile came back. She stood and Cole closed the distance between them. He picked her up and twirled her around once, as he always did, careful not to bump into Meagan.

By the time he set her down, Meagan had edged away from them both until her back touched a bookshelf built into the wall.

He knew he was smiling when he held out his hand and said, "Meagan, this is Sadie, my little sister."

23

Saturday, January 3
8:30 a.m.

Lucias floated on top of the world. Today was the day. He would take the flowers to Meagan, then he would take the money to the drop-off and get paid. With the commission he made today, he'd be able to buy another bed for the trailer. A better bed, a bigger bed, for when Meagan came to live with him. He couldn't decide if he should go ahead and buy one and surprise her, or wait until she was with him to help him choose just the right one.

"I'm here to pick up my order," he announced to a woman in the flower shop who looked strung out on too much coffee. Her eyebrows begged for a set of tweezers and her hair was long overdue for whatever women did to color in the roots. He pulled out a business card and laid it on the counter. "Raymond Lester here," he said, pulling the lapels of his plaid jacket together in front, enjoying the way the syllables of the name rolled through his lips. His first choice had been the name Norman, but after he watched *Psycho* several years ago, he decided he didn't want a name associated with someone frightening like that. People might get the wrong idea. "I called in an order last night for the biggest and best flowers you have."

"Yes, sir," the woman said. Her smile was huge and her teeth didn't seem to all fit inside her mouth. "I wasn't sure if you was a prank call or not, but I made it up anyway, just in case." She left the room and returned with a massive collection of flowers held together in a foot-high pink vase. "Is this what you was wantin'? Sure hope so. Took me all morning to put it together."

He looked over the long stems and full blooms of lilies and roses and a bunch of other flowers he couldn't name. "It's perfect," he said. Meagan would have to love him when she got these. How could she not? He would get to see her reaction in less than fifteen minutes. If she cried with joy, he would remove his grey wig and the makeup that disguised him as older. He'd show her his face and tell her that she was his heart's desire.

He pulled his wallet from the inside pocket of the tweed jacket. "How much?"

"Well, you said you had a lot of money, and you wanted the best..."

He tapped his foot. "How much?"

She named a price. "That's ridiculous!" he sputtered.

"Not for all them flowers!" she argued. She pulled the vase from his hands and turned to take it away.

"No, wait." He put a hand on each side of the vase and tugged enough to keep her in the room. "I don't have that much on me right now." She hesitated and he pulled three twenty dollar bills from his wallet and laid them near the register. "You can have that now and I'll pay the rest this afternoon. I'm getting more money today."

The woman snorted and pulled the flowers away from him. "Fat chance," she said. "I'm not stupid. You pay all or nothing."

"But I won't have the money until this afternoon!"

She mimicked his voice with a whine. "Then come back and get the flowers this afternoon!"

He snatched his money back and stuffed it into his wallet. "I'll go get the money now. Don't sell those flowers to anyone else. I'll be back by ten." He ignored whatever nonsense the woman mumbled at him and stormed out of the shop toward his car. His contact wouldn't be at the drop-off until noon, but Raymond would find a way. Raymond was clever and sneaky. He wouldn't make Lucias delay the most important moment of his life for something as stupid as money.

24

Saturday, January 3
10:00 a.m.

"Knock-knock."

"Who's there?"

Cole's eyes gleamed with mischief. "Interrupting cow."

"Interrupting cow wh—"

"Moooo!"

Meagan felt as if someone had thrown her into a snow globe and shaken it up. Cole's younger sister doubled over with laughter on the couch next to her, while Cole ruffled her hair with his un-bandaged hand. Sadie Fleming leaned her waif-like body over to put her head on Cole's shoulder. "Tell another one," she begged.

He wrapped his big arm around her shoulders. She couldn't weigh more than ninety pounds, and curled up next to Cole she looked as small as a child. "I've already told you six," he said with a laugh. "That's all I know."

"Then tell me a story." Meagan watched the girl lift her big, dark eyes in an idolizing gaze at her brother. "The one you used to tell when we were little."

"Okay, peanut," Cole said. He pulled her close. "Once upon a time..."

Who was this man? Unable to fully believe Cole's transformation to loving, caring big brother, despite how his sister clung to him or how tenderness filled his voice whenever he spoke to her, Meagan shifted toward the far edge of the couch in a small, subtle separation from the pair and observed her surroundings. The shelves were stocked full of books, their yellowed pages and worn bindings suggesting second-hand donations. Both the paintings on the walls and the carpet had seen better days, but whoever had created this haven managed to make the environment positive and homey. Meagan would feel comfortable sending a teen trauma victim to such a place.

Cole had not explained much about Shady Grove, but all the girls who passed by or sat reading in the room were survivors of something terrible. Meagan had worked with enough trafficking victims to recognize the aura of deep pain, shielded but never completely hidden. She knew if she talked to the staff, she would find people with her same passion—to help victims not only survive but overcome. Curious, she rose and approached a woman dressed in baby blue scrubs. "Would you have a brochure or something with information about this place?" she asked.

"I'm afraid not." The woman smiled as she made a notation on a laminated chore sheet on the wall behind her. "We are a small facility and can only take in a few girls at a time. We take boarders who are at high risk for continued exploitation, and only after extensive profiling. Most importantly, we only take girls who are willing to get clean, stay clean, and follow the rules while they are with us. It's their choice to stay or not." A bell hung by a handle on the wall next to the sheet. The woman lifted it off the hook and rang it. "Since Shady Grove opened, we've had so many applicants, we've never had to advertise. If you'd like to know more, you're welcome to walk around and ask questions, but please don't ask the girls about their past. Many of them have been deeply wounded and betrayed, and we try not to trigger those memories."

At the sound of the bell, two girls put bookmarks in books and returned them to their shelves. Another two cleaned up the checkers game they had been playing. Cole checked his watch and said, "Ten-thirty. Time for your nap."

The other girls left and the room emptied except for the three of them. "No," Sadie said. She crossed her arms and poked out her bottom lip. "I don't want to take a nap today. Not while you're here."

"You have to," Cole said, his voice calm. He uncrossed her arms and pulled her to a standing position. "It's the rules."

"Will you be here when I get up?" Meagan feared the girl would burst into tears. She wondered how old Sadie was.

"I promise," Cole said. "And I'll make something special for you for lunch."

Sadie's eyes lit up. "Mac and cheese?"

He hugged her. "Of course. Now go on."

The woman in scrubs re-appeared in the doorway and led Sadie from the room. The moment she was out of sight, a shadow seemed to fall over Cole's face and Meagan saw the pain emerge. He had hidden it well all morning.

Meagan stuck a hand into her yellow bag and brought it out wrapped around a bottle of ibuprofen. "Want some?" she asked.

He glanced down as if he'd forgotten she was there. His gaze stayed on her face for several beats, then drifted to her outstretched hand. "Yeah," he said. "Thanks."

She popped the top and dropped two pills into his hand. He took them down dry and almost smiled when her nose scrunched. "Learned to do that in the military. Pain is more readily available than water sometimes."

"Which branch were you in?" She rose and walked with him from the main room through a smaller sitting room and into a kitchen designed for large-scale cooking.

"Marines." He gestured around the empty room. "We have the place to ourselves for the next half hour."

"Why did you leave the military?"

He looked back at her, studying, and she wondered if he could see through her eyes and tell she knew about his injury from the bombing. And about the woman spy. He surprised her with a sudden smile. "Tell you what, you answer five of my questions, and I'll answer three of yours."

She sat on a bar stool with a laugh. "I'm no math expert, but that doesn't seem fair."

"It isn't," he responded with a grin. He used his right hand, the one not bandaged, to pull a box of macaroni and cheese mix from the third cupboard to the left. Retrieving a pot from under the sink, he set it under the faucet, then reached around her for a serving spoon. "But life isn't fair sometimes. Take it or leave it."

"You seem to know your way around this kitchen."

He filled the pot halfway with water and dumped the macaroni in. "I should. I make mac and cheese every Saturday for Sadie."

"So you're a nice brother but not much of a cook."

He put the pan on the stove and set the burner. His smile did not hide the sadness around his eyes. "She was just a kid when our mom left. I was a young teen, but I got a side job sweeping in the back room of a grocery store. The owner paid me off the record to avoid child labor laws. We lived on Ramen noodles most nights, but on Saturday I'd splurge and get a box of mac and cheese, and we'd celebrate like it was a gourmet meal. It's still her favorite food." He turned and leaned a hip against the counter as he faced her. "Her short term memories are affected by the years of drug use, so she doesn't always remember that I come every week. On the bright side of that, it's special for her every time I come and every time I make this."

Meagan blinked away tears and swallowed hard. "Where was your father?"

Cole's face hardened. "Gone most of the time. Making money. Drinking it away. We were better off when he wasn't around than when he was."

She could tell more was being left unsaid than said, but didn't pry further. The macaroni began to boil. She sat up straighter on the stool and tried to lighten the atmosphere. "So you said you had five questions for me? Or were you just throwing out a number?"

He looked relieved at the change of subject. Turning to stir the boiling noodles, his own voice lost some of its heaviness as he said, "I'll start with five, but often answers to questions lead to more questions."

She joined him at the stove. "Well, you only get five in our deal."

He breathed in deep, like he smelled something nice, and she felt her heart engage when he smiled at her. "I'll take it for now. Question one: who was the white-haired lady in the blue van that came to your house the day I drove by?"

"Oh." He wanted to ask investigative questions. She told herself to ignore the disappointment that it wasn't something more personal, and moved to the refrigerator to look for a carton of milk. "We call her the bath lady. She comes twice a week to give Pops a bed bath now that he can't get around much and his skin is so susceptible to damage." Meagan set the milk on the counter next to the stove and went back for the butter. "So you won't have to waste another of your questions," she said with a glance his way, "she's not the white-haired lady in the muumuu on the plane, and we aren't in cahoots or anything. She's a nurse practitioner and I can give you her name and info. She'd have a solid alibi for the entire time I was in India."

He stirred the noodles with an absent nod. "That's good to hear. Question two: did your grandmother really die four months ago?"

Meagan set the butter on the counter, her eyes down. "Yes. Of cancer."

"I'm sorry."

She kept her face averted. "I miss her," she whispered.

From the corner of her eye, she saw him set the spoon aside and move toward her, an arm out in the same motion he had used earlier before he hugged his sister. She held her breath, wanting to be held and comforted, but afraid to want either from him. He stopped before touching her, returned to his place in front of the stove, and she let the breath out.

"I'm sorry," he said again. "That must have been hard."

She nodded and pulled a measuring cup from where it hung from a hook on the wall. With a spoon from a nearby drawer, she measured out a fourth cup of butter. "Did you know your grandmother?"

He shook his head. "No. Not my grandfather either, or any relatives. My dad and mom were both runaways when they met. I wish we had. It would be good for Sadie to have someone besides me."

Meagan thought of what she had seen over the course of the morning, thought of her own childhood wish for a strong big brother. "She has a lot, having you," she said.

His hand stilled over the pot and his eyes met hers. Today they were less green and more hazel, muted by his dark sweater. "Thank you."

The air was charged with too much emotion. Meagan turned away and hunted for a mixing bowl. "So what's question number three?"

"Why did you cut your hair and change the color right after you got back?"

She set the bowl on the counter with a little too much force. "Why do you want to know that?"

He went back to stirring.

"The noodles don't have to be stirred the whole time," she pointed out.

"I know," he said. "Usually I bring a book to read while Sadie naps." He continued to move the spoon in a circular motion, saying, "It looks suspicious. You go to India with beautiful long, dark hair, and when you get back chop it off and dye it a different color. Like you're trying to look like a different person. Like you have something to hide."

"Oh brother." She slapped spoonfuls of butter into the bowl. "You've never been a woman in Asia, have you?"

"Uh, no, on both counts." His grin came back. "I've never been a woman or been to Asia."

She fought a smile. "Well, if you had, you'd learn fast that in the part of India where we work, lighter skin and lighter hair are considered more beautiful." She touched her bangs, brushed aside now that she didn't need to hide the bruise any longer. "My natural hair shade is blonde and my natural skin color is pasty white. I went out the first time looking like that and I had men following me down the street, offering to marry me."

He chuckled and she scowled at him. "It was embarrassing, and it didn't help that I'm taller than just about everybody in the whole country. My presence causing such a stir created problems with the work we were trying to do with the women in the brothels. So before I left I vowed I was never coming back unless my hair was dark and I had a tan."

He had not stopped chuckling. "Why didn't you accept one of the proposals?"

She spooned the rest of the butter out of the measuring cup, then used the cup to measure the milk. "I'm not marrying a guy who would have to stand on tiptoe to kiss me." He laughed at that and she added, "Not to mention guys who propose to girls they've never met aren't exactly my type."

When he stopped laughing, she glanced his way. His eyes were on her face and his voice was low as he asked, "What is your type, Meagan Winston?"

25

Saturday, January 3
10:30 a.m.

Lucias dared not speak over a whisper. "It's Raymond. Tell the boss I'm here early."

The boy on the asphalt beside the metal trash bins stood as quickly as if a shock of electricity had run through the puddle under him and zapped his pants. The kid took off down the alley and out of sight. Lucias hunched his shoulders, uncomfortable out in the open. It wasn't normal for the contact to tell him to come during the day. Too risky. Either of them might be seen. And now he was early and the contact might make him wait until noon just to punish him. People in higher positions were like that. They lorded over those underneath them and bossed them around. Lucias knew he could handle the top jobs right now, but the contact said Lucias had to prove himself before he could get promoted. He hadn't minded the low jobs because they kept him near Meagan on her trips. But once Meagan was with him, she wouldn't travel any longer and the trips would be lonely without her.

He would refuse to go anymore. He would demand a better job. They had no right to keep him down like this, make him do the hard work and only get a small percentage of the profit. He deserved better.

With sudden resolve, he squatted next to the farthest trash can, careful not to let his pants drag in the puddles. He set his briefcase on a dry section of asphalt and put in the numbers to open the lock. When the top opened to reveal the stacks of rupee notes, he pulled five or six large stacks from the pile, hid them in secret pockets he'd sewn into Raymond's jacket over a year ago, then rearranged the money to make it look like nothing had been touched. He earned those stacks with his little gift. The connection would have a whole new money maker if he knew what was good for him. If the connection decided to reward him with more money, all the better. He picked up the small glass bottle and turned it in his hand, admiring the pretty colors.

The sound of shouting caught his attention. It came from down the block, from where the boy had run. Lucias did not know the exact address where the connection stayed, but the sounds came from close enough to its vicinity that Lucias knew he shouldn't stay. He closed the briefcase and threw it into the plastic recycle bin behind the trash cans, covering it with newspaper and empty plastic bottles. He'd never needed to do that before. The connection said the recycle bin was the emergency drop-off spot only if he couldn't hand the briefcase over in person.

Words reached him, yelled from a distance. "Drop your weapons! Police!"

Lucias didn't need to hear more. He had no weapon, and he wasn't staying around to be caught by people who did. He ran from the alley out onto the street leading to where he parked his car. It was torture to slow his feet and walk along with the flow of traffic, but Lucias told Raymond it was what he had to do. Raymond was impulsive and that got him into trouble. Lucias reminded him that if they ran, it would draw attention. Raymond worried that the connection might not find the briefcase, but Lucias said it wouldn't be his fault if the police found it instead. If they did, Lucias would wish he'd taken more of the money for himself. But he had enough now for the flowers and the next few weeks, until he was due for a smaller job in the city. The small jobs kept him supplied between trips, and were easier. He would teach Meagan about the business. They would work as a team and be successful and rich.

"Forget about it for now," Lucias whispered to Raymond as he neared the car. "We'll go exchange this money and get the flowers, hide the rest of it in the usual place, and then we're going to Meagan's house with the biggest pink vase you've ever seen. She's going to love us. You'll see."

Saturday, January 3
10:45 a.m.

What man was her type? Meagan scrambled for words to say that didn't sound like she was describing Cole Fleming all the way down to his choice of sweater. "I like guys who are honest." She threw him a look. "And who can cook gourmet meals. And fix pipes. Was that your fourth question?"

His smile spread. "No. I rescind it."

"You can't. I already answered it."

"No you didn't. Not really. My fourth question is, what were the color codes you and the other girl used in your shop that first day I came in?"

The stovetop timer went off and Cole turned off the burner and carried the pot of noodles to the sink to drain. Meagan watched him, hesitating. "I don't think I'm allowed to tell you that." She tilted her head and considered his profile. Several red lines scraped across his cheek and jaw. She wondered where else he hurt. "Did you have all these memorized, just waiting for a time when we'd make mac and cheese together?"

"No, I just have good recall when it comes to things I want to know."

"And you want to know about me," she stated, one eyebrow up and a hand on her hip.

He set the pot down and looked at her, his gaze direct. "Yes, Meagan. I do."

Silence stretched between them and Meagan shifted back to her task, only to realize she had nothing else to do. She reached across him for the packet of cheese powder and blushed when she encountered the solid muscle of his right upper arm. She spilled some of the powder opening the packet, then spilled more trying to pour it into the mixing bowl.

He watched as she added the hot noodles and mixed it together. The butter melted as it swirled in circles. "How about I guess about the codes and you can tell me if I'm right or not?"

She stirred faster, not looking at him. "You're the investigator."

"Code red meant something happened that needed your attention but it wasn't an emergency," he said. "I surmise that based on how you immediately looked concerned, but not afraid. You also looked toward the back room, as if someone was waiting there for you, possibly someone who needed your help. Knowing the work you do, I would guess it was an escaped girl, but one you already knew because there was no curiosity on your face, only care."

She moved her spoon around the top edges of the bowl to catch the last bit of cheese powder. "You do have good recall."

He moved around her to the refrigerator and pulled out two bottles of water. "Deducing the code blue is a little harder." He set the bottles on the counter overhanging the bar stools. "When your friend said, 'code blue,' she looked at me and then at you. Then you went pale, looked at me, and asked me to leave. I would guess code blue means a certain kind of danger, possibly from the person in your presence?"

Meagan did not know how to respond. She opened cupboards. "Where are the bowls?"

He reached over her to the cupboard closest to the ceiling, bringing his body much too near her own. "I'll assume by your silence that I guessed right." He pulled down three white ceramic bowls and placed them in front of her on the counter.

"Assume whatever you want," she said. She stood perfectly still to avoid another brush against him. "What's question five?"

He was near enough now to whisper. "Where are your parents and why aren't they the ones living with your grandfather?"

She scooped the yellow-sauced macaroni into the three bowls, putting extra in one. Cole's young sister would benefit from eating all of it, though the meal was far from nutrient rich. She opened the fridge and searched for raw vegetables or something healthy, and found her choice of carrots, broccoli and celery. "That's more like it," she said, pulling out the carrots. As she washed and began to peel them, she answered Cole's question. "My parents are an archeologist-anthropologist team." She cut the peeled carrots into smaller sections. "Dad digs for historical treasure and mom delves into the secrets those treasures tell about people and culture. Their work on a few key sites over the past five years gained them recognition in pretty high places, so when a routine dig in Egypt a few months ago unearthed—pun-intended—traces of a possibly undiscovered culture, my parents were called in. It was not long after Nana died, and I think they needed a new focus. Her long battle with cancer was hard on them both." She broke off a section of a carrot and munched on it. "The dig is scheduled to last six to nine months. They've never been gone for such a long stretch of time, but this was the opportunity of a lifetime."

"And your grandfather?"

"He couldn't stay in his house without someone living there who could run his errands and get his prescriptions filled. Most importantly, someone had to be around to help in case of an emergency since mom and dad don't even have cell phone service where they are. We get an email from them maybe once a month."

Cole gathered the shreds of carrot peels and threw them in the trash can against the far wall. She breathed easier with him at a distance. "And that person was you," he said.

She shrugged. "He wanted so much to stay in the home he and Grandmother shared almost fifty years. I hadn't found a place of my own yet, so it worked for everybody."

He came near again. "And when the time comes, will you stay, or is your heart someplace else?"

She reached up to the high cupboard for another bowl and barely caught it when it came falling out. "Let's not discuss where my heart is or will be." She collected the carrots and placed them in the fourth bowl. "Besides, your five questions are up. It's my turn to ask three."

"Okay."

He was back in his place right behind her. She kept her eyes on the carrots. "What is your real job?"

"That's not an open topic."

She gripped the counter. "Where is your father now?"

His voice was hard as steel. "Stepfather. I don't know."

She turned her body and faced him. Looking up into his eyes, she whispered, "What happened in Iraq?"

26

Saturday, January 3
11:00 a.m.

"I don't talk about Iraq."

Meagan stood at the counter, macaroni and cheese forgotten, and asked softly, "Why not?"

He bent at the waist and leaned his forearms on the counter across from her, one foot propped onto the rung of one of the barstools. A shadow fell across his face. "A man shouldn't have to defend his integrity to the people who know him well."

"What about the people who don't know him well?"

"They don't matter."

"Some of them do," she said, moving to sit on the second barstool. "Some of them should."

He kept his eyes on his clasped hands. "People should give the benefit of the doubt. Innocent until proven guilty, right?"

"It's a nice sentiment, but not realistic." She remembered their lunch and brought a bowl to set in front of each of them. "If it worked in real life, I wouldn't have to try to convince the FBI that I'm not an international drug seller. When the evidence is there, people tend to think you're guilty until proven innocent."

Cole looked out the window. "Why don't you try a different question?"

She bowed her head and gave a silent prayer before biting into the noodles. "Why did you bring me here?"

At that he faced her and came close. With her sitting on the stool, and him standing beside it, she had to crane her neck to maintain eye contact. He sat on the other barstool and their faces were almost level again. She counted several more scratches on his skin. "I wanted you to see what drugs do to people. How destructive they are."

"Cole, I already know that." She set down her spoon and rested her arm on the counter, not hungry anymore. "The evil of human trafficking is often layered with drugs. I've worked with minors pimped out by family members to maintain a drug habit. I know how terrible it is." She slid off the barstool and stood near. "You still don't believe I didn't do it."

His voice was husky. "I want to believe you, but that's probably why I shouldn't."

"I don't sell drugs, Cole."

Meagan heard a gasp and turned to see the woman in scrubs just inside the kitchen doorway, Sadie at her side. "Cole!" Sadie said, rushing to her brother and throwing her arms around him. "You made me mac and cheese!"

The woman remained rooted to her spot, her eyes on Meagan, her face white. "Are you okay?" Meagan asked.

She shifted her gaze to Cole. "Can—can I talk to you a minute?"

"Sure." He looked puzzled, but removed Sadie's hands and said, "Be right back. Go ahead and start your lunch." He glanced at Meagan, then followed the woman in scrubs from the room.

"You came with Cole, right?" Sadie asked, her curious eyes on Meagan's face, then on her bowl of macaroni.

"I did."

She tilted her head. "Has he ever brought you before?"

Meagan shook her head.

"I didn't think so." Sadie filled her spoon and took a large bite. "I don't think he's ever brought anyone else here. You must be special. Are you special?"

"Not really." Meagan smiled and shrugged. "I'm just me."

The girl smiled back. "I like you. Your eyes aren't hiding things. And you haven't been watching me all morning." She rolled her eyes. "Sometimes I get so sick of being watched all the time."

Meagan nodded again, her voice wry. "Lately, I know just what you mean."

"Are you going to marry my brother?"

She coughed. "I don't—"

"He'd be a great guy to marry," she said, digging into her bowl of food with surprising gusto. Meagan offered her own bowl and the girl took it. "When we were kids, he took care of me, like a dad. There was this one time, one summer, some people came to our neighborhood and invited us to a Bible club. We lived in a bad part of town and people were always shooting or fighting. I think sometimes they made up reasons to fight just because they were bored. But for that week, every morning, Cole took me and a bunch of other kids who lived around us to the park and we got to hear good stories like the guy who got swallowed by a whale and the three guys who were thrown into a fire but they didn't burn up. And Jesus. I loved the stories about Jesus. They said He loved kids. All kids. I didn't think anybody but Cole loved me."

Meagan wrapped a hand around Sadie's. "Jesus does love you, very much."

"Oh, well..." She turned and hunched over her bowl. "I used to believe that, when I was little."

"Jesus still loves you, Sadie."

"Yeah?" She put down her spoon. "Where was He when all of this happened to me?" She pulled her long sleeve upward and revealed scars. "They said God had plans for my life. What kind of plan is this?"

Fighting tears, Meagan silently begged help from heaven before she spoke. "I don't know why God didn't stop it, Sadie. I wish He had. I wish He would stop every evil person out there from hurting people like you." She took Sadie's hand again. "But the one thing I do know is that He was there with you every moment. And now you're here and He wants you to be free."

The girl began to cry. "But I—"

Cole returned to the kitchen. "Sadie?" His voice held concern. "Are you alright?" She leaned against him and he pulled her close. "What's the matter?"

Through her tears, Meagan heard her sob, "I miss Jesus."

Cole looked to the woman in scrubs who had followed him back into the kitchen and now stood between Sadie and Meagan. "Just ten minutes?" he asked.

She looked at Meagan, then at him. "I'm afraid not," she said. "But you can call her tonight."

He nodded, accepting her words. He put his hands on Sadie's shoulders and pulled her away enough to look into her face. "I've got to go now," he said, bringing another round of tears, "but I'll call you after supper tonight, okay? Write down everything you want to talk about, and we'll talk as long as you want."

"Promise?"

Meagan put fingers to her lips, hurting at the pain displayed on Cole's face. "I promise."

"Sadie, come with me," the woman said.

"Just a sec." Cole's young sister pulled Meagan into a hug. She whispered in Meagan's ear, "He thinks it's his fault, because he was gone. But it isn't. It started before he left."

The woman called Sadie's name again and ushered her from the room, carrying the full bowl of macaroni and cheese Cole offered. He had not taken one bite. He turned to Meagan and said, "I'm sorry. She overheard our conversation."

Meagan stood. "What conversation?"

"About the drugs." His Adam's apple bobbed. "We've been asked to leave the premises."

Meagan watched Sadie accompany the woman back down the hall. "We?" she asked.

"You." He rotated his left shoulder and winced. "I shouldn't have brought that up in here."

She cleared the bowls and spoons left on the counter, needing something to do. "I guess that proves the point I made earlier. Seems like everyone assumes I'm guilty except for the people who know and love me." She did not want him to see how it bothered her to the core to be blamed so readily.

He helped her with the dishes, then escorted her to Steve's car. They rode in silence through the gate but when she reached for the door handle to go back to her own car, Cole said, "I'll follow you home."

"You don't need to."

"The real criminal is still out there, Meagan. I don't want him running you off the road next. Let me follow you home. I won't ask to come in or anything."

She put on her winter gloves and wrapped her scarf around her neck. "All right. Thanks."

27

Saturday, January 3
11:00 a.m.

The interrogation room: a place of power. Steve stepped inside, letting his silence add to the tension. The new prisoner sat still but his eyes shifted from the empty black table to the blank white walls, to the mirror hiding Steve's team, to the obvious security cameras. *Let it sink in*, Steve said internally. He moved to lean over the man's shoulder. *Get good and scared.*

"State your name," Steve ordered. He tossed a weighty file folder onto the table.

"Jerod."

"Got a last name?"

The prisoner looked to the right. "Smith."

Liar. Steve sat on the edge of the table at an angle so he towered over the suspect. The man did not look up at him, but kept his eyes on the table, on the folder. His left foot angled to face the doorway, but the man wasn't leaving until Steve got some answers. Steve pulled three papers from the file and slapped them on the table. "Tell me about these people, Jerod."

The prisoner picked up each paper and looked at the name and description. "I don't know any of them," he said.

Steve watched him rub the back of his neck with a wavering hand. *Lying*. "How did one guy get three falsified passports? Did you make the passports for..." He held the first paper two inches from the man's nose. "Agatha Mooring?" Second paper. "Raymond Lester?" Third paper. "Damion Smith?" He dropped the three documents in front of the suspect. "Are they family? Maybe a brother, Jerod *Smith*?"

"Don't have no brother," Jerod mumbled. "I'm telling you, I just picked up the money today and that's all. Hodge always picked it up before, but you arrested him, so they asked me to do it this time. I don't know nothin'. I just went to get the money."

His arms were crossed but his eyes had gone up and to the left as he talked, which implied, unfortunately, that he was telling the truth. "Hodge said he didn't know anything either." Steve leaned down and got in the man's face. "So who has the information I want? Give me a name and we might make a deal. No name, and you're in jail as an accomplice in an international drug operation. That won't sit well with a judge."

The prisoner put his palms out. "Don't you get it? They don't tell us any names. We don't see any faces. We just get our job assignments, do the job, and get paid."

"How'd you know Hodge's name?"

Jerod bent his head and looked at his hands. "He's my brother."

"You said you didn't have a brother."

"I lied."

This was going nowhere. Steve could just imagine the guys behind the mirror pulling off their earphones and heading out for a coffee break. He had to get something before they gave up on him. "So you're saying your brother's job was to pick up the money, and since he's in the clink now you got the job today, but neither of you have ever seen the guy who brings the money, or the guy you give the money to?"

"Didn't say that." Jerod shifted in his chair again. Now both of his feet faced the door. "Hodge, he saw the guy a few times. Had to count out the money and then give the traveler his cut. Hodge used to sift a little extra for himself before he left it at the next drop-off place, but don't tell him I told you that."

Steve sat across from Jerod at the table and leaned forward. "Did your brother ever tell you anything about the guy, the traveler? A name? Description?"

Jerod shrugged. "No name. He told me once the guy was white, and older than he thought. Hodge used to make fun of his old-guy jacket."

"What was funny about it?"

The man smirked. "It was plaid, like from a hundred years ago or something."

Steve reached for the file and pulled out a still they'd made from the international flight surveillance camera. "Like this?" he asked, showing Jerod the picture.

Jerod shrugged. "I guess. I never saw it, but that does look old and dumb, like Hodge said."

A knock sounded from behind the mirror. Steve stood. "Wait here," he said.

"Like I have a choice." The prisoner held up the picture and shook his head. "That is one ugly jacket."

Steve left the room and walked around the outside corner where two of the men assigned to his case, Phil and Quinn, stood at a small table covered with monitors and cables. Both took their headphones off and Phil said, "We got a couple of calls."

"Did they tell us anything helpful? All our leads have stalled."

"Our guys in Florida found Darla Moore. She hasn't been to Georgia in years. Moved away and left her kid when he was fifteen. She says he'd be the one using the car now. His name is Lucias Moore and he lives on a gravel road off Sugarsnap Drive."

"Sugarsnap. How quaint." Steve was already putting on his jacket. "Let's go for a visit."

The second man, Quinn, stepped forward. "We also got a call from the DEA. That bottle of colored sand they found in the briefcase isn't sand."

"Drugs?"

"Opium. India is a big manufacturer of it. Looks like our guy is not just delivering product overseas, but smuggling product back."

"You stay here," Steve told Phil. "Get Jerod 'Smith' into the system and find everything you can on Lucias Moore. Does he have a record? Get me a photo and work on getting a warrant to search his house. Get one for a Meagan Winston while you're at it. Quinn, you're with me. We'll check out this address, see if the car is there, and try to get some information out of the guy. If we find any evidence today, we'll bring him in and search the house later."

Steve's phone rang. He picked up the call on the way to the car. "Steve Campbell."

"It's Stephanie. I need you to bring the car back so I can use it."

"Can't." Steve and Quinn got in the car and Steve turned the key in the ignition. "I'm on a case."

"It's Saturday."

"We just got our first big lead—the name of the guy who was on at least two of the flights to India, and who delivered the drug money this morning."

"Well that's just peachy, but I need a dress for tomorrow. I don't have anything to wear to a church."

You mean you don't have anything to wear that fits anymore. Steve shifted into reverse and pulled out of the parking space, holding the phone between his shoulder and chin.

"You're going to get a crick in your neck doing that," Quinn warned.

"You may not need to go to church after all," Steve told her. "It looks like Meagan Winston might have been telling the truth that she didn't have anything to do with this."

"Oh, no you don't." His wife's familiar nag tone came through loud and clear. "I finally have something to go to and I'm going to look good when I go. You can pick me up on your way to wherever you're going and drop me off at the mall."

Steve gripped the steering wheel with one hand at the twelve o'clock position, and clenched tight fingers around his phone with his other hand. If it had been a drink can, it would have crumpled. He started to tell Stephanie he was not dropping her off at the mall and picking her up like she was some teenager, but a glance at Quinn in the passenger seat made him change his choice of words. "Fine. I'll be there in less than ten. Be ready."

He hung up and avoided another look at his fellow agent, keeping his eyes steady on the road. "I have to pick up my wife on the way." He could feel Quinn's smile beside him. Now would be the time to ask the kind of small-talk questions Steve hated. Was Quinn married? Did he have kids? Did his wife drive him insane, too?

Stephanie was the small-talker, and she was in high gear from the moment she got in the car. It was no mistake how she ignored her husband and talked to Quinn the whole drive. Steve didn't mind. With Quinn in the car, she'd be sweet and friendly, and Steve wouldn't have to defend himself against whatever her latest accusation was.

"The gravel road is half a mile ahead," Quinn said after he checked the GPS map on his phone.

"Where are you going?" Stephanie asked.

Steve's phone rang and he looked to see the number on the caller ID. He took the call. "Phil, what have you got for me?"

Phil got right to the point. "We've heard back about the Indian rupees. They're counterfeit, all of them, but I don't think our criminal knows it. We got word from a bank that someone exchanged almost a thousand dollars' worth this morning—after we confiscated the briefcase."

Steve pulled off onto the gravel road and slowed to keep the car steady. "Any leads on that?"

"The bank manager pulled up his security video and told me over the phone that the man was white, older, had light hair and wore a plaid jacket that the manager said looked like tweed."

"That's our guy. So the manager didn't know the rupees were fake?"

"Not until afterward. That's why he called it in. I'm sending someone to verify the information and get a copy of the video."

"Get the rupees for me as well. Good work, Phil." He closed the call and was reporting the new information to Quinn when Quinn gestured toward the back seat. "Are you sure it's a good idea to bring your wife to this guy's house?"

Steve caught Stephanie's eye through the rearview mirror. "Why didn't you remind me? We passed the mall five minutes ago."

"I didn't think you'd just forget about me back here."

He gunned the engine a little and the crunch of tire displacing gravel gave sound to his frustration. A lone trailer came into view, set a ways off the drive. "Too late now. You can wait in the car." To his surprise, she did not argue. He drove off the road and they bounced over uneven ground until he was yards from the run-down building. He parked the car at an angle facing the double-wide. The guy had chosen a good spot. All Steve could see in every direction were trees and a section of the gravel drive. Was this where the meth lab was? "Lock the doors when we get out," he told Stephanie. He checked his gun, radioed in his location, then he and Quinn exited the car. Steve led the way to the front door, which sat crooked on its hinges, and knocked. “FBI. Anyone home? We have some questions for Lucias Moore.”

The unmistakable sound of shoes crushing dried leaves came from behind the trailer. Pulling their guns, Steve motioned for Quinn to go around the south side of the trailer and he’d take the north. He was just at the edge of the front panel of the double wide when he heard a vehicle start. He ran. “Behind the trailer!” he shouted to Quinn. “Block the car!”

Quinn was too far away to do anything but watch when the grey Oldsmobile raced around the trailer toward the road. Steve was running back around to the front of the trailer when he heard his wife’s scream.

28

Saturday, January 3
11:15 a.m.

Lucias swerved onto the main road and pressed hard on the gas pedal. Had they jumped into their car and followed him? Lucias had seen their guns. He'd almost hit their car, parked right in his path, in his haste to escape.

How did they find him? He recognized the man who had come running just as he pulled away. He was one of the two who took Meagan that afternoon, but not the one Agatha had run off the road. That guy was dead. Lucias had done his research on this other guy. That building where he worked belonged to the FBI and the man's name was Steve Campbell. He'd found that out easily enough by sending Agatha into the building with a fruit basket. A few smart questions and he'd left with a name. The secretary had not even noticed Agatha kept the basket for herself.

Why was Steve Campbell at his house? Lucias looked into his rearview mirror and saw Raymond. "What are we going to do?" he asked. He still had his money; they wouldn't get that from him. He had arrived only minutes before they did, and was about to put the first bills between the wooden slats of the emptied hive left there from a previous owner's beekeeping days when they arrived. No bees produced honey there anymore, but if people ever did come to the house, they would fear going near the hives, making it a perfect place to store cash.

He kept one hand wrapped around the curved top of the flower vase so he could take the turns sharp without it falling over and the water spilling out. With a quick look at the flowers came an urgent desire to go to Meagan. If he was with her, he could calm down. Feel better. He pulled off to the side of the road just before he reached her drive and put the car in park. Leaving it running, he popped the trunk and ran back to retrieve the wads of cash hidden under the tire. It was a good place in general, but if the FBI was after him, they'd find it there for sure. He bundled the stacks inside his partially-zipped coat and fought the wind back to the front passenger seat. The passenger door, still mangled some from the wreck, took extra strength to open. Inside, he considered the section of upholstery that had a slash in it from that night long ago, the night Claudia had laughed at him. He stretched open the torn section and jammed the bills inside.

Once the seat cushion was back in place, Lucias returned to close the trunk. Before he did, his eye caught the colored powder in a sealed sandwich bag, the extra he had bought in India for himself. Could he keep that hidden under the tire and, if the police checked, tell them it was a souvenir? Or a drink mix?

A police car came toward him on the road and Lucias slammed the trunk shut. The squad car slowed next to him and the policeman put his passenger window down to call out, "Need help there?"

"No," Lucias said, keeping his face to the side as much as possible. "Just checking my spare tire."

"Good idea, but next time check it at home or in a parking lot, okay? You're too close to the road to be safe."

"Okay, thanks." Lucias got into the car and clenched his hands against the wheel to get them to stop shaking. If the officer had checked his trunk, he'd have found the powder. Lucias had to get rid of it. The policeman drove on and Lucias searched his mind for options. He couldn't just pour it out on the ground. Snow was still piled up alongside the road and since the section of powder he'd taken from the bottle was red, it would show too much. He could visit the bathroom at Meagan's house and flush it down the toilet, but that would be such a waste. He moved the car forward, but then stopped when the huge vase of flowers tilted to the side. That was it!

He stopped the car again and went back to the trunk. He lifted the tire and reached for the small bag that would incriminate him in any court of law, and carried the bag back to his seat in the front. Opening the bag, he poured the powder into the water under Meagan's flowers. At the florist shop, the lady had given him a small packet of white powder to put in the water. "Flower food," she'd called it. He had left the packet at the store, wary of anything that looked so much like cocaine. But now, if for some reason someone found traces of the powder in the water, he could just claim it was flower food. A few days from now, he would go back to Meagan's house and offer to change the water for her. Then he could take his powdered water home and drink it in intervals. It might not work as well, but would be better than wasting it altogether.

Thus resolved, and rather proud of himself for outwitting the police and the FBI in one afternoon, he turned his car back onto the road and drove with a smile toward the home of the woman he loved.

Meagan was going to be so happy to see him.

29

Saturday, January 3
11:15 a.m.

Steve called in an APB on the grey Oldsmobile while he ran around Lucias' trailer to the car where Stephanie continued shrieking. Her voice could get like fingernails running down a chalkboard. He opened the car door to the backseat. "What's the matter? What happened?"

"Where did you go?" Her hands clutched his shirt front. "He almost ran into me!"

That was it? "You're not hurt? Nothing happened?"

He noticed for the first time that she was wearing makeup. And she'd dressed in jeans and a nice shirt. "That maniac could have killed me!"

"Okay, well, he didn't, so that's good." Quinn caught up to him at the car. "Quinn, let's take a look around and see if we can find anything." He turned back to his wife. "Do you want to come with us, or wait here in the car?"

She shook her head with vigorous enthusiasm. "This place is scary. I don't like it. Can't you take me to the mall and then come back here?"

"We need to find what we can while we're here. It won't take long. You can stay in the car, but if you get scared, come find us." He shut the car door and holstered his gun. They didn't have a warrant yet, but they would soon. If they left now, the guy might come back and remove evidence. Steve didn't see any "No Trespassing" signs. There wasn't a law against wandering through the woods. "Let's go check around outside, Quinn. We need to find those stacks of money he got from exchanging the rupees. And if we could find a stash of his drugs, we'd have enough to arrest him when he gets back."

They split up, rounded the structure, and met again behind the home. Steve looked at the piles of clutter and trash and made a face. "The unpleasant side of investigation."

Quinn smiled. "I.e. digging through the trash. Shouldn't we wait for the warrant, though?"

Steve wasn't above bending a rule or two if it meant moving forward. "If we find something, one of us can wait here till the warrant comes."

"If you say so." Quinn chose a smaller bag. "I'll take this one."

"Yeah, give me the big jobs."

"You could leave and take your wife to the mall."

"Ha ha."

Quinn laughed. "Looks like your bag is all dishes. Are they broken?"

"Not all broken, but definitely all dirty."

"So we can rule out our guy being a neat freak."

"What, the trailer falling apart and empty toilet set out in the yard didn't give that away?" Steve pointed across the back yard, if it could be called a yard. "Are those the things people keep bees in to make honey?"

"I think so. They don't look like they've been used in at least a decade."

"We should check them out." Steve re-tied the trash bags and was starting toward the wooden hives when he heard another blood-chilling scream. "What now?"

Quinn had his gun out already. "That sounded for real." He took off and Steve followed, vowing next time to just take the woman to the mall. They came within sight of the car, but it was empty. Steve did a one-eighty turn and his jaw dropped when Stephanie bolted out the door of the trailer.

"What were you doing inside?" he asked.

She was pale as skim milk. "I tried closing my eyes and resting in the car, but I kept hearing sounds." She gestured toward the trailer, then grabbed at his arm. "The door was open so I thought you were inside. I went in, but then I saw a spider. Two spiders. Huge ones."

He was going to have to bribe Quinn to keep from telling this to everyone at the office. "Spiders?" he said. "You're screaming about spiders?"

Quinn headed for the door. "If the door is unlocked, we might as well check it out, since the warrant is coming."

Steve ignored the twinge of guilt. It wasn't really a lie. The warrant would come. Eventually.

Quinn turned to Stephanie. "Do you want to come with us?"

"No." She grabbed a handful of her hair in each fist, a sure sign she was, as she liked to put it, freaking out. On one of their first dates, she'd told him she was deathly afraid of spiders. He always thought she was exaggerating. "No, you couldn't pay me to go back in there. I'll wait here."

He handed her the car keys. "At least go back to the car and turn the heater on. It's got to be in the thirties out here."

She accepted the keys and turned without another word to either of them. Steve could see even as she walked away that she continued to pull on her hair. He chewed the inside of his cheek and said to Quinn, "We're dropping her off at the mall before we go anywhere else." He pushed on the trailer's front door and it swung open. "I guess we should go hunt down two spiders, or at least pretend to, for her peace of mind."

"I'll go in first," Quinn offered. He pulled his gun but kept it at his side and Steve did the same. It sounded like spiders were the biggest threat inside the house, but they were trained to take precautions. If he'd been a criminal and heard a scream like Stephanie's, he'd have been out the door in a second.

Quinn stepped inside. Steve entered behind him and coughed. "Uugh, do you smell that?"

His partner nodded. "Mold. Musty old carpet. Drugs. And ketchup. Gross combination. Wish I'd brought a mask."

Steve stepped over an empty dog bed and took a look in the kitchen. The counters were lined with Styrofoam plates and cups, and bags of plastic silverware lay in a pile on the table. "Guess that explains the dishes in the trash."

"Steve, you need to see this."

He made his way out of the kitchen area toward the sound of Quinn's voice. "Find a spider?"

"Not yet."

"Then what did you—" Steve came to a halt and stared. "Oh, man." On the far side from the couch, above a small square TV placed on a chair, the wall displayed at least twenty photographs of a slim woman with long, dark hair. The photos were taped to the wall with clear packaging tape. Every one of them had red marker slashed across the woman's face in the shape of an X.

Quinn waved him over. "Look at the floor here."

Six inches deep out from the baseboard under the photo wall, torn portions of more photos lay scattered on the floor. Quinn picked up several, then dropped them. "All the same girl," he said. "Black straight hair. Mid-twenties I'd guess. Dresses professionally. The angles and distance of the photographs make me think of the kind of pictures our surveillance team gets from a distance."

"So he's either in the security business, or he's stalking this girl." Steve pointed at a few torn photo edges still taped to the wall. "Between the red Xs and the fact that he ripped at least half of the photos off the wall and tore them up, it's not a big leap to assume his obsession with her didn't turn out the way he'd hoped."

"We should find out who this woman is. She may be in danger."

Steve picked up one of the smaller torn photos. "We can't run facial recognition on any of these pictures. Her face is just a red X." He crossed the room to the two remaining doors. One led to a small bathroom. The other was locked. "Why would a guy leave his front door unlocked, but lock his bedroom door?"

Quinn put his nose close to the door. "I don't smell a dead body. We need that warrant. When's Phil going to get here?"

Guilt flickered again at the look Quinn gave him when Steve admitted the warrant wouldn't be ready until Monday. "We'll come back first thing Monday," Steve said. "I have a feeling we'll find something important behind this door. For now we can take some of those photos in for prints."

"We can't take anything, Steve. You know that. And we need to leave now."

"But this girl might be in trouble." Steve waited for Quinn to cave but he didn't. "Fine. Let's get out of here." On his way back through the living room, Steve noticed a framed photo on a table next to the couch. "Maybe there's a face on this one," he said, coming closer and picking up the frame. His mind seemed to stall at the familiar face, then pedaled double time. He quickly set the photo back in its original place. Another frame lay face down next to it. He picked it up and looked at the photograph of a smiling woman with her arm around a young boy. "This must be the mother," he said. "Let's find a photo of Darla Moore once we're back in the office and verify this is her."

Quinn frowned, but he took a picture of the photo with his phone, then nodded his chin toward the framed picture that was still upright. "She's not the girl on the wall, is she?"

Steve shook his head. "No, she isn't."

"Should I take a photo of her, too?"

"No need to." Steve put the mother's picture face down again on the table and turned to go. "Her name is Meagan Winston, and we're going to her house right now."

30

Saturday, January 3
11:30 a.m.

Raymond's jacket provided little barrier against the cold, but even still Lucias found himself sweating. He parked outside Meagan's home and went around to the passenger side to get the flowers. The door screeched and complained, but Lucias pried it open, got the vase in hand, and kicked the door shut. He looked under the flowers to make sure the powder had dissolved. Seven steps got him to the porch stairs. Another six brought him to the front door. He adjusted his jacket, checked his wig, and held the vase down so he could best see her face when she opened the door.

He leaned to the right and used his elbow to ring the doorbell. "Coming!" a feminine voice called, and Lucias' heart pounded so hard the flowers in his hands vibrated from the force.

The door opened and Lucias' smile dissolved just like the red powder. "Where is Meagan?" he asked.

"I beg your pardon?"

The woman was older than Meagan and seemed vaguely familiar. She might work at Meagan's shop. Silently, inside his head, he ordered Raymond to remember they were supposed to sound like professionals. "I have a delivery for Miss Meagan Winston," he said. "Can I bring it inside? It's heavy."

The red-haired woman looked at him in that judging, suspicious way and Lucias felt his fists want to clench. He saw his old co-workers' faces, their hesitation and fear. He hadn't let them stop him then and wouldn't let this woman stop him now.

A male voice called from somewhere out of sight. "Let him in, Kelsey," the voice said. "Bring the flowers in here so I can see them."

With that invitation, Lucias moved forward, forcing the woman to step back and allow him to pass. The warmth inside the home made the fragrance of the flowers more potent. Meagan was going to love them. The woman directed him to an adjoining room where an old man sat in a recliner with his feet propped up. Lucias knew he was Meagan's grandfather from all those nights watching through their bay window with his binoculars. "Well, now, that's a vase a flowers," the man said, folding and setting aside the newspaper in his hands. "Do I need to sign for them or anything?"

"No." Lucias held tight to the vase. "They are for Meagan. I need to give them to her. Where is her room?" He had seen most of the downstairs of her home over the past two years, but he'd never seen inside her upstairs bedroom. Was it a girly color like pink, or a passionate color like red? Did she have pictures hanging on the wall? Were there any pictures of him?

No, there couldn't be. Every flight but that last one, he'd been in disguise. He should mail her a photograph to put on her wall. Of him, Lucias Maddox Moore. She could put it up next to a picture of her, and they'd be together, the beginning of forever.

The woman's voice interrupted his happy thoughts. "Meagan's not here right now." Lucias did not like her. Her presence, the way she looked at him, made him nervous.

"When will she be back?" He could wait. He could sit on the porch and wait all day. If they made him leave, he could wait in the car. He'd refuse to give the flowers to anyone but her.

"Don't know," the old man said. "She's off with that soldier of hers and didn't say when they'd be back."

He almost dropped the vase. "The sol-soldier?"

"Cole Fleming." The man reached for the card in the bouquet but Lucias pulled back. "Are the flowers from him? He's a fast mover."

They are not from Cole Fleming! Lucias almost shouted. *They are not from anyone but me!* Lucias was the one who loved her. Lucias was the person she belonged with. How dare she go somewhere with another man?

"I thought he got killed in an accident," Lucias said, his voice coming out a little too high to be casual.

"Where did you hear that?" The woman tried to get him to look into her eyes. Lucias turned his back on her, but not before he saw her suspicion grow into something like fear. His palms went clammy and he had to set the vase down before he dropped it.

"I have to go," he said. His disappointment was beyond expression. The man he'd run off the road was still alive, and he was with Meagan. Lucias did not even know where she was. How could he watch over her, protect her, if she ran off like that?

He jerked open the door and stomped down the porch steps back to his car. Something had to be done. And soon. Cole Fleming had ruined his perfect moment and would have to face the consequences.

Killing him hadn't worked, but death wasn't the only way to destroy a person.

31

Saturday, January 3
11:45 a.m.

Meagan's stomach hurt. Poor Sadie had one day a week to spend with her brother, and Meagan had ruined it. Why hadn't she thought of the fact that talking about selling drugs in a recovery facility was foolish?

But at the time she and Cole had been alone in the kitchen. She had not guessed her words would be overheard. She drove home praying for help. Her life had been so good. Secure and predictable, just the way she liked it. Now she felt like Joseph in the book of Genesis, unjustly accused and—

Wait. Joseph got thrown in jail and was there for years before being let out. On second thought, she didn't want to associate with Joseph's situation at all. "God, are you trying to teach me something through this? Is it a test of some kind? What am I supposed to do?"

The quiet joy of her home coming into sight was therapeutic. She'd go inside and make some hot chocolate, and ask Pops to tell her a story of the good old days. She might even take a nap.

She parked in her usual spot in front of the shed, deliberately not looking at the dilapidated structure. So many things needed to be fixed, painted, repaired, but that took either personal skill or money to pay the people with the skills. She had neither. The shed would collapse one day and she'd have to deal with it then, but hopefully that day would not come anytime soon. She had enough to handle right now.

Cole parked his car, or rather Steve's car, next to hers. He stepped out and closed the door with his left hand. He winced and Meagan approached to say, "You need to see somebody about that hand."

"It's fine."

"Yeah, that's what Pops says about his legs. And his first heart attack wasn't really a heart attack. Like the two other ones don't count if the first one didn't." She crossed her arms. "You need to go to a doctor."

"Doctors don't see patients on Saturday."

"Go to Urgent Care then."

"Trust me, Meagan." He held the bandaged hand in his good one. "I've had a lot worse. This is not a big deal."

She saw him lift his shoulder and move it in a slow rotation. "Is that where you got hurt in Baghdad?" She reached out and almost touched him but her hand stopped to hover near his shoulder.

He frowned and she put her palms up. "Sorry, I forgot that subject is off limits. Can I ask you a question about Sadie though?"

His head dipped once in a slight nod.

"Why is she in Shady Grove? I mean, what happened to make her need to go there?"

He turned away from her and leaned his forearms on the top of the car. "Someone drugged her and her friends at a slumber party, then while they were under the influence, took pictures of them."

She put a hand to her mouth. "You mean..."

His face showed deep pain when he looked back at her. "Internet pornography." He turned away. "She was twelve."

Meagan stepped closer and put her hand on the tense muscles of his arm. "It wasn't your fault," she whispered.

He looked at her and his voice carried agony. "It was."

She reached up with her other hand and wrapped her gloved fingers around his tightly gripped fist. "But Sadie said—" Meagan heard gravel shifting and looked to see a maroon Toyota Camry coming down the drive. "What—" She lowered her hands and put them in the pockets of her coat, her question left unfinished. They stood in silence while the car came near and parked facing the house. After squinting to look through the tinted windows, she asked, "Is that—"

"Steve."

The ache in her stomach spread. "Did you ask him to come here?"

"No."

Steve stepped from the car, along with another man, and both made their way to where Meagan and Cole stood. "What are you doing here?" Steve asked Cole.

"I—" Cole looked at Meagan, then back at Steve. "What are you doing here?"

"We found some important evidence," the other man said. "Hey, you're the guy who called in about the grey Oldsmobile, right?" He put his hand out and shook Cole's. "I'm Quinn Phillips. Good work. We traced the car to Florida, then back here to a guy who—"

"Don't tell them anything, Quinn," Steve ordered, his mouth tight. "One of them is still a suspect and the other isn't on the case with us anymore."

Cole stood upright, Steve stepped forward to face him, and Meagan watched the unspoken challenge pass between the two men. She had no desire to try to break up a fight. "If you didn't come here to tell us what you found, what did you come here for?" she asked Steve.

The front door to the house opened and Kelsey stood in the doorway. She called out, "Your grandfather says to bring them inside, Meagan. You all must be freezing."

Steve looked at Meagan. "You might as well let us come in. I'll have a warrant to search your house by Monday."

She stepped back and wished she could lean on the solid wall of Cole's chest behind her. "You don't need a warrant. I've told you I'm not part of this. Search all you want."

With a nod toward his partner, Steve led the way to the house and they both flashed their badges and introduced themselves to Kelsey as they stepped inside. Cole touched her arm and said quietly, "I told you I wouldn't ask to come in, so I'll say goodbye for now. Thanks for coming with me this morning."

Meagan looked at the front door, left open after the two men entered. She should go shut it before Pops caught a draft. "I was going to offer to re-bandage your hand, since you're a stubborn male and refuse to go to the doctor." She had decided Cole Fleming was a man worth trusting. Here was a test to see if she really believed it. "You can—you can come in."

"Are you sure?"

She bit her lip, but nodded. He walked with her up the porch steps and into her grandfather's home. The thought of the FBI searching inside the house did not make her stomach feel any better. It was foolish, she knew, but she felt more secure having Cole there with her.

Steve stood in front of Pops, an eight-by-ten printed photo in hand. "Have you ever seen this man before?"

Meagan came to stand beside his recliner and looked at the picture, surprised to see it was the man in the plaid suit from the plane surveillance. Quinn had said they'd found evidence. Were they pursuing someone other than her?

Hope built inside her until her grandfather said without hesitation, "Sure have. He was here just this morning."

"What?" Meagan asked in disbelief. Steve looked at her with open suspicion. "What do you mean, Pops?"

"He brought flowers. Got pretty unhappy when I told him you weren't here."

Kelsey entered the room and looked from her grandfather sitting in his recliner to the men standing in front of him. She crossed to where Cole stood near the fireplace. "You said the car that had been following Meagan was a grey Oldsmobile, right?"

Cole nodded, his eyes studying Meagan. "That's right."

Meagan felt like her mind switched to slow motion when Kelsey said, "Some guy brought you an enormous, gaudy vase of flowers this morning. He wanted to put them in your bedroom."

She shivered. "Did you let him?"

"Of course not." Kelsey stepped from the room and returned with a huge pink vase. An eclectic combination of large flowers stemmed out from it in all directions. She set the vase on the coffee table in the center of the room and they all stared at it. "Meagan, he knew about Cole's car accident. He got all flustered when he found out Cole wasn't dead, and when I asked him how he knew about the accident, he said he had to go." She walked to the bay window and looked out. "I watched him. He drove a grey Oldsmobile." She glanced back at Steve and Quinn. "I wrote down the license number if you want it."

"I'd like to see it," Quinn said. "We can check it with the one Cole called in."

"It's on a sticky note in the kitchen. I'll get it."

"Before you do that," Steve said, "can you confirm that this was the man?"

He handed her the photo of the man in the plaid suit and Kelsey nodded. "That's him. Same outfit even."

"What was he doing at my house?" Meagan asked, rubbing her hands up and down her arms. "Is it cold in here? Why did he bring me flowers?" She took the photo and held it. Her hands shook and she gave it back to Steve. "Is he your new suspect?"

"He's one suspect," Steve said. He looked over the flowers. "Did a note come with them?"

Kelsey re-entered the room and handed the sticky note to Quinn. "Yes." She pushed away large orange lilies and white carnations until she found the small card. She handed it to Meagan. "I didn't open it."

Meagan held her breath as she tore the miniature envelope. She read the note inside. Her heart thudded and her lungs emptied of oxygen. "I don't—I don't understand."

Steve held out a hand for the card. She gave it to him with reluctance and he read aloud, "We make a great team. I love you." His eyes pierced her. "Want to explain this?"

"I—I can't. I've never met the guy. I've never even seen him except in the flight surveillance videos you showed me." Her throat closed up. She fell into a chair, hands on her cheeks, and looked from one person to another, stopping at Cole. "What is happening?" she whispered.

Cole's eyes held concern, but Steve's did not. "You said we could search the house. Are you still okay with that?"

"Yes, go ahead," she said. The two men left the room and Pops reached over and took her hand. "Pops, I'm so scared," she said, putting her free hand over her eyes. "What does this guy want with me?"

"I don't know, pumpkin," he said. "But fretting about it won't fix it. Let's pray." Kelsey joined them and Pops looked over at Cole. "I take it you're the handsome soldier who came to visit the other night. Glad to see you made it all the way inside. My little granddaughter has only brought two other guys inside to meet me. I didn't like either of them. We'll see how long you last. Come and pray with us."

Meagan was glad she still had a hand over her face so no one could see that it was on fire. Cole must have come over and completed their circle, for Pops began to pray. His voice soothed and his words comforted. She placed herself under the refuge of the everlasting arms, and by the time her grandfather finished, she was able to add her amen to his words.

"We'll trust God on this," he told her. "He's never let us down before, not in four generations. He's got a plan for this as well."

"Thank you, Pops." She hugged him and avoided looking at Cole. The men returned, Quinn now with rubber gloves on, a small bottle of sand-art in hand.

"Where did you get this?" he asked.

She smiled at the memory. "In India. The brothel children made it for me."

Quinn's glance at Steve held information Meagan wished one of them would say out loud.

"I need to take your sand-art bottle to our lab," Steve said. "And I'd like to take the vase in to get fingerprints." He looked at Kelsey. "You're the only one besides the suspect who has touched it?"

"That's correct."

"I would like my bottle of sand back when you're through with it," Meagan said, "but keep the vase." She looked at the bouquet and shuddered. "Take the flowers, too. I don't want them." The men were near the front door when Meagan called them back. "I just remembered something. Wait here, please."

She ran upstairs to her room, opened her closet door, and searched through the laundry basket until she found the pair of jeans she had worn the day Cole hammered her car. She dug into one pocket, then another, until she found the crumpled note. On her way down the stairs, she heard Cole tease Steve, who held the vase, about his taste in flowers.

"Stay out of this, Cole," Steve said.

"I was just joking."

"I'm not talking about that," Steve barked, shifting his weight from one foot to the other. The vase had to be heavy. "Stop being everywhere and searching things, and stop hanging out with my suspect. This case is mine. So butt out or else."

Cole's voice lowered. "Or else what?"

Quinn must have already gone out to the car. Steve set the vase down on the small table in the hallway and stood nose-to-nose with Cole. "You're *not* taking this job away from me."

"I don't want your job," Cole said. "I'm just—"

She stepped on a creaky stair and they both looked up. "I have a note," she said. "Someone left it for me at the store. It might be from this same guy." She gave it to Steve. "Would you *please* tell me what is going on?"

He pocketed the note and pulled out his phone. "You and Lucias Moore are working together in the drug trade, that's what's going on. As soon as I find that grey Oldsmobile, and as soon as I find the evidence I need about you, you're both going to jail."

"But I told you, I don't even know this guy!"

His finger swiped his phone twice and he held it up for her to see the screen. "No? Then how do you explain him having a framed picture of you on a table in his house?"

The blood drained from Meagan's face. Her mouth opened but no words came out. Cole came to stand beside her. "Meagan?"

"Lucias Moore is our main suspect." Steve said. He shut down the phone. "And if I find what I think I'll find in that bottle of sand. I'll know for sure that you—" He pointed at Meagan. "—are his accomplice."

32

Saturday, January 3
1:00 p.m.

"Things are finally getting somewhere," Steve told Quinn before dropping him off at the office. "Get the vase and the sand to the lab. I'll pick up Stephanie, take her home, and be back here by two."

"You got it." Quinn shut the door and Steve headed out on the road toward the mall.

So the guy in the plaid jacket was Lucias Moore. Steve sent Stephanie a text to meet him outside the Food Court and thought through the possibilities. They'd find Lucias' prints on the vase, and opium in the sand-art bottle. On Monday, they'd take the warrant to Lucias' house and get whatever he was hiding in his bedroom. They'd take prints off the photos on the wall and match them to the prints on the vase.

If all went well, he'd be making two arrests on Monday. Closing a case of this caliber would have to move him up in the ranks. He'd be given harder cases, bigger cases. Journalists would start to know him by name. Co-workers would ask for his help specifically when they hit on a hard-to-crack investigation.

By the time he picked up his wife, Steve was smiling. She climbed into the passenger seat. "You look happy," she said. She reached back to set a large bag from Belk in the backseat.

He glanced her way. "You look pretty pleased yourself."

"I am. I got a super cute dress. It wasn't the size I wanted, but the color is pretty."

"That's good."

"Don't you want to see it?"

"Aren't you going to wear it tomorrow?"

She sighed and crossed her arms. "Never mind."

What had he done now? Steve waited for some tears or a nagging comment. After two minutes passed, he decided the silent treatment was worse. "So, we got some good evidence today," he said. She kept her gaze out the side window, but he figured that was a good thing. If she kept quiet, maybe he could think through things clearly for once. "Meagan, the girl you're going to scope out for me tomorrow, is running scared. I've got her on the hook. I'm going to do a polygraph test on her next week, but it will just be for the official file. I don't need the wires to tell me when she's lying."

Stephanie turned and looked at him. "What do you mean?"

They were halfway home. A few more miles and he could be on his way back to the office. He wanted to get as much done on this case as possible today, since Stephanie would have the car tomorrow. "A person's sensory recall comes from a specific part of the brain," he told her. "The right side is where the brain manufactures new ideas. The left side is where it remembers things. So if you question a person and they look up and to the right, they are creating a story."

"Lying."

"And if they look up and to the left, they are searching a memory."

"Telling the truth."

Steve tapped his fingers on the steering wheel in time to the music on the radio. "There are lots of other ways we're trained to tell truth from lies, things like body language and facial expressions. The eye one works best in my opinion, though, unless the person is left-handed, in which case the right side and left side are opposite."

"So how do you know if a person is right or left-handed?"

He almost rolled his eyes. "It's pretty easy to tell."

"What if they're faking it? Or what if they're ambidextrous, what then?"

"It's not that—"

"Or what if they learned that tactic, so they're pretending to be right-handed when they're really left-handed? What if they're dyslexic?"

"What? What would being dyslexic have to do with anything?"

"I don't know. You're the expert. You tell me."

This was why life was easier at the office. "Here, we're home. Let's talk about this some other time, okay?"

She reached back for her bag. "You're not coming?"

"This case is hot right now. I've got to get back."

"Of course you do."

She always seemed to be sighing these days. "I'll see you later tonight," he said. "Want me to bring home dinner?"

"Will you be home by dinner?"

"Probably."

She looked at him like she knew better. "I'll make myself a sandwich."

"Suit yourself." He turned the car around, glad he had a reason to go back to work. When it came to wanting respect, or appreciation, there was a lot more chance of getting it at the office these days than at home.

Saturday, January 3
1:00 p.m.

"I just called in reinforcements," Kelsey said. "Brianna's bringing pizza and an old movie. We're going to eat ice cream out of the carton and forget everything that just happened."

"It's a great idea, but not possible," Meagan said. She hadn't been able to stop wringing her hands since the FBI agents left. "Some guy is trying to trap me, or set me up, or something. Why else would he say he loves me and we're a great team? I've never even met him!" She pulled her hands apart and looked at her palms. "My hands are dry. I need some lotion." She stood and faced Cole, who hadn't moved from his spot near the fireplace. He'd be plenty warm by now if there had actually been a fire in it. "And why did those guys seem so interested in my sand-art bottle? There are a lot of secrets everybody seems to think I should know, and I don't know a thing!" She bit her lip and asked Pops to hand her a tissue to blow her nose. "I'm going to make some hot chocolate."

"Make some for me," her grandfather said. "And bring me some of that pecan pie your friend brought over."

"You're diabetic, Grandpa."

"Just cut me a sliver then."

Kelsey followed Meagan into the kitchen. "Sorry. Guess I shouldn't have brought the pie. Is a sliver okay?"

"Yeah." Meagan opened the fridge and pulled out the pie. "But he'll eat three slivers if you let him."

"I'll only eat two," Pops yelled from the living room.

Meagan leaned onto the kitchen counter and her laugh was a little too close to hysterical. "What am I going to do, Kelsey? How do I fix this?"

"I don't think there's anything you can do at the moment, which is why we're going to distract you with a forget-about-it party."

"A what?"

"I grew up with three sisters. Whenever one of us would get our heart broken, or have an extra bad day, we'd throw a forget-about-it party. We'd dress in our pjs and eat ice cream out of the carton and watch old movies."

Meagan's response was emphatic. "I'm not wearing my pjs with Cole Fleming still here."

Kelsey laughed. "He's already seen them once."

"An embarrassment I'd like to avoid repeating, thank you."

The door swung open. When Cole entered the kitchen, Kelsey dissolved into laughter and Meagan blushed furiously. "Did I interrupt something?" he asked.

"Not a thing," Kelsey said. "I'm just headed up to get Meagan's slippers for her."

"Kelsey..." Meagan warned.

"The ones with the bunny heads?" Cole smiled. Meagan wanted to crawl under the kitchen table. "They're cute."

"Hey, Meagan!" Pops called from the other room. "See if that man of yours can fix the leaky pipe while he's in there."

Could her face get any hotter? She put a hand to her brow and shook her head. "Let's get that cut of yours bandaged so you can leave."

His grin was huge and once again made him look like a little boy in a big man's body. "I'm in no hurry," he said.

Meagan had no response for that. "I'll go get the first-aid kit." She fled the room, sidestepping Kelsey at the bottom of the stairs with the slippers, and kept going until she was in Grandpa's room with the door shut behind her. Chaos, everything was chaos now. She had to do something, was willing to do something, but what? March down to the FBI office and demand that Steve give her some information? Track down the flower delivery guy and threaten him with her mace? "God, I've tried to create a stable environment for Pops, to keep his heart as stress-free as possible. Now we've got FBI agents searching the place, Kelsey trying to get me to forget, and a really, really good-looking guy who is as secretive as he is charming in my kitchen." She dropped to sit on Pop's bed. "Lord, would you give me some wisdom, please? Is it okay to trust Cole Fleming? He doesn't seem like the guys we encounter in our work, but I know the heart can be deceitful." She pulled the first-aid kit from under the bed and opened it, sorting through the materials. "Everything is just so wrong right now. How do I make it right again? Steve thinks I'm with the bad guy. Nobody seems to recognize this bad guy might be after me. And he got inside the house today..." She pressed her fingers against her eyes. She couldn't cry. Not now. She had guests.

Get busy, Meagan, she told herself. *Do something.*

Her mother had always said, "You can't hike the Appalachian Trail right this second, but you can take one step right this second." What was a step she could take? She looked around the room, searching for inspiration, and her gaze fell on the old-style phone hooked to the wall above a small table with a pad of paper on it. She pulled the earpiece off the wall and punched in numbers she had memorized just in case.

"Gainesville Police Department. How may I help you?"

Meagan took in a deep breath. "I need to know what to do to get a conceal-and-carry permit, and also how to get a restraining order." She wrote the information on the pad and thanked the person before hanging up. On Monday, she would start the process of getting a gun, and if this plaid-jacket guy got anywhere near her home again, she'd have the law to help protect her and Pops from him.

Surprised at how much better taking that one step made her feel, Meagan gathered up the first-aid supplies and headed back toward the kitchen, where Cole Fleming waited.

33

Saturday, January 3
1:30 p.m.

Cole enjoyed the look of pleased surprise on Meagan's face when she returned. "You made the hot chocolate?"

"It wasn't hard." He smiled. "I can cook as long as there are packets or boxes with instructions on them."

She laughed and the sound churned up a longing that surprised him. When was the last time he set aside the mire of work and just enjoyed a few hours of something good? The Bible said to think on things that were good, and just, and pure, and lovely, and a few other words he couldn't remember. He had lost that focus. The darkness too often pulled him under. How could he work for justice and not get overcome with evil?

"You're thinking awfully hard," Meagan said. "Afraid I'll diagnose that you need stitches in that hand?"

He looked up at her from where he sat. Every day he was becoming more convinced that Meagan Winston was something good. Good and just and pure and lovely. He would forget everything else today and think on her. "Your hot chocolate's going to get cold."

She sat across from him at the table and lifted the mug, wrapping her hands around its warmth and taking a sip. "Just right." She smiled. "Should I take the other mug to Kelsey?"

"She's got one. She and your grandfather are watching football."

"You can join them if you'd like," Meagan offered.

He wanted to stay where he was. "I'd rather see what I can do about that leaky pipe of yours. And I should look at it before you work on my hand. Wouldn't want to get a fresh bandage dirty and you have to redo it."

"That's considerate of you." She glanced at the sink. "I've tried fixing that pipe several times already. The house was built in 1952, so stuff all over the place needs work. I Google home repairs, and the guys at Lowes know me by sight now, but even at that I can only manage temporary solutions. One of these days the whole place might fall down on my head." Meagan took another sip. "You fix pipes?"

Her voice was conversational, but wary. He chuckled. "Not officially, but in Iraq if something broke, we knew we'd better figure out how to fix it ourselves. We didn't have manuals and couldn't Google out there, so I got pretty good at wrangling repairs myself. Good enough that I'm willing to give your pipe a try. One of the connections may just need to be tightened."

"That's possible. Nobody's ever given me an award for my muscle strength."

It felt good to laugh. "Why don't you hire somebody to come fix things, instead of trying to do them yourself?"

"Money." She blew into her cup. "I already feel guilty just having such a spacious, beautiful home compared to most of the people in the world. When so many people live on a dollar a day, how can I fork out a thousand dollars to fix the roof? When it comes to choosing a new roof or dozens of children being rescued from the brothels..." She looked straight at him. "Is there really anything to consider?"

Cole wished Steve could hear Meagan, see Meagan, right then. He'd know she could not be connected in any way to a crime that hurt other people. "What about your grandfather's medical expenses?"

"Insurance pays for those, thank the Lord. That's an expense I don't have to worry about."

"I thought Christians weren't supposed to worry about anything."

She considered his comment. He waited to be asked about his personal beliefs, but instead she said, "That's true. I shouldn't worry. I should pray about things and let the Lord provide."

"Can't God provide for the kids in India and for a new roof?"

Her full lips spread into a smile. "You've got me there."

The scene in the room was getting too cozy, feeling too good. Needing to distance himself, he finished his hot chocolate and took his mug to the sink. "Let's take a look at those pipes."

Saturday, January 3
2:00 p.m.

Steve looked at the photo Quinn brought in of Darla Moore. "Something's not right here," he said. "Are you sure this is current?"

Quinn nodded. "This year. I know what you mean. Our guy in the plaid suit is about the same age. He can't be her son."

"This throws a wrench in things." Steve shoved the photo away. "Pull her file for me. And see what Phil found on Lucias Moore." He noticed the red light blinking on his desktop phone and stood. "I've got to go see Baine."

"Uh-oh. That can't be good."

Steve agreed but wasn't going to say it. "He probably just wants an update on how the case is progressing." He left the room and crossed two hallways to get to Baine Zimmerman's large office. Baine wasn't the head of the division, but close enough to make an agent's palms sweat. "You wanted to see me?" Steve said when ushered inside.

"Your description of the photos in your suspect's home today brought up a memory," Baine said. "Please, sit." Steve sat and Baine continued. "Three years ago, back when I was with the PD in Atlanta, we had a case go cold, and when you mentioned the photos, I remembered one of our suspects had an unusual name. Lucias."

"What kind of case?"

"Homicide."

Steve kept his face interested but passive, hard to do with adrenaline shooting through him. "Lucias Moore?"

The man set a bulging file on his desk. "I got the file sent over. I want to hand this case back, Steve. The Atlanta homicide team never got any solid evidence tracing the murder to your suspect, but I think if they re-open the case, and we have a more experienced team of agents working on the drug side of it, we might be able to land this guy."

Had lightning struck, Steve couldn't have felt more singed. "You want to take the case away from me? But we just got some great evidence. We're moving fast, and I have two suspects."

Baine nodded. "I know."

Steve had to convince Baine of his value. "Quinn and I know this case inside and out. Transferring it over would waste time. We'd have to get another team up to speed on what we've found, and—" He forced himself to stop before he begged. "Sir," he tried again, pretending a calm, detached demeanor. "I believe I can close this case. I ask that you give me three more days before you decide to hand it over."

"Two days." Baine opened the folder and flipped pages. "I'll give you until five p.m. Monday."

"That will be enough," Steve said. "Thank you. We won't let you down."

"I trust you won't." Baine slid the file toward Steve. "You'll want to familiarize yourself with the murder. See if you can find anything in there that shines light on our current investigation."

"Yes, sir."

Steve took the folder and left before Baine had a chance to call him back. Back in his office, he set the folder on his desk next to a pile of papers Quinn must have dropped off from Phil's part of the investigation, and opened the drawer to his right. Behind the pencils, sharpener, and box of refill staples, he found the stress ball some co-worker had given him as a joke when he first arrived. "You're going to need it, working here," the man had said with a laugh. Steve wasn't laughing now. He squeezed the ball with a count and didn't stop until he reached one hundred.

He opened his filing cabinet and used his fingers to step a path across the lettered tabs toward M. It wouldn't hurt to go over all the information they'd gathered so far. At the F tab, his index finger hesitated, and on impulse, Steve pulled out the file marked "Cole Fleming." He set it on the desk and frowned. Cole had become a burr under his saddle. Steve should never have asked for his help at the beginning. Once Cole decided to help, there was no stopping him until the job was done. Hadn't Steve learned that the hard way? Wasn't Steve the one who'd had to rescue Cole from himself?

As if on its own accord, his hand reached to open the file, and Steve stared down at the newspaper clippings, the partial truths, the implicating questions. Cole had never responded to any of it, had never given any kind of statement, and Steve knew why. If the media ever got hold of the real story...

They were scheduled to move out in ten minutes, but Cole was far from ready. He stood like a statue next to his bunk, a note in his left hand. "It's from her," he said.

Steve pulled on his boots. "That woman you named Delilah?"

"She's warning me to stay off this mission. My life depends on not being part of the envoy today."

Steve froze. His voice came out hoarse. "We knew someone was funneling information to the enemy." Women had seduced men out of their secrets for centuries, but Steve would never have guessed Cole would succumb to the oldest and most powerful tactic in history. "Cole, you didn't—"

"I have to stop her."

Horror pumped through his veins when Cole dropped the note and sprinted to the door. "Stop her? You have to stop the envoy!"

Cole had left him with no recourse. If Steve reported that the mission was compromised, he would have to say why, and it would destroy Cole's career. He would have to trust Cole to succeed, but he placed his team in the back of the line that day, just in case. The bombs went off forty-seven minutes later. His team suffered only one casualty, Cole himself, found more dead than alive under a pile of rubble.

Later that day, Steve would lie for him, would tell the authorities that Cole had not gone AWOL, but was acting under orders, following a tip about a potential suicide bomber...

Steve returned Cole's newspaper clippings to their place, took out the file on Lucias Moore, and with a firm push, closed the file cabinet. He set the two files on Lucias side by side, opened the old one first, and told himself to stop wasting precious time and focus on the task at hand.

It was a good thing Stephanie wasn't expecting him for dinner. If it took all night, he was going to learn everything he could about his suspect. No new team was taking his investigation and getting credit for solving his case.

34

Saturday, January 3
4:00 p.m.

Meagan opened the front door for Kelsey's husband. Nathan wore a jersey and carried a twelve-pack of Mountain Dew. "I heard there was pizza and a ball game," he said as he stepped inside. "How could I resist that?"

Kelsey welcomed him into the living room with a kiss. "You heard wrong. It's pizza and an old classic movie." She laughed when Nathan groaned. "But Meagan's grandfather is watching football right now, and I have a feeling he'd vote on your side."

"I would, too."

Meagan tried not to smile as Cole entered the room and the two men shook hands. "I don't know who you are," Nathan said. "But if you're voting for the game, you can have all the Mountain Dew you want."

"Nathan, this is Cole Fleming," Meagan said, coming to stand beside Cole. "He's...he's..."

"I'm here to fix the pipes," Cole said with a laugh. "And I think I finally did."

"Really?" He'd been tinkering under there for over two hours.

"Cole Fleming? That name sounds familiar." Nathan looked to his wife with a puzzled frown that after a moment cleared. "Oh," he said. "You're the guy who came to see Meagan in the shop. The taller-than-Meagan guy."

Meagan had to sideswipe the conversation right away. "Cole, can you show me what you did to the pipes, so I'll know how to fix them next time?"

"What, you doubt my abilities?"

She smiled. "I doubt the pipes." She practically pushed him back into the kitchen so he wouldn't see Kelsey jabbing Nathan's shoulder and telling him not to embarrass her.

"Embarrass her?" Nathan said in a whisper that wasn't soft enough. "Are they dating or something?"

Oh heavens. "Go enjoy the game," Meagan said loudly. "Brianna's on her way with pizza." If she could keep Cole in the kitchen for a few minutes, Nathan would get absorbed in the game and not be inspired to talk for a while.

Cole stepped into the kitchen, laughing. "Seems all your friends, and your grandfather, are rather interested in my presence here."

She knew her face had flushed bright pink. "They've been trying to set me up for years." She hoped her voice sounded casual. "Ignore anything they say that's embarrassing."

"I'm not the one blushing."

Meagan felt the heat run up her ears. "You're making it worse." She busied herself with the first-aid kit. "If you're done with the pipes, I should bandage your hand now."

He laughed again. "You're a very interesting person, Meagan Winston."

If he kept looking at her like that, the way she looked at her bunny slippers, she was going to be red from head to toe. "That's just because your friend thinks I'm a criminal."

Shock waves surged through her hand when he reached across the table and touched her. "I don't think you are."

Her eyes lifted and she saw that he meant it. "Thank you," she whispered.

The moment stretched with his hand around hers until he cleared his throat and said, "Let me show you what I did with the pipes." He opened the two cupboard doors under the sink and directed her attention to the middle. "See this section here?"

"The curvy part?"

He chuckled. "Yes. You've got three 'curvy parts' before the pipe goes into the wall, and all of them could use replacing."

"But then how did you fix them? You didn't leave to go to the store."

He kneeled and used a rag to wipe the pipe. "Nope. Thought I'd save you some of that money you need for the kids. I cleaned out the old fixtures and sealed them with some plumber's putty I found way in the back of the cupboard. It was old, but still worked after a good stir. No one should use this sink for at least two hours, then after that we'll test it to see if the putty holds."

She told herself not to be quite so glad that he would be staying the rest of the afternoon. "Thank you for doing this. I appreciate it." She tore off the bottom of the grocery list held to the fridge by a magnet, and wrote, "DO NOT USE" on the scrap. With a piece of tape, she secured the makeshift sign to the faucet.

Cole stood and smiled at the sign. "You're welcome. Consider it a contribution to your cause."

It occurred to her that they were standing close, alone in the kitchen. If they had been dating, it would be the perfect time to steal a kiss.

"You're blushing again."

Good thing the man couldn't read minds as well as faces. "I'll go wash my hands in the bathroom and then we'll work on that cut on your hand." She escaped his presence for the second time, thinking how strange it was that one could feel the desire to run away from someone and run toward them at the same time.

Saturday, January 3
4:00 p.m.

Quinn popped his head into Steve's office. "I heard we're getting bumped off the case."

"Not yet." Steve motioned him in. "We've got till Monday afternoon. Come and look at this."

Quinn came in and looked at the file from across the desk. Steve turned an eight-by-ten photo so he could see it right side up. "This is Claudia Conners. Look familiar?"

"She looks like the girl all over our suspect's wall."

"That's what I thought. She went missing three years ago. They never found her body, but the photos that the murderer sent to her home address were graphic enough to declare her dead. They're in the file if you want to see them."

Quinn looked at one and quickly closed the folder on the rest. "Was this an FBI case?"

"No. There was no reason for it to come to us at the time."

"So why's it here now?"

Steve pulled out another photo. "This is the guy they think killed her, but they couldn't get any solid evidence to convict him."

"Hmm." Quinn picked up the photo and looked it over. "Light hair, thin, mid-twenties or younger, looks like he's never spent an hour out in the sun. Who is he?"

"This," Steve said, taking the photo from Quinn's hands, "is Lucias Maddox Moore." He set out their photo of the man in the plaid suit and two more grainy photos, taken from airline surveillance, of the woman with white hair and the hippie man. "Take a good look."

Quinn leaned over and Steve saw the moment he connected the dots. Quinn pointed at the photo of the young man. "This is our man." He touched each photo. "And this, and this, and this. We're only after one guy here."

"Yes." Steve stacked the photos, his face grim. "And Lucias Moore, our international drug runner, is probably also a brutal murderer."

Saturday, January 3
4:00 p.m.

Lucias spent the afternoon in the mall parking lot. It was a safe place to think. Steve and the other guy might still be at his house. They had seen his car. Had seen Raymond. Lucias couldn't go home until he had a new plan.

He needed a new friend. A new friend with a new name and a new look. And a new car. If he had a new car, he could be invisible again, and that was important. He needed to be invisible to the rest of the world until he could reveal himself to Meagan. Then they could face the world together.

It was agony that he hadn't been able to stay and see her face when she got his flowers. He shouldn't have gone away. He should have forced that woman to let him stay.

Things were getting out of control. He tilted the rearview mirror and looked at Raymond. "You've been found out," Lucias told him. "So you have to go. I'll miss you." Lucias put his car in gear. He wouldn't miss the car; he hated the car, and Agatha had banged it up anyway. "Thanks, Raymond," he said as he drove, "for being smart enough to get those extra stacks of rupees from the briefcase. You scared me when you did it, but now we have enough money to make a really good plan."

Money gave a man power. Lucias had enough for a down payment on a car, new clothes, even enough to buy information. He would create a beautiful strategy, one that would put everyone back in place, where they should be, for him to continue to pursue Meagan.

He'd left her a note and sent flowers to prepare her heart for him. Now he would prepare her mind.

35

Saturday, January 3
5:00 p.m.

"Thank you, Kelsey." Meagan closed the empty pizza box and threw it like a Frisbee toward the door. "And you too, Brianna."

"What about me?" Nathan asked before yelling at the defense to block the punt. "I brought drinks."

"You too, Nathan."

Pops finished off his second piece of pizza. "It's my TV."

"You too, Pops."

Cole grinned. "I fixed the pipes."

"Okay, okay." Meagan laughed. "Thank you, everybody."

Kelsey snuggled up against her husband on the couch and stole a sip of his drink while he bemoaned an incomplete pass. "I knew you'd enjoy a forget-about-it party if you let yourself," she said.

"You were right." Meagan dug a spoonful of mint chocolate chip ice cream from the carton. "I don't think I've ever thrown a pizza box in my life. I may just leave it there until tomorrow."

"Wow, you're branching out," Nathan said. "Next thing you know, she'll be coming down in those bunny slippers I've heard about."

Meagan threw a balled-up napkin at Kelsey. "Sorry!" Kelsey said, dodging the napkin with a laugh. "It just slipped out the other day."

Cole drank the last of his bottled water and stood. "Anybody need anything from the kitchen?" Meagan watched him go, concerned at the sudden sadness in his eyes. She rose and followed him, picking up the pizza box on her way.

"I knew you couldn't leave it there," Kelsey called out with a grin. She put her hand out to her husband. "You owe me five bucks." He took her hand and kissed it.

Meagan found Cole in the kitchen, fiddling with the pipes under the sink. "You said they needed two hours to dry. It hasn't been that long yet."

"I know. Just thought I'd check them." He didn't lift his head.

"Is something wrong?"

He stilled. She waited, unsure if he'd heard her. When he cleared his throat, she sat at the table. "What is it, Cole?"

He looked at her then and she thought of a young boy making mac and cheese for his baby sister, pretending it was a gourmet meal so she'd feel special. "This whole afternoon." He cleared his throat again. "These people, and you." He shrugged but the gesture was offset by the husky drop in his voice. "It's like family. What I've always imagined family should be like."

"You miss it," she whispered.

He shook his head and turned back to the pipes. "You can't miss something you never had."

His bandaged hand rested on top of an overturned bucket set on the floor outside the cupboard. She touched it, placed her hand over his, and he went still again. When he turned to her, his eyes held unshed tears. Meagan felt her own respond in kind. She knew what to say when teenage girls sobbed in her arms, but had no idea what to say to this giant of a man who may have never allowed himself to cry in his entire life. "Brianna brought the pizza before I could get to that cut on your hand," she said softly. "Now might be a good time while we wait for the pipes to dry."

He nodded. "Okay." He blinked several times, moved the bucket back into the cupboard, and by the time he sat at the table, the corners of his mouth were turned upward. "Just no stitches or anything that involves needles."

"You've got a deal." A great cheer came from the adjoining room. "Should we go back in there so you can watch the game?"

Cole's eyes locked with hers while he shook his head. Meagan caught herself twisting the gauze in her hand, unable to look away. "Meagan..." he said.

Nathan burst into the kitchen. "You missed it!" he told Cole. "Best play of the game. There are only three minutes left in the fourth quarter. It's going to be a tight finish." He tossed his empty drink can into the trash. "If it goes into overtime, we may have to order another pizza."

He left and Meagan's eyes turned back to Cole. He smiled and she felt her insides quiver. "I guess we should—"

"Come on, Cole!" Nathan yelled from the living room. "The linebacker just got an interception on the twenty-five yard line!"

Cole stood and his smile spread, but it was still directed at her. "Yeah," he said. "We probably should."

He led the way back to the living room and Meagan followed, hoping she wasn't glowing or anything. She had to go back for the first-aid kit she'd forgotten, then had to go back for the gauze she'd dropped on the table when Nathan came charging in.

Kelsey and Brianna shared the large green couch with Nathan, so all that was left was the smaller paisley-covered love seat. Meagan hoped no one would comment on them sharing it. Cole sat on the far side, closest to Pops in his recliner. She tucked herself into the near side, close to the edge, and unwrapped his hand to survey the cut. "Yikes," she murmured. "Whatever got you, got you good."

"A window and I got in a fight." He glanced at the cut. "The window won."

"I see that. Looks like you put something on it?"

"Antibiotic stuff."

"Good for you. It's beginning to heal."

With gentle touch, she cleaned the wound, rubbed more ointment into the area, then covered it with gauze and wrapped it. He watched her; she could feel it, but did not dare look up at him. When the bandage was secure, she turned his hand palm down, then up again. "I think this will do. Try to not get it wet." She smiled and glanced up. "No snowball fights."

He smiled back and it took several seconds for her to register the unnatural silence in the room. She glanced around. "Is the game over?"

Every eye in the room was on the two of them. Meagan felt the blush coming. "What?"

"It's getting kind of warm in here, don't you think?" Nathan commented. Kelsey jabbed him in the arm. "Ow." He poked her back and she giggled.

"You know, when Meagan was little..." Pops began.

Meagan braced herself. "Whatever he says," she leaned over and whispered to Cole, "it's bound to be embarrassing."

He chuckled and she caught herself grinning at him until she remembered everyone was still staring. She let go of his hand and scooted farther toward the edge of the couch.

"She came home one day crying like her little heart was crushed," her grandfather continued. "I asked her what had happened and she said she'd broken up with her boyfriend. She was in third grade. I asked her why, and she told me she broke up with him because he was too immature."

His belly laugh always got Meagan laughing too, no matter how humiliating his story might be.

"Now when she got to high school, she had the same problem. None of the boys were serious enough about life for her. She always had passion, little Meagan did, even that year that she wore blue eye shadow every day and I called her 'siren eyes' because when she blinked she looked like a police car."

"Grandpa..."

"I used to ask her why she didn't find some guy in college. She told me guys weren't looking for a girl who wanted to go to India." He looked on her with pride. "She went to India anyway."

Kelsey cleaned up the cans and paper plates. "And I'm sure glad she did. We love having her on our team."

"This is starting to sound like a eulogy," Nathan said, tossing his second can into the trash bag Kelsey held open. "You guys are getting me choked up."

Their guests cleared out too quickly to not be obvious. "See you tomorrow at church, Meagan," Kelsey said with a hug.

Brianna waved from the doorway. "See you Monday at the store."

"Seems all your friends had important things to do just now," Pops commented. "Since I'm not too old to know a setup when I see one, I reckon I'll rest my eyes here and take a little siesta."

Meagan didn't bother to try to hide the blush anymore. "Oh, Pops, don't tease."

He laughed and said to Cole, "If I didn't tease her, she wouldn't know I loved her. Now you two go somewhere else so I can sleep."

Cole began a polite goodbye, but Pops interrupted to ask Meagan to get his neck pillow from his room. On her way back, she heard him tell Cole, "...loyal to a fault. The people she loves, she'll defend them to the teeth and stick with them for life. But she's slow to make that choice." Meagan felt her eyes widen. Grandfather's voice was as serious as she'd ever heard it. "The guy who deserves her is the guy who can make her love him so much she won't be too scared to admit it. Nobody's ever gotten close." She walked in to see him pat Cole's arm and his voice went back to its usual tone. "Wish you the best!"

Meagan raced into the kitchen before Cole turned and saw that she had heard part of their conversation. What was the deal with everyone trying to set her up lately? Did they think she was lonely? Miserable? Incomplete? She was going to have a talk with Pops. And then with Kelsey. And Nathan. And Brianna. Maybe she should just write the lecture and print copies to hand out at the store and save herself some time.

"I think you're all set up now," Cole said as he came into the kitchen.

"You're telling me," she grumbled, then startled. "Wait, what?"

"The pipes. They should be dry now. Try turning on the water in the sink."

"Oh, right." She turned the knob and bent down to look at the pipes underneath. "No leak. That's great. Thank you. You saved us a lot of money, and me a major headache."

"You're welcome. Thank you for letting me stay. It was a great day."

Her smile toward him fell. "I'm sorry about what happened at Shady Grove this morning."

"It wasn't your fault," he said. "I'll call Sadie tonight. She might not remember the morning at all."

"So if I went back, she wouldn't remember me?"

He closed the cupboard doors. "You're thinking of going back?"

"No, I mean, I just—oh brother."

He smiled. "I'm sorry for the way Steve is acting."

She shrugged. "I guess it's his job. If I were him, I wouldn't trust me either. Not after reading that note."

Cole removed the taped paper from the faucet and threw it in the trash can near the door. "You're sure you don't have any idea who it might be from?"

"I'm sure. And that scares me."

He frowned. "Do you have someone you can call if there's trouble?"

"There's always 9-1-1, of course, and I can call Nathan and Kelsey."

"How far away do they live?"

"About twenty minutes."

"How long does it take 9-1-1 dispatches to arrive?"

She thought of the last heart attack Pops had and shuddered. "Almost ten minutes. We're a little ways out here."

Cole's frown deepened. "Do you have a gun?"

"Not yet. I'm going to get one." She wrapped her arms around herself. "I hate guns."

He pulled another strip of paper from under the grocery list, wrote something on it, and handed it to her. "I have a gun, and I live closer than your friends do. If you're in trouble, call me."

She looked at the numbers on the paper and all the uncertainty Kelsey's efforts had kept at bay came rushing back. Her voice was whisper soft. "I hope I'll never have to, but thank you."

He seemed to sense her fear and put on a smile for her. "That's rough on a guy's ego—give a girl your number and she says she hopes she'll never have to call you."

Meagan shook her head at him but smiled back. "Are you related to my grandfather?"

He sent a searing look her way and she felt like one of those old Southern belles must have before they swooned. "I sure hope not," he said.

36

Sunday, January 4
10:00 a.m.

Stephanie wobbled her way up the steps to the church's main entrance. She should have worn flats. Steve hadn't even noticed her whole new look except to throw out, "It's nice to see you dressed for a change," a comment definitely not worth the broken ankle she might get wearing these heels.

The flared skirt of her turquoise and black dress fluttered around her knees. She smiled at the man who held the door for her and asked him where she might find the women's Sunday school class. He was probably in his spot near the door to be helpful to visitors like her, but she wouldn't discount the possibility that the interest in his eyes might be because she looked attractive.

That morning, she'd tucked her wedding ring away in her top dresser drawer. Steve had commented on her bare hand, but she had countered, "I wouldn't want anyone to ask me who my husband is."

"You could make up a name," he'd said with a frown that almost looked like he cared.

The makeup and the dress and the tight control-top hose squeezing her into a size closer to what she wanted to be infused a confidence she'd thought was gone forever. "No," she said with a triumphant smile at his consternation. "I'd rather be single today."

He had not liked that answer, and she enjoyed the sweet taste of victory. She had not minded when Steve made her drop him off at the FBI office. It gave her a chance to show a little leg and leave him to worry how much would show when she sat in church—without him. His frown stayed in place the whole drive. He harped about how his case was life or death and how important it was that he solve it by five o'clock Monday.

She might just forget to pick him up, as he'd forgotten to come home so many, many times. It would do him good to wait for her, to wonder if she was having fun out there, not thinking of him at all.

The Sunday school room was more like a community center, large, with a kitchen on one side and room for twenty or so tables in the open area. A circle of eleven or twelve chairs had been set up in the middle. Only four of the chairs were filled so far, but Meagan Winston was in one of them. Stephanie sucked in her stomach and approached the group, careful with each step so she didn't introduce herself by falling flat on her face.

A woman named Kelsey talked with her first, and Meagan joined in, but Stephanie found herself distracted by the conversation the other two ladies were having.

"He's such a slob," the one woman said. She had long eyelashes that looked suspiciously fake. "How hard is it to pick up a pair of socks? I find them everywhere. In the cushions of the couch. On the floor. One week I refused to pick them up, and he didn't even notice! He just kept going until finally I collected them from all over the house and dumped them on top of his side of the bed."

"How many were there?" the second woman asked. She leaned forward and the charms on her necklace jingled like wind chimes.

"Eight pairs! Can you imagine?"

Stephanie knew she was supposed to be talking with Meagan, asking her questions about India, but she was hooked into the two women's conversation. They sounded like they felt as frustrated as she did. "So what do you do when you try to get your husband's attention and it doesn't work?" she heard herself ask.

The two women stopped and looked at her. "I gave up a long time ago," the second woman said with a sigh that might as well have come from Stephanie's own mouth.

"Well, I'm not giving up," the eyelash lady said. "I'm not his maid. We've been married two years now and he still—"

A phone rang and Stephanie turned to see Kelsey rifling through her purse. "I'm sorry," she said. She looked at the number and surprise crossed her face. "It's from India." She took a look around the circle, which by now had nine women counting Stephanie, and handed the phone to Meagan. "Would you take it?" she asked. Meagan nodded and left the room, speaking softly into the phone.

So much for getting information out of Meagan for now.

Kelsey began to address the group and Stephanie settled in for a half hour of boredom. She was shocked from the get-go when Kelsey said, "How many of you get irritated at your husbands because of something they regularly do or don't do?"

Every hand went up except Stephanie's. She wanted to put both hands up, and a foot or two, but at the last second remembered she was playing single today.

"How many of you have tried to get your husbands to change?"

Again, every hand went up and a few complaints came out.

"I tried that too," she said. "It got me angry, defensive, resentful, and about ruined my marriage. How's it working out for you?"

Silence. The women looked down, fidgeted with their purses, or inspected their clothing for stray specks of lint. Stephanie wondered if she should go out into the hall, see if she could hear Meagan's conversation. Steve said they needed the name of Meagan's contact in India. She could be talking with the contact right now. But Stephanie couldn't just walk out without a reason.

Kelsey smiled. "I was praying one day about this exact thing," she said. "I complained how my husband took me for granted, and didn't love me like he used to, and I felt like he just wanted a cook and a maid and I was sick of it."

A few of the women gasped. "But Kelsey," the eyelash woman said. "Your marriage is perfect."

Stephanie jolted at Kelsey's peal of laughter. "Oh, Margaret, if you only knew! My marriage is made of two selfish sinners, and the only reason it's any good today—and I have to say, it's great—is because of the Lord."

Here's where the religion speech comes in, Stephanie thought. *Give to the church, or feed the poor, and your marriage is going to be fixed. Please.* She crossed her arms and leaned back.

"So for weeks I prayed that God would get my husband's attention, and you know what happened?"

Several women asked, "What?"

"He got mine."

She let that sink in. The lint-picking women got busy on their clothing again. After a full minute or two, she continued. "You see, my husband likes to leave his clothes on the floor next to his bed, or draped over a chair. He doesn't see any need to put them away since he'll probably wear them again. And if he doesn't wear them again, he forgets about them, so they stay in a pile next to the bed FOR-E-VER."

A few women laughed. Stephanie kept waiting for the religion part.

"But God sent a passage to mind one day that I quite honestly did not want to hear. It's Colossians 3:23-24. I have it here. 'And whatever you do, do it heartily, as to the Lord and not to men, knowing that from the Lord you will receive the reward.' And one more passage...Luke 6:38." She seemed to notice the lady next to Stephanie was sharing her Bible with her. "This is Stephanie, everyone," Kelsey said with a sudden gesture in her direction. Stephanie knew her face got a deer-in-the-headlights look. Now she'd never be able to sneak out. "Stephanie, would you read that verse for us?"

The lady sharing her Bible pointed and Stephanie read quickly. She wanted all the attention offmusad her as soon as possible. "Give, and it shall be given unto you; good measure, pressed down, and shaken together, and running over, shall men give into your bosom. For—" She halted. "Bosom? Isn't that, like, the word for boobs?"

A choking sound came from several directions. Stephanie clapped her hand over her mouth and mumbled behind it, "Oh, crud. I bet we're not supposed to say words like boob in church."

Kelsey's laughter was joyful, not mocking. "Stephanie," she said. "I'm glad you're here." She looked down at her Bible. "That's an old word. Other versions say the giving will be 'poured into your lap.' And the rest of that verse says, 'For with the measure you use, it will be measured to you.'" She looked around the room. "God showed me that my husband wasn't leaving his clothes on the floor to make my life miserable. But I, grumbling and complaining while I picked them up, was the one who was selfish and angry. My wrong in resenting him was much worse than his wrong in being forgetful or inconsiderate. I was not only damaging my relationship with my husband by my stubborn refusal to accept this one thing; I was harming my relationship with God."

Stephanie had the chance to openly stare at the others because all of their shoes suddenly seemed to be of great interest. She wanted to laugh at them, but then thought of Steve, of how he spoke to her in weary tones first, then angry ones, but only after she lashed out the anger she always seemed to carry around with her anymore. Oh. She dropped her head to stare at her own high-heels.

"Dear ladies," Kelsey said, "do you want to have your husbands do the things you want or stop doing the things that bug you, or do you want a happy marriage?"

One young woman asked, "But why should we have to choose? Why can't they just do what we want out of love for us?"

"I used to ask the same thing, but God switched my question around. Why couldn't I let that one thing go out of love for Him? And I don't mean him—my husband. Out of love for Him—my Savior."

Stephanie looked up and saw a smile of peace on the woman's face. She was talking nonsense, but no one could say it hadn't worked for her.

"I started picking up or folding his clothes, and as I did, I said out loud, 'I'm doing this for the Lord.' After a week or two, when I picked up his clothes, I'd pray for him. Now I see his clothes and I smile and I am glad for the reminder to pray for the man I love more than anyone in the world. You see, when I stayed stubborn and demanded something from him, we were both miserable. When I gave up and gave out of love for God instead, my attitude changed. And you might be surprised what a good attitude will do for your marriage. There are things he wished I would do—like clean out my hairbrush, which I think is a total waste of time but it bugs him to no end—and he started doing it for me. Hmmm." She grinned. "See a pattern here? We reap what we sow. Good produces good. Anger and resentment produce more of the same."

Stephanie realized she was on the edge of her seat. "It can't work," she said. "It's too easy."

"Not hardly," Kelsey responded. "It's one of the hardest things you'll ever do, because it means setting aside what feels like your rights and giving when you want to get." She surprised Stephanie with a hearty laugh. "Goodness, that wasn't our Sunday school lesson at all today. I didn't plan to ramble on like that, but—"

Kelsey's words faded to silence. Stephanie followed her gaze and saw that Meagan had returned to the room, phone against her ear, her eyes red. She walked through the circle as if she didn't see any of them and handed the phone to Kelsey. "It's Pakshi. You know the woman they were trying to get out this week?"

"Rachita?"

Meagan nodded then burst into tears. "He killed her."

37

Sunday, January 4
10:30 a.m.

Lucias had long ago memorized Meagan's schedule. They both were creatures of habit and liked routine. But sometimes change was good. Lucias had made a change, a big change, and he knew Meagan would like it.

He parked his new black Sedan right next to Meagan's VW bug. He'd never had his car so close to hers before and it sent shivers of delight through him. She was inspiring him to greater courage. He'd left Agatha, and Raymond, and even Damion behind. He was Lucias now, armed with information, dressed to kill, ready to implement his plan that would get Meagan away from those men and straight to him and him alone.

Phone in the pocket of his new black suit pants, he swept his hair from his forehead and strode toward the church building. Every Sunday for at least a year, he had waited in the parking lot for her to emerge. Not today. Not anymore. He walked inside, saying pleasant things to random strangers, hating them all for taking Meagan's attention away from him for two hours every week. Once they were together, she would not need to come to church. She would not need all these extra friends. Lucias would be her everything, as she was his.

He found a pew toward the back of the main auditorium and took a seat, watching for Meagan's entrance. He would stay back for now, but not for long. It was almost time, and he was ready.

Sunday, January 4
10:35 a.m.

Kelsey jumped up and left the room, continuing the phone call while Meagan sobbed. Everyone else seemed as lost as Stephanie. One lady walked over to the kitchen area and returned with a box of tissues. She handed them to Meagan, who thanked her, her voice clogged with tears.

As subtly as possible, Stephanie pulled a pen from her purse and wrote the two Indian names Meagan had said on her palm.

"We were so close to getting her free," Meagan said. She blew her nose but the tears kept coming. "She had believed in Jesus and was full of hope."

"Who—who killed her?" someone asked.

"Her husband."

Stephanie's gasp joined the others. Meagan lifted her tear-stained face and said, "It's so awful in that place. That man, he didn't want her to be free. He started a kitchen fire and called it an accident." She buried her face into a fresh tissue and her shoulders shook with grief.

The woman with the eyelashes murmured, "And I was complaining about socks." She borrowed the tissue box from Meagan and wiped hard at her eyes. Her lashes did not come loose, so Stephanie decided they must be real.

Meagan lifted her head. "If your husband doesn't beat you, if he doesn't spit on you, or sell you to other men, or threaten to kill you for grasping the slightest hope..." Tears dripped onto her skirt. "Thank God for him. You are blessed."

One of the women put an arm around Meagan and prayed out loud. Stephanie bowed her head along with the others, but her mind was not on the prayer. Steve was no saint, that was for sure, but he wasn't the monster she had worked up in her mind over these last months. Could Kelsey's way work? Stephanie wouldn't be doing things out of love for God—she hadn't spoken to God since the baby died—but the principle of the thing seemed sound. Do something nice for someone and they're more likely to do something nice back. Was it worth a try?

"Thank you," Meagan said when the prayer ended. Her shoulders hunched over, the way Stephanie had sat when the baby had come far too early, and she'd wanted to keep the pain contained. "It seems God knew she would never be safe, even at our safe house, so He delivered her forever, to His home. I should be glad for her. She is free now, and he can't ever hurt her again."

A chill ran up Stephanie's spine. These women were strange. They talked backwards. When Kelsey returned, also crying, and the women gathered to pray again, Stephanie slipped out of the room and wandered the hall. She would see about getting information from Meagan after the service. For now, she needed some breathing room from these people and their upside-down ways.

She had come to get ahold of information, not to have a God who let women die, who let babies die, get ahold of her.

Sunday, January 4
10:50 a.m.

"Meagan? Are you all right?"

She was not all right. Not even close. Meagan looked up and saw Cole Fleming hurrying her way. It did not even register that she had never seen him at her church before, and when he was within arm's reach, his face a mask of concern, she did not question the desire to bury her head into his shirt and cry until there were no tears left.

He had an arm around her and her face was against his shoulder when reason returned. She jerked away. "I'm so sorry," she said breathlessly. She used the wadded-up tissue in her hand to wipe at his shirt where some of her makeup had smeared. "I've ruined your shirt." A fresh rain of tears fell. She looked around and realized they were in the church lobby, surrounded by people, many of whom looked at her with the same concern Cole had. She wiped her hair out of her face. "I should go home. I'm a horrible mess."

"Meagan," he said. He put a hand on each of her shoulders. "Meagan." When she looked in his eyes, he asked, "What happened? Can I help? Is it your parents? Your grandfather?"

She shook her head. "It's me. My life is falling apart." She sniffed. "A friend just got murdered, and somebody is stalking me, and Steve thinks I'm a criminal and Grandpa told me to stop bossing him around this morning, and I ran out of milk." She sobbed out in a choked whisper, "I'm just so tired."

Cole took a look around. "Come with me," he said, guiding her into the auditorium, his warm, solid arm around her shoulders. He found a spot for them both on one of the back pews, set near the corner of the building, out of the way and far less noticeable than they were in the lobby.

"Thank you," she said, balling her tissue in her fist and squeezing until her fingernails dug deep into her palm. She blinked and tried to gain control of herself. "I'm sorry. I shouldn't fall apart on you like this."

"It's okay." He pried the tissue out of her hand and used it to wipe her cheeks. The motion was tender and she fought more tears. "Sadie cries on me all the time."

She held out her hand for the tissue and used it, despite it being soggy, to wipe the last of the moisture under her eyes. Her face had to be a train wreck. She looked at him and thought to ask, "What are you doing here at my church, Cole?"

"Isn't everyone welcome at church?"

"Of course. I just meant—"

"I'm teasing." He smiled and angled to face her better. "I hope it doesn't scare you, like I'm following you again—"

She felt her lips turn up at that memory. When had things changed so much in her opinion toward him?

"I've been visiting churches since I moved back in the area. We never went to church growing up, so I didn't have one to come back to." He leaned over and arranged the hymnals in the little back-of-the-pew shelf to stand with equal distance between each one. "I am a follower of Christ, but a struggling one, and the joy I've seen on your face...well, it seemed the church you went to would be a good one to try. I hope you don't mind."

"I don't mind." Something shifted in her heart. He was a believer who wanted to grow in his faith. That was the number one most important thing when it came to a man she could lo—

She reigned in those wild thoughts before they ran somewhere dangerous.

"I won't keep you here if there's a place you always sit."

She shook her head. "I typically sit closer to the front, but I'd rather stay here today." Would he think she meant with him? "In the back where less people can see me," she clarified. "I hate crying in front of people."

His gaze traveled over her face. "You're beautiful," he said simply.

She blushed and put the tissue up to her cheeks. As it was still wadded up, it did not cover much. "Don't be ridiculous."

"I'm not," he said. "I think—"

Organ music announced the first song. Meagan stood and tried to focus, to gain a higher perspective. She sang the hymns, and shook hands during fellowship time. During the sermon, the pastor talked about the Good Shepherd and Meagan spent the time praying to Him for guidance and care. Never had she felt more like a lamb in need of carrying.

38

Sunday, January 4
12:00 p.m.

"What do you do for lunch on Sundays?"

The service had ended and Meagan, a little more clear-headed, stood and took the arm Cole offered. "The bath lady stays with Grandpa till three. I think she likes taking a break and watching church services on TV with him. So I go to a little cafe near here. They have a sunroom that makes me feel like I'm sitting outside and getting fresh air."

"Mind if I join you?"

"Hey, Meagan!"

Meagan turned to see their Sunday school visitor headed her way. "Hi...Stephanie, right?"

Tugging on her dress, the woman was out of breath by the time she caught up. She leaned over to adjust one of her spiked heels. Her feet had to hurt. "I was wondering if you and I could talk over a cup of coffee, or—" She stood and stepped back, her mouth open. "Oh!" Cole had turned and Meagan looked to see his face register surprise as well. Odd.

Meagan looked from one to the other. "I was going to the cafe down the street, and—"

"The one with the sunroom?" Stephanie sent a nervous glance toward Cole. "I've always wanted to go there."

"We could meet there," Meagan said. "Cole, do you want to meet us there, too?"

"Uh, sure."

They walked across the street and to the parking lot. Meagan noticed a black Sedan parked beside her little bug. "Did you get a new car?"

Cole looked the vehicle over like women looked at the new jade earrings for sale at Rahab's Rope. "I wish. I'll probably only get enough money from insurance to buy something used, not to mention I'll have to replace all the CDs which drowned with the car, and my jacket."

"Hard to conceal-and-carry when you're wearing a sweater," Stephanie commented, then her gaze skittered like she'd said something wrong.

Meagan's eyes felt swollen and her brain seemed headed for the same fate. "Do you two...know each other?"

"Yes."

"No."

Cole shrugged, but he sent a glance toward Stephanie that anyone could see had a question in it. "Her hus—"

"We met at a bar," Stephanie interjected. "A long time ago." Megan let the awkward silence linger. "Well," Stephanie said with a bright smile. "I'll see you there." She took off, her speed hindered by her shoes.

Cole offered Meagan a ride but she shook her head. "No thanks. I'd rather drive."

She opened her door and was about to climb in when Cole's phone beeped. He checked it and frowned. "It's a text. Quinn says I need to come in to the FBI office. Steve's found something important and wants me to look at it." He reached out his hand, as if to touch her cheek, but pulled it back and adjusted his sleeves, rotating his shoulder. "I guess I have to take a rain check on lunch."

Meagan rubbed her eyes. "I hope he found the real suspect, and this will all be over soon."

"I'll do what I can to help end this for you." He put his large hand onto her shoulder. "Try to take it easy today," he said. "You've been through a lot."

She whispered her thanks with a tremulous smile, and watched him go with a sigh.

Sunday, January 4
12:00 p.m.

Lucias' body shook with barely controlled rage. If he didn't have everything set up so beautifully, so perfectly, he'd allow the boil inside him to erupt and destroy Cole Fleming right where he stood between Lucias' new Sedan and Meagan Winston's car.

His hand, Lucias' hand, had touched her today. It was the first time. Such a meaningful moment. Lucias had discovered the church had a three-minute break between songs when people walked around shaking hands or hugging one another. Fellowship, they called it. It was the reason Lucias had come inside. When the man told them to shake hands, Lucias had walked down the aisle behind the pews to where she sat in the back on the opposite side. He had put his hand out. Held hers inside his. It was almost more than he could bear.

And she had not cared. Had hardly looked at him. She had missed the entire moment because of Cole Fleming, who'd had the gall to ask her a question just then and divert her attention back to him.

Lucias imagined ways of watching Cole die, laughing inside as his ideas graduated from generic to gruesome. That man would regret taking Meagan from him. He would beg forgiveness for daring to put his arm around her. Lucias put his hands into a circle and squeezed tight. Cole would pay. Meagan was vulnerable right now. Lucias didn't blame her for wanting someone near, for feeling lonely. Didn't he understand that feeling?

By tomorrow at this time, she would understand that it was Lucias she should lean on, Lucias she should cling to.

He cheered inside when she shook her head no at Cole and started to get into her car. He knew where she would go, where she always went on Sunday afternoons. If Cole Fleming would just walk away, Lucias could get into his new car and go be with her. The thought of touching her soft skin again made his breathing quicken.

The parking lot cleared. Cole drove away in Steve Campbell's car and Meagan left in her VW bug. Lucias made his way to the new black vehicle that matched his new black suit and the shiny black weapon concealed under it. All just like Cole Fleming's, only better in every way.

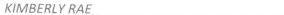

39

Sunday, January 4
12:40 p.m.

"I'm sorry about your friend in India." Stephanie sipped her latte, relieved to hear Cole wouldn't be coming. She tried to think how Steve would manipulate the conversation to get the information he wanted. "Do you go out there a lot?"

Meagan stirred honey into her hot chai tea. "Twice a year. It's always strange coming back, getting used to things costing so much and people being so different."

"So you...spend time with a lot of Indian people while you're there?"

"Certainly. Our Indian partners are amazing. Most of the time we're learning from them rather than the other way around. We have access to more resources than they do, and think of ourselves as suppliers and mediators from the people who care here in America, to the people working in the trenches in India."

"Is there—is there a certain person who is in charge out there?"

"Several." Meagan went on to describe the work, and then began talking about the children, and Stephanie had no idea how to get her back on track. Steve should have just interrogated her. He was good at bullying people into giving him what he wanted.

Except her, she realized. He hadn't been able to get her to give him much of anything but a lot of heartache. He was a jerk sometimes. Most times lately. But never intentionally cruel. She caught herself tearing up.

"Are you okay?" Meagan reached across and touched her hand. "You seem to be remembering something sad."

She was never going to get a name out of Meagan Winston, so she gave up and said, wistful longing in her voice, "I...had a baby...almost. She was five months along." She hadn't talked about the baby to anyone but Steve. "I was going to name her Rebecca Anne." She put her head in her hands. "How can you love God when He takes away the thing you want most in the world?"

"Oh, Stephanie, I'm so sorry."

Stephanie felt the grief well up, still as fresh as the day it happened. "People say time makes it better. They lie. Nothing will make it better." She lifted her head and said with raw emotion, "And I want to just scream and scream at God for letting it happen." She heard her own words and stood to her feet. "I should go. I've probably blasphemed or something and you don't even know me and here I am unloading on you..."

Meagan grasped her arm. "Stay, please. I understand. More importantly, I think God understands."

She let out a bitter laugh. "Shouldn't you get struck by lightning for saying something like that?"

Meagan smiled. "If so, a lot of the people in the Bible would be fried to a crisp." She pulled a small Bible out of her large purse and opened it to somewhere in the middle. "Stephanie, I go to India and see horrible things, things I don't tell anyone when I come back. People want to hear the good stories, the rescue stories. They don't want to know the terrifying darkness some of these women live in every day. The suffering of the children. Sometimes I want to shout up to heaven and ask where God is and why He has abandoned those people."

Stephanie sat back down. "You do? Really?"

Meagan nodded. "On this last trip I met a family in the brothels that had lived there three generations. The little girl's mother was a prostitute, her grandmother had been a prostitute, and her great-grandmother. The little boy's father was a pimp, along with his grandfather and great-grandfather. They wouldn't even consider the option of their children leaving that filthy, disgusting place. Talked like it was an honor to continue the family business. Like it would be good when the boy was old enough to negotiate the sale of his sister's body. I have never felt so helpless in my life. Where was God? Didn't He care about these kids? Didn't He care when the generation before were kids, and the one before that?"

Stephanie could only nod. She was surprised when Meagan pulled a worn, folded sheet of paper from her Bible and slid it across the table to her.

"I take this with me every trip, verses from God's Word, so I don't give in to despair."

Stephanie turned the paper to face her and read aloud, "My God, My God, why have You forsaken Me? Why are You so far from helping Me, and from the words of My groaning? O My God, I cry in the daytime, but You do not hear; and in the night season, and am not silent." She looked up at Meagan. "That's exactly how I feel," she whispered.

Meagan nodded. "Keep reading."

"He has not despised nor abhorred the affliction of the afflicted; nor has He hidden His face from Him; but when He cried to Him, He heard." When was the last time she had cried out to anyone but Steve? She skimmed the next sections on the paper. The words went from despair to hope, from fear of God's silence to assurance of His presence. At the end were three final words: "God is love."

"You may have given up on God," Meagan said softly, "but He hasn't given up on you." Her phone rang in her purse, but she ignored it. "I told you what I did about India so you would know I'm not throwing you a hollow platitude to make you feel better. God loves you, Stephanie. He was with you when you lost your baby." Her eyes filled with tears. "He hurt with you."

The phone rang a second time. Stephanie put a napkin to her eyes and tried to keep from weeping. "Go ahead and answer it," she said. "I need a minute."

"Okay." Meagan pulled her phone out and put it to her ear. "Hello? Quinn, is something wrong?"

She walked away. Stephanie eventually lowered the napkin and went back to the top of the paper, reading through the words again, wondering if God could truly be near as Meagan said.

Sunday, January 4
12:50 p.m.

"Listen carefully, this is important."

Meagan stepped outside, letting the door swing shut behind her to block the noise inside the sunroom. "Quinn, you don't sound like yourself. What's going on?" He'd summoned Cole, and now was calling her? Why wasn't Steve the one on the phone?

"Steve told me to call you. He couldn't get himself to tell you in person. Meagan, you need to stay away from Cole Fleming."

She stopped in her tracks. "What?"

"Cole Fleming is not who he pretends to be. He is not a good man."

Meagan grasped an outdoor bench. "But Steve's been working with him. They grew up together—"

"The FBI has been trying to catch him for years. Steve has pretended to be his friend to get close to him and find out things."

"Like what?"

"That's classified." Quinn's voice sounded muffled, like he was outside talking in the wind. It was a clear day where she was. "Has he ever told you about his real job?"

She winced. "No."

"Has he ever told you about the bombing of his battalion in Iraq?"

"N-no, but I read about it..."

"He doesn't talk about it to keep from incriminating himself. Steve is telling the papers everything right now. The story will be all over the place tomorrow. We're trying to get Cole to play his hand."

Meagan fought dizziness. She held onto the bench and vaguely noticed a car just like Cole's parked across the street. But Cole's car was in the river. A blond-haired man in a slim-legged black suit talked on his phone next to the car. She grasped on the thought that he should wear a coat. A couple walked by, the girl gushing over something the boy said. They didn't look cold either. Neither did the old man hobbling across the street. What was the temperature? She was shivering.

Quinn continued talking, warning her away from Cole, suggesting she call the police if he tried to come near her.

"This can't be true, Quinn." Meagan dropped onto the bench. "It can't be."

"It is, Meagan. Cole Fleming is bad. If you don't believe me, I guess I'll have to tell you—well, Steve told me not to tell, but—"

"But what?" Meagan leaned forward, hugging her knees. "What, Quinn?"

"Cole's job, the reason he keeps it secret, the reason he keeps his sister holed up away from everybody."

The tears were falling before he said a word. "No..." she whispered.

"It's porn. He drugs girls and takes pictures of them. He got his start at a slumber party years ago, using his sister as bait to get other girls. His dad sent him away to Baghdad to protect her."

"No," she said more firmly and stood. She put a hand over her mouth so he would not hear the sob breaking from her. "No, I don't believe you. Sadie said—"

"Cole's sister was doped up at the time. She wouldn't remember anything that really happened. He's probably been getting close to you to get access to more girls. Just get a newspaper in the morning. You'll see for yourself tomorrow in black and white that he's a liar."

Meagan hung up the phone. She couldn't hear any more. In a daze, she looked around and tried to remember where she was. She glanced through the window of the cafe and saw Stephanie sitting at a table inside, the paper of Bible verses Meagan clung to most in her hand. Meagan needed that paper.

Back inside, a rush of uncomfortable heat blasted her from an overhead vent. She took wooden steps to their table. "Stephanie, I'm sorry, I have to go. Something has...happened."

"You look like you've seen a ghost," Stephanie said.

"Worse." Meagan couldn't ask for the paper back. Stephanie needed it. She would go home and write a new one, a longer one. It would give her mind something to do while her heart broke.

"Are you going to be okay?" Stephanie stood and put a hand on her arm. "What happened?"

Meagan could barely form the words. "The thing I feared most just found me."

40

Sunday, January 4
2:00 p.m.

Meagan drove aimlessly for an hour. She turned off the praise CD in her car. She ignored the ringing phone. Numb from the heart out, guilt finally propelled her toward home. She had stayed away longer than usual and Pops might be worried.

Through the fog in her mind, she heard the sound of an ambulance behind her and pulled off the road to let it pass, then continued on her way. How was she going to keep Pops from knowing she was in pieces? It would be wrong to fake a headache. On second thought, she wouldn't have to fake anything. Her head pounded and nausea crawled up her stomach. She could set him up with a good movie and he'd nap in the recliner most of the afternoon. She'd escape to her room and...and what? Pray? Cry? Grieve the loss of newly born hopes?

Part of her still said none of it could be true. He could not be so duplicitous to have fooled all of them. But how could she refute the information? Quinn knew things that no one but Steve could know.

The sound from the ambulance siren did not recede into the distance. As she turned onto her drive, it got louder. "Oh no," she whispered, reaching across the passenger seat to grab her phone out of her purse. She looked at the missed calls. Four from home. *No, please. Please.*

She pressed her foot on the gas pedal. The house came into view, an ambulance and fire truck parked in front of it. The siren stopped but red lights flashed across the yard like heralds of doom. She parked the car and ran. The bath lady met her on the front porch. "Meagan! I was worried. I tried to call you a bunch of times."

"Is he okay?" Her voice came out like a little child's. A frightened child's.

"It's nothing terrible," the woman said, her hands reaching out to grasp Meagan's arms. Meagan had seen her do that to Pops more than once. It was a calming gesture, meant to reassure and help the person focus.

It did not work today. "I'm so sorry I wasn't here." Two paramedics came through the door guiding a stretcher. "Oh, Pops." Meagan rushed to his side.

"Aw, don't you worry. Nothing happened worth all this fuss and noise," her grandfather said. She was relieved to see his speech was not impaired. It wasn't a stroke. "A guy gets a few pains and some extra pitter-patter in the gizzard, and she calls in the cavalry." He chuckled. "It was probably just that pizza we ate yesterday."

"He doesn't seem to be in danger," the bath lady said. Her name was Angela but Meagan never thought of her by her name. "But I wanted to take him in and get him checked out, just in case. If this is a pre-heart attack, maybe we can head it off at the pass."

Meagan's chest was experiencing its own pain. "Are you taking him to the hospital?"

"I want him to get checked in for at least twenty-four hours." She put her hands out. "Don't get scared. It's just a precaution. I have other patients I have to see, and he needs to be monitored until we're sure everything is stable."

She nodded. She knew she was in no condition to be trusted to take care of anyone right then. "Okay. Thank you. I'll change and go straight to the hospital."

"Don't. Give yourself a couple of hours at least. They won't let you in until after they're done running tests. There's no sense wearing yourself out in a waiting room. You know how long these things can last sometimes."

The paramedics had Grandpa strapped inside the ambulance. Pops lifted his hand and opened his mouth. She waited for words of wisdom. Something to hang on to.

"If I die, I'll be surprised," he called out. She laughed for his sake. They closed the doors and the ambulance drove away, lights still flashing but sirens off. That was reassuring. The sirens would be blaring if they felt any sense of urgency.

The fire truck cleared out and an unnatural silence fell over the area. "It's going to be okay," the bath lady said.

Nothing is okay. Meagan forced a smile and waved as the woman made her way to her blue van and drove on to other people in need. Meagan stood in the cold, not wanting to go inside the empty house, but not wanting to stay outside either. Her phone rang. Afraid Pops might have digressed to a heart attack already, she accepted the call.

She should have checked the number. The last person she wanted to talk to was Cole Fleming.

Sunday, January 4
2:30 p.m.

"Meagan, it's Cole. I hope I'm not interrupting your time with Stephanie."

"N-no."

She sounded like her nose was stuffed up, or she'd been crying again. He felt a pang of sympathy. She'd had a rough day.

His own was turning out not rough, but confusing. He had arrived at the FBI office to a set of locked doors. Steve wouldn't answer his phone, and Cole tried calling the number Quinn had used to text him, but no one responded to it either. "I'm sorry for having to run out on you. I was looking forward to lunch together. Are you free for dinner?"

"No."

He waited for more information, but all he heard was a sniff and then the sound of her blowing her nose from a distance.

"Um, how are the pipes holding up?"

"Fine."

"How's your Grandpa doing? He's a great guy. I'd like to get to talk with him again sometime."

"You can't." Her voice broke. "He's on his way to the hospital."

"Oh no." He had walked back to Steve's car. It was going to be nice when insurance got back with him and he could get a vehicle of his own again. "Can I help? Would you like some company at the hospital?"

"No."

He could hear her crying and it tore into him to think of her alone. "Meagan, I've got all evening free. I'd like to be there for you if I can. I could bring supper, or—"

"No, Cole. I don't—you can't—" Something slammed in the background. "I don't want you to come."

Her voice was colder than the weather outside. "Meagan, can you explain?" Something had changed. "Is this about what Stephanie said about the bar? We did meet at one, but that was because I showed up to get St—her future husband. He got drunk and passed out on the floor near the pool table the night before their wedding. I tossed him over my shoulder and took him home, where he woke up enough to say he was terrified of getting married. Then he threw up all over my shoes. Not my favorite memory."

"Please, Cole." He heard her let out a little sob. "Don't call me anymore. I know everything."

The phone went dead. She'd hung up on him. Cole put his hands out in a gesture of sheer bafflement, then had to grab the steering wheel to keep from running off the road.

"What just happened?" he asked aloud. He wracked his brain through the ride home, but arrived no closer to an answer, just a feeling of great loss.

Sunday, January 4
2:45 p.m.

Lucias didn't like to see Meagan cry, but it was for the best. She hadn't known Cole Fleming long, so it would not take much to forget him. Lucias, however, had been with Meagan for years. His attachment to her was strong and lasting. He held his binoculars up to his eyes and watched with glee as she turned to go inside her home but then noticed the manila envelope he'd left on the seat of the rocking chair on the porch. She bent to retrieve it, looking it over on both sides. He had not written her address or a return address on it, just her name, in flowery letters he'd taken painstaking care to create and place in perfect lines on the envelope.

She sat on the rocking chair and Lucias exulted. It would be much harder to see her facial expressions if she went inside to open it. She tore the side edge and pulled out the photo. His heart beat so hard it almost burst through his chest. She was looking at him, at Lucias' face, for the first time. This morning had not counted. She had not really seen him. This was the moment he'd imagined. This was the beginning of their love story. Now she knew who had wooed her. He had written his love on the back of the photograph. She was turning it over now.

Her eyes went wide and his heart soared. She was surprised. She was not crying anymore. Her heart must be telling her that Cole Fleming did not matter. Not at all. She had someone else who loved her. Someone who had proven it. Soon she would smile and he would know pure joy.

She stood and, before he had a chance to think what it meant, went inside. She closed the front door and he could no longer see her face. Could not see her smile.

He readied the car to move to another location where he could look in through the bay window, but the shades to the window shut as he watched. Right before his eyes, shades, blinds and curtains closed all over the house. What was she doing?

With a loud curse, he threw his binoculars. They cracked against the passenger window of the car then fell onto the seat. He yelled and banged his hand against the dashboard. She was not supposed to do that. He needed to see her. How could he know how she felt about his photograph if she hid inside the house?

Her grandfather was gone. She was alone. If it had been any other day, he would go to her now. It would have been the perfect moment. Just the two of them. In her home. He'd get to see her room, where she slept. His pulse raced. He wanted to go now. He wanted his perfect moment today.

But then all his work would be wasted. He had to wait until the plan unfolded completely. Everything was in place. After tomorrow morning, he would act. Tomorrow afternoon, he could prove in person what he'd written on the back of his photo.

"Soon you will be with me. Forever."

41

Monday, January 5
8:30 a.m.

Steve yawned. "I need coffee." He pulled into a fast food drive through and ordered the largest option on the menu. "You want some?"

"Nah, brought some from home." Quinn held up his thermos. "Did you ever go home? You were still working when I left at eleven."

"I got an hour or two of sleep on the floor of the office. My jacket makes a lousy pillow."

"You're going to fall asleep on your feet today."

Steve paid the fast food worker and took his extra-large coffee. "I pulled more than a few all-nighters in the military. I'll be fine now that I have this." He took a sip, jerked back, and put the drink in the middle consul. "So fill me in on your side of things."

Quinn clamped his thermos between his feet on the floor and opened the file on his lap as Steve maneuvered through traffic. "Our buddy Jerod isn't the sharpest pencil in the box, so letting him go was a smart move. He led the DEA right back to his base, where his contact soon showed up to punish him for losing the Indian rupees."

"So they've got Jerod and the contact now?"

"Yeah, and the contact is mad as a hornet and willing to confess anything to make a deal. I talked to the DEA this morning and they're confident they'll have the meth lab soon and that side of this case will be closed. They still need the Indian contact for the international side."

"Which leads to us, and Lucias Moore."

Quinn pulled the file underneath to sit on top of the stack and opened it. "We heard back from the lab. The bottle of sand from Meagan Winston's house showed up to be just sand. No drugs."

"Hmm. Surprising. And the prints on the vase?"

"Lucias Moore, as we expected. But the unexpected thing was the flowers."

Steve tried his coffee again. Still too hot. Stephanie said he acted like a bear just out of hibernation without his morning coffee. He should have called her yesterday to tell her he was working all night, but by the time he thought of it, it was too late to call without waking her up. He'd send a text after they searched Lucias' house. "What about them?"

"The lab was working on the vase when they noticed the white carnations had turned pink. They tested the water and found red food coloring and opium. It matched the kind in the briefcase."

"In the water?"

"I thought that was strange, too."

The coffee had cooled enough to not burn his tongue. Good enough. Steve stopped at a red light and guzzled half the cup. "The sand bottle in the briefcase wasn't full. My guess is he took some for himself. But why put it in water and deliver it to Meagan?"

"Maybe we'll find an answer in his house."

Steve parked in front of Lucias' run-down trailer. "I doubt we'll need to bring the warrant. I don't think he's been here since we showed up last time." The door was still unlocked. Steve pushed it open, a hand on his weapon. "FBI. We have a warrant." He took a careful look around. "Clear," he called, and Quinn entered behind him. Quinn worked the kitchen while Steve took the living room. He chose one of the crossed-out photos on the floor and bagged it. "I spent half the night reading about this murder case."

"Claudia's?" Quinn joined him. "The kitchen's clean." He coughed. "Let me rephrase that. The kitchen's dirty, but clean of evidence." He looked at the photos on the wall. "Find anything interesting?"

"Just that the murder happened three years ago, Lucias got fired not long after, and his first flight to India was thirteen days after that."

"He moved on fast."

"I'm done with this room. Let's find what's behind that locked bedroom door." Steve crossed the hallway, senses on alert. "No sounds or extra smells." He picked the lock and pushed the door open. A spider fell from the door frame and landed on Steve's shoulder. Quinn went inside the room while Steve fell against the wall brushing the thing off. It landed on the worn Berber carpet and disappeared. "That was a big one."

"Not as big as this." Quinn pointed his chin to the wall behind Steve. Steve turned and did a double take. A chill ran across his shoulders.

Meagan Winston smiled at them. From floor to ceiling, secured onto the wall with clear packaging tape, the image of her was at least eight feet wide and as many feet high.

"She's looking into the camera," Quinn commented.

"He didn't take this photo," Steve said. "I remember it from their store's website." He backed against the opposite wall and held his phone up to take pictures. The image only displayed her from the shoulders up, making her face bigger than the bed in the room. "How did he get an image this size?" He moved closer and ran his hand along the photo. "It's not one picture. The whole thing is made of poster-size photos that he connected with glue or something. The resolution must have been high to make these with this quality. She's only a little pixilated." If she was out on display like this, what was the man hiding under his bed?

"That kind of project would take a long time and a couple hundred bucks to do," Quinn said. "A labor of love?"

"Or lust." For some reason, the huge image made Steve's skin crawl. "Let's check out the rest of his room and get out of here."

"Where to next?"

"Depends on what we find." Steve wished he hadn't left his coffee in the car. "We only have until five today to prove we can stick this case, so let's hope we come across something good." He rummaged through the drawers in the one dresser in the room while Quinn checked under the bed.

"Man, this guy needs a maid service. Even a laundry basket would be a start." Quinn pulled piles of dirty clothing out and tossed them against the far wall. "I don't think we'll find anything in here except smelly socks and—wait a minute." Quinn pulled plastic gloves from a pocket, put them on, then dropped to his stomach and elbow-crawled deep under the bed. "I found a box." He backed out and looked through it. "It's letters. Signed from Claudia. The homicide team is going to be pumped to get these."

Steve had reached the bottom drawer of the dresser. He pulled out a similar box. "What do you want to bet we'll find more letters in here?" He opened the box and pulled a sheet of paper out. He skimmed over it, then quickly folded it and put it back. He closed the box. "Let's go. We've got what we need."

Quinn stood with the box of letters from Claudia. "Where to?"

"Meagan Winston's house."

42

Monday, January 5
8:30 a.m.

"How's your grandfather doing?"

Meagan sat at the table in the store's back room across from where Kelsey and Brianna shared their breakfast with Alexia. "He sounded great on the phone. I'm going to stop by to see him as soon as I leave here."

"I'm glad to hear you'll be going home," Kelsey said. "It's your day off, and you look like you could use some sleep."

"That's a nice way of putting it." Meagan glanced in a mirror set near the rows of necklaces waiting for clasps. Her eyes were bloodshot, with dark purple half-moons underneath. "I look like I got run over by a truck."

"It's been a difficult weekend."

Kelsey didn't know the half of it.

"Did you hear?" Alexia rose and gave Meagan a hug. "My pimp's parole got denied! He's back in jail."

"Thank God for that," Meagan said. Her words came out brittle. If they had been visible, the letters would have cracked and fallen to the floor like a broken mosaic. "One less guy out there preying on soft-hearted girls and breaking their hearts."

Brianna cocked her head. "You okay, Meagan?"

She sat at the table and diverted attention by saying, "I came by to tell you that I think I should stay away from the shop for a while. With the investigation still in process, I don't want to draw any attention that will put a shadow on Rahab's Rope."

"Meagan, we're not worried about that. We're behind you." Kelsey buttered her biscuit. "They'll figure out you're innocent and that will be the end of it."

"Maybe not." Meagan told them about the photograph left on her porch. "Whoever this guy is, he's getting braver. I don't want him coming here to look for me and endangering..." She sent a pointed look at Alexia, who had gone across the room to throw her biscuit wrapper away. "...any of our friends."

"You have a point there," Kelsey admitted, "but it just doesn't feel right, like we're sending you away until you prove your innocence."

"We all know that isn't the case. I'll stay away to keep our girls safe. That's the most important thing right now. They're vulnerable, and men like him—" She refused to think about Cole. The morning paper would be there soon. She had to be gone before it came. She could not bear to read the devastating truth in front of even her closest friends. "Men like him know just how to gain a vulnerable girl's trust and exploit it. I won't let him do that here."

"But will you be safe at home, alone?"

"I've got Steve Campbell's number in my phone now. I'm going to call him later this morning and tell him about the photo."

"And you can call Cole, too," Brianna said with a grin. "I think he'd be more than willing to help protect you." She waved her hand in front of her heart. "He is one handsome guy. Shame he's too old for me."

"I—I need to go." Meagan gathered her belongings and wrapped her scarf around her neck. "Keep me posted, okay? And let me know if there's work I can do from home."

Kelsey rose and hugged her. Meagan felt like a block of wood, afraid to hug back. She was one blink away from losing it. She couldn't collapse into a weeping mess in front of Alexia. She was supposed to be one of the leaders, one of the strong ones. "Lord willing, this will all be over soon," Kelsey said close to her ear, "and you'll be back here where you belong. I'm praying it will be taken care of this week. We need you here when I leave for India on the eighth."

"Thanks." Meagan left the store, aware at some subconscious level that she should be paying more attention to her surroundings. She got in her car and, once the engine was running, turned the heat on high. Some guy out there was fixated with her. If he walked up to her car that instant, she was not sure she would even care.

What could he say or do that would make her feel worse than she already felt?

She took the familiar route toward the hospital, dreading her arrival. By the time she got to Pop's room, he would be reading the morning newspaper. There was no avoiding whatever would be printed on it.

Monday, January 5
9:00 a.m.

Cole parked Steve's car and stepped into the cold air to face another Monday morning at a job he hated. Today felt like a Monday times two. He'd stopped at the gas station on his way, but the usually friendly cashier glared at Cole like Cole had just maimed his favorite pet. He'd gone next to the diner, and still didn't know how to think about what happened there.

"I'll take the usual, Jack," he'd said when he walked in.

"No room today." Jack's voice had a gruffness to it Cole had never heard.

"Everything okay with you?" Cole knew Jack's son had gotten in some trouble with the law recently. "How's Billy doing? Have they decided on a court date yet?"

"My boy may have done some shady things," Jack had said, crossing his arms and blocking Cole's path to an empty booth. "But he's no traitor to his country." Heads had turned and Cole felt whispers rise from the tables all around him, like a swarm of locusts waking up and immediately busying themselves devouring the landscape. He saw a man at the table behind Jack set down his newspaper and rise. He adjusted his Vietnam veteran's cap and moved to stand behind Jack. "You'll need to be on your way, Cole," Jack said.

Two more men had left their chairs and now stood behind Cole. For some reason, everybody in the diner seemed prepped for a brawl to start. Cole had not felt such hostility since Iraq. "What's going on, Jack?"

"Just that there's no seat and no food here for you today. Be on your way now before trouble starts."

"But I—" The men closed in tight enough that the only route available was the one that led outside. "Can't I even ask—" The man behind him grabbed him by the collar of his jacket. "Hey, I just bought this yesterday. Don't—"

Cole had found himself roughly escorted from the premises. He could have downed three of the men, and Jack, but he had no reason to fight any of them. Why did they all act as if they had reason to fight him?

He'd skipped breakfast and gone straight to work. Before he could get to his desk in the one-story building, Matt Sinclair, one of the newer recruits, met him with a newspaper in hand.

"Have you looked at today's paper yet?"

"I've had enough negativity this morning." Cole did not stop except to grab a drink at the water cooler. "Why start with everybody else's bad news?"

Matt refilled his coffee mug from the half-empty pot on the counter adjacent to the water. When Cole sat at his desk, Matt wandered over and set the paper down. "I'm afraid it's not everybody else's bad news today. You're the cover story, man."

Cole stared at the front-page image of him carrying an MK19 Grenade Launcher, his face fierce, his uniform and his skin covered in sand, a woman in a figure-hugging green dress sending the camera a sideways glance in the background. "They photoshopped that woman in," Cole said. "No female in Baghdad went out in public dressed like that."

"You'll have a hard time convincing anyone of that, or that the story isn't true." Matt leaned his weight on the edge of his desk. "They used a lot of technical terms, made it sound good."

Cole flipped the paper open and scanned the accusatory paragraphs, the questions about where the woman got her grenade and other explosives, the story of how he was seduced into giving away his own envoy's position to a terrorist, and how a fellow officer and childhood friend had lied to protect him. That fellow officer had finally come forth to tell the truth, that Cole Fleming was guilty of sharing military secrets with the enemy. Why else would he have run away from his own battalion's mission that fateful day they were all targeted to be killed? "It's missing the part that no soldiers were killed that day," Cole ground out. "And the only one seriously wounded was me."

"Guess they thought those facts weren't important."

"Didn't fit their conclusion, you mean."

Matt leaned over and said in a low conspirator's voice, "So did you do it?" Cole stood so quickly, his hands fisted at his sides, Matt fell off the desk and backed a step away. "I was just kidding, man."

Cole uncurled a hand long enough to grab the newspaper. "Mind if I take this?"

Matt's hands were both out and he moved farther away. "Go ahead, you can have it."

"Thanks." Cole traced his path back toward the door. "Tell the powers that be that I'm taking my first vacation day." He heard the low growl in his voice and did not bother to mask it. "But it won't be for a vacation." He let the door slam behind him and pulled out his phone as he marched toward the parking lot. Steve's number went to voicemail after the first ring, but Cole hung up before speaking. This was a matter to deal with in person. Cole's knuckles went white on the steering wheel as he drove to the Federal Building. He strode inside to find Steve's office empty.

"Where can I find Steve Campbell?" he asked a man in a cubicle across the hall.

The agent did not look up. "Steve's working a case."

Cole wanted to yank the man's designer toupee off his scalp. "I know. I was in here last week helping. Where is Steve now?"

"Are you FBI?" The man swiped his bangs out of his eyes and regarded Cole. "You're the one who called in about the grey Oldsmobile."

"That's right." A glance to the right revealed another agent headed down the hallway with a newspaper in hand. Cole didn't have much time. "I need to find Steve right away, but he's not answering his phone."

"Does it have to do with the case?"

Cole put his hands flat on the man's desk and leaned over him. "It's very important."

"He called in a few minutes ago. He and Quinn searched the suspect's house and are now going to another house. A Meagan

Winner or Winsome or something. I can check the record if you need the address."

The agent in the hallway looked at him, then at the paper. "I know the address," Cole said. "Thanks for your help." He departed without a backward glance.

Fifteen minutes would get him to Meagan's house, where Steve would have to put his precious investigation on hold while he explained what lie he'd told to protect Cole, what truth the lie was meant to hide, and why he had suddenly decided to destroy the honor of Cole's name.

43

Monday, January 5
9:00 a.m.

"Oh, Pops." Meagan pulled her chair close to his hospital bed and laid her head down on the edge of the mattress. "I was afraid he wasn't the man I thought him to be, but I never dreamed it could be as bad as this." She felt him pat her head and wished for the past, when she was a young, pig-tailed girl and a pat on the head was enough to make her feel better. "I wanted him to be..."

His hand rested on her hair. "Your Prince Charming? Your perfect man? Meagan, my girl, every person on this earth, including the man you will promise to love until death, is flawed and sinful at the core. You want someone who knows that and has been redeemed by Jesus, and is going to live the rest of his life by God's strength and for God's glory. Is Jesus the Lord of Cole's life?"

She kept her head buried in the mattress. "He said so, but—"

"Then if that's the case, let's look at this situation from a practical standpoint instead of a weeping female's."

"I'm not weeping," she mumbled into the sheet.

"You were either yesterday or this morning. Your eyes look like overripe tomatoes."

She lifted her head. "Thanks."

He patted her hand then held up the newspaper like he was displaying it for a report. "First thing: the soldier who gave this information did not give his name, which makes me doubt his word. Second: this entire article is based on the unnamed soldier's word. There are no quotes from other soldiers, superior officers, or eyewitnesses. Third: the so-called journalist created conclusions based on conjecture, not facts." He smacked the headline and dropped the paper to lay across his lap. "The entire piece is highly suspect and brings to mind the old but wise adage, don't believe everything you read in the papers."

"But Pops, this is just the last straw. Quinn already told me..." Meagan slumped in her chair and wiped at her eyes. "He told me terrible things about Cole. Things I don't want to believe, but how can I not with them all piling up like—like—"

"It seems to me someone might be trying to discredit him."

A machine behind Pop's head beeped a staccato rhythm. A nurse entered and Meagan gestured to the piece of equipment, one of about twenty connected to her grandfather. "Is something wrong?"

"His oxygen monitor just got dislodged." The nurse smiled and clamped a small device back onto Pop's middle finger. "Most of these machines make strange noises. Don't worry, if something was really wrong, you'd know it."

She exited and Meagan resumed her slouch on the chair. Both her physical and emotional state seemed defined by fatigue. "I can't see it being a big conspiracy," she said, rubbing her eyes. "There are too many angles. Why would anyone go to that much trouble?"

Her grandfather pushed a button on the side rail to elevate the foot of his bed. "We could try to figure this out all day, but there's really only one question to answer and one thing to do."

"Let me guess. The question is, when am I going to learn that a man who seems too good to be true probably is, and the thing to do is to never be stupid enough to let my heart get involved again."

He chuckled. "You're pretty stuck on this guy, aren't you?"

She sighed. "What's the one question, Pops?"

He rolled up the newspaper and sent it flying. It hit the wall and missed the trash can by a foot. "Have you prayed about him?"

"Yes." She'd been up most of the night. "What's the one thing to do?"

He pushed the call button for the nurse and asked for a cup of vanilla pudding. The nurse answered no to the pudding but said she would bring him some crackers, her voice at such a high volume Meagan wanted to plug her ears. Did she think the speaker was broken? He adjusted his pillow and said, "The Bible gives clear instructions on what to do in a situation where someone has wronged you. You go to them and tell them what they've done."

"But he knows what he's done."

"That's the instructions. You go to them, and tell them what they've done, and give them a chance to ask forgiveness."

"But Pops—"

He reached over the bed rail and took her hand. "In all my years, Meagan, whenever I have obeyed these instructions, either the person has repented and asked forgiveness, or the person explained the truth of the situation and I found out I had been the one misjudging them. Either way, the relationship was restored. Remember that skinny little woman who came and cleaned the house for us when your grandmother first got cancer?"

"Yes. Her name was Valerie. What does she have to do with—?"

"She dropped a figurine one day. Her hands had arthritis and they cramped up on her. The figurine broke and she felt terrible, but your grandma said it wasn't important, and she meant it. A few months went by and your grandmother hired someone else to come and clean. The first lady—Valerie—she told someone who told someone else who told your grandma that she knew it was because of that figurine she broke. Your grandma was so upset; she didn't care a whit about the dumb little ceramic thing. She called the woman right away and explained. You see, your grandma had heard that Valerie's knees had been giving her trouble and didn't want to make things worse for her by asking her to clean a house with so many stairs."

"This is about things a lot more important than a broken figurine, Grandpa."

"The point is to not decide you know the truth before you ask the person directly involved."

"But people lie. How are you supposed to know if they're lying?"

"That's what the praying part is for." He gripped her hand. "Meagan, I've prayed for you since the moment I heard you existed inside your mother. I have asked God to watch over you and guide you. I know He has not left you, not one moment, since you became His. He will help you know the truth."

She put her cheek against his hand. "I'm afraid to trust my heart."

"That's a good thing," he said, his voice kind. "You can't trust your own heart. But you can trust God's."

The nurse returned carrying a tray laden with crackers, water, and a small paper container of pills. "The excitement never ends around here," he muttered. "I'm going to eat this unappealing snack, then take a nice long nap until they come to poke and prod me some more." He swallowed the pills. "You get going," he told Meagan. "Go home and get a nap yourself. When you wake up, give that man a call and find out the truth. It may be just as bad as it seems, or it may not. But don't decide on another person's word."

"Okay, Pops." She rose and kissed his cheek. "Keep praying."

"I will. And if you need a shoulder to cry on, you know where to find me." He looked down at his tray. "I'll be right here, with my measly packet of crackers. If you come back, bring me a sliver of pie, would you?"

"I'll pretend I didn't hear that."

"Aw, come on. The rapture could come at any minute. I don't want this to be my last meal."

The nurse started on a lecture about blood sugar management. Meagan left the hospital room and shuffled down the corridor to the exit doors. She was thankful it would be a short drive home. She needed sleep, a few hours where she could forget Cole Fleming and Steve Campbell and the frightening man who left his picture in her rocking chair.

The drive was uneventful, but the moment her home came into view, Meagan knew she would get neither sleep nor the desired hours of forgetfulness.

Steve Campbell sat on her porch.

Monday, January 5
9:15 a.m.

Could fury turn to heat, Lucias' binoculars would melt and meld to his eyes. Steve Campbell had walked into Meagan's house—his Meagan's house—picking her lock like a common criminal. Steve would see her kitchen, her bathroom, her bedroom. That was Lucias' dream. For Steve to see it first burned within him like hate, a spark that ignited when Steve's partner stepped out of their car holding a distinct cardboard box wrapped in yellow paper with daisies on it.

Lucias pulled away without them seeing. He ignored the speed limit and dared the law to follow him back to his trailer. He left the engine running and tore inside, his eyes swinging left and right. In his living room, only forty-six torn portions of Claudia's photos lay on the floor. They had taken one. Lucias knew which one; he had them all memorized. Had they taken Meagan's? Her framed photograph remained perched on the end table near the couch, but it stood at the wrong angle. They had touched it. Touched her.

He ran to the bedroom, his breath clogged in his throat, and was able to release it only when he saw that her face, her smile, on his bedroom wall had not been marred or a portion of it taken. He spread his palm on the bottom ridge of her lower lip and rested his head against her cheek. "Why are they at your house, my love?" he whispered. What could they want with her?

His clothes lay scattered across the floor. Someone had searched under his bed. His heart began to race. Had they found Claudia's box? He dropped to his knees and dug through the remaining clothes under the bed. It was gone. He rotated and jerked the bottom drawer of his dresser open. He had not been imagining it. Steve had taken his box. His most precious possession.

Lucias' hands were shaking as he dialed Meagan's number. She did not answer, but he could not wait. The FBI could arrive any minute. "Meagan," he said when the phone went to voicemail. His voice was breathless, but he tried to keep from sounding afraid. "They've been here, to my house. They've seen you here. They have your letters. You have to get away. Don't go home. He's there. Go someplace safe. I'll contact you when I have a place for us."

He hung up and stood. He should pack, but there was no time, and Steve Campbell had what he needed most. Lucias raced back through the house, stopping only to take the framed photo of Meagan and a pillow from the couch. Motel pillows were always too thick. They suffocated him.

What about money? Hiring his source to get the information from the FBI and leak the story about Cole Fleming to the papers had cost everything he'd had left. He would have to go to Atlanta and get a quick deal to run, just enough to get him through a day or two, until he could safely return.

"Don't give up, Meagan," he said aloud. His trailer shrunk to toy size in his rearview mirror. "I'm coming back for you."

44

Monday, January 5
9:15 a.m.

Meagan stood several feet from the porch steps, wary of approaching her own home. "Steve, there's something I need to talk to you about," she said.

Steve rocked the chair back and forth with a false air of calm. His entire body was rigid. "I have something to talk to you about, too."

The way he said it, the way his fingers clenched, made her not want to come any closer. Why was he at her house anyway? "Quinn called me yesterday," she said. "He told me—"

At the sound of wheels on gravel, Meagan turned and saw Steve's car. "Oh no," she whispered. She whirled quickly to Steve. "Is it really true, what you told Quinn to tell me about him?"

Steve frowned. "About who?"

"About Cole. In Iraq." She gripped her purse in front of her like a protective shield. "And with his sister. Is it true?"

Cole parked the car nearer the house than was practical and in one smooth move was out and on his way toward Steve, newspaper in hand. He barely glanced at Meagan. "Why did you do it, Steve?" he said, his voice low and hard.

"Do what?" Steve stood, transferring his frown from Meagan to Cole.

Meagan stumbled out of the way when Cole marched to the porch steps, up them, and stood eye-to-eye with Steve. "I want to know why the guy who used to be my best friend just lied my name through the mud."

"What are you talking about? Who lied? About what?"

Cole shoved the newspaper, and Steve, into the rocking chair with such force Meagan feared it would topple. Steve gripped the arm rails and kicked to find footing. Cole stood over him as Steve looked at the paper in his lap and Meagan saw his face go white. "Where did you get this?" Steve's voice was hollow.

"It's the cover story on every paper in the city."

"I didn't do this, Cole." Steve looked up at him. "I swear, I never—"

Cole snatched the paper back and shook it in Steve's face. "No one else could have. And what were you talking about, lying to rescue me? What did you think I needed you to lie for?"

Steve threw his arms out. "That woman seduced you just like the real Delilah! You gave secret information about our location to her. Do you know what the military does with soldiers who collaborate with terrorists? Somebody had to save you."

Cole gripped Steve's shoulder and Meagan saw pain cross Steve's countenance. "You actually believe that I gave away our envoy's location to a woman I knew worked for the enemy? You think I would send my own men to die because she—" His voice held disgust. "—turned my head?"

"Did-didn't she?" Steve tried to pull his shoulder out from under Cole's palm but couldn't. "I didn't tell the press, Cole. I vowed to myself I'd never tell."

"This has gone too far, Steve. Whatever—"

Meagan let out a cry of alarm when her own front door opened and Quinn stepped outside. "What are you doing in my house?" she asked. Three men were on her porch and she was still on the ground, as if they had taken possession and she was now a stranger needing an invitation. She moved to the bottom of the stairs. "And Steve, why did you have Quinn call to tell me those terrible things about Cole, instead of telling me yourself?"

Quinn's gaze scanned from Steve to Cole to her. "I didn't call you," he said. "I don't even know your number."

"You texted me yesterday," Cole put in. "Told me to come to the office because Steve had something important to show me." He held up the paper. "Was it this? Because it would have been nice if you'd let me in the building when I came so I could have stopped this pile of trash from getting printed."

"What are you talking about?" Quinn let the screen door go and it banged shut behind him. "I don't know your number either."

Cole turned to Meagan. She noticed he had bought a new jacket. This one fit his wide shoulders. "What terrible things did he tell you?"

Quinn shook his head. "I didn't tell her anything!"

She climbed the steps but Cole still towered over her. "He said I'd know by what the papers said this morning that you were a liar. And he said...he said..." Her eyes stung.

"Maybe she's organized this entire thing to try to get us off the investigation." Steve joined Quinn at the door. "What did you find?"

"She who?" Meagan asked. "Me? Why would I make up something to break my own heart?"

"Meagan..." Cole moved close. He held out the paper. "This isn't what really happened."

"Your job," she cut in, hearing Quinn say her name to Steve behind her but too intent on Cole's dark green eyes to care. "Tell me the truth. Do you—do you work with—with—" She swallowed, took in a long breath, and let it out in the question she dreaded to have answered. "Does your work have something to do with—with—pornography?"

His forehead creased and his eyes looked deep into hers. "Meagan, it's not what you think."

"Is it true?" She gulped down a sob. "Yes or no?"

The newspaper got crushed, inch by inch, as he clenched his fingers into a fist, flexed them, then clenched again. "Yes, but not the way it sounds."

The sob she had stifled rose again. She felt it tear through her and there was no hiding the crushed hopes in the sound that emerged. "How can there be any way that isn't terrible?" She backed away when he tried to touch her arm. "Go away, Cole Fleming. Do not ever come near me again. I will pray that Sadie never learns the truth, and—"

"Sadie?" He was near again, this time with flame in his eyes. "You will not tell Sadie anything about what I do."

She moaned and staggered through the three men to open the screen door.

"Stop for a minute," Steve announced. He put out his hands, one palm against Cole's chest, one out toward Meagan. "Cole, I plan to find out who's behind this story getting leaked to the press, but right now we've got more important priorities that have to be dealt with."

"More important?" Meagan watched a muscle work in Cole's jaw. Would her heart ever heal from this? From him? She went inside.

"Meagan Winston." Steve followed her and Quinn followed him.

"You should ask before you come in somebody's house." Meagan rubbed her aching temples and went to the kitchen. She opened the refrigerator. Where had she put the cold pack? Oh, she'd taken it to Pops that morning in case he needed it.

"We have a warrant."

She grimaced and searched through the junk drawer for something to knock the edge off her headache. "Have at it. I haven't received any more flowers, but see if you can find something else interesting."

"We already have." Quinn motioned for Steve to come with him into the hall. Meagan filled a glass of water and downed two pills. She left the kitchen to find them and saw Cole through the open front door on her way by. He still stood on the porch with the crumpled newspaper in his hand. For the sake of her pounding head, she refrained from yelling at him to go away.

Quinn and Steve stood near the coffee table in the living room. Quinn held a box wrapped in faded yellow paper covered in little white flowers. "That's not mine," Meagan said of the box.

"We know." Steve reached down to the table and picked up the photograph that still ran chills down her spine. "But this is."

"*That's* the thing I need to talk to you about," she said. "Some guy—" Her phone rang in her purse, still slung over her shoulder, and the ring echoed in her head. She set her purse down on the couch and pointed at the photo. "He left this yesterday when I was—"

Steve flipped the photograph over and read the words, then said, "We've got his picture in your home, a note from him to you, this box of notes from you to him, and—"

"What?" Meagan crossed to stand on the opposite side of the coffee table. "What notes?"

Quinn pulled out one of the papers in the box and opened it. Cole entered the room but Meagan ignored him. "My dearest Lucias," Quinn read. "Thank you for protecting me from the two men who were bothering me today. I think you are smart and I can't wait until the day we are together, forever. With love, Meagan."

She had to pull her dropped jaw up enough to speak. "I didn't write that! I don't even know this guy!"

"He left you flowers that had opium in the water," Quinn said.

"Opium?" Meagan's legs would not hold her up. She dropped onto the couch.

"Your face is plastered all over his bedroom wall," Steve added.

"It is?" Cole asked. Steve pulled out his phone, swiped it twice, and showed it to Cole.

His eyes widened. "That's in his room?" Steve nodded. Cole's voice dropped enough to be frightening. "Is it as big as it looks?"

"Bigger."

Meagan wrapped her arms around herself and looked out the window into the woods surrounding her house. Was he out there somewhere, watching? Was he always watching? Was she losing it?

The phone dinged in her purse; someone had left a message. "Mind if I check your phone?" Steve asked. Meagan shook her head, watching like a bystander in her own life as Steve dug through her purse, Quinn looked through a batch of letters she supposedly wrote, and Cole stood to the side, his face so seemingly sincere, his eyes so full of apparent care. She looked away.

Steve pushed buttons. "Your phone is different than mine," he said and handed the phone to her. "Would you play the message you just got on speakerphone? And then I'll want you to show me how to look through your call log."

She sniffed. "It's probably the hospital. My grandfather's there you know, and I'm glad he's missing this whole horrible mix-up." She punched in the password to access her voicemail and clicked the phone on speaker.

"Meagan, they've been here, to my house," a voice said. "They've seen you here. They have your letters. You have to get away. Don't go home. He's there. Go someplace safe. I'll contact you when I have a place for us."

"That's the voice that called me yesterday," Meagan whispered. She pointed at Quinn. "He said he was you." She put her head in her hands. "What on earth is going on?"

A hand took her arm. She thought it was Cole and started to pull away, but then glanced up to see it was Steve. "Meagan Winston," he said, pulling her to her feet. "You're under arrest. You have the right to remain silent..."

She stared, her mind blank. Cole came to stand by her side. "What are you arresting her for?" he asked Steve.

Steve led Meagan to the front door. "Aiding and abetting Lucias Maddox Moore in possession and distribution of meth across international borders, and possession of illegal opium from India with intent to distribute in America. Also she's a possible accessory to attempted murder if she was part of the plan to run you off the road." He looked from Cole to Meagan. "And she's a possible accessory to the murder of Claudia Conners."

45

Monday, January 5
9:45 a.m.

Cole followed Steve and Meagan to the car. She hadn't said a word since Steve read her the Miranda rights. "Steve, this has to be a mistake." He opened the door for them with a scowl. "Do you have to cuff her? She's not dangerous."

"She might have inspired a guy to murder someone," Steve said in a clipped tone. "Sounds dangerous to me. Stop interfering."

There was no arguing with Steve when he was sure of something. Cole turned to Quinn. "Why does he think she might have some connection to a murder?"

Quinn explained about the Claudia Conner's investigation. He reached into the backseat of the car next to Meagan and pulled out a second box almost identical to the one he held under his arm like a football. "One box has letters from Claudia to Lucias in them." He lifted his arm a little to indicate the other box. "This one has letters from Meagan. I haven't had time to read them all since we came straight here from his house, but some of them talk about how she's glad he chose her instead of Claudia and how she could make him so much happier than Claudia could. They sound borderline obsessive, if you ask me."

"That's not Meagan at all."

Quinn shrugged. "You haven't known her long. She could be a totally different person in secret."

"Can I read the letters?" Cole held out his hand for the box but Quinn did not release it.

"They're evidence."

Cole leaned to look in Steve's window. He was in the driver's seat with his seatbelt buckled. "Steve, let me go over the letters and give you a summary."

Steve shook his head. "I don't trust you to be unbiased." He leaned out the window. "Come on, Quinn. We're losing time. The deadline is five."

"I can have the letters read and summarized by three," Cole offered. "It will give you time to focus on other evidence."

"Why aren't you at work?"

Cole held up the newspaper.

"Oh." Steve drummed his fingers on the dash. "Let him have them, Quinn." He stared Cole down. "But I want all the evidence you find. Don't leave anything out."

Cole took the two boxes from Quinn, then looked Steve in the eye. "I've never lied to you, Steve. Or kept secrets you needed to know."

A look of guilt or shame crossed Steve's features. He yelled for Quinn to hurry and drove off without speaking to Cole again. Cole caught a glimpse of Meagan's face in the backseat as they passed. Her eyes were closed, her hands behind her. Steve shouldn't have put her in handcuffs.

Cole prayed as the car faded from view. Was this arrest aligned somehow with his story in the newspaper? Was someone trying to keep them busy with false evidence to keep them off the real trail?

Quinn said he hadn't texted Cole or called Meagan.

Steve said he hadn't given the Iraq story to the media.

Meagan said she had not written the letters in the box.

What if Lucias Moore was orchestrating all of this, and he, Steve, and Quinn were playing right into his hands?

46

Monday, January 5
1:00 p.m.

"Are we ready?"

"I don't like small rooms." Quinn wiped his upper lip with the cuff of one of his sleeves. "How about you ask her the questions and I stay on this side of the glass where it's airy? I'll write lots of notes."

Steve adjusted the video monitor until Meagan Winston was perfectly centered. He needed some coffee. "How did you get accepted by the FBI if you're claustrophobic?"

"They didn't ask about that during my polygraph test." Quinn tapped his earpiece. "I guess I'll get on in there. Hearing everything you say twice is getting annoying."

Steve sat in front of the monitor but nudged the screen aside. He'd do better watching Meagan through the glass. "Let's get started."

He had expected Meagan to fidget, to scratch at the cuff on her arm or pull at the galvanometers secured with Velcro around two of her fingers. She sat like a mannequin as Quinn asked the initial questions. "She's too passive. I think she's going to try to beat the test. Ask her if she's got her toes pressed against the ground."

"Meagan, are you pressing your feet to the floor?"

She did not look up from the table. "No." Her voice was wooden.

"Ask her if she's squeezing her buttocks."

Quinn had to cover a laugh. He glanced at the glass. Steve knew he could not see through it, but nodded anyway. Quinn asked the question and Meagan's eyes darted up. "Did you seriously just ask me about my rear end?" she asked.

If Steve had to guess, she was surprised and offended at the question, which would mean she had not been trained on how to manipulate a lie detector test. "Ask her a question we know is true."

"Meagan, do you work for a ministry called Rahab's Rope?"

She went back to looking at the table. "I do."

"Do you work with Kelsey and Nathan Peterson?"

"Yes."

"Do you consider them friends?"

"Among my best." Her eyes flickered. "Quinn, can I ask you a question?"

Quinn looked at the glass. "It's not procedure..."

"Did you really not call me yesterday?"

He shook his head. "I have never called you, Meagan. Did you really think the call was from me?"

Steve leaned forward. The computer screen in front of Steve showed Meagan's blood pressure, respiratory rate, and electro-dermal activity all remained steady. "I really did."

"We need to make sure the test works on her. Ask her a personal question, something she feels strongly about."

"Meagan, do you believe pornography is an innocent pastime?"

Even before she spoke, needles began to fly on the graph. "Pornography feeds human trafficking," she said. She sat up straight and leaned toward Quinn. "Women and children are victimized and abused for a multi-billion dollar industry." She curved her fingers into a fist on the table. The needles ran wild. "Don't you know that people's brains are literally affected by pornography, like they are by drugs? Eventually just watching isn't enough. It leads to violence, and even at its initial phase, it destroys real-life relationships."

Steve tapped his fingers against his chin. "Calm her back down."

Quinn put his hand near Meagan's. "Unfold your hand please, Miss Winston." She did and sat back with a sigh. He checked the graph, then asked, "Meagan, how often do you travel to India?"

"Every six months."

"Why do you go?"

"To get children out of brothels and give victimized women the hope of the gospel."

"Did you take drugs on your last trip?"

"No."

"On any of your trips?"

"No."

"Did you bring opium back from India on your last trip?"

"No."

Quinn looked over at the graph again, then at the glass. Steve didn't know what to make of her. She spoke about the drugs dispassionately. The machine indicated truth. "Ask her about Cole."

"Meagan Winston, did you believe the story in the newspaper about Cole Fleming this morning?"

Her heart rate increased. "I—I didn't know what to believe."

"Do you have personal feelings for Cole Fleming?"

Steve didn't need the graph. Her eyes glistened and he could see even from a distance that her breathing quickened. "I—I—don't want to," she whispered.

"You don't want to have feelings for him?"

She looked away. "I don't want to answer that question."

Steve moved to stand with his nose almost against the glass. "Either she's the best polygraph manipulator I've ever seen, or the machine is reading her accurately. Ask her about Lucias."

"Meagan, are you in partnership with Lucias Maddox Moore?"

"No. I've never met Lucias Moore and I've never even seen him except for in that photograph that showed up on my porch yesterday." She wiped her eyes but then her hand stopped in front of her face.

Quinn noticed the needles arch higher. "What is it?"

"Yesterday, at the cafe..." She pressed her fingers to the bridge of her nose. "Across the street, a man who looked like the picture was talking on the phone. I noticed because his car looked like Cole's old car." She focused on Quinn, her eyes gone wide. "A car just like that was parked next to mine at church before that. Quinn, could he have been that close? He's been inside my house, on the plane when I fly, he knows my phone number, and now he knows where I park at church?" She held her hand out straight and watched it shake. "Why, Quinn? Why is he doing this? Is he trying to set me up so he can go free?"

The door to Steve's section opened and an agent Steve knew by sight as Anderson Cray, but had never spoken to in person, entered.

"You're a long way from the Criminal Investigation Division of the building," Steve commented.

"The DEA got the meth lab," Anderson said. He joined Steve at the window. "That connection your buddy Jerod led us to gave us names and locations for everyone up the line except the actual lab and the guy who mixes and packages the meth."

Steve pulled out his earpiece. Meagan had started to cry and would be useless for information for a few minutes. "How did they get the final name and lab location?"

"At two this morning the police pulled over a red Chevy Blazer for speeding. The officer called in the name and plate numbers, and the DEA got out there fast. It was one of the names Jerod's connection had listed as high on the chain. They found three pounds of meth, five pounds of cocaine, and a thousand ecstasy pills in the guy's trunk under his spare tire. Between that and the thirteen thousand dollars in his glove compartment, the guy was looking at maximum security for ten to fifteen years unless he gave up the meth lab and the guy who cooks up the drugs. They raided the lab at noon and brought in six more guys, including a scientist and pharmacist."

"That's good news. Thanks for letting me know."

The agent crossed his arms and looked inside the room where Quinn and Meagan seemed to be having a conversation rather than a one-sided interview. "I didn't come just to let you know about the lab."

"Oh?" Steve saw the needles on Meagan's graph skitter wide and fast again. What had Quinn asked her?

"We supplied the DEA with our information on the case. They interrogated the six men from the lab, plus the three they'd already arrested." He gestured toward the glass. "Not one of them recognized Meagan Winston's photo or her name. They also didn't know anything about Claudia Conners." He stepped closer to the glass and examined the scene. "Whatever Lucias Moore's connection with both women is, it's personal. If she is helping him with the drugs, it's on his own dime."

The agent left and Steve waited to reposition his earpiece. He sat and checked his watch. Only two and a half hours until five. He only had one idea left. If it worked, it might be enough to get Baine to let him continue the case to the end. If it failed, Baine would take the case, and Steve's credibility with it.

Quinn looked up in surprise when Steve stepped into the small room. He sat in the only empty chair available and said, "Newly arrested prisoners get a phone call." He waited until Meagan looked him in the eye. When she did, he said, "I need you to call Lucias Moore."

47

Monday, January 5
2:00 p.m.

Cole entered the store and approached the brunette behind the cashier counter. "Could you tell Kelsey or Nathan that I'm here?"

Meagan had said her name was Brianna. Cole could see she was nervous. "The newspaper article isn't true, Brianna," he said. "I know that a lot of the people you encounter lie well, and use lies to exploit the girls you try to protect, but I'm not one of those people."

Brianna gave him a tentative smile. "Well, I haven't actually encountered anybody like that, but I guess I'm kind of always looking out for that first one. I'd rather it not be you."

He smiled back. "I'm with you on that. Did Meagan ever explain to you that I didn't really lie about being with the FBI?"

"She said—"

The door to the back room of Rahab's Rope swung aside and Kelsey came into view. She stopped short. "Cole. I—I didn't expect to see you."

"I'm sure it's not a pleasant surprise." Cole gestured toward the newspaper lying on the cashier counter. "I don't have time to explain about that right now, I'm afraid. Meagan got arrested this morning, and—"

"What?" Brianna put a hand to her heart. "She didn't do anything wrong!"

"I intend to prove that," Cole said, his jaw set. "But I need your help." He turned to Kelsey. "Would it be better to talk in the back? I don't want to cause problems being in your store today."

Cole's gaze followed Kelsey's scan of the room, taking in the glances and whispers customers sent their way. "That might be best." She waved at a customer she knew and said to Cole between her teeth, "Leave the store through the front door and come around the back. I'll be there to let you in."

He dropped a quick nod and took his leave. Outside, military habits took natural place. By the time he reached the back door, he had camouflaged his route and location, checked the area for suspicious vehicles or pedestrians—the grey Oldsmobile was nowhere to be seen—and had three exit possibilities if the need came to retreat.

Kelsey cracked the door. "I'm inclined to trust you, Cole," she said. "But you should know I've called Nathan and he's on his way. Our conversation here will include him on speakerphone."

"That's wise," Cole acknowledged. "In your line of work you can't be too careful."

"I agree."

She led the way to a table near a wall lined with iron pegs that held hundreds of necklaces. Cole wasn't knowledgeable enough about jewelry to know which ones were completed and which were still in process. "Is Nathan on the speakerphone now?"

She pressed a finger to the phone on the table. "Yes."

"Good. Hi, Nathan." Cole set the box he'd been carrying on the table. "I'll try to be as succinct as possible. The FBI arrested Meagan this morning for partnering with a Lucias Moore in the drug trade, and also as a possible accessory to murder."

The phone remained silent but Kelsey's cry filled the room. "Why on earth...?"

"As I said, I'll keep this succinct. Meagan can give the details later." He opened the box and spread several of the letters across the surface of the table. Kelsey sat and surveyed the letters while Cole continued. "Steve found these letters in Lucias' home, along with a box of letters from a Claudia Conners, a woman who worked with Lucias until she was murdered three years ago. The law was never able to convict Lucias of the crime, and soon after it, he started the flights with Meagan to India."

Kelsey held up one of the letters. "But these aren't Meagan's handwriting."

"That's what I need your help with," Cole said. "I've spent the past few hours reading every letter from both boxes. They're all from the same hand. Since Claudia couldn't have written letters after her death, the letters had to have been written by Lucias."

"This guy is getting scarier by the minute."

Nathan spoke through the phone. "So he's writing letters to himself supposedly by the women he's interested in?"

"And the first woman he was interested in—obsessed with if you ask me," Cole said, "ended up dead."

Kelsey shivered noticeably. "That's terrifying."

Cole rubbed his bad shoulder. "Here's a letter from Claudia." He pulled a paper from his inside jacket pocket. "I left the rest of hers in the car. Let me read it for you." He had to try hard to keep from making a face as he read aloud, "Dearest Lucias, I love you. You are smart and handsome and strong. I can't wait for us to be together, forever. When will you finally tell me that you love me? When you do, I will kiss you and say I have been waiting for you all my life."

"Yikes." Kelsey sat and propped her chin on her hands. "It sounds rather elementary, similar to the note that came with the cards, and the one he left for Meagan here at the store."

"Right. Steve has those two notes, plus the photograph. I'm sure we'll be able to match the writing on those to the writing on the notes in both boxes. But I was wondering if you had a sample of Meagan's handwriting to take to Steve this afternoon. It would solidify that the notes supposedly from Meagan aren't from her at all." He didn't add that the notes supposedly from Meagan mentioned him, and were following a parallel pattern to Claudia's. Both sets started out friendly and full of praise. They encouraged Lucias to declare his love, saturated ad nauseam with cheesy clichés like, "My heart beats only for you," or, "You are my whole existence."

"Of course." Kelsey stood and crossed to a small rectangular table stacked high with catalogs and order forms. Methodically, she opened the drawers lining the underside of the table and searched through them.

Cole sat in the chair closest to the phone and kept his voice low. "I won't deny that there is real danger here. Meagan's letters go beyond Claudia's, and the most recent show that Lucias is feeling a growing impatience." Claudia's box held three letters of frustration before they ended with her death. Meagan's most recent ones held that same frustration, sometimes in identical wording, but they numbered five.

"Here it is." Kelsey carried a slip of paper to Cole. "I knew I had an order she'd filled from one of the house parties we host. It clearly shows her handwriting."

"Thank you." He placed the order along with Claudia's letter back into his pocket. "I'll do everything I can to get this resolved. Soon." He packed Meagan's letters back into the box and rose. "I'm on my way to the Federal Building now."

"Is Meagan there?" Kelsey asked. She tapped the catalogs to even out the edges of the stack.

"As far as I know. Steve wanted to do a polygraph test."

The back door opened and Kelsey pivoted to face her husband. "Nathan. You made good time. Can you stay here for the afternoon? I'd like to go see Meagan. I'm sure she could use a friend."

Nathan hugged his wife and received instructions on the orders Kelsey had started. "I'll see you there, then," Cole said to Kelsey. "I'm glad you'll be coming." As much as he wanted to comfort Meagan himself, it was not his right, nor would attention from him be her desire. Though he would never stoop to writing himself letters with her name at the end, he understood one thing about Lucias Moore. The idea of winning Meagan Winston's heart was enough to inspire a man to action.

He picked up the box and tucked it under his arm. "It's time for me to go."

48

Monday, January 5
2:30 p.m.

They had his letters. How was he going to be able to sleep in a strange place without his letters to read before bed? He had his pillow, but that was all. None of his clothes. Not even his toothbrush.

An ugly woman with yellow-stained teeth and a flap of skin hanging from her chin like a turkey asked, "Can I have a credit card number?"

"I don't use credit cards." He hadn't in years. They made a person easy to find. "I'll give you—" His phone rang and Lucias frowned. Steve Campbell had discovered his number. The FBI had already called twice during his drive, but he hadn't answered. Steve had probably forced Meagan to show him her phone. They had probably listened to Lucias' message to Meagan. Just the thought made his temperature rise. "Just a minute," he told the turkey woman.

He set his pillow on a dingy chair in the lounge area and pulled his phone from his pocket. He would answer this time, tell Steve to stop antagonizing Meagan. "Yeah?" he said. He leaned his elbow on a window frame, then moved back. His shirt sleeve pulled up a layer of dust.

"Is—is this Lucias?"

His hands went damp and he wiped them on his pants. Meagan! He'd know that voice anywhere in the world. She had never said his name before. Had never called. What should he say? He couldn't start with I love you.

"Hello? Is anyone there?"

"I'm—I'm here." He spoke to her. To Meagan. His heart nearly exploded. He looked around the motel lobby with new eyes, seeing it as he would if Meagan were there with him. Three chairs, all in need of new upholstery. One glass coffee table with scratches. Five windows, all with dust half an inch thick on the sills. A cockroach scurried for cover under an elevator door with an "Out of Order" sign. One outdoor stairway. One counter. One nasty old woman wanting his money for a night in this rat hole. "Meagan, I have a better place planned for you. I wouldn't make you stay in a dump like this. When we're together—"

"Lucias." Her voice was breathy and stirred his soul. "The FBI arrested me."

His mind stalled and went blank. They had Meagan in their clutches? Her voice broke through his sudden terror. "Lucias, they have arrested me because of you. Because of the drugs. And because of a woman named Claudia who was murdered."

"They read your letters," he accused, his terror turning to fury. "They read how you praised me for rejecting her and choosing you instead."

"What should I do, Lucias?" Her whisper was a dart that shot through straight to his heart. "They're asking so many questions."

"Don't tell them anything. I will take care of you. Don't worry."

"They're coming. I have to go."

The call was over before he could say what was on his heart. He tried to call back but no one answered. He rushed back to the counter where the yellow-teethed woman still stood. "I'll give you twenty dollars cash now and pay the rest when I check out."

"You don't pay, you don't stay," the woman said. Had she practiced that arrogant little phrase?

Only his love for Meagan stopped him from reaching across the counter to wring her scrawny, sagging neck. If he got arrested for murder, he couldn't help Meagan get free. "Listen to me." He leaned over the counter and put just one hand around the front, wrinkled part of her neck. She gurgled and he wanted so much to squeeze the life out of her. "You don't want to say no to me." He increased the pressure until she nodded, eyes bulging in fear. He loved that look. Maybe when he and Meagan were together, they'd go on a spree before they settled somewhere. They could steal fancy cars, take money, and enjoy watching people fear and die in their wake. What a vacation they could have then. Better yet, a honeymoon.

"I'll take the twenty," the woman choked out when he let her go.

"You'll take nothing now," he said, alive and full of power. He would avenge his love, rescue her from the oppressors. "You can hope I will pay you something tomorrow when I leave."

He took his pillow to room forty-nine. Once inside, it was time to get serious. He summoned help. Raymond was gone and Damion was too unpredictable. He needed someone he could trust. When she came, he felt a sense of peace. All would be well.

"Agatha, Meagan needs us." He leaned back against the rickety headboard of the bed and held his pillow against his heart. "We have to make a plan."

49

Monday, January 5
3:00 p.m.

"Meagan, are you okay?"

Meagan rushed across the hallway to embrace her friend. "Kelsey! I'm so glad to see you. They made me call him! It was horrible." Her insides still shook. "Hearing his voice, pretending I was whatever sick fantasy he'd created in his mind..."

Kelsey hugged her again then took her hands. "Do they really think you're working with him?"

"They did when they brought me in, I know that." She looked back to where Steve had stopped to talk with Cole Fleming. Cole handed over the box of letters, then gestured and leaned forward as he talked. Whatever he was saying, it was important to him. When he had walked into the building with Kelsey, she hated how her heart betrayed her. If he was anything like the man she had been told he was, she should feel nothing but disgust for him. But Quinn had said those phone calls came from Lucias, not him. It was possible none of what he said was true. "Now, I don't know what to think," she told Kelsey, "about anything."

"You know what to think about the things that matter most," Kelsey said. She sounded like she was giving goodbye advice, and when Meagan glanced back again, she saw why. Steve marched toward them, his mouth in a grim line. "Remember," Kelsey said quickly, "you are loved with an everlasting love. No one and nothing can take that away or make it fade."

Steve grasped Kelsey's arm. "I need to ask you to leave, ma'am. No visitors for the prisoner."

"We're all praying for you," Kelsey called back as Steve escorted her to the door.

"Wait!" Meagan said with a sudden step forward. "Kelsey, will you visit Pops? He doesn't know about any of this. He'll be worried if I don't come see him."

"I'll put his mind at ease," she assured, adding with a look at Steve, "without giving anything away."

"You can't stay here either, Cole," Steve said on his way back. "I've got to get her to the county jail for the night. Baine is waiting for my report at five."

"Have you thought about my condition?" Cole asked.

"I have, and I agree to it. I'll be there in the morning with a representative of the press."

"Who has a good camera."

"Yes."

Steve turned to unlock the door to his office. Cole faced Meagan. "I'm here to fight for you, Meagan." His jaw worked. "And tomorrow I'll fight for myself."

Her whole body tensed when his large hand cupped her jaw. "And Meagan," he whispered, "I work in the porn industry the way you work in human trafficking." He pressed a light kiss on her forehead and left before his words could find home in her thoughts.

"Okay, Miss Winston," Steve said. He had placed the box of letters on his desk and was locking his office again. "Let's get you to jail."

Monday, January 5
5:00 p.m.

Steve paced outside Baine's office. The moment the door opened, he bypassed the secretary and deposited the boxes of letters on the large imposing desk set in front of floor-to-ceiling windows. He gave his report, concluding with, "I have a photo and handwriting sample for Lucias, a voice sample on his accomplice's phone, and the accomplice herself is being processed in our county jail as we speak."

"Good work," Baine said. He had not risen from his seat, and now leaned forward to stack the boxes one on top of the other. Steve waited for him to open one and look at the letters, but instead he said, "I'll want everything you have. All your files. All your evidence."

"S-sir?" Steve wished he had been asked to sit.

"You've handled this case well, and I'm convinced the DEA can go from here with your accomplice to get what they need to close the drug case. We need to focus on the murder investigation now." He slid the boxes to the side. "Can you box up everything and have it on my desk before you leave today?"

"But..." Steve's right hand floundered, feeling for something solid to keep him upright. He grabbed hold of the back of a chair. "But I know everything about this case. I—"

"That's why you'll be on call and available to consult whenever needed." Baine leaned back in his chair. "And when you're not needed, you can start on the other cases waiting in a stack on your desk."

At least three arguments readied in his mind for expression, but Steve knew none of them would do any good. Baine had already turned to his computer, something Steve had done numerous times to show someone at his desk that their conversation was over. Steve reached the door without tripping over his shoes or running back to beg for twenty-four more hours.

"Oh, and Campbell?"

He stopped at the door but did not turn. "Yes, sir?"

"You'll want to make sure everything of yours is ready to transfer back to your cubicle. Agent Simmons will be returning by the end of the week. He'll want his office back."

Steve made sure to close the door carefully behind him, and kept his face devoid of anything that showed how Baine's last words were lemon juice on an already painful cut. He returned to his office and packaged up every piece of information and evidence he had for Lucias' case, and marched it back down the hallway. He set it on the secretary's desk. "Baine wants this," he told the woman. She nodded with a blank expression and went back to her typing.

He returned to the office that would only be his for another day or two, and just to rub the lemon juice in, he boxed everything of his on the desk, as if he'd been fired, and set the box on the chair nearest the door. If they called him to leave and go back to his little square of space first thing in the morning, he'd be ready. He'd take his box and his filing cabinet, and head back to the bottom rung of the ladder again.

He was not sure why he drove home instead of to the nearest bar. Maybe because it would be easier to pick a fight with Stephanie than a drunk stranger. He trudged up the stairs to the apartment and opened the door. "Oh, excuse me, I'm in the wrong—"

"Hello, Steve."

The woman who stood there was his wife, but Steve had a hard time believing he was in the right place. "What happened?"

She smiled. "I thought I'd make some changes."

Change would be a cleared spot on the couch big enough for him to sit without something poking into his rear. This was a transformation. He could see the floor, all of it except for the places covered with furniture, and the furniture was cleaned enough for company. And Stephanie, she was in her new dress. Her hair was up in some kind of twist and her eyes were bright. She had shoes on. He thought of asking if they were having guests, thought of asking if it was their anniversary. "What happened to the stacks of books?" was what came out.

His wife blushed. Steve couldn't remember the last time he'd seen that. "I realized they weren't helping. A lot of things I did weren't helping me get what I wanted, so I thought I'd try a different way."

Here it came. The divorce papers. Or the blackmail. I'll look nice and I'll clean the house, but you'll have to do something to keep it this way. "What do you want?"

"Well, I've been talking to God about us, and—"

"Oh, come on, Steph. You went to church one time. Now you're talking to God? Did He tell you to get all cleaned up? And then clean up your jerk slob husband?"

She blinked. "No, that's not what I—"

"Is this some way of manipulating me?"

"No!" Her eyes glistened. "I just wanted—"

"Never mind," he cut in. "I don't want to know. Whatever it is, I can't. Whatever you want me to do, I'll fail." He still had his hand wrapped around the knob of the door, which stood wide open.

"Steve?" She stepped toward him. "Honey, why are you so upset?"

Honey? Why did she have to start being nice to him now, now when he needed to tell her that everything was slipping away?

"I went to the grocery store after church yesterday," she said. Her voice was soft and hesitant, like when she approached a stray she feared would run off. "I can make dinner. We could talk. About us."

Us. The word was quicksand waiting to suck him under. She stepped closer. Would she want a hug or a kiss, like the old days when he was happy to come home? He felt remorse rise like a bad case of heartburn. "I—I have to go," he said. "I can't—"

"Can't what?" She reached the door just as he abandoned it and raced down the stairs. "Steve, where are you going?"

He did not respond. What good would it do to tell her that he couldn't pretend, not tonight? The case was stripped from his hands. His one big chance to make it, gone. And Cole...his best friend...

Steve knew where he needed to go. The one place to forget it all. He drove there, walked inside, and ordered a drink. And another. And another.

50

Monday, January 5
8:00 p.m.

Meagan thought of unhappy, war-jostled Lucy Pevensie in *The Chronicles of Narnia* when Lucy told her siblings, "The sheets are scratchy." Meagan wanted to say the same of the orange material of her prison uniform. It looked like a set of scrubs five sizes too large, as ill-fitting to her body as the holding cell was to her sense of security.

But she was too old to play Lucy Pevensie. Meagan had her own war to endure, and needed to do it with maturity or at least the appearance of it.

"Wassup, girl?" A woman with an enormous mass of hair sidled up next to Meagan. "What you in for?"

Meagan tried not to cough at the cloud of smoke that permeated the air around her. "Drug trafficking."

"You fooling me? You ain't got no piercings. No tattoos." She pointed at her own generous collection of body art designs. "The girl I buy from has a big silver dumbbell through her eyebrow. And her tongue's pierced. Her ears hang down because she stretched big ole holes in them, like as big as Oreo cookies. And up the sides of her ears, she's got three..."

Meagan pulled her knees up on the hard bench and would have wrapped her arms around them, but the handcuffs attached to her waist chain prevented it. "I hate, hate, hate this place," she whispered.

The woman leaned in and Meagan coughed. "Aw, it's your first time, ain't it? Hey, everybody, she's a first timer."

Her yell had no effect on the other women in the large cage the policeman had sent her to wait in while she was being "processed."

Sixteen women filled the containment. Most stared with vacant eyes at the TV hanging in the corner. One shrieked into a telephone attached to the wall. Two women leaned back-to-back on a bench near the far corner and somehow managed to sleep. Meagan couldn't hear herself think over the three prisoners arguing to her left.

As far from comforting as Steve and Quinn's presence had been that day, she had still hated to see them go that afternoon. Before they left, a little after four, Steve had pulled a policeman aside and she'd heard phrases like, "...a place to keep her for the night," and, "...FBI will take responsibility." The policeman had protested about something and Steve's voice had risen as he said, "I can't stay and explain. I have to get back. Just put her somewhere, okay?"

He'd marched out, a reluctant Quinn behind him, whose backward glance of apology toward Meagan gave her some measure of dignity to cling to. The policeman had not been happy to be stuck with her, that was made clear. He handed her off to a female officer, who frisked her, took her watch and jewelry, and sent her to take a shower with lice shampoo that smelled like floor cleaner. She exited in a jumpsuit that labeled her a criminal and she'd been sitting in this large cage ever since.

"It's all your fault!" the woman on the phone yelled. She slammed the receiver against the wall so many times, a guard had to come in to subdue her. Another tried to fix the phone that now hung in multiple parts connected only by wires. The arguing women stopped to cackle and point at the scene. Meagan put her head down on her knees. "God, please get me out of this place."

"Meagan Winston?"

Her head shot up and the woman beside her hooted with laughter. "Hey, cop!" She shoved a thumb toward Meagan. "This girl done thought you was God comin' to rescue her!"

"That's a first," the policeman said. "Come with me, Miss Winston."

"Time to get your glamour shots." The woman patted Meagan on the shoulder. "It ain't so bad, if you don't mind being locked up, bored to death, and not allowed to do nothing. You get free food, and you can catch up on sleep. Did you know a snail can sleep for three years? I'd like to be a snail some days. Working nights ain't no picnic. Sometimes I—"

"Put a cork in it, Louise." The policeman opened the gate and ushered Meagan down a bare hallway to a small room where she was told to stand against a white wall. The flash made her wince. "Stand to the side." She turned and thought of the woman back in the holding cell. This was about as far from glamorous as it got. Another flash, then the officer directed her to a table to be fingerprinted. "Is this really your first time in a jail?" he asked. "You've got no record."

He pressed her finger down in a rolling motion and lifted it. "I guess I do now," she said, looking at the machine that scanned her thumbprint. Black ink must be old-fashioned. "Yes, it's really my first time."

"We don't usually get prisoners handed to us in person by the FBI." He removed the waist chain and handcuffs and led her out of the small room to another hallway. If she'd been inclined to try to escape, she was already far enough into the maze to know she'd never find her way out. They reached a large door, but the policeman stopped before opening it. "What are you really in here for?"

She thought about Joseph in the Bible, how later he said God had meant it for good. "I honestly don't know why I'm here," she said. "I'm trusting God has a purpose in it."

His eyebrows lifted. "You think God sent you to jail? That's rich."

"I think God allowed it." She scratched her head. The lice shampoo had dried out her scalp. "I don't know why, but I'm not giving up hope that He will use it for good somehow."

"Might as well." The policeman led her through another door to a large area filled with individual cells. "It's not like you can change anything yourself anyway."

She acknowledged that irony but did not laugh. Her eyes took in a scene she'd never expected or wanted to see. She thought of pet shops, which had always distressed her as a child, seeing the animals in cages, so confined, waiting for someone to set them free. Here the cages were larger and the occupants human. And she would be one of them. She bit her lip and fought tears.

"Don't cry," the officer said in a quiet voice. "It's your first night. Don't look weak at all. You set yourself up for a lot of trouble that way, especially if you're going to be here for a while."

"Okay," she whispered, appreciating the advice but not sure she was physically capable of following it.

"Did they set bond on you yet?"

"No bond. Steve said we'd figure everything out in the morning."

He gave her a once over. "You're on first name basis with the FBI. Are you a secret agent going undercover or something, and the tears are just for show?"

She shook her head. "As far from it as you can imagine."

"Well, thanks to your Steve buddy not giving us a classification, you'll get to spend the night in an individual holding cell until we find out what section of the prison to book you into. It's going to be a cold and lonely night." He kept a hand on her arm as he led her across the main area, through another door, into a hallway lined with small rooms. Her visions of old western jail houses were laughable compared to the reality of this place. The cells here had no bars to rattle, just rooms with blank block walls, and heavy doors that slid and locked into place with an eerie, echoing click. No windows. No natural light. No natural anything.

Her hands had gone numb from clasping them so hard. She sat on the one mat in the room and watched the door close. "Cold, yes," she whispered into the silence that followed. "But not alone."

51

Monday, January 5
11:00 p.m.

Agatha helped Lucias develop a great plan. "My Meagan will be rescued, and I will be her hero," Lucias said. "I'll tell her all about you." He left the dingy motel room and took quiet steps down the outdoor stairs to the ground floor parking area. The fenced-in pool, empty for the winter, did not even have a cover over it. "Hey," he told the lady at the front desk when he entered the lobby from outside. "Someone could fall into that pool and get hurt."

The woman behind the desk shrugged. "Not my responsibility." She had to be twenty years older than the first old lady had been. The first one's skin had sagged; this one's practically dripped from her face like she was melting. That was a fun thought.

He refocused. "I need to use your computer. It has Wi-Fi, right?"

"Nope," she said, picking at her teeth using a fingernail with polish half chipped off.

"You have to have Wi-Fi."

Her teeth broke her nail and she spit the broken part off onto the floor. "I mean no, you can't use it."

She was arguing with the wrong person. Someday he would come back to this motel and make both these women regret complicating his life. "I'll give you ten bucks if you look up something for me." He'd only have ten left, but if the cocaine delivery he'd set up for two a.m. in Atlanta went well, he'd be set again.

The hag eyed his ten dollar bill. "Look up what?"

"Just a phone number."

She snatched the bill and turned the computer monitor. "Look it up yourself. But I'm watching you."

He moved the keyboard within easier reach and typed, "Director FBI Gainesville GA" in the search engine. He enjoyed how the woman sucked in some extra air and moved a few feet away from him when she saw what came up. Let her think he was a secret agent. Maybe he could play that and get out with room service and a zero on his bill. He wrote down a phone number and moved the keyboard back, waved at the woman like Raymond would have done, and made his way outside again.

There, next to the empty pool that he might only imagine still emanated a lingering smell of chlorine, he put in the number and waited with delight for the message and then the beep.

"This is Lucias Maddox Moore," he said, smiling up at the night sky, imagining the fear on their faces when they heard his voice. "Steve Campbell has someone I care about. Her name is Meagan Winston, and if Steve himself does not walk her out of your building by noon tomorrow, with an apology, a lot of people will die. You might be one of them." He had to pause and put his hand over the phone so they would not hear him laugh. "I don't know where your office is, but I do know where I put the bomb. Your building isn't so hard to get into. Steve's folder on Cole Fleming was very helpful, by the way."

He had more to say but the phone beeped a second time and the call was disconnected. He leaned on the fence railing and grinned. He'd paid a cleaning person a pile of money to get that folder from Steve's office. The guy would never have agreed to place a bomb, but the FBI director wouldn't know that.

"Tomorrow, Meagan," he whispered into the night. "Tomorrow at noon."

52

Tuesday, January 6
1:00 a.m.

Stephanie rolled onto her back and stared at the ceiling. Let her marriage fall apart. Steve didn't care. Why should she? All that work: hours of cleaning, building up hopes, dressing up, for what? "Is this how You come through for people?" she demanded upward. God didn't answer. She didn't know why she thought He'd listen in the first place. God was probably like Steve; He always had something more important to do.

Why couldn't she just go to sleep and forget it, forget him? Steve could fall asleep in three minutes flat, even after an argument. It wasn't fair. She shouldn't be the only one who cared about their relationship.

Her phone vibrated on the bedside table and Stephanie wanted to ignore it. She didn't want to talk to him, hear another excuse why work mattered more than his wife. She grabbed the phone and did nothing to disguise the anger in her voice. "What?"

"Stephanie, it's Quinn."

She sat up and for some reason ran her hand through her hair to make herself look more presentable. "Don't tell me," she said. "He's spending the night at the office."

"He isn't at home?"

"Isn't he with you?"

"I wouldn't be calling you in the middle of the night if he was," Quinn said. "Baine's been trying to reach him for an hour."

Stephanie remembered meeting the intimidating man once. "What's happened?"

"I don't know, but whatever it is, it's important enough that he called me and told me to find Steve."

She scooted off the bed, the phone still to her ear. "He left here before supper and hasn't been back. I assumed he went to the office."

"That's where I am. Any other ideas where he might be?"

"Where else does he go but to the office?"

"Stephanie, did Steve tell you we got taken off the case? Baine's sending it to a homicide team in his old police department."

She opened the closet door and grabbed the nearest sweater and pair of jeans. "No, he didn't. I could tell he was upset about something, but he just up and left and I—"

"Where would he go if he was really down, or angry?"

She threw the clothes on the bed and rummaged through the laundry basket next to the dresser for a pair of socks. "I think I might have an idea where he went. Give me half an hour. If he doesn't call you by then, check back with me."

"We'll wait to hear from you."

The last place she wanted to go in the middle of a freezing cold night was a bar. It was a good thing Cole had gotten a rental and returned Steve's car that afternoon so she had her own car to drive. Steve was probably passed out somewhere. She'd sober him up enough to talk, but he wouldn't win any points with Baine, calling in drunk. She drove to Steve's usual place and found him in his usual booth. Even when devastated, he was still predictable.

Stephanie wasted no time. "Steve, how drunk are you? You need to make a phone call."

His bloodshot eyes filled with tears the moment he saw her. "Stephanie, I'm a horrible person. You never should have married me. I'm sorry. I'm so sorry."

"If only you'd remember these speeches the next day," she said, pulling the bottle out of his hand and setting it on a separate table out of reach. "Come on, I've got to get you home."

"No, I have to tell you." He gripped her arm with surprising strength. "I'm not as drunk as I look." He hit his head against the table. "Or as much as I'd like to be. I had to think. Had to remember. I can't remember. I don't know for sure."

If she couldn't get him up, they'd have to just call from there. She sat and pulled out her phone. "Listen, Steve. Quinn called. He said—"

"Quinn wasn't there. It was Cole, in Iraq. I lied to protect him, but he didn't do it. Today he said he never told her the location. I lied for him because I wanted him to be the guilty one."

"What are you talking about?"

"I never could measure up to him. I was jealous. What if it was my fault?"

"Was what your fault? Steve, I need you to concentrate. Quinn called and—"

Steve slid from the seat onto the floor and put his head in her lap. "You shouldn't love me. You shouldn't have cleaned the house for me. I wanted so much to do something right, but I've done everything wrong. Everything."

Stephanie sighed and made a phone call. "Quinn, he's in no condition to talk to Baine," she said when Quinn answered. "I'll get him home, get him some sleep, and have him check in with you in the morning to see if Baine wants him to call or come in."

"Do you need help?"

She looked down at her husband, who wept on her jeans. "We've done this song and dance before." She helped Steve stand and put her arm around his waist so he could lean on her as they walked, wishing she hadn't yelled at God earlier. Quinn's help would have gotten Steve into the car easier, but only God could help them out of the pit their lives had become.

Tuesday, January 6
6:30 a.m.

Cole flexed his shoulder. The heavy ache told him it was a wet, humid morning, but his eyes had already clued him in on that fact. A few degrees colder and children all over the state would be squealing in delight over a rare snow day home from school. Instead the cold slushy rain landed in steady splats against his windshield, and then onto his hair and jacket as he ran from the car into the hospital.

"I'd like to see Gerald Winston," he told the receptionist, who until his arrival had been nodding off at her desk.

She yawned. "It's not visiting hours."

"I know." He stomped his feet to get the water off and noticed mud on the floor. He looked behind him. "Sorry for the trail of mud prints I just tracked in."

"No problem." She offered him a sleepy smile. "It's not my job to mop it up."

He fished a business card out of his jacket pocket and handed it to her. "I'm with the Department of Justice," he said. "I've got a busy day and this is the only time I can see him. Is there any way...?"

She set her wide eyes on his card, then up on his face. "S-sure. He's on the third floor. Tell the lady at the desk that you're there. Hopefully he's awake." She leaned forward and whispered, "Is he in some kind of trouble? I saw your gun when you pulled out the card."

"No, he's just a friend I'm visiting." He buttoned his jacket and gave her a smile. "Thanks for your help." He took the nearest elevator to the third floor and was shown to a room by a young intern in scrubs. She opened the door, yelled good morning to Meagan's grandfather, who was awake, and slipped Cole her phone number on her way back by him.

"I saw that," the older man said after the girl was out of earshot. He laughed at Cole's look of chagrin. "You make friends quickly."

"I'm glad you're awake." Cole tossed the strip of paper in the trash.

"Blondes aren't your type?"

"Strangers aren't."

"Good for you." The man Meagan called Pops pushed the button to maneuver the back of his bed up, enabling him to sit and face Cole. "Have you brought word of Meagan? Kelsey was all secretive. Funny how young people try to protect old people, even though we old folks have been through twice as much living and have heard twice as much bad news. I was born during a World War. That should count for something."

"Meagan really wanted to come see you," Cole said, sitting in a chair beside the bed. "The FBI has her...detained right now. Part of the investigation."

"Don't talk in code, boy. This old body may be going decrepit on me, but my mind's still working fine. I talked real loudly when they first brought me in, so they all think I'm half deaf. Everybody shouts when they come in to give me instructions. Hurts the ears." He chuckled. "But when they want to keep secrets, they don't bother to whisper. I know for a fact my test results all came back fine, and I was set to be released, and next thing you know a couple guys in black suits show up. The doctor goes out in the hallway and it's all hush, hush talking, and now I'm here 'until further notice.'" He shifted so he could look Cole in the eye. "I just want to know one thing. Is she safe? Is someone taking care of her?"

Cole maintained eye contact. "She is safe, sir. And I'm doing everything I can to catch the real criminal so she can be free of these charges and get you both home."

"Sounds good to me. Can't sleep with them coming in every five minutes to poke me or take my temperature." He pulled the sheets aside and set one foot out to air. "But Kelsey already came to tell me Meagan was okay. Why are you here, young man?"

A nurse entered and set a breakfast tray on Mr. Winston's lap. Cole waited as he thanked God for his food, then said, "To be honest, I came to ask you to pray for me. I've got to tell a story this morning, of an event I'd rather not revisit."

"A bad memory?"

He nodded. "Very. It's important that I do it, though, and since my own father isn't around to ask..." *And he'd sooner punch me in the face than pray for me.* "I came to ask you. I'm as nervous as if I were heading into battle today, and I need the Lord's help."

"Well, son, you came to the right place." The man put his aged hand on Cole's shoulder. "I've never liked how people say they'll pray for you but then they leave and you know they'll probably forget. You asked me to pray, so I'm going to pray now." He did, aloud, and a place deep inside Cole ached worse than his shoulder. What he would have given to have a father like this man. When finished, Meagan's grandfather lifted his head and smiled. "And since I'm here with nothing better than infomercials to watch on TV, I'll have extra time for praying this morning. Can't even get a decent weather report."

"Cold and rainy. That's about it." Cole stood and wiped down the sleeves of his jacket. "I appreciate your prayers, sir. Thank you."

"Don't take this to mean more than it does, say, regarding you and my granddaughter, but I've been praying for you since that first day you came to the house. God's got a plan for you, son, a good one."

Cole did not know what to do with the strange flip-flop his stomach did at that information. "I'd better go. Thanks again."

"If you come visit later, bring some pudding or something." He saluted and called out as Cole left, "Like the last time I saw your nose, so long!"

Tuesday, January 6
7:30 a.m.

An hour after breakfast, without explanation, an officer entered Meagan's cell and accessorized her orange jumpsuit again with a waist chain and handcuffs. He escorted her from her room, down hallways, out to a small area adjacent to the large holding cell that now contained a mere three women instead of the sixteen it had the previous night. The place where she was directed was not a room, more like a large cubby within a room. A built-in concrete block bench ran the length of the cubby area in a horseshoe shape. Steve Campbell sat on the back line of the horseshoe, downing a large cup of coffee, and a stranger with a news-station-sized video camera sat on the right. Cole, who had been pacing the tiny space, two steps over and two steps back, surprised her with open emotion in his eyes as she appeared. He cleared his throat and waited for her to sit before he did. "Are you okay?" he asked, his gaze drawn to the steel circling her wrists. "Were you able to sleep at all?"

"A little." She thought of saying Steve was the one who looked like he hadn't had any sleep, but then she hadn't seen herself that morning. She might look worse. "I always have trouble sleeping the first night in a new place."

One corner of Cole's mouth lifted. "Even one as nice as this?"

She glanced at the camera-toting stranger, who looked uneasy, as if he feared her imprisonment might be contagious. "Remind me not to ask your recommendations on vacation spots," she said to Cole.

He chuckled but quickly sobered. "I'm sorry all of this happened to you, Meagan."

She shifted and the chain clanked against her handcuffs. The sound startled Steve, who had almost fallen asleep over his coffee. His head jerked and he squinted at the police officer. "You can go," he told him.

The officer locked his knees and crossed his arms. "Until you release her, I'll be staying right here with the prisoner."

"We're taking her out as soon as we're done here."

"You are?" Meagan would have brought a hand to her mouth, but the waist chain kept her restrained. "Did you catch Lucias?"

Steve looked like he wanted to chew on a bullet. "We've got a long day ahead of us. There will be plenty of time to get you up to speed later."

She noticed his careful look at the cameraman and kept her questions from finding voice. It was enough to know she would be out of this horrible outfit and all it meant soon. "Thank You, God," she whispered.

"Have you been talking to my wife?" Steve growled. "About God?"

Meagan looked his way with a puzzled frown. "I've never met your wife."

"Actually you have," Cole put in. "Stephanie, the woman you went to the cafe with Sunday afternoon."

"She's his wife?" She turned to Steve. "Why didn't she tell me?"

"Yeah," Cole added. "That's one more thing Steve and I need to discuss."

"Not now." Steve drank the last of his coffee and tossed the cup to the policeman, who did not react. The cup fell to the floor and a bit of coffee dripped out. "Would you at least step out of earshot?" Steve asked the officer.

The man did not budge. "We've made an exception already letting the prisoner meet with visitors outside the regular visiting area with protective glass. I'm sticking to protocol on this and you will respect it, or she can go back to her cell."

"I don't have time to argue about this." Steve motioned to the man with the camera. "I've got to get to Baine for our meeting at nine."

The stranger brought his camera down onto his lap and pushed buttons. While he was busy, Meagan scooted a bit toward Cole and asked, "Why are you doing this, Cole?" He could have called a press conference and had the media swarming around him. "And why here?"

The journalist positioned his large camera on his left shoulder and Cole leaned near Meagan to say, "Remember when I said it didn't matter what people thought had happened, and you said it should matter what some people think?" She nodded. He looked deeply at her, then down at his hands as he said, "It matters to me what you think."

53

Tuesday, January 6
7:45 a.m.

Cole rubbed his hands on the knees of his suit pants in vain effort to quell the nervous tightening in his stomach. He had no time to gauge Meagan's response. Steve, who looked like he could use a couple of aspirin, kicked his fallen cup aside and announced, "Let's get this started." He pointed to each of them in turn. "You talk," he said to Cole. "You video," to the cameraman. "And you two," he finished with a jab toward the policeman then Meagan, "be quiet. No questions or comments. We've only got forty-five minutes max."

Cole wiped perspiration from his hairline. It was time. He had not spoken of that day since his report forty-eight hours after it happened. His eyes found Meagan's, and he told himself to talk just to her, to make sure she knew he was not the man in the newspaper article.

"I can only give so many specific details, but I'll tell you what I can," he began. "We were a Special Purpose Marine Air-Ground Task Force with the initial role of advise and assist. I'll state our general location as Baghdad, but we were actually a few miles out. Our job was to train soldiers in the Iraqi army. We were instructed to remain on base unless under orders to leave for a mission. ISIS started hitting the base with artillery and rocket fire. We were informed ISIS had obtained and was using Chinese-made shoulder-mounted surface-to-air missiles, and had also captured some 155 mm howitzers." At Meagan's blank look, he added, "They can fire up to about nine miles. We were in trouble."

He ran a hand through his hair and continued. "My battalion got the assignment to scout several areas and identify ISIS targets for air strikes. We were successful enough, and secretive enough, that the enemy sent in a spy. The enemy had downed several aircraft, one of which had documentation and information crucial to—" He stopped and rubbed clammy palms over his face. "I don't know why I'm talking all technical. The problem was that if ISIS got possession of the stuff in that one plane, a lot of American soldiers would die. Our job was to get to the plane, get the stuff, and get it back to the base, preferably without any of us getting killed along the way."

He sent a quick glance to the camera. "The enemy knew we were going after something important, but they didn't know what or where. They sent a woman to try to find out where our troupe was headed, and what we were after."

This was the part that mattered. Steve sat as still as stone, and Cole knew his mind was in Baghdad, reliving the sand and heat and bombs and fires, the fear of death each day so thick in the air you thought you could taste it. Steve would need few words. The policeman and the cameraman—Cole had little regard for whether they understood or not. But Meagan, he wanted her to see, to be there, to know what really happened. Cole leaned over. He put his elbows on his knees and his head down. He closed his eyes and sent his mind back to that day in Iraq.

His lungs burned and sweat trailed down both sides of his face. The heat threatened to put him on the ground, but he had to reach her in time. He forced his screaming calves into a final sprint to the building and lunged inside, too breathless to speak, able only to put both hands forward in a silent appeal to the beautiful woman dressed in green, who had a line of explosives strapped to her thin waist.

She stood twenty to thirty feet away near the doorway, her head out to view the oncoming line of tanks that carried his fellow soldiers.

"Please," he gasped, taking in huge gulps of air, needing to talk so he could convince her not to do this. "Please."

Her head turned and she looked on him with eyes full of sorrow rather than surprise. "I told you not to come. You had to know I would get the location." One tear slipped down her cheek. "Most men are not like you." Her head dropped. "I wish they were."

He finally had enough breath to create more words and he spoke quickly. "You don't have to do this. I can take you someplace safe, away from here. You can start over again. Hear about a God who loves you." He had wandered from God the same time he left his father, but looking at this woman, so cloaked with despair, it was the clearest thing in the world that she needed Jesus. How strange that he could see it for her when he'd refused so long to see it for himself.

"I have heard of your Jesus," she said, checking the position of the envoy again before saying, "If it were only me, I would go with you. Learn of Him. Be free. Maybe even forgiven." The roll of the tanks rumbled the earth beneath their feet. "But my family is shamed and this is my only hope of giving them honor. Our faith says this is the one way I am sure of being accepted into heaven."

"That's not true," he insisted with urgency. "Please, just give me a chance. I can help you and your family. This isn't what God wants you to do."

"I am not acceptable any other way."

He reached for his radio to call Steve to abort the mission. His hand grasped air. The radio, and his equipment pouch, were back in the bunker, on his bed next to the Modular Tactical Vest constructed to save his life in a situation like this. All he had was his M9 Beretta pistol. He took it out and pointed it at her. "I don't want you to die like this."

She revealed the grenade in her hand and what air he had remaining left his lungs. "Run," she said. "This is my destiny, not yours. Run!"

His hands shook. The tanks were close enough he could hear commands being ushered from the lead vehicle's commander. "Please..." he begged. Sweat beaded and dropped from his face like tears. "Please."

"I'm sorry." She pulled the pin on the grenade and closed her eyes. "Allah akbar," she whispered, and turned her body to the doorway.

He knew what would happen. She would run into the street and face the lead tank. The grenade would go off, blasting shrapnel through her body and igniting the other explosives. Her death would trigger the death of many others.

With a shout of both warning and regret, he pulled the trigger. She dropped to the ground and he ran.

Two seconds later, her grenade exploded. The building contained the grenade's destruction, but not the explosions to follow. Flames burst through windows and doorways, then the walls crumbled and red heat mixed with death exhaled from the building. He did not stop to watch. He ran for his life toward the refuge of the nearest building, and had reached the edge and turned left to hide behind the stone wall when he was lifted into the air and thrown. Pain ripped through his left shoulder. Shrapnel cut ribbons of his clothing. He slammed onto the ground and cried out in agony. Rocks and sand rained down on him. Before the flame could settle, his body gave way to unconsciousness.

Cole breathed in and out, choosing details that would sound like a report instead of a memory. He heard the contained panic that traced the edges of his words, and only as he neared the end did he realize that at some point Meagan had reached for him. He looked down and saw his own hand covered hers completely. He should let go. His grip was probably cutting off the circulation in her fingers.

He lessened the pressure but did not release her hand. Eyes still on the floor between his feet, he continued. "I woke up in one of our tanks. The ride back to the barracks was excruciating. Once the medic there had worked on me enough that I would survive the trip, they flew me to America."

For the first time since he started talking, he looked up. Steve was pale, a layer of moisture dampening his skin. The cameraman stared in silence, his camera somewhat off to the side as if he had forgotten to either put it down or keep it trained on Cole's face. Meagan wiped tears from her cheeks.

"You saved their lives," she said.

His head dropped. He let go of Meagan's hand to rub his shoulder. "Not all their lives."

She touched his arm. He could not bear to hear a hollow reassurance, so he spoke to Steve. "I hallucinated those first days. They had me on a lot of morphine. But I do remember, at least I think I remember, someone telling me none of our men were killed, none of the tanks were damaged beyond repair, and only a few men suffered minor injuries."

Steve wiped his face with the back of his hand. "That's right."

Cole spoke quietly. "I don't remember you lying for me. And I don't know what you would lie about."

"I thought you had told her the location of the envoy. I thought that you were responsible; that's why you ran to stop her that day." Steve would not look at him. He stood. "We'd better go." He handed a business card and a sheet of paper to the man with the camera. "Make sure this video gets to every major news source in the city. Pass along my contact information if anyone has questions. I vouch for the truth of this testimony and renounce the falsehood of the article in the newspapers yesterday. The source did not have accurate information."

The man nodded, packed up his camera, and left after shaking Cole's hand. Cole stood. "Steve, we—"

"I have to get to the office. Baine has me back on the case and I need to strategize with him about a noon deadline."

Cole knew Steve was being deliberate in his lack of information, knowing if he got Cole to ask for details, it would keep Cole from asking other things. Too spent to push further, Cole nodded. "I've got the week off, so I can help. Vacation time." Steve missed the irony, but he noted Meagan did not. Her face radiated sympathy. The chains connected to her handcuffs clinked as she stood. She did not speak, but touched his shoulder one more time on her way by him, a slight but comforting gesture.

The police officer, who had remained silent, shook Cole's hand the moment he rose from the bench. This was why he hated talking about Baghdad. It changed the way people saw him. They treated him like a hero, but he had failed. He had risked men's lives to try to save a spy. He'd failed to bring his radio so he could abort the mission. He'd shot a woman. He'd aimed at her thigh to bring her down rather than kill her, and that had been foolish. She might have dragged herself out the door and thrown the grenade at the lead tank. And what if he had not run fast enough in the first place, and arrived too late to do anything but see his fellow soldiers blown to pieces?

Shame could run in opposite directions at once. He wished he had been able to save the woman from choosing a destiny that was a lie. He also wished he had reported her after their midnight meeting, when she confessed she was a spy. "She fell in love when she was a girl. The boy convinced her to meet him in secret one night. She did and was discovered. Her reputation was destroyed and she was labeled an outcast." At the stricken look on Meagan's face, he realized he was speaking his thoughts aloud. "She had no place to go and ended up on the streets, where she became what her community had already claimed she was. Along the way she got recruited by the enemy." He frowned. "Or more accurately, was told to do what they wanted or she would die. They promised redemption with the suicide bombing. She kept saying she had no other choice."

Steve cleared his throat. "You couldn't have saved her Cole. Some people are past saving."

Meagan's wince mirrored his own. "I don't believe that anymore."

Steve reached down for his discarded coffee cup. "Maybe you should." He looked around for a trash can. "I've got to get back. Cole, you get Meagan checked out of here, or whatever the process is called. You can take her by your office if you still want to, but don't take long, and then bring her to the Federal Building."

The relief on Meagan's features hit Cole hard. She smiled and said, "You really meant it when you said I'd get released."

Steve did not seem to hear. "Speed up the process, will you?" he said to the officer. "And Cole, get her stuff in a bag, but keep her in the uniform, and make sure that when you show up at the building, she's wearing the chain and handcuffs."

54

Tuesday, January 6
9:00 a.m.

Meagan remained silent as Cole and the policeman gathered her things and had her sign paperwork. When Cole had talked about Iraq, her heart had responded to his deep pain. The moment Steve mentioned Cole's office, however, doubts pummeled her again. There was so much she did not know about Cole Fleming, so much she feared to know. Would her heart allow her to recognize a lie if he told it?

"The handcuffs are yours but the waist chain belongs to the prison," the officer told Cole. "You'll need to bring it back when you return the uniform." He crossed his arms. "Mr. FBI didn't tell me when that would be."

"I think he might not know," Cole said. "Things have gotten kind of hairy with his investigation."

The officer smirked but refrained from saying more. Cole held the door for Meagan and then helped her down the outside stairs. It was ridiculous how cumbersome a simple thing like stairs could be when wearing handcuffs and a waist chain, and getting into his car was even worse.

Needing to fill the silence, Meagan said, "This is a nice car. Yours?"

"Just a rental for now." He drove out of the prison parking lot and Meagan hoped she would never see the place again. "I don't seem to have much time for car shopping lately." He put in a CD and Meagan recognized it was the group he said was his favorite. "I'm not into mint green myself, but it was the cheapest option I could get right away."

"It'd make a fun nail polish color."

"Exactly." He glanced over at her with a smile, but it fell when his gaze dropped to her hands. He turned the wheel and stopped the car on the side of the road.

"What's the matter?" she asked.

"I can't stand seeing you in those cuffs." He reached across and opened the glove compartment. It dropped onto her knees and he clammered around behind a hammer and two more CDs to pull out another set of handcuffs.

"So you're going to add a second set?"

At that his smile returned. "I'm hoping the standard key will work on yours." He removed the key from his set and tried it on the cuffs on her wrists. With a click, she was free. He pulled the cuffs and the chain off and tossed them in the backseat while she rubbed her wrists and stretched her arms.

"Thank you."

He pointed his chin toward the backseat before maneuvering the car into traffic again. "Remind me to put those back on before we take you into the Federal Building. I'm not sure what Steve's plan is, but I have a feeling I won't like it."

"Since it involves me wearing this hideous outfit, I already know I don't."

"Would it help if I said you look cute in orange?"

"No."

He laughed. "Then I won't say it." He pulled into a fast food parking lot. "I'd take you someplace nice since you just got out of the slammer, but you don't seem to want to show off the new clothes. How does a drive through biscuit sound?"

"Wonderful. With grape jelly please."

He ordered for them both and she tried to hide when he drove up to pay. He noticed and offered her the coat draped across the middle consul. "I hate wearing coats. You might as well use it."

She thanked him and pulled it across her lap to cover as much of her outfit as possible, but then removed it once they had their food. "I'm tempted to purposefully drop jelly on this jumpsuit. It would serve Steve right to have to get it cleaned."

"No comment on that."

With her first bite, jelly dripped from the biscuit and landed on her leg. Cole laughed and she hunted for a napkin to wipe at the stain. "I promise I did not do that on purpose. Really." She dipped the napkin in her water and attacked the purple splotch. "Will this go on my permanent record, do you think?"

He did not answer and she glanced up to see he was pulling into a parking lot. "Where are we?"

His face was hard. "My workplace."

Tuesday, January 6
10:05 a.m.

Cole avoided looking at the building and ignored the tightening in his gut. "Meagan," he said, wishing he could get his voice to sound less solemn. He walked around the mint-ice-cream-colored car and opened the door for her. "What I'm going to tell you and show you today needs to remain a secret. Can you agree to that?"

He could see hesitation in her beautiful eyes, shadowed by dark circles. She clasped her hands in front of her, as if still wearing the handcuffs. "I—I can't promise that until I know what it is." Her eyes locked on the nondescript building. It sported a sign with a computer company logo. "The windows are tinted," she said. "You can't see inside."

"That's purposeful." He took her hand and her surprised gaze traveled to his face. "I work for the Department of Justice. We are a specialized unit here that sometimes partners with other agencies, like the FBI, but we keep this location and what we do here under the radar for the safety of the workers and their families. I will take you inside if you promise you will not share our work or especially our location with anyone."

She searched his eyes and he let her. Her hand remained in his, and after enough time had passed that he started to shiver, she said, "I promise that unless I see illegal activity, I won't tell anyone."

"Good enough." He opened the passenger door she'd shut and pulled out his coat. "You should wear this."

"Aren't you cold?"

He put it over her shoulders. "My jacket is thicker than that jumpsuit."

She snuggled into it and he wondered if it would smell like vanilla when he got it back. Her walk was slow toward the building. "Are you frightened?" he asked.

The wind blew and she brushed hair out of her face. "Embarrassed. Are there people in there? I look like a clown who forgot her wig and big floppy shoes."

He laughed out loud. "Well, I've seen worse."

"If you're talking about my pajamas, beware."

They were at the door, Cole still chuckling, when she stopped and whispered, "Okay, yes, I am afraid."

He reached up and gently touched her cheek, letting his eyes linger on hers until the wind blew cold air and some sense back into him. "Come inside." He held the door open and watched closely as Meagan took tentative steps into his building. He tried to see the interior from her perspective. Drab. Dark. No decorations. About as opposite her setting at Rahab's Rope as it got. "Only four guys work in this section, including me," he explained. "None of us have much of a knack for making a place feel like home."

She stood in the center and turned counter-clockwise until she had surveyed their entire section, complete with four desks, each with a chair and wastebasket, and little else. "I'm glad to hear none of you think this is homey."

"To me, at least, this place will never feel like home." He led her to his desk. "It feels like war. Or the middle of the night just after a nightmare." He pulled over a second chair from the desk to his right. "The guys must be in a meeting right now."

"That's a blessing. You won't have to explain your visitor who looks like she escaped from prison."

"A shame. We could have made up a good story."

She sat at his desk and looked up at him. "So what is the mystery of what you do, Cole Fleming?"

Why did he want to tell her everything? Why did it feel important that she knew who he really was? He sat and rolled his chair close to hers. He turned on his computer and felt the familiar tension when their site came up. Meagan gasped at the young girl on the screen, her face so innocent, like Sadie's once was.

"Cole..."

Meagan's hands gripped the armrests. She slid her chair backwards. He turned it so she was facing him rather than the computer. "We call her Cupcake." Meagan winced and he rushed on. "She's not real. She's a digital girl. We upload her and within seconds get hits from men all over the country who are willing to pay to watch her." He shut down the screen. "I don't need to tell you the details. You can guess. It makes me sick, but this little girl is helping us track, arrest, and convict child predators. That's my job, Meagan, to find creeps who harm children and put them away."

Meagan eyes were full of tears. "And she's not real?"

"No. She's not real."

He heard a little sob then Meagan put her hands over her face. She stood and took a few steps away from the desk. He followed. "I just—" She began to cry. "I was so afraid you—" Her hands fluttered a bit and then she whirled and they were around his neck.

Out of instinctive response, he wrapped his arms around her waist, and once the stunned feeling wore off, he became aware of how very good she felt. He tightened his arms around her small frame. "Meagan..."

"Hey! Sorry."

Cole looked behind to see Matt, the co-worker whose chair he'd borrowed, standing two feet into the room in an awkward pose, as if he'd tried to stop mid-stride and had not quite succeeded. Meagan pulled away from Cole and searched for a tissue, wiping her eyes with her hand when she did not find one. Matt started to smile but his gaze dropped to her clothing and his eyebrows went up. "Uh...Cole? We don't usually have visitors in here."

"It's okay," Cole said. He turned to Meagan. "There's a box of tissues in the bathroom. I'll get it for you."

She sniffed and he felt guilty for leaving her with Matt instead of letting her escape to the bathroom herself. But he needed a minute. If she had left, Matt would grill him about Meagan's presence and especially about what might have happened had he not shown up just then. Cole needed to get his heart rate back to normal so he could pretend holding Meagan, even for a few seconds, had not been a complete distraction. He'd forgotten where he was.

It was no wonder the other guys never brought their wives to work. He grabbed the tissue box and headed back to his desk, where Meagan's cheeks blazed almost as bright as her orange outfit. Had Matt said something to her, or could that telltale sign of emotion be because of him?

55

Tuesday, January 6
11:00 a.m.

Cole drove, speaking on the phone to Steve in such solemn tones Meagan would have worried had she not been so consumed with Matt's comment. "We all agreed not to tell the full details of our job to anyone but wives or fiancés," he'd said. "And none of us have brought anyone inside the building." She had gestured toward the prison uniform and told Matt she was a reasonable exception, but questions had flooded her mind ever since.

What had she been thinking, throwing herself at Cole like that? Embarrassment burned up her neck and across her cheeks. Cole finished his call and Meagan searched for something to say in safe, small-talk territory. "Could we stop by the hospital before we go meet Steve? I'd like to check on Pops."

"I'm afraid not." He kept his focus on the heavy lunch traffic as he switched lanes. "He's been secured in a special area of the hospital and is under guard day and night now."

"Why?" She tucked Cole's coat up tight to her chin. "What happened?"

"Nothing has yet," he reassured. "It's a precaution, but the danger you're in should be taken seriously. From what Steve just told me, we shouldn't stop at a hospital or anywhere but the Federal Building right now. And even that makes me nervous. This guy is a madman."

"Lucias?"

Cole nodded. "He called the director last night and threatened to blow up the Federal Building if you're not released with an apology by noon."

She shuddered and pulled the coat tighter. "What is he thinking? Why is he doing this?"

"He's in love with you."

She scoffed. "That's impossible. He doesn't even know me."

"I wish that were true." He veered to the right to pull off the exit. "I've read his letters, Meagan. The man is obsessed with you." She wasn't sure if his frown was for the bottlenecked traffic on the road, or if it was for her. "I didn't want to tell you," he said, "but his letters have me concerned. He talks about me in the most recent ones, and even though the words are supposed to be from you, he's clearly heading for jealous rage any time he sees you with me."

She could not seem to get warm. She held her hands out to the heat coming through the vents, and resisted the urge to get Cole's hammer from his glove compartment and hold it in her lap. She should have applied for a gun back when she had the chance. "Isn't it bad, then, that you're with me right now?"

"That's why Steve called me. He and Baine just finished reading the letters. He wants us in Baine's office immediately, where he can put you under guard and explain their plan to both of us." He parked the car as close to the building as he could. "I hope Lucias isn't here watching already. We don't want to make him angry, since he's a fuse waiting to be lit, but there's no way I'm letting you walk across the street into that building by yourself." He reached into the back and she cringed at the clanging of the chain and handcuffs. "I wish I didn't have to do this," he said, his voice low. He kept his eyes on the chain as he positioned it around her waist.

"Me too." She held the chain out for him to attach it to the cuffs. "If a bomb does go off, I'm not going to be able to run very well."

His eyes found hers and their gazes locked. "I will not leave your side," he said. He had both her hands cradled inside his. His face moved slightly toward hers, but he came to an abrupt stop and looked out the back window, side windows, and the front. When he bowed his head and prayed aloud for her safety and a sense of peace, then asked for courage to protect her and wisdom to fight for her, she felt tears threaten. He said amen and lifted his head. "Are you ready?"

She wasn't. She wanted to stay there, in his mint green car, her hands cocooned in his.

The phone rang and she thought the cliché about jumping out of one's skin was not as far-fetched as she'd always believed. Cole answered and she could tell it was Steve's voice on the line. Cole put the car in reverse and backed out of the parking space. "There's a secondary entrance around back," he said to her. "We can drive the car right up to it and there will only be a few feet where you're exposed between the car and the building. Lucias stipulated 'by noon' not at noon, so they're assuming he's been waiting for us and knows we're here now."

She slunk down in her seat. "What about you?"

"I'll park and be right behind you."

"But you'll be exposed, and it sounds like he's angry with you right now, not me."

He glanced her way with a half-smile. "I'll be fine."

"Yes, you will." She tried to cross her arms. The cuffs resisted. "You promised you wouldn't leave my side, so I want you to take me inside and have someone else park the car."

He started to grin, but when he looked her way and his gaze took in the chain and cuffs, he sobered again. "Yes, ma'am," he said, then added with a soft sigh, "I look forward to the day when you're home again, with your grandfather, in your horrible pajamas and those cute bunny slippers, safe and sound."

She blinked moisture from her eyes. It would do no good to cry now. Cole hadn't brought the box of tissues with them. "When that day comes, you're invited over for homemade macaroni and cheese and peanut-butter fudge."

They reached the back of the building. Steve, Quinn and another man stood just inside the doorway. Steve's gun was out and ready. Quinn's was out and at his side. Cole stopped the car and gave her one long look. "First we have to get through today."

Tuesday, January 6
11:30 a.m.

Idiots. Lucias wished there really was a bomb in the building so he could get Meagan out and blow the rest of them to bits. He'd seen Meagan the moment Cole drove her into the parking lot in that stupid girly green car. He knew the exact moment Cole almost kissed her, and the exact moment he stopped and looked around. If Lucias had the skill of a sniper, Cole Fleming would be slumped over his steering wheel right now, blood dripping out of the hole in his head.

Now he had to wait while they talked inside about whatever useless plan they were surely creating. They would try to trap him, but he was smarter than they thought he was. He had his own plan.

The front door to the Federal Building opened and Lucias held his binoculars with one hand at a time while he wiped the other hand on the material of his seat. He needed dry skin to grip the binoculars hard, to not miss one second of his victory, to see every detail and know just when Meagan left the parking lot and was free to be with him. He had originally decided to hide under a blanket in her backseat and surprise her after she had driven a few miles away from the FBI, but her car wasn't there. They must have arrested her at home, or had someone take her car away. She would walk from the building to her store, and he would arrive just as she reached the sidewalk. She would get in his car and he would take her away, and they would be together forever. If there was a cloud nine, he would be on it.

Four men in dark suits, coats open, walked through the door and down the stairs. Their heads turned like robots with laser scan eyes, as if Lucias would be foolish enough to be in sight. Next came Cole and the man Steve had brought to Lucias' house. Both wore earpieces. Cole said something, his hand to the earpiece. He checked his watch and Lucias checked the clock on his dash. Eleven forty-nine. They were cutting it close. Cole opened his jacket and put a hand to his gun and Lucias wanted to attack the big soldier. Why had he been the one to drive Meagan to the FBI? After that article in the newspaper yesterday, Meagan should have not wanted anything to do with the man. She continued to make unwise choices. He would have to talk with her about that when they were together.

She appeared in the doorway and his heart beat hard. She looked afraid. Steve held her arm and they walked down the stairs together, behind Cole and the other guy, with the four robots covering their sides. Meagan was a burning sun in the night sky, her orange prison uniform bright in the middle of all those dark suits. Some horrible person had put a chain around her and handcuffed her beautiful, feminine hands. He would ask her who had done that to her, and they would make that person pay.

At the bottom step, Steve stopped Meagan. He put a key in the handcuffs and opened them. He removed the chain from her waist. Lucias leaned forward and watched Steve's mouth move. That would be the apology he had demanded. Now Steve would say goodbye and Meagan would walk away.

Steve extended his hand and she shook it. Lucias would rather she had slapped his face. Steve gave her a bag that probably contained her clothing and personal items and she walked toward the road, but she did not turn to go to her store. Why was she not doing what she was supposed to do?

Lucias' hands shook. He gripped hard on the binoculars. Harder. They snapped in two.

She got into a car. An FBI car. With Steve Campbell, his partner, and that hateful Cole Fleming.

He yelled a curse and pummeled the steering wheel with his fists. "Meagan, Meagan," he wailed. "Why are you destroying my love for you?"

56

Tuesday, January 6
12:00 p.m.

Meagan had almost stopped shaking. The sight of her grandparents' home, so welcoming and safe compared to prison gates and barbed wire, made her want to run inside, climb into bed and have a good long cry.

Cole opened the door for her and he and Quinn flanked her the few steps from the car to the porch, then up to the house. Steve followed, telling someone on the phone that they had arrived and would be setting up a secure perimeter within the hour.

"Are you sure this is necessary?" she asked Quinn, who stood at her left side, not quite as grim-faced as Cole on her right.

Cole put a hand on her back and ushered her inside. "I don't know about Quinn," he said, not giving the other man time to speak, "but I'm convinced this Lucias guy is a murderer, and the fact that he murdered the last woman he was obsessed with should scare you."

"Are you trying to make this worse?" She yanked at the sleeves on her orange jumpsuit. At least the chain and handcuffs were off now. What she wouldn't give to go upstairs and change into her pajamas, drink a cup of hot chocolate, and sit in complete silence for hours. After she had her good long cry. "I already about shook into pieces leaving the building. What if he'd had a long range rifle or something?"

"That's not his MO," Quinn put in, checking the living room and then the kitchen in such a serious set of moves she began to feel nervous in her own home. "Clear. Claudia was murdered up close. He used his hands."

Cole's hand on her back tightened and, whether consciously or not, he pulled her close to his side. She determined to at least pretend to be strong. "Well, then, I guess I should be grateful I have three men keeping him out of reach." She wanted to be thankful they were there, protecting her, but the need for their presence did not make it feel any less like an invasion into what once felt like a safe haven. Would she ever be able to walk in the woods around the house again, or sit in the living room with the curtains open at night, without wondering if someone was watching?

Not until Lucias Moore is behind bars. To make that happen, she had to follow their plan. *Just two days,* she told herself.

"You probably want to get out of that outfit," Cole said.

She tried to smile. "Yeah, it's got a jelly stain on it." His eyes on her were kind and at that moment the thought of burying her head into his shoulder and being held was more tempting than even the silence or the good cry. But Steve and Quinn might think she wasn't capable of carrying out the plan if she fell apart in front of them now, or even if they heard her losing it up in her room, so with wooden steps she climbed the stairs to her bedroom and changed into her most comfortable non-pj clothing. She stuffed the jumpsuit into a plastic bag.

"Meagan?" Cole's voice just outside the door startled her, but it shouldn't have. She should expect to not be given much personal space for the following two days. "You about finished?"

"Almost." She ran a brush through what little hair she had, and checked in the mirror to see that she did, indeed, have big dark circles under her eyes. Well, maybe if she looked terrible, Lucias would find some other woman to follow around.

The thought of him being there, inside the house, had her shaking again. Was this how Alexia felt? She talked about her pimp like he was everywhere. It was no wonder so many of the girls were terrified of testifying. Some were too afraid to escape in the first place, certain without a doubt that if they tried to leave, they would be found and punished.

"I'm sorry, Alexia," she whispered. "I cared, but I never really understood."

"Meagan?"

Meagan reminded herself that Alexia was safe in a recovery shelter, and Cole waited for her in the hallway. She opened the door and stepped around him to get to the stairs, pretending she did not see the slight outstretch of his hands. If she found solace in his arms right then, she knew she would not be able to keep from crying. "Let's go see what weird gadgets Steve and Quinn have set up downstairs to make my perimeter secure, whatever my perimeter is." She glanced back at him. "And then I'm making some fudge." Crying she would not allow, but comfort food, that was another matter.

Tuesday, January 6
2:00 p.m.

"I can't do this," Brianna said, clutching the basket, wanting to drop it and run. "They need to find someone else. Don't they have people who do this kind of thing?"

"Yes." Kelsey's voice was calm, but Brianna could tell she was more nervous than she acted. She had repositioned the beading on the necklace in her hands three times. "But he has been in here before. Remember the note? He'll get suspicious if we suddenly have a whole new set of staff. Especially if they're as big and imposing as Cole Fleming."

"Don't they have any girls in the FBI?"

"I'm sure they do, but like I said, we need to be the people out there. We're doing this for Meagan."

Brianna bit her lower lip and tried to keep her chin from quivering like a little girl's. "But he might be a murderer," she whispered.

"Which is why we prayed, a lot, before agreeing to do this. God is here with us, and He's stronger than this man." She put her hands on Brianna's upper arms, something Brianna had seen her do with many young girls in distress. She'd never expected to be in their camp. "This is what we do, Brianna. We put ourselves at risk to help women targeted by predators. Only this time we're working to protect someone we already know and love."

"I know." But she had chosen to intern at the store to fight evil without having to encounter it firsthand. What if he pulled out a knife, or a gun?

"I'd better get back out there," Kelsey said with a quick hug. "Don't forget to keep watch, right?"

"Right."

Kelsey slid the door open and returned to the main area of the store, sliding the door back so only an inch or two remained open. Brianna took her place there, basket in hand, and watched. She would have found the concept of stalking the stalker funny if her teeth weren't chattering at the thought. "God, please help us do this right," she whispered. "I'm so scared I'll say the wrong thing and give it all away." If she did, would he up and kill her? Was she more afraid for herself than for Meagan? "Help me to have the right heart for this." She quoted some of Kelsey's favorite ministry verses in her mind, about defending the rights of the poor and needy, and how the Lord loved justice.

The bell rang and an elderly woman entered the store. Brianna's heart stuttered then sped. The FBI agents had said that Meagan's stalker would probably be dressed either as an older man in a plaid suit jacket, or as an old lady. Could this be him? The lady walked over to the side wall display of fair trade spices and chocolate bars. She chose one of the bars and moved toward the register. That was suspicious. She had not looked at anything else in the store, and Brianna did not remember seeing her there before. Most shoppers took their time.

Brianna told her legs to move, told her arms to push aside the door. Lead weights seemed attached to the tops of her feet.

"Is that all for you today?" Kelsey asked. She threw a look toward the door to the back room where Brianna stood.

The lady dug change out of her purse and Kelsey glanced at the back room again, her eyes sending a message like a mother would to a child who lagged behind. *Get up here,* it said. Another look. *Now!*

Brianna willed her body into action. She opened the door and carried her basket to the cashier counter. "I brought—I—I brought this for your trip Thursday," she said, knowing she sounded like a school-aged kid with stage fright. "Presents for you before you go to India."

"I'm not going."

The lady dropped her purse and muttered as she bent low to retrieve it. Kelsey went around the counter to help her and Brianna did not know if she should say her next line or not. Kelsey picked up and held the woman's purse while the woman reached for something else on the floor that Brianna could not see. Brianna started to ask Kelsey why she wasn't going on her planned trip, but Kelsey shot her a look and shook her head. Brianna stood and thought about murderers and criminals while the lady paid for her chocolate bar with quarters and dimes, then hobbled from the store.

When the door shut behind her, Kelsey put a hand to her mouth to cover her laugh. "That wasn't our guy," she said.

Brianna's heart finally slowed its frantic sprint. "How do you know?"

Kelsey's eyes shone with laughter. "When she leaned over, her dentures fell out!"

The bell rang again and there was no time for Brianna to run to the back room and watch from afar. Three women entered. One of them was elderly. Should they suspect her?

Another woman came in behind them and Brianna fought the urge to retreat. She stayed as they shopped, said her part when it was time, then escaped once the only shoppers left in the store were too young to be possibilities.

Safely in the back room again, she glanced at the clock. Only twelve minutes had passed? She still held out hope that he wouldn't come, that he would go someplace else to get information, maybe Meagan's house, though he would know by now she had agents staying there. He could call the airport and sweet talk some Delta receptionist into reading the passenger list to him. No, he wouldn't do that; he didn't know about the flight. She bit her lip again. The FBI was right. There wasn't much else he could do other than come to the store.

The front bell rang again and she picked up the basket she'd dropped. How many old ladies were going to visit Rahab's Rope that afternoon? When this one neared the register, Brianna prayed for courage and stepped into the store room again.

Tuesday, January 6
2:20 p.m.

Lucias drove for two hours, in such a rage he almost ran out of gas without noticing. Meagan was causing him problems. If Raymond were still alive, he'd tell Lucias that Meagan was making his life unhappy and he needed to move on, but Agatha wanted to give Meagan one more chance. Agatha liked Meagan.

He filled the tank at a station, glad to have cash again thanks to his run in Atlanta. The minutes standing in the cold air cleared his mind. He knew where to go next.

A headache was making its way from behind his eyes up across his forehead and down around his ears. He knew he would only have an hour, two at the most, before it would blind him to everything but getting a fix to make it stop. He stopped at a second gas station and told Agatha she would have to hurry. Agatha did not want to wear something different, but he explained to her that it was not safe to return home to get her regular clothes and hair. The FBI might have agents watching for him. She complained, but put on the new outfit and the new wig for his sake, once he told her he could not get Meagan away from those creeps without her help.

Agatha wore her new outfit into Meagan's store. The bell on the door jingled in its annoying cheerful way. Lucias counted four other customers inside. Meagan's good friend, the woman with lots of freckles, stood behind the cash register. He meandered, looking at the earrings, then the scarves. The headache got worse and his left eyelid started to twitch. The dark-haired girl who worked at the store came in from the back room, carrying a basket. She took it to the woman at the register and he moved to a section of wall hangings, close enough to hear their conversation.

"...it's tradition," the girl said. She set the basket on the counter. "Hot chocolate mix and a bagel for your breakfast on Thursday."

The woman pulled a small card out of the basket and read, "Have a great trip! We're praying for you. Love, the team." She hugged the dark-haired girl. "Thanks, Brianna, but I'm not going on this trip to India."

"What?"

He moved closer, to a pile of books for sale. He picked up the one on the top of the stack and pretended to look it over.

"Kelsey, you've had this trip planned for months," the girl said. "Why would you cancel it at the last minute?"

The woman named Kelsey shook her head. "The trip isn't canceled. Meagan is going."

He dropped the book and it landed with a thud on the floor. The dark-haired girl stepped toward him. "I'm sorry," she said. "We're just chatting away. Do you need help with something?"

"No, thank you, sweetie pie," Agatha said. *Don't overdo it*, he told her. "These old hands can't keep hold of things like they used to. I'm fine, though. Don't let me bother you."

The girl smiled. "Well, let us know if you need anything." She went back to the register and Lucias set the book on top of the stack again, careful to not draw any more attention. The Brianna girl lowered her voice and said something to Kelsey. He had to come closer to the register to hear her.

"...she is at her house, but all those FBI guys are there, too."

Kelsey's focus was so intent on Brianna, she did not even see him step closer. "They won't leave her alone," Kelsey said. "Even though they let her out of prison today, they're staying at her house. She called me and told me she can't stand it. I suggested that she take my place on this trip to India. They can't follow her out of the country."

"And they're going to let her go?"

"They can't stop her. There isn't any evidence to convict her anymore."

Brianna pulled the card from her basket. "Well, I guess I don't need this now." She dropped the card into the trash can next to the cashier counter. "Meagan doesn't like bagels. I don't think I'll take her the hot chocolate either." She picked up the basket. "I don't know about you, but I don't want to go over there when her place is crawling with guys carrying guns."

"I called and asked if we could see her off at the airport, and they said no."

Brianna crossed her arms. "That's mean. We're her best friends."

"I guess they have their reasons." The Kelsey woman noticed Agatha and seemed startled. "Are you ready to check out?" she asked.

Agatha didn't know what to do. Lucias grabbed the nearest item and set it on the counter. Some kind of headband or something. Kelsey rang up the purchase while the dark-haired girl took her basket back into the other room. Agatha talked about silly things while Kelsey put her item in a pretty little bag with a ribbon on it.

"Thanks for stopping by," Kelsey said.

"Have a nice day, sweetie." Agatha turned and Lucias made her trip over the waste basket. It fell over. "Oh, I'm so clumsy."

"It's okay," Kelsey said. "I'll get it."

"No, no." Agatha kneeled down and put the papers and torn tags back in. "I've got it."

"You have a nice day, too," Kelsey said before Agatha left the store. Agatha was careful to wave with her empty hand, keeping hidden the hand that held a small card with well wishes for a Thursday trip.

It was fate. Lucias smiled in triumph. Thursday was January eighth.

Meagan's birthday.

57

Tuesday, January 6
7:00 p.m.

Cole offered to help Meagan clean up after their supper of chicken wraps and sliced peppers. It was the only thing he could think of to create some sense of normalcy for her.

"I used paper plates so there wouldn't be much to clean up," she said, shrugging and circling the kitchen. "But maybe that was a bad idea. Now I don't know what to do with myself."

"The fudge was delicious."

"Thanks." She shrugged again. "I throw a few ingredients in a bowl and microwave it, then stir. It's an easy recipe I got off Pinterest one night when Grandma couldn't sleep." She wiped the table and dumped the crumbs in the trash. "That reminds me. I want to order a CD from that singing group you like. What was their name?"

"You mean the Mylon Hayes family?"

"That's right. I couldn't remember. Do you think they'd get it to me overnight if I paid the extra shipping?"

He broke off another square of fudge. "I'm sure they would. You in a hurry?"

"Everything feels kind of urgent lately." She avoided his gaze. "Would I be allowed to call Pops? I can't recall the last time I've gone so long without talking with him. Even when I'm in India, I call every couple of days."

"We've checked your phone for bugs, and I'm sure they've checked his phone in the hospital. I don't see why not." He followed her into the living room where Steve and Quinn had found a game to watch. Though they tried to keep the equipment to a minimum, it was still glaringly obvious that the law had settled in to stay for a while. The living room looked more like a stakeout than a home.

"You can call," Steve said, "but don't give any information about Thursday, and stay where we can hear you." He muted the television and Cole could see the displeasure on Meagan's face. She picked up her cell phone from where it sat on the coffee table, connected to tracing equipment, and was dialing numbers when it rang. She jumped, but then answered it, leaving Steve and Quinn scrambling for their headphones and the recording device.

"It's just Brianna," Meagan said, frustration in her voice. She added to the phone, "No, I'm glad it's you. My handlers thought I was dumb enough to answer a phone call from the bad guy without letting them set up first." She tried to turn away but the cord attached to the phone yanked her back. "I have to warn you, if you stay on the phone long enough, the FBI will know exactly where you are."

Her smile, slight as it was, soothed some of the stress in the air. Cole crossed the room to edge the curtain aside. Was Lucias Moore out there?

He dropped the curtain back in place and turned just as Meagan hung up the phone. "She said it worked, she thinks, but not to ever ask her to do anything like that again."

Steve stood. "They're sure he came into the store? You should have let me talk to her."

"They did the whole routine three times, but she said she was almost one hundred percent sure the last one was him. To quote her, 'No old lady in the world has legs that hairy.'" Meagan handed the phone to Steve with a grin. "You can call her if you want and talk about his legs some more, or his falsetto voice, or the curly wig that was put on crooked."

Steve looked like he'd stuck a lemon wedge in his mouth. "I'll take your word for it."

Meagan called her grandfather and talked for a few minutes. "Can I go up to my room now?" she asked when the call finished. "I need to order something online, and I want to send a few e-mails. I may not be in the store, but there's plenty of work that I can do from home. The e-mails piled up while I was in jail."

Cole grinned. She stood with her arms crossed and her face pressed into a scowl, like a teenager asking to break curfew. He wished she had put on her bunny slippers, but then again, something about her wearing them made her look young and vulnerable, and he wanted to pull her into his arms and protect her from all the evil out there. It was better she kept her slippers in her room and he kept his mind on other things.

That personal advice became harder to keep late that night when she wandered into the kitchen where he had set up a temporary office after Steve and Quinn had gone to bed. She startled and he stood. "It's just me," he said quickly, his gaze taking in her flowery robe and fleece pants with kittens on them. That night she wore just a t-shirt under the robe instead of a long nightgown. The bunny slippers nearly undid his carefully maintained composure. He gestured to his computer. "I can leave if you were hoping for privacy."

"What are you doing?" She opened a cupboard and pulled out a box of herbal tea bags.

"Work."

She put a hand to her stomach. "Oh."

He clicked a button to minimize the window he was in, and slid the laptop to the side of the table. "Can't sleep?"

"I'd rather stay up than have more of the dreams I started with tonight."

"Understood." He considered her for a moment, then said, "If you need a distraction, could I...could I tell you about Sadie, and what happened to her?" He never talked about Sadie, but somehow Meagan kept wedging into his carefully protected cavern of secrets.

She returned the box of tea bags back to the cupboard, and looked back at him only long enough to nod once. She opened another cupboard and pulled out a box of macaroni and cheese. "How about I make some for you?"

He could not explain why his throat clamped up on him or his voice went hoarse. "I'd like that."

While Meagan found the ingredients to add to the box mix, Cole sat, leaned back, and tried to keep his voice steady as his words took them both into the darkest, most enclosed part of his past.

Tuesday, January 6
11:00 p.m.

Relief or guilt? Steve knew he'd feel one or the other when Stephanie answered the phone. "I'm sorry it's so late," he said when she picked up on the second ring. "I should have called you earlier. I don't know why I don't think to do that." He checked to make sure the guest room door, where he'd stationed himself, was fully shut. "I can be a real jerk sometimes, I know that."

"Are you drunk again?"

There was the guilt. He'd gotten used to associating the feeling with her. Maybe that was why he stayed away so much. "I'm not drunk. I'm at Meagan Winston's house." He told her about the changes in the case. "I have to be here until Thursday morning. I'm sorry for not telling you sooner. I should have."

"Steve, are you okay?"

Her voice sounded wary. She probably thought he was at a bar, lying through his teeth. "What do you mean?"

"You just—you don't apologize for things. Ever. Has something happened?"

What was he supposed to say? *My best friend told a story this morning and I found out I hate myself.* "Yeah, sort of. Listen, could you...would you want to come over tomorrow? There's something I'd like to talk to you about, and I don't want it to be over the phone."

He waited long seconds before she said, "I could pick up breakfast and bring it over."

"That would be great. I'd like to have you here."

"Will Meagan mind?"

"I think she'd like to have another woman around. But I'll ask her in the morning just to make sure."

"Okay. Anything specific you want for breakfast?"

"Whatever you bring will be fine."

Silence again. Then, "Are you sure you're okay?"

How did she pick up on so much even over the phone? "I just—are you still praying? You know, about us?"

"Well, kind of." She didn't sound as enthusiastic as she had before. He could hear her soft breathing and was surprised at the sudden, strong desire to have her near, to pull her close and spend the night with his arms around her, thinking only of her. How long had it been?

"If you pray tonight," he said, "say one for me, okay?"

The one word came through quiet. "Okay."

"Thanks. And I'm sorry for running out on you yesterday. The house looked real nice. And you did, too."

He heard a sniff and the guilt cut deep. "Goodnight, Steve."

"Goodnight." He closed the call and sat on the guest bed in the dark, thinking of his wife, wondering if her prayers would get through, and if he should dare adding one of his own.

58

Tuesday, January 6
11:40 p.m.

Meagan scooped macaroni and cheese into two bowls and made her way to the kitchen table. She placed one in front of Cole, who stared at it like a long-forgotten memory. "What happened next?" she asked.

He put his hands around the sides of his bowl. She did the same with hers and felt warmth seep into her skin. "He started hitting me more often, for lesser reasons. After a while, it was for no reason at all. Sadie would scream and try to get him off me, but he was usually drunk by that point. He'd pass out eventually and she'd clean me up." He kept his face down, looking at the noodles in unnaturally bright yellow cheese sauce. "She would cry and I'd hate him. If I had been old enough, if I'd had a steady job, I would have gotten us both out of there, away from him."

Meagan kept her voice soft. "Did your father ever beat Sadie?"

He shook his head. "She was his real daughter. I was just a step-kid. He doted on her. Used to show people her picture and brag about how cute she was, what a pretty woman she would become." He put his head in his hands. "I left the day after high school graduation and joined the military. I cut out because I thought she would have it better without me around, with no one for him to target. I never guessed...I should have known..." A shudder ran across his shoulders.

She reached across to him, but pulled back when the kitchen door opened and Steve appeared. He stopped short. "Didn't know anyone was up. I can come back later."

"No, it's okay." Meagan took in a deep breath and gestured to her bowl. "Want some mac and cheese?"

He shook his head but smiled a little. "Did Cole make that?"

"Meagan made it for me," Cole said.

"That's a switch."

Meagan looked at Cole. He had his attention back on his computer. Emotions he probably did not want to feel played across his features. "I was telling her about Sadie," he said, his voice gruff, his bearing showing military control again. "Just got to the leaving home part."

"Cole spent two tours of duty writing her letters," Steve said to Meagan. "After a few years, she stopped writing back." He lowered his voice. "Broke him up pretty bad when he found out what happened."

Cole stood. "I'm going to the bathroom. Fill her in on that part while I'm gone, will you?" He made an abrupt departure.

Steve took his chair. "I got back to the U.S. while Cole was still recovering from the bomb blast." He ate a few spoonfuls of the food in Cole's bowl. "He was out of it for a long time, so I was the one who took the call when it came."

"About Sadie?" Meagan was not as concerned about hearing that part of the story as she was about the man who could not bear to tell it. "She was on drugs by then?"

Steve nodded and took another bite. "From what they told us, it—"

"Who are they?"

"The same people Cole works for now. Sadie's dad got her started doing drugs with him, then he started selling. He got behind on payments with the wrong people and needed fast money, so one night when Sadie had a slumber party with some friends, he drugged them all and took some pictures. After that, he would force her to plan sleepovers and repeat the process. He kept it up until people got suspicious, and then he just focused on Sadie, keeping her high so she didn't know much of what was going on. He got enough hits online that he caught the attention of the internet task force. He had gotten real cocky by then and bragged online about his 'business' success. One night an officer who posed as a john hooked up to come visit Sadie at her dad's place, and they busted the dad and got Sadie out. They found a pile of drugs and camera equipment, enough to put him away for a while, but because Sadie was incapacitated at that point, there was nobody to testify against him. He got out on a legal loophole right before Cole got released from the hospital."

Meagan's whole body felt wired tight. "What did Cole do?"

Steve stared down at the bowl much as Cole had earlier. "He was in no shape to do much of anything yet, but he came back to Gainesville, put Sadie in a secret recovery facility before her dad could find her again, and went on a rampage looking for the man. He worked the streets and I'll be honest, I was afraid what he'd do if he found the guy." He ate three more bites, scraping the last of the sauce from the bowl with the spoon. "After two months of that, the task force recruited him. Said he'd learned more in those two months about the underground internet trafficking market than they had in a year. He agreed on the terms that he be allowed to use the job to search for his step-father." Steve put the spoon into the bowl and looked at it as if he wondered who had eaten Cole's snack. "That's been his whole life ever since."

The kitchen door opened and Cole appeared, too exact for the timing to have been a coincidence. Steve mumbled an apology for scarfing down his food, set the bowl in the sink, and said goodnight.

Meagan stood and turned to face the man who had suffered as much or more than his sister. The kitchen was lit only by one dim light over the stove, but she could see the pain, unhealed pain, still in Cole's eyes. She picked up her bowl and held it out to him. "Steve was hungrier than he thought. Do you want mine?"

Cole looked down at the bowl. "You made mac and cheese for me," he said.

"Yes." The bowl wasn't warm anymore in her hands. She tried to think of what to say, what would help. Her toes wiggled inside her slippers.

"No one ever made mac and cheese for me before." His voice was a whisper. "I always made it. No one ever made it for me."

She saw the unshed tears in his eyes. Setting the bowl back on the table, she reached out and did what her heart had wanted to do all day. The moment her arms circled his waist, he pulled her against his chest, crushed her to his heart. She cried for him, for the boy forced to become a man far too soon, for the man who suffered still. When she lifted her head and looked up, she saw his own face was wet. She pulled her hands free to wipe his cheeks. He closed his eyes as her fingers swept over the contours of his face. "When this is all over," she said softly. "I will help you find Sadie's father. I will help you catch him."

His arms still around her, he leaned to rest his forehead against hers. "So my sister can be free."

She brought her hands down to settle against his heart. "So *you* can be free."

Wednesday, January 7
8:20 a.m.

Stephanie had just put the car in park when Steve was at her door, jacket open and gun exposed. He opened the door for her, scoping the area with what she used to tease was his eagle-eye vision. She had never seen him act like this on her behalf. "Steve, I'm not the one getting stalked," she said, collecting the bags of food and the cardboard contraption that held four cups of steaming coffee. She juggled the bags, but gave up and said, "Would you pause being Mr. Protective and carry something?"

He stopped viewing the area and seemed to see her for the first time. "Stephanie," he said, as if surprised. She never would understand this man. "Good morning." His gaze traveled over her face and hair. "You look pretty."

She blushed like a pre-teen and felt even more unnerved when he continued to stare. "What are you looking at?"

He cocked his head. "At you."

"What for?" She let a little bitterness creep in. "You haven't looked at me on purpose in a long time."

"That's because I'm an idiot."

This was a day for surprises. They stood with hesitant gazes on one another until Stephanie said, "Weren't you worried somebody was going to shoot us or something?"

Steve came to attention. "Right." He took the coffee carrier and she carried the bags inside. "Breakfast!" he called out.

"Is everybody up?" she asked.

"Baine called at seven this morning wanting a report."

"Nice of him."

Quinn emerged and followed them into the living room. Cole was already there in a recliner, a Bible open on his lap. "Where's Meagan?" Steve asked.

Cole set the Bible aside with a half-smile. "You're the FBI. Aren't you supposed to know?"

"I'm coming!" Footsteps pattered down the stairs and just as Meagan came into view the doorbell to the front door rang inches from where she stood. She shrieked. Stephanie felt Steve's arm snake around her waist and move her behind him. He pulled out his gun and Quinn and Cole followed suit.

"Meagan," Cole said low. "Come stand behind me."

She stood frozen in place, her eyes huge.

"Meagan," he repeated. "Walk. Now."

She followed instructions and positioned herself behind Cole's wide shoulders, her hands curling around the arm he stretched out in front of her torso.

"Hi," Stephanie whispered to her as Quinn made his way toward the door. "Didn't mention it before, but I'm Steve's wife."

Meagan's eyes never left the door, but she nodded. "Nice to see you again."

"I brought breakfast."

Quinn looked through the peephole in the door. Steve shifted to peer around the bay window's heavy curtain. "Man in uniform," Steve said. "FedEx truck. Package in hand."

"Who's there?" Quinn called out.

"I've got a package for a Meagan Winston," the man said. "I need a signature."

"Oh, that's my CD," Meagan said. She moved to go around Cole but he held her back.

Quinn opened the door a crack. He held out his hand for the small envelope. "I'll get it signed for you." He closed the door and brought a clipboard and pen to Meagan. "Just sign this. Don't open the package." He carried the signed paper back and opened the door enough to return the clipboard and pen to the man. The FedEx employee glanced inside and his eyes went wide at the gun in Cole's hand, then his gaze traveled up to Cole's face.

"Say, aren't you the guy in the paper this morning?" He reached to his back pocket but came up empty. "I've got one in the van. You saved your battalion from a woman suicide bomber. That was really—"

"Thanks," Quinn said and closed the door with an abrupt thud. Steve snatched the envelope from Meagan's hands.

"Hey! That's mine."

"It could be from Lucias. A trap of some sort." Steve disappeared with the envelope.

"He's probably gone to test it for arsenic or something," Stephanie said with a shrug. "Sorry. He tends to overreact."

"I do not!" Steve yelled from the kitchen. "I'm just getting a pair of scissors to cut this open."

She grinned at Meagan. "So like I was saying, I brought breakfast, and coffee."

Cole loosened his tense posture and pointed his gun at the floor. "Steve overreacted."

Meagan giggled and Stephanie groaned. "Of all the things to drop. I should have had him carry the bag of biscuits. At least we could have salvaged those." She picked up the Styrofoam cups and tried to stack them back in the container. Two had broken open and coffee puddled on the floor. "I'm so sorry, Meagan."

"Don't be." Meagan pulled napkins from one of the bags and mopped up the dark liquid. "This carpet is shag from forty years ago. I'd love to replace it."

"If Steve stays much longer, you'll probably have to."

"I heard that." Steve returned to the living room, CD in hand. "Is this the one you ordered?"

Meagan looked at the Hayes family photo on the sleeve. "Yes."

"I'm going to test it just to make sure. If Lucias somehow hacked into your internet account, he might have discovered your order. This could have a secret message on it, or some kind of drug that affects you if you touch it."

Stephanie watched with the others as Steve put the CD into the player near the coffee table. Southern Gospel music poured out and Cole smiled. "It's their new one. I really need to order that soon."

"Are we in the clear?" Meagan asked. She pushed the stop button and retrieved the CD. "I'll take this upstairs. Stephanie, make yourself at home. And Steve," she said, pausing at the bottom of the stairs, "if you get bored later and want to scare us all to death again, you can go get my mail out of the mailbox and test it for drugs or teeny explosives."

Steve took one of the non-broken cups of coffee from Stephanie. "Ha ha."

Meagan smiled. "I won't order anything else while you're here," she said. "I promise."

"That might be wise," Stephanie quipped, "for the sake of your carpet." Steve finished the first cup of coffee and reached for another, but Stephanie held it back. "These are for the other guys."

"I need it more."

"That's your problem."

Steve growled. "A guy can't get any respect around here."

Meagan's laughter rang down from the stairs. "That sounds like something Pops would say."

Stephanie looked around and felt a surprising ache. Steve was smiling. He laughed with the guys, with her. They acted like friends. Like family. Had her prayers mattered to God after all?

The good feeling dissolved when Steve's smile fell. He looked at her, sober again, and said, "If you've got the time, I need to tell you something." His gaze included Cole and Quinn. "All of you. Grab a biscuit. This may take a while, and by the end of it you might need an extra cup of coffee, too."

59

Wednesday, January 7
3:20 p.m.

Meagan opened the window, alerting Cole to her presence with a wave so he didn't fall off the ladder. "Are you okay?"

"Sure." He had both arms extended, using an old broom to shovel leaves out of the gutter that ran to a peak above Meagan's bedroom window. "This is an easy job. Fixing the loose shingles on the roof, now that will be tough."

"I mean about Steve." She saw his face shutter closed. She leaned onto the windowsill and put her head outside. The ladder balanced against the siding about an arm's length away. "It had to be hard to hear that all this time he thought you had given away secrets to the enemy."

He did not look at her. "I'm not sure if that was harder, or hearing that he might be the one who did."

She shivered but did not think it was due to the cool afternoon air. "What will happen to him now?"

"He's safe as far as prosecution," Cole said, knocking another pile of leaves out of the gutter. They fluttered around him to the ground. "For one, he's out of the military. For another, he doesn't actually know if he told her anything. All he knows is that he went to the bar the night before the mission, she got him drunk, and he woke up with a hangover and a tank load of guilt over what might have happened." He attacked a stubborn batch of piled-up pine needles. "The only person who could convict or absolve him is dead. So in that sense, it's over. But some things don't ever end."

Meagan brushed a wayward leaf from her arm. "I hope I'm not gossiping," she said, "but do you think this will hurt his marriage?"

Cole finished the section of gutter and dropped the broom. She waited while he climbed down the ladder and moved it to rest just below her elbows on the open windowsill. When he stepped up to his former position, broom in hand, his face was level with her own. "Steve's marriage has been hurting ever since he started drinking heavily. Since that might have begun that night, I'd say yes." He reached up and swept the broom across the gutter over her head. Leaves rained down around them. "Drinking destroys people and their relationships." He frowned. "Guilt can do that, too."

"I hope things change for them," Meagan said. "Stephanie seems really nice."

He lowered the broom and looked at her. His frown deepened. "You shouldn't be visible like this, Meagan. I know you're tiny, and Quinn says it's not part of Lucias' MO to shoot from a distance, but I'm not okay with you presenting yourself as a target."

She laughed. "Tiny? I'm five eleven."

"I didn't say short." He smiled and touched her arms where they crossed on the sill. "Put your head back inside and shut the window, please."

She gazed into the surrounding woods and felt fear trickle down her spine. "Only if you come inside, too."

"I have work to do. This house of yours needs some serious attention."

"I know. And I'm grateful. But clean gutters aren't worth your safety."

"You don't need to worry about my safety."

"Then do it for my sense of sanity." She pulled her head in and stood upright, but bent down again to say out the window, "Do you really think I'd be okay sitting inside while you're out here making yourself a very not-tiny target?"

With a chuckle, he let the broom fall to the ground. "I'll come in on one condition."

"Who says you get a—" A shrill noise rang out, startling her. She banged her head against the upper window frame. "Ouch."

Cole pulled his phone from his pocket. "Steve, why are you calling me? You can't be more than thirty feet away." She waited as he listened, chuckled, and whispered to her, "He doesn't want to come out in the cold." She smiled at first, but her nervousness grew as he remained outside talking. And talking. About something inconsequential compared to the danger that she hadn't even thought of until he mentioned it. Now she couldn't think of anything else.

She waved her hands at him to come in. Tapped his arm. Thought about smacking him if that would get his attention. After several minutes passed and he still talked Steve through fixing some piece of equipment inside that wasn't functioning, she blew out a breath and ducked back inside to find the notepad on her bedside table. She wrote a quick note and went back to the window, slamming it against the glass hard enough to catch his eye.

"Tell Steve to tell you to Get Inside Now!"

He grinned. "I'll come take a look at it," he said to Steve. "Be right there." He pocketed his phone and said with a smile, "You should have written code blue or something on there."

"You're not in danger from the person you're standing near."

The smile in his eyes had her toes curling. "I'm not so sure."

She flushed. "And code red is when one of the girls is in danger. There isn't a code for the situation you're in. I guess Kelsey figured if you stood outside in broad daylight when a stalking maniac was on the loose, you'd have the sense to know you were in danger and come in." Her volume had increased with each word. She wanted to shake the stubborn man.

"You should make a code for that," he said, ignoring her growing frustration. "Like green or something."

"Green? Shouldn't it be yellow, like a caution light? Green means go."

He laughed and pointed at the note still in her hand. "What's with the capitals on some of the words?"

"If I tell you, will you get off the ladder?" She touched the note. "We teach our girls if they need to send us a message but can't say things openly, to write a longer note and capitalize the words that matter. I've practiced it so many times with them, it's gotten to be a habit when I write messages. I have to go back through my e-mails and take out the capitals." She frowned and tossed the notepad backwards toward the bed. "But we shouldn't be talking about this right now."

"I'm really not worried, Meagan. Lucias is probably hiding somewhere, making some crazy plan for tomorrow morning."

"Then why'd you scare me back inside?"

"You're different. We're all here to protect you."

"Which you can't do if you get shot, or fall off the ladder for that matter. Please come inside, Cole."

"You didn't hear my condition yet."

She huffed a sigh. "Fine. What's your condition? I'll give you some fudge."

"You have to promise to let me come back when this is all over and fix some things around here."

The shiver running across her this time was one of pleasure. "Why?"

He regarded her with a smile. "Let's just say your house is a nice place to be." He swept his arm toward the yard and shed. "Besides, I need the practice working on a house. When Sadie gets out, I want to get a place for her and me. We never had a real home, and I want her to know some stability. She needs to be able to start over in a place that feels like...like..."

"Like home."

"Yeah." He started down the ladder. Finally. "Like family. A safe place where she can have hope."

She put both hands on the window to close it. "And love."

"Yes," he said. He paused on the ladder and his eyes found hers as she slid the glass shut. She saw his mouth move. "And love."

60

Wednesday, January 7
11:20 p.m.

Meagan woke to the sound of gunshots and her own scream. The insistent pounding sounds came again, from the other side of her bedroom door. *It's just knocking. Get a grip on yourself.* She grabbed her pajama pants from where she'd draped them on the chair and held them against her chest. "Who is it?"

"It's Cole. Are you okay?"

What was Cole Fleming doing outside her room in the middle of the night? She imagined opening the door and being pulled into a kiss and her face flamed. "What do you want?"

"Can I open the door?"

"No!" She threw her bedcover aside and yanked her robe, which had been draped on the chair next to the pants, over her lavender t-shirt. She stepped over the slippers set next to the chair and rushed to the door, opening it and realizing at the exact moment Cole's eyes dropped to her legs that she'd left her pants where they'd fallen from the bed. She shut the door in his surprised face and ran back to the bed, grabbed the pants from the floor and put them on, then rushed back. She flung open the door a second time, re-tying her robe.

"Your phone is ringing downstairs," Cole said without preamble. Now that the door was open Meagan could hear it. "Steve thinks it's Lucias."

What a fool she was. Cole wasn't thinking about romance. He was doing his job. "Oh." She joined him in the hallway but he gestured toward her feet.

"Don't forget your slippers. It's cold on those wooden stairs."

She blushed but went back to slide her feet into the fuzzy bunnies. When she returned to the hallway, Cole looked down and smiled. She should have bought new slippers, and new pajamas, when Kelsey had suggested it. "The phone stopped," she said. "What do we do now?"

It rang again and Steve appeared at the bottom of the stairs. "Can I answer it?"

She was surprised he asked. "Go ahead. I sure don't want to talk to him."

Steve returned to the living room, out of sight, and Meagan rubbed her hands up and down her arms, giving up when she realized her hands were just as cold. "I want to know what he's saying, but I don't want to know." She faced Cole. "I dreamed Steve and Quinn waited at the wrong plane and I ended up flying to India with Lucias three rows behind me in that nasty old wig. We landed and—" The dream had been more vivid than a real memory, the colors sharp, the noises loud. She shivered.

Cole put his hands on her arms and rubbed warmth into them. "What happened when you landed?"

She shook her head and shut her eyes tight. "You don't want to know." She tried to smile. "I want to be like your little sister and ask you to tell me a story to distract me from whatever they're saying downstairs."

His gaze grew tender. He moved to sit on the top step and invited her to join him. He did not pull her into his arms as he'd done with Sadie, but he did put one arm around her shoulders. She decided to stop caring about her pajamas and her slippers, and snuggled against his warmth. Tomorrow she would feel the embarrassment, but tonight she was just too cold and too scared.

"Once upon a time," he said and she smiled. "There was a boy who wanted to grow up to be a brave man. He wanted to stop bad people and rescue the innocent. He wanted to become strong, very strong, so he would be able to protect the people he loved."

Meagan could hear Steve's voice rise in the living room, but did not strain to understand the words. She leaned her head against Cole's shoulder. "Did this boy grow up to be a soldier?"

"He did. And he learned everything he could about fighting, but only because he wanted to fight for those who couldn't fight for themselves."

"That sounds a lot like our verse at Rahab's Rope."

"I'd give anything to work there someday."

She glanced at his face. He looked as surprised as she at his words. "Is that part of the story?"

"No. I wish it was." His eyes were shadowed. "I can't ever become who I want to be until Sadie's father is brought to justice." He looked down at her face and she longed to reach up and trace the thin red line that ran across his cheekbone, covered by a light brown scab. All the smaller scrapes from the car accident had healed. "Your ministry, Meagan," he whispered, "is what I've always wanted to do." His breath touched her face. "To rescue kids like Sadie. To help them live free and stop the pattern of bondage for future generations. I don't want to spend my days in the hole I'm in, pretending to be like the men I want to take down. I want to help get people out of captivity, but I feel captive myself." He gazed at her lips, then his eyes trailed up until they met hers. "What do I—?"

Steve yelled and something in the living room slammed. Cole removed his hand from her shoulder and she sat up just as Steve and Quinn both entered the hallway. "We were so close," Steve said. "Four more seconds and Quinn would have had his location."

"He knew exactly what he was doing," Quinn said. "He had it timed just right."

Meagan didn't want to know but felt she should ask. "So it was Lucias?"

Steve nodded. "He asked to talk to you."

"What did he want?"

Steve's expression was far from pleased. "We recorded it. You should probably come and listen."

61

Wednesday, January 7
11:23 p.m.

Lucias was sick of Steve Campbell and the FBI. "Just let me talk with her!" he shouted. He wiped spit off his phone. They were making him angry and that made his headache worse. "I know she's there. Is she with him?"

"With who?"

Steve Campbell's fake calm voice was like fingernails on a chalkboard. "Don't act stupid," Lucias said. "Cole Fleming has been helping you manipulate my Meagan from the beginning. And now you're holding her prisoner in her own home. I want to talk to her. Make sure you're treating her as well as she deserves."

"She's just fine. But you don't sound fine. You sound upset. Why don't you tell me why—"

"Don't start that psychoanalyzing stuff on me." Lucias kicked the wall. He'd stayed in the junky hotel a second night and the wall now had two holes in it. "You're not going to get me talking so you can trace this call."

He wanted to put his pillow against Steve Campbell's mouth and shut it forever. When Steve said, "You killed Claudia Connors, didn't you?" he pulled his knife out of the bedside drawer and slashed his pillow in three places.

"Stop! Just stop talking!" He stabbed the mattress of the bed again and again. "Give the phone to Meagan right now!" he screamed.

The idiot's voice rose. "Are you planning to kill Meagan, too?"

"Shut up! You can't keep her there forever!" He cut a slit in the sheet and tore it, hoping Steve could hear the sound of his rage unhinged. "I will get her from you. She is mine!"

The alarm on his watch went off. He hung up the phone and threw it against the wall. Shreds of sheets in his hands, he clenched both fists and roared. They did not know who they were dealing with. Tomorrow morning he would show them. He would show them all.

Wednesday, January 7
11:35 p.m.

The recording ended and Steve pushed the stop button on the machine. Meagan dropped to sit on the loveseat in the living room, curling into a fetal position. "He's insane," she whimpered, putting her head on her knees. "I can't—I can't go tomorrow. I just can't." She lifted her head to look at Steve, Quinn, and Cole, who all stood over her, Steve with her phone in his hand, Quinn holding his headphones, and Cole with his hands in his pockets. "He's crazy and obsessed and no matter what you do, he's going to get me."

"We should rethink this, Steve," Cole said. His eyebrows cinched together. "There's got to be another way to catch him."

Steve sat next to her on the loveseat and looked her in the eye. "There is risk involved, I won't deny that," he said. "But we need to get this man behind bars and we need to do it soon. Right now we don't know where he is, and our only hope of drawing him out is you." He stood and looked at Cole before saying to her, "We can't force you to do this, and considering I suspected you as an accomplice, no one would blame you for not wanting to help me. But I am asking you to help. I need your help. I can't think of any other way to bring this man to justice."

"Justice. You picked the right word," she said, certain her tone radiated how pathetic and helpless she felt. She probably looked like Alexia her first days in the safe house when her pimp was still hunting her. "You know I'm going to do it. I just really, really don't want to."

"Thank you, Meagan." Steve put her phone into his jacket pocket. "I'm going to bed. I'll keep your phone with me in case he calls again, but if it's okay with you, I won't come and get you if he does. I think we've all heard enough from him for the night."

She nodded and he left the room, followed by Quinn. Cole put out a hand and helped her to her feet, and she walked with him to the stairs, murmuring, "I keep telling myself that if Lucias gets caught, they can catch the contact overseas who is buying his drugs. If I stop Lucias, I'm helping kids in India."

His grip tightened around her hand. "I keep thinking if I stay up all night, maybe I can come up with a different plan."

"Everything's already in place, and you know it's a good plan. It just also happens to be really frightening." They reached the top of the stairs and stopped outside her door. "You do this kind of thing all the time. It probably isn't scary for you like it is for me."

"You'd be surprised."

She wavered at her door. "I can't get his voice out of my head." She looked up at Cole, allowing the fear to show in her eyes. "I'm scared of going to bed, of what I'll dream."

He touched her face then surprised her by pulling her into his arms. "I'm going to be right there with you tomorrow. I won't leave your side."

His embrace was gentle. She rested against the solid bulk of his chest and listened to the rhythm of his heart. He ran fingers down her temple and behind her ear, as if brushing aside a lock of hair. She realized his hand was no longer bandaged. That same hand traveled to her chin and lifted it, and she felt a new kind of danger, an intoxicating kind. His other arm tightened around her waist and the hand on her chin urged her closer.

She closed her eyes and his lips touched hers with soft warmth. His thumb ran a trail along her jaw line, sending shivers through her. He pulled back just enough to whisper, "You should get some sleep. We're leaving early in the morning."

She nodded. "Goodnight, Cole," she said, but did not move to go.

They stood close for several moments, neither pulling away. Cole finally stepped back, but before he turned and left for the night, he touched his lips to hers once more, and murmured against them, "Goodnight, beautiful Meagan."

62

Thursday, January 8
6:04 a.m.

By six the next morning, Meagan was dressed in her Indian clothing and had changed her hair to brown with a temporary dye that would wash out with a good shampoo. When she joined Steve and Quinn in the living room, both sporting two-day beards, Steve commented, “You must be an early bird.”

“Not usually.” She refrained from telling him dreams had woken her at four and she had decided to forgo more of the same and read her Bible until five instead. “Today’s a big day.”

As she walked from the living room to the kitchen, the doorbell rang. She looked through the peephole. “It’s your wife,” she told Steve.

“Stephanie’s here?” He stood and came to look through the peephole once Meagan stepped aside. “I don’t believe it. And it looks like she has coffee. Bless the woman.” His phone beeped. “Can you let her in? Baine’s calling. I’ll be right back.”

“Happy Birthday, Meagan,” Stephanie said when Meagan opened the door. “Wow, you look exotic. The dark hair suits you.” She held up her bag of biscuits. “Knowing Steve is always leaving at the last minute, I brought breakfast so you could eat on the way.”

“That was thoughtful of you.” Meagan said. “How did you know it was my birthday?”

Stephanie reached down next to her feet and picked up a basket with a balloon tied to it. “This is how.”

Cole came down the stairs, looking fierce and businesslike at the same time in his black suit and tie. Meagan blushed when he sent a secret smile her way. “It’s your birthday?”

She nodded. “And Steve’s making sure it’s a memorable one.”

"So is someone else." Stephanie handed the basket to Meagan. "Who's it from?"

Meagan pulled out the small card and read it with a smile. "It's from the team." She opened the bag set in the center of the basket and pulled out packets of hot chocolate and two blueberry muffins. "Hot chocolate. Just what I needed this cold morning before we go. Should I make some for everyone?"

"Don't make any for Steve," Stephanie said. "He thinks anything without caffeine is worthless sludge." She grinned. "I, on the other hand, appreciate the value of chocolate in any form. I'd love some."

Cole raised his hand. "Me, too." He stuck his head into the living room. "Quinn, want some hot chocolate?"

"Naw, I'll take coffee. Thanks."

Meagan carried the basket into the kitchen and set it on the table. The cheerful balloon floated up to bounce off the light fixture. She had put water on the stove to heat when the kitchen door opened and Steve appeared. "Cole said you got a basket from outside," he said. "You should have left it there and called me to come check it. You don't know for sure that it's from your team."

"But I do," Meagan countered. She held up the note. "This is Brianna's handwriting. And after last night I doubt Lucias was in the mood to go buy a balloon and decorate a basket for me this morning."

"Let her enjoy the gift," Stephanie said, coming into the kitchen with the bag of biscuits. "Stop overreacting."

"I'm not. I just—oh fine." Steve reached for two Styrofoam cups of coffee. "If you all are having hot chocolate, that leaves more coffee for me."

He left and Meagan and Stephanie were alone. "Are you scared?" Stephanie asked. "I know I'd be shaking in my boots. And I don't even have any boots."

"I am," Meagan admitted, pouring hot chocolate mix into three mugs. "But not like I was last night. I know I'm in good hands."

"I don't know. Steve looks pretty beat." Stephanie smiled. "Cole, however, seems extra alert, and particularly focused on you."

She was blushing again, so turned and kept busy pouring hot water into the mugs. "I'm sure the guys will do their best," she said. "But I was talking about God."

"Do you really believe He's watching over you?"

Meagan handed a mug to Stephanie. "I wouldn't have the courage to go today if I didn't know for certain God is coming with me."

"When this has all settled down, I'd like to talk to you more about—"

Steve made his way into the kitchen again. "It's time to go."

Meagan looked at the clock. "Already?" She transferred her and Cole's hot chocolate to travel mugs.

"Quinn and I are going in my car," Steve said. "You and Cole come in his. Remind Cole to park no closer than two but no farther than six spaces away from us. If I can't find parking spots close to the entrance I'll call in for permission to use reserved ones." He gave his wife a peck on the cheek. "Thanks for the coffee. See you when we get back." He headed back to the living room. "Cole, I need you to..."

Stephanie shook her head and laughed. "He's such a hopeless romantic."

Meagan nodded toward Stephanie's mug. "Do you want yours in a travel cup?"

"I'm fine." Stephanie smiled sheepishly. "I actually drank all mine already." She rinsed out the mug and set it in the sink. "I hope today goes well. I don't know what you're planning but Steve said it was a big deal. You're helping him land this case and he's grateful."

"I hope I'm going to help him. We'll see." She took in a deep breath. "I feel all jittery, like I'm going on a first date."

"Well, you've got an hour-plus ride with Cole to the airport, so maybe it is one in a way."

She let the breath out with a laugh. "A very strange, scary, not-fun way." She joined the others in the hallway and handed the mugs to Cole to hold while she put on her coat and gloves.

Stephanie said goodbye and reached for the doorknob, stopping to say with a smile, "Cole, your second date had better be much more fun than this. Just warning you."

She laughed at Meagan's flushed cheeks and disappeared. "What did that mean?" Cole asked her.

Meagan took her mug and gave herself a moment by drinking a sip. Once they were outside, she could pretend her cheeks were red from the cold. “Nothing. Let’s get going.”

63

Thursday, January 8
8:50 a.m.

"Everything about this feels wrong." Cole knew he was scowling, and as much as he wanted to help Meagan be brave, he could not keep the worry from his voice. "This airport is too big. There are thousands of people here."

"We couldn't change the airport," Meagan said with a calm he did not share. "I always fly out of Atlanta. It has to look like all the other trips." She glanced back. "I even packed stuff into my suitcases and carry-on to make sure they were as heavy as usual."

"Changing your hair was a smart idea, too." He reached over to pull one of her suitcases for her. "Want me to carry the bag?"

"I got it." She smiled. "I have a little goodbye present in there for you. Thought it would make it look more like I was really leaving for a while."

He slid an eyebrow up. "I'm curious, but you should save it for another time. We don't want him angry, and he definitely would be if it looked like you thought I was special." She blushed and he grinned. "I'm not saying I would mind if I *was* special..."

They joined other passengers with too much luggage in one of the large elevators, and as the people-packed container rose, Cole took hold of Meagan's hand. It was the first moment since they had left the house that Cole was certain Lucias was not watching them. She did not glance his way, but her fingers gripped tight around his and he found himself praying for God's protection, aware more than ever before that he could not guarantee his own ability to protect her. There were too many variables. Too many dangerous possibilities. They didn't even know what disguise Lucias would be wearing.

The elevator doors spread open and Meagan removed her hand. He wanted to pull it back, close the doors, go back down, get in his green rental car, and drive back to the safety of her house. This plan was too risky. He should have stayed up all night and thought of some other option.

She led the way down the long, wide pathway from one terminal to the next. He stayed as close as possible but they were like fish in a crowded river. People rushed toward them, around them, alongside them. He stayed so focused on keeping her in sight he almost ran into her when she stopped in the middle of the pathway. She pointed to the ladies restroom and handed over her suitcase and carry-on. "Be right back," she said, disappearing before he had an opportunity to panic. He stood next to the entrance, gripping the pulled up handles of her suitcases, staring down every woman who went in after Meagan and earning more than one disturbed glance in return.

The moment she appeared, his lecture started. "You can't run off like that, Meagan. You just put yourself in danger."

She looked embarrassed. "Sorry, but I really needed to go."

He had more to say, but refrained, handing over one suitcase and pulling the second himself. "Do me a favor and run through the plan again."

"We went through it three times on the drive here."

"I know, but my heart is still pounding from you going AWOL and I need the distraction." He also needed to find a bathroom himself, but was not leaving Meagan Winston, not for a second.

"Okay." She switched her suitcase from one hand to the other and walked a little faster. He took a moment to admire her in her bright red outfit with its flowing Indian scarf. She said she'd chosen the ensemble so they'd be able to spot her easily, but Cole didn't think he'd have a hard time spotting her anywhere in any color. "You and I say goodbye at the ticket counter, where you flash your special permission from the FBI to go through security when they ask you what you're doing at the gate. Then you stay there to watch, and tell Steve and Quinn, who are in the tunnel thingy leading to the plane, when you see anyone suspicious. As soon as Lucias is in the tunnel, you stop anyone else from going in."

"Remember, he might not be in one of his usual disguises today. We have to look at everyone with suspicion."

"That's your job," she said, moving aside to keep from breaking up a large family walking together. "My job is to look clueless and happy, and to walk down the tunnel not scared out of my skin that he's probably behind me."

Cole really hated this plan. "And then what?"

She stopped and frowned. "I have to use the restroom again."

"We're almost there. Then what?"

"Then as soon as I step onto the plane, Steve and Quinn will arrest Lucias in the contained environment where other people will not be endangered. They'll contact you, and you'll have already contacted the security people who already know about all this, and they will take Lucias to prison and you and I will go home." She shifted her weight from one foot to the other. "I really need to go to the bathroom, Cole."

He wanted to argue, but he was in the same predicament. "The guys and girls bathrooms aren't close enough together. We need to find one of those family restrooms that's just one stall and I can wait outside for you."

"Do you know where one of those is?"

"No." His body sent urgent messages to his brain. "I promised I would not leave your side."

She touched his chin with a small smile. "I think, all things considered, I'll let that promise slide for a minute or two."

He swept the area with a look. He almost told her to wait there while he went, and then he could watch the door while she took a turn, but she'd be more vulnerable standing in the open pathway than in a restroom stall. "Okay," he said, fighting the urge to do what Sadie used to call the potty dance. "We'll both go, but quickly. No hanging out at the mirror to fix your lipstick or anything. Be back here in thirty seconds. I'll take the suitcases. You take your carry-on. It has your phone in it, right?"

She nodded, handed her other suitcase over, and rushed away. As he made a beeline for the men's room, his phone rang. He let the call go. Once he was back in the main walkway between terminals, watching impatiently for Meagan to appear, he checked his missed call. Steve must be wondering why they were four minutes behind schedule. He returned the call and Steve's words turned his veins to ice. He dropped both suitcases and ran across to the ladies room, jostling against several people but not noticing. "Meagan!" he yelled. "Meagan, if you don't come out right now, I'm coming in there!"

He waited four seconds for her to respond, ignoring the stares and points, his angst increasing as women exited the restroom and fled away from him. Were they coming out because of his threat to come in, or for a more frightening reason?

"Meagan, are you in there?"

"I'm here."

He released a harried breath, but her next words filled him with terror.

"With Lucias."

64

Thursday, January 8
9:04 a.m.

Steve broke into at a run so abruptly, he almost dropped his phone. "Quinn, come on!" he yelled behind him. By the time Quinn caught up, Steve had called security and put them on high alert.

"What is it?" Quinn asked.

Steve had to shout to be heard as they dodged the hundreds of people coming and going through the terminals. "Stephanie called me."

"I know," Quinn said, "but—"

"She drank some of that hot chocolate that came in the basket this morning."

"Yeah. So did Cole and Meagan." Quinn ran to push the elevator button before the door closed but Steve grabbed his arm and directed him toward the stairs. They took them down two and three at a time.

"Stephanie said she's been going to the bathroom non-stop for the past fifteen minutes."

They barely made it onto the shuttle and Steve grabbed one of the poles and bent over to catch his breath. "I called Cole and he'd just been in the bathroom, too."

Quinn wiped his forehead with his jacket sleeve. "And Meagan?"

Steve felt his stomach tighten into a knot of anxiety. "That hot chocolate was for her. We can assume it was to get her into a bathroom right about now."

"Did Cole give their location?"

"No. I've got security meeting us out front. We need to have eyes on every exit from the airport."

"There's no way—"

The shuttle doors opened and Steve announced, "Stand back! FBI." He barreled through the waiting crowd and only checked back once to see if Quinn made it through behind him. They ran through baggage claim and to the nearest exit door leading to the duel-level parking deck. Two security guards met them on the sidewalk and Steve showed his badge. "Did you see them?" He had e-mailed digital photos of Meagan, Cole, and Lucias in his multiple disguises to the entire security team that morning.

The men shook their heads and radioed to others along the line of exit doors. "Nothing here," one said. "I'll check with the guards in the North Terminal."

"There's no way," Quinn repeated. "This is Atlanta. Do you know how many exits there are in this airport?"

He looked to the left and right. The airport, and its exits, ran farther in both directions than he could see. "Look at all those cars, Quinn. Thousands of them." Steve ran a hand through his hair. "If he gets her out of the airport, we'll never find them."

Thursday, January 8
9:06 a.m.

Meagan gripped the bathroom counter so tightly she lost all feeling in her hands. In the mirror, behind her and offset to the left, stood Lucias Moore. His wig was a dark shade of red and hung down in a bob to his shoulders. A hat with a dotted veil hid part of his face. His dress was not a muumuu, but still hung large and bulky on his small frame. Meagan thought of Brianna's comment that no old lady had legs that hairy, and she wanted to let loose a hysterical, panic-stricken laugh. She'd run for her life if he didn't have a weapon holding her still. Not a gun. Not a knife. Security would not have let those dangerous items through. But they could not confiscate the weapon of words.

He smiled at her in the mirror. "I know this isn't the perfect moment, Meagan," he said with a soft, high voice that screamed through her. "I promise, once we are away from this place, from all those men planning to trap me, I will make this a birthday you will never forget."

You already accomplished that. She closed her eyes. *God, help me! I don't know what to do.*

"Meagan," he whispered, saying her name again and again until she opened her eyes and looked at him through the mirror. His smile was a clown-like contortion with his pink lipstick and white powdered cheeks. "We'll be together, and everything will be wonderful."

She looked him in the eye. The man. The murderer. "I don't want to go with you."

"They make you say things you don't mean." He reached up and touched her hair. She flinched. Angry fire blazed in his eyes and she forced herself to remain still as his hand ran down her head and across to her shoulder. "That's why we have to leave right now. I'm taking you away from them. You belong with me. Everything will be all right."

She heard a shout. Her name. Lucias's hand on her shoulder clamped hard and he quickly covered her mouth with his other hand to stop her from crying out. Her breathing came in quick gasps that left her lightheaded.

Cole's strong voice, loud and filled with fear, called her name again. "If you don't come out right now, I'm coming in there!"

Lucias held her tight in his grip and turned to several women emerging from the stalls. Two more stood at sinks a few yards away. "If you don't want to die a terrible death," he said with eerie, articulate calm. "You will leave right now. I know it will be hard to go without washing your hands, but I assure you..." He stepped forward, his hand still tight over Meagan's mouth. The women stared as if mesmerized. A toilet flushed and another woman emerged. Her eyes went wide and she gasped. "Being a little dirty is much better than being a bloody heap of torn flesh on this hard tile floor." He stood very still and said, "Go. Now."

They ran. Lucias released his grip. Meagan leaned against the wall and wrapped her arms around herself.

Lucias spoke to her. "You know what you have to do. Go ahead, Meagan. Obey me." He touched her hair again. "The bomb is under his car, waiting for him to chase after you. And don't try to warn him about it. I also have something special set up where his sister lives, in that nice little place where she hides. There's a third at your red-haired friend's house. It's outside, but their house is small, and I've got it on a motion sensor so it won't be wasted. It won't go off until someone opens the front door."

His smile spread wide and revealed lipstick on two of his teeth. He adjusted his wig and hat, took a look in the mirror, and held up a small makeshift device, saying to his reflection, "Everything can be controlled wirelessly these days, Agatha. Just the push of a button, even from so far away, and I can set the motion sensor on one, the ignition trigger on another, or make all of them blow up, just like that."

Cole's voice rang out a third time. "Meagan, are you in there?"

Lucias turned and ran his free hand over and down her head again, like he was petting a cat. "If you don't want them all to die, Meagan, you have to keep me happy."

"I'm here," she called out, her voice emitting her despair. "With Lucias."

65

Thursday, January 8
9:12 a.m.

Cole had not felt such helpless fury since the day he'd found Sadie huddled behind a dumpster, her skinny exposed legs lined with scars from razor blades, her paper-thin arms layered with bruises from heroin addiction. "Meagan, tell Lucias I want to talk with him. Ask him to come out."

Her voice trembled and he switched his gun from his right hand to his left so he could clench his right hand into a fist, ready to break Lucias' nose with a hard punch the moment his face came into view.

"Cole." Her voice came with an echo now that the bathroom was mostly empty. "Answer your phone."

It rang and he holstered his gun but left his jacket open so he could retrieve it at a moment's notice. "Meagan?" he said the second he put the phone to his ear. "Are you okay? Has he hurt you?"

"Listen to me, please," she said. He thought he could hear Lucias breathing in the background and pressed his fist against the wall until he felt physical pain. "You have to do what I say. Don't ask questions. Go at least thirty steps away from the bathroom."

"No. Meagan, I should never have left you in the first place. That hot chocolate this morning; it had something in it. This was all his plan. I'm not moving one foot from—"

"Cole, please." This time there were tears in her voice and he was aware that his throat ached, and his hand, and his shoulder. The worse ache was behind his sternum and to the left. "Please just do it," she pleaded. "Please."

Tense, reluctant, he stepped backwards once, twice, three times, unmindful of the people who had to move out of his way.

"I'm walking, Meagan. I'm going to hang up so I can call Steve and tell him our location."

"No, don't! That's why he's making me call you, so you can't call anyone else. You have to stay on the phone with me. Tell me when you're close to the opposite wall."

He continued stepping backwards, not able to get his body to turn away from the bathroom, from her. Two security guards ran from his left toward the opening that led to the ladies room. Cole watched them try to assess the situation without alarming the crowd.

"Cole," Meagan said. "Are there FBI officers outside the bathroom?"

"They're airport security guards. Two of them. Meagan, if you walk out now, we could—"

"Tell them they have to leave."

"Meagan, I—"

He heard a struggle and a small gasp of pain. "Tell them!"

Cole pulled out his security pass and motioned the guards over. He covered the speaker on his phone with his hand. With low and quiet tones he told them, "We have a hostage situation. The criminal is Lucias Moore. Hostage is—" His throat closed up and he had trouble speaking. "Meagan Winston." He quickly gave the men Steve's number. "Tell him where we are. Tell him—"

She appeared in the doorway and Cole felt like every muscle in his body hardened to stone. Lucias stood behind her. What kind of weapon did he have? How had he gotten it through all the security checkpoints? If Cole charged forward with the two security guards, could they get him down? Not without risking Meagan's life if he held a gun or a knife to her back.

Cole could not see well enough. People filled the gap between them, only a few noticing the security guards. The rest pulled their suitcases or pushed strollers, on their way to or from one of the hundreds of flights that morning. He wouldn't even have a straight path to her if he tried to run Lucias down.

He put the phone back against his ear. "Meagan, what kind of weapon does he have? Is he holding it against your body?"

"Don't try to rescue me, Cole. And don't let the security guards call Steve or anyone else. Tell them."

He turned slowly, hoping one of the guards would have made the call by the time he spoke. The one had his radio to his mouth. The other held out a map of the airport, a finger at their location. *Please say it*, Cole begged internally. *Tell them where we are*. "You have to stop the call," he said, stretching each word. The men looked at him, then at each other, then at Meagan and Lucias in the open bathroom entrance. The man with the radio clicked a button and put it away. Cole turned his body and said through his teeth, "Do they know where we are?"

He shook his head to the negative and Cole turned back to Meagan, his eyes stinging. "Tell me what to do, Meagan. What does he want? I'll get it for him."

"He wants me."

Confusion flooded Cole when she stepped away from Lucias and walked toward him. Was Lucias letting her go? Behind her, he saw that Lucias had no weapon of any kind in his hand. His confident smile at Cole raised the hairs on Cole's neck. If he didn't have a weapon, the security guards could tackle him and Cole could pull Meagan safely away.

He had thought of four possible scenarios, all with good endings, by the time she was close enough to speak to him without raising her voice. "Give me your phone, Cole," she said. Tear marks ran down her cheeks and Cole wanted desperately to pull her into his arms and run. He shook his head and reached for her hand. She pulled away. He glanced and saw Lucias, in his off-kilter red wig and veiled hat. Lucias clenched his fists and stomped his foot. His eyes were full of hate, but Cole could not have cared less. He reached for Meagan's hand again and would not let go. "Come stand behind me, Meagan. We'll send the guards to take him down. Even if he runs, we'll alert the entire security personnel team and have guards at every exit and every—"

"Cole, stop," she said. "Let go of my hand."

"No. I'm getting you out of here."

"You can't." New tears fell and the ache in his chest turned into a deep, sharp stab. "Cole, please listen to me. His weapon isn't here. He's got a remote. One is in his hands, but he has another one somewhere else. They're all already set. Even if you could capture him before he pushed the button, he's the only one who can deactivate the timers and the motion sensors. Don't you see?"

"No, Meagan, I don't. What are already set?"

"The bombs."

Bombs. He felt it, the flashback wanting to come, and forced his lungs to breathe, to not allow the memory or the fear override his ability to think. He had to be able to think right now. Meagan needed him. "What kind of bombs and where are they set?"

"He won't let me tell you, but Cole, you have to trust me that too many lives are at stake. Lives of people we love." Her eyes were speaking but he could not read the message. Who could she mean? The list of people he loved was very short. He felt the blood drain from his face. She saw and nodded. Her tears ran freely and she did not wipe them away. "We have to do everything he says," she whispered. "It's the only way. Maybe after he takes me away, maybe if he gets bored with me, he'll let me go."

He could see she did not believe that any more than he did. He looked at Lucias, who leaned casually against the far wall, knowing they all were puppets in his new game. "Meagan, I can't let you go with him. I can't."

"You have to." She reached up and touched his cheek. "I would never be able to live with myself if other people's lives were lost to save mine. Don't you understand?"

He did, but hated it with every tightened muscle he had. "Meagan..." There was nothing left to be said, and yet everything to say. "Meagan," he said again, his voice husky and raw. How could he let her go?

She took his phone from his hand, then held her hand out for the security guards' radios. They looked to Cole and he had to nod his head. They gave up their equipment and Meagan turned to Cole again. "Set your watch for five minutes." He did. "You have to promise you will wait right here until those five minutes are up. You can't contact Steve or anyone else. He says he'll know if you borrow someone's phone." She wiped at her eyes with her arm, her hands full with the radios and both of their phones. "I doubt he's telling the truth, but we can't risk it. Promise me?"

Saying those two words was the hardest thing he had ever had to do. "I promise."

Lucias called her name and she shut her eyes tight. “Pray for me,” she whispered. She turned without opening them, but then looked back for a fleeting moment.

He could not fight the pain. Her eyes said goodbye.

66

Thursday, January 8
9:18 a.m.

Steve paced on the sidewalk, ignoring arriving passengers unloading baggage from their trunks and casting irritated glances at him. A man walked his way with a contained gait that brought Steve rushing to his side. "You know something."

The man nodded. He was not in a security uniform, but the way the guards nearby came alert at his presence, Steve guessed him to be top-level staff. "We've had a situation reported by several women who were in a bathroom when a man wearing a wig told them to get out or he'd kill them. The man had his hand on a woman's mouth. The woman was described as tall, thin, with short hair. Another report came in about a man in a suit carrying a gun. Same location."

"That's got to be them." Steve gestured Quinn over. "Where are they?"

"The incident took place in Terminal A at the restroom between gates eight and nine. We've called security in that section and have had no response. We're sending three new teams there now."

Quinn joined them. "I've called Cole's number five times. No answer."

"What about Meagan's?"

"The same."

Steve addressed the man again. "Has your team been alerted to the situation?"

"Not yet. We need to be careful. This airport runs over two hundred and fifty thousand people through every day and that's just passengers. The last thing we want is widespread panic, which is what would happen if word of this spreads."

"Evacuate them."

The man shook his head. "That would play into his hands. There'd be no easier way to sneak through than being in the middle of a crowd of thousands of people running for their lives."

"He has a good point." Quinn made another call, waited, then closed his phone. "Still no answer."

Steve paced again. For the first time in his memory, he had no plan. "So what do we do?"

"We wait for the three teams to get to the location and send us a report, then we go from there."

"Wait?" He stopped and stood, but could only maintain the position for four seconds. He turned to pace again. "That's it?"

"You could pray if you're the praying type."

Steve thought about that. "I'm not, but I know someone who is." He swiped his phone and waited for an answer. "Hey, Stephanie. I need you to call Meagan's friend, Kelsey."

Thursday, January 8
9:21 a.m.

Meagan kept her eyes closed and prayed through their shuttle ride from the terminal to the main area that held baggage claim and led to the parking decks. When the doors opened, Lucias nudged her forward. They stepped outside and he put his arm out, bent at the elbow. "Take my arm, Meagan," he said. "I don't want you getting lost." She fought nausea at the idea of touching him but put her arm through his. "See," he said with a smile. "I'm a gentleman."

He led her toward the escalators. Both the up and down were packed with people. They shared a stair and Meagan pretended to trip so she could grasp the moving rail with both hands. At the top he put his arm out again and she knew it was folly to refuse him.

"Um, Lucias?"

"I'm Agatha, sweetie," he said. Then he stopped in the middle of the open way, where people were greeting new arrivals or saying goodbye to departing friends and family. "No, Agatha," he said in a mild voice. "You need to go now. She's with me, not you."

A chill ran down Meagan's spine. She stared, along with a few others, as Lucias yanked off his hat and wig and threw them to the ground. He turned and smiled at her, his light hair flat and damp against his head, an inch of skin at the top of his forehead pale in comparison to the caked-on makeup covering the rest of his face. His lipstick had not worn off, and his appearance there in his bulky dress and cloppy old-lady shoes drew attention. Meagan wanted to pray that people would remember them so when Cole caught up they could tell him where they went, but she knew such a prayer was wrong. At least three lives depended on her not being rescued from the man. *God, help me be brave. You said there was no greater love than to lay down your life for your friends. I don't think he wants to kill me, Lord, but what if he wants...?*

"I'm here, Meagan," Lucias said, seemingly unaware both of the stares of those passing by or the reason for them. "I have been waiting for this day for a very long time. I feel so—" He stopped. "No, this is not the right place. It has never been the right place. We have to go somewhere else. Someplace beautiful and romantic and perfect. You'd like that, wouldn't you?"

She chewed on the inside of her cheek and nodded. Yes, she would like that, but only if it was with Cole. "Lucias," she said with a hesitant touch on his arm. She pointed a few feet away. "I need to go to the bathroom again."

"I'm afraid I can't let you do that."

"You can come with me. I'm not trying to run away." How did one communicate with a madman? "Remember the hot chocolate you sent me this morning? You're the reason I have to go. Remember? The hot chocolate worked. You picked something that worked very well."

His chest puffed out with pride. "I did, didn't I? Okay, we'll go together. Where's Agatha?" He searched around and found the wig and hat on the floor. "Poor Agatha, I mistreat you sometimes, don't I?" He put the wig and hat on and walked with Meagan into the restroom. He stood outside her stall and talked in a high voice about Lucias' sad childhood and his neglectful mother. Meagan finished and washed her hands as he talked of Claudia, how she was not right for Lucias and he—or Agatha—had been worried about him.

"I'm ready," she said.

"I'm not, not just yet."

Meagan could not decide whether to be horrified or disgusted as Lucias proceeded to have an argument with Agatha over who would get to walk her to the car. Lucias won and Agatha's wig and hat ended up in the trash. He jerked two paper towels out of a dispenser, got them wet, and wiped them over his face, removing some of the makeup, smearing the rest. "I didn't think to bring another outfit," he said. "But that's okay, isn't it?" He smiled at her like an enamored boy. "Love goes beyond the way a person looks or what they wear."

Back in the main area, they walked together between baggage claim roundtables. Meagan found her fear growing as they neared the multiple sliding glass doors with red exit signs over them. Lucias chose one to the left side of the building. As they walked through, cold air enveloped them and Lucias shivered. "Agatha should have brought a coat," he said, jumping up and down a few times. "She forgets things. I'll talk with her about that." He looked her over. "You don't have a coat either. That's not smart. You could get sick out in the cold."

"I stuffed it into my suitcase." She looked to the right. Several security guards were in sight. One glanced their way. His eyes went wide and he immediately put his radio to his mouth. "It's back at the terminal."

"Well, we can't go back for it." Lucias grabbed her by the arm, his touch suddenly rough. He must have noticed how the quartet of visible security guards had their eyes trained on them and all four were on their radios now. "We have to go."

Thursday, January 8
9:23 a.m.

Cole's watched beeped, ending the longest five minutes of his life. He took off at a dead run, not caring if the security guards were with him or not. The first airport boarding desk he saw, he ran to it, flashed his pass, and asked to use their phone. After a quick call to Steve, not even giving him time to respond, he tossed the phone back at the stewardess and sprinted for the stairs that led to the shuttle. Lucias could take any of the hundreds of route possibilities, but Cole could not waste time theorizing. He endured the torture of standing still on the shuttle from the terminal to the baggage claim area, then yelled for people to move aside as he tore up the stairs. Hundreds of people milled in the main area. He saw a security guard near the bathroom several yards away. Unwilling to wait the seconds it would take to run the distance, he shouted, "Did you see a man in a red wig?"

The security guard shook his head but a woman sitting on a bench beside the restroom nodded. He rushed to her side and dropped to his knees in front of her. "Was he with a tall woman carrying a red bag?"

"Yes. I noticed him because he threw his wig on the floor. I've been waiting for my granddaughter to arrive, you see. He looked ridiculous in that dress. I think you should arrest him."

"I agree." Cole got to his feet. "Which way did he go?"

She pointed toward the South Baggage Claim area and he called back his thanks as he ran, dodging people, scanning the area for Lucias or Meagan. He saw neither, but he did see Steve, pacing outside the middle exit doors. Cole was breathing heavily by the time he got through the doors to Steve's side. Quinn was with him, and multiple security guards. "Have you seen them?"

"Would I be standing here if I had?" Steve asked. "Tell me what you know."

Cole had no interest in talking. "Where would he take her? Where would he have parked?"

A call came over a security guard's radio. Cole's hope flamed to life as all five security guards received calls and reached for their radios, too. The first one listened and told Cole, "We've got a sighting. They're outside the airport." He looked around Cole's shoulders and pointed. "There."

Cole turned and would have run but Steve grabbed him and held him back. "We have to be smart about this. Stop thinking like a man in love and think like a soldier."

He didn't want to think like a soldier. He didn't want to think at all. Or talk. Or make a plan. All those things took time, time Meagan might not have. "They're across the street," Cole said, his jaw tight. In a few more steps, they'd be in the parking garage. "Talk fast."

67

Thursday, January 8
9:31 a.m.

Lucias and Meagan crossed the lanes for arriving cars and took the stairs down to the underground section of the hourly parking deck. Meagan felt the tears threaten again when Cole's mint-green car came into view, parked across an aisle and five spaces diagonal to Steve's. Lucias led them right to Cole's vehicle. "If he hadn't been so distracted by you, he would have seen me following him this morning."

It had not even occurred to her. She turned and looked for his black sedan. "Where is your car?"

He pointed two aisles over. "Right there. But before we go, I want to show you something." He got on all fours next to the car, his dress pulling up to reveal very white legs. "Come down and see," he said. She knelt and bent over and her heart beat hard. He had not been lying, not about this bomb at least.

"Pretty, isn't it? People say that money can't buy happiness." He stood and looked down on her. "But it can buy the things that will make you happy." He held out both hands and she forced herself not to cringe as she took them and rose. "And today," he said, looking deeply into her eyes, "it's going to make me very happy to watch Cole Fleming die."

She covered her mouth with both hands to stifle her cry. "But I came with you! I did what you said."

Anger hardened his gaze. "I told you not to care about him. He just makes problems for us. He needs to go."

God, help me. Help me think of something, please!

"Wait!" she said. "I—I had a present for him. Can I—can I leave it in his car?"

"Why would you do that? He's going to blow to pieces. Why give him a present?"

"Well..." She tried to make her mouth move into a smile. Fake as it was, it seemed to please him. "If he dies and I didn't get to say goodbye, I might miss him. But if you let me leave a present and a note saying goodbye, then it will be better. You want me to say goodbye to him forever, right?"

He adjusted his dress and thought for a moment. "Okay. But I get to read your note before you put it in the car."

Her hands shook as she opened her carry-on. She fumbled and dropped several items before finding the CD. The Hayes family smiled from the photo and Meagan begged God to use them to save Cole's life. Tearing out a paper from her small notebook, she wrote with quick, sloppy handwriting. She had to get this done fast. Cole's five minutes were up and he would be coming. If he caught up with them, God only knew what terrible things would happen.

When she had packed the night before, she had taken most of the items off the small desk in her room and thrown them in to fill her bag. Now thankful for what last night was a random choice, she retrieved a roll of tape and used some to secure the note to the CD. "It's ready."

"Let me read it." He took the CD from her and read out loud. "Dear Cole, I have to Go Right Now. Lucias wants me to Run Away with him. Goodbye forever. Meagan." He grinned at her, then read the bottom. "P.S. I like your Green car, but I think Yellow would be better."

Her heart pounded wildly. Would he notice the capital letters? Would Cole remember? Would Cole understand that the green and yellow were both the colors they'd talked about in their new code about being in danger right where he was?

God, please...

"This isn't a romantic note at all," Lucias said. He handed the CD back to her and she gripped it tight. "I like it for him, but I hope you write better ones to me. I can teach you wonderful things to say, like how my heart is yours for all time and eternity, and how—" His eyebrows narrowed and he frowned. "Agatha reminded me we need to go. Throw the present in the car and let's leave."

She pulled on the door handle and wanted to sob. "It's locked."

"Oh well, you can leave it on the ground, or on the roof of the car, or just throw it in the trash. It won't matter anyway."

He tugged on her arm, but she stopped him. "I have an idea." She pulled the tape back out of her bag, and taped the CD to the driver's side window with the note visible. She was sectioning off a second piece of tape when she heard a shout. Lucias dragged her away.

God, please let it stay and not fall to the ground!

The shout came from above, and as they ran toward Lucias' car, she looked up to see security guards swarming the area. Cole came into view, his eyes trained on her as he raced down the stairs. Steve and Quinn followed.

Lucias jerked her arm and pain shot through her shoulder. They reached his car and he unlocked the doors. "Get in," he ordered. "Now!"

He opened the passenger door and pushed her to get inside, but she turned to look one more time. Cole reached the bottom of the stairs. *Run to Steve's car,* she wanted to scream. *Don't go to yours!*

He made a beeline for the green car and she did scream then. Cole gave her one look, glared a challenge to Lucias next to her, and pushed the button on his remote to unlock the doors. He opened the door and started to get in.

Lucias had stopped pushing her. "Just turn the key, Cole," he whispered beside her. "That's all it will take."

Meagan screamed Cole's name.

Cole paused and noticed the CD taped to the window. He reached around the door to pull it off. Steve and Quinn had caught up and stood near the trunk of the car. Security guards spread into a wide circle around their section of the lot.

"I should go, I know," Lucias said. Meagan looked over and could see he was not speaking to her. "But I just can't resist. It's my first bomb killing. I have to watch it."

She was sobbing out loud, clinging to the edge of the door to stay standing. Cole read the note, looked at her, then yelled at Steve and Quinn, "Run!"

"No!" Lucias shouted. His skin instantly mottled red and the veins of his neck stood out. He grabbed Meagan by the face and smashed her head against the car. "You tricked me!" he shrieked.

Needles of agony shot through the back of her skull. Meagan fought to stay conscious. She opened her eyes and watched in horror, unable to get her arms to move to stop him, as Lucias lifted his remote device and pushed a button. No one heard her scream then. Cole's car exploded in a deafening blast. The windows shattered and fire belched out. Where was Cole? Meagan strained to see but her vision blurred. Where was he? Was he alive?

"Get in!" She felt Lucias' hands on her, shoving her into the passenger seat. "You're just like the rest!" he shouted. "I'm finished with you!"

68

Thursday, January 8
9:31 a.m.

Cole's ears rang so loudly he barely heard Lucias shouting. A car door slammed and he groaned. Another slammed and he rolled onto his stomach and told his limbs to work, to push him up. He had to stop at a kneeling position until the wave of dizziness passed. He looked at his car, now a burning shell. Meagan had saved his life.

He stood and staggered two steps to where Steve lay sprawled on the pavement, injured but conscious. Quinn rose to his feet half a parking space beyond Steve, the least damaged of the three. Steve pulled keys and his phone from his pocket and threw them both to Cole. "My car. Go."

Cole did not wait for clarification. He dashed, limping, for Steve's car. He heard the squeal of tires and Quinn's shout of warning behind him. He dove to the side and rolled, dropping Steve's phone. The black sedan swerved toward him, clipping the bumper of the car at his left shoulder. He slid to the right as bits of metal scattered on the asphalt. Lucias sped away and Cole jumped to his feet. He grabbed the phone from the middle of the road and ran across the two spaces left to Steve's car. He used Steve's key remote to unlock the car as he ran. He wrenched open the door, threw himself inside, and jammed the key in the ignition. With a quick check behind, he backed out, then burned rubber after the sedan, his hand on the horn to ward off the car coming toward the lane from the side aisles. The side car stopped and Cole put his foot to the floor.

The black sedan shot toward the ticket booths. If Lucias got through them and down the access road to I-85, Cole knew he would never be able to stay on them. Not in twelve-lane traffic. He would lose her, and Cole had no hope that Lucias' anger would cool on the drive.

No one had ever found Claudia's body. Wherever Lucias took Claudia, that was Cole's guess where he would take Meagan. To kill her.

He found his own phone number on Steve's speed dial and called it, causing a slight waver in Lucias' driving. Meagan had his phone. Lucias was probably searching for it, or yelling at her to get it out.

The parking ticket booths stood like sentinels in a line to their left, raising and lowering their striped metal arms to detain or allow cars through to the access road. The three closest had a line of cars two deep. The farthest one had one car moving up to the window to pay. The second farthest had just emptied.

Cole felt heat surge through him at Lucias' voice when he answered and yelled, "You'll never get her from me! She's mine! Forever!" Lucias drove at full speed toward the empty booth. He swerved sharp to the left to face the opening. Cole saw the man inside the booth open his mouth wide. He pulled the door to the booth open and raced away, his hands out to stop approaching cars from running over him.

"Meagan!" Cole shouted into the phone. He aimed for Lucias' driver's door and hit the gas. "Duck and cover!"

The front hood of Lucias' car was inside the booth area when Cole rammed him. Cole's car hit the backseat on the driver's side and the black sedan lurched, crashing into the next booth. Metal screeched and tore. Cole's air bag inflated and caught his head, sparing him a concussion. He fought it with his hands and tried to open his door. He had to get to Meagan.

As he kicked at the door from the inside, he heard sirens and thanked God for the help. The door finally opened and he fell out, forcing the nausea and dizziness away, faltering to his knees only once before he reached Lucias' totaled car. Steam escaped from the engine and the right back tire had cocked to an unusable angle. He looked in only long enough to see that Lucias had his own face in an air bag. His fists beat the air and Cole could hear him shouting obscenities.

Only Meagan's earlier words about there being other people in danger kept Cole from leaving Lucias right where he sat and rushing to her side. Cole opened the driver's side door and hauled Lucias out by the collar of his dress. He checked to be sure no devices were in his hands and dropped him onto the pavement. "It's a good thing those sirens are getting close," Cole ground out. "You'll be safer in their hands than in mine."

A security car braked next to Steve's mangled vehicle. As soon as guards exited and had their weapons aimed at Lucias, Cole left him and ran around the sedan to the passenger door. He had not heard a sound from her side of the car, and hadn't been able to see past the bag when he dragged Lucias out. "Meagan?" The door was tight and he had to pry it open. "Meagan, can you hear me?"

He looked in and for a moment his heart stopped. Her air bag had released, but she was under it, curled into a ball mostly on the floor underneath the dashboard, her hands over her head. He reached out, terrified he'd touch cold skin and discover he had killed her. "Meagan?" he whispered. She muttered something and his heart started again. He kneeled and pulled her from the car, moving to a sitting position on a concrete slab between the booths and holding her in his lap. She had her head in her hands. "I'm sorry," he said. "I couldn't think of what else to do. If he got you away, I knew he'd kill you. I had to stop him, but I'm so sorry I hurt you."

She shook her head and when she lifted it to look at him, he sucked in a breath. "Oh, Meagan."

"You got me away from him," she said, looking at him through her right eye. Her left was red and swelling shut. "Thank you."

Her head lolled to the side and his fear came back. "We've got to get you to a hospital right away."

She curled up against him and he felt her head shaking no against his neck. "Have to go home first. Have to change."

He pulled back to look at her face. "Meagan, you're hurt. Maybe badly. We need to get you to an emergency room."

"Yes," she said, her words starting to slur. "But have to change first."

"Change what?"

She snuggled against his chest and he thought she'd lost consciousness, but then her soft voice said, "I'm wearing underwear covered in baby chickens that says 'chicks rule.' I can't go to the hospital with..."

Her voice trailed off and through his fear and pain he felt himself smile. He pulled her close and whispered into her hair, "Meagan Winston, I think I'm going to fall in love with you very soon."

69

Thursday, January 8
5:00 p.m.

"He's gone again?" Steve shook his head. "For a guy who said he wouldn't leave your side, he sure disappears a lot."

Meagan pressed both hands to her bruised ribs. "Don't make me laugh. It hurts."

Stephanie followed Steve into the hospital room. "Meagan, I am so, so sorry." She set a bouquet of pink carnations onto the oversized windowsill. "If I hadn't said Steve was overreacting, he would have taken the hot chocolate and none of this would have happened."

Brianna and Kelsey giggled as they fought to fit through the door next, each carrying balloons and individual-sized cartons of ice cream. Kelsey dropped her package of plastic spoons and she and Brianna jostled like bowling pins as she bent to pick them up. Once inside, Brianna sobered. "No, it's my fault," she said, emptying her gifts on the bed over Meagan's feet so she could give her a gentle hug. "I never should have put that fake note in the trash where he could get it. I didn't even think—"

"I was standing right there," Kelsey said after her own hug. She gave a carton of double chocolate to Meagan and handed her a spoon. "I should have picked up on him knocking the trash over. I should have seen—"

Steve backed into a corner, arms crossed and looking disconcerted about being stuffed in a small area with so many teary-eyed women. "Well, I'm not going to say it was my fault, if that's what you're all waiting for."

Meagan smiled. "Stop, all of you, please. I spent the last two hours thinking through all the things I should have done to keep this from happening, but I've decided to just thank God that I'm alive, the bombs at Shady Grove and Kelsey's house got disabled without anyone getting hurt, and Lucias is in jail."

"And will be for twenty to life, if I had my guess," Steve said. He nudged Stephanie to hand him one of the small cartons of ice cream. She murmured something and he added, "She can't possibly eat them all before they melt."

Brianna handed a container of rocky road to Stephanie with a smile. "We brought enough for everyone."

Stephanie passed it back to Steve. "What do you mean, twenty to life?"

"On the way to the prison, the police got a recording of him ranting and screaming. He yelled a lot of things about Meagan and Cole, but then he started talking about his mother and then Claudia. Then they said he started arguing with, like, three people in his head. I think he forgot anyone else was there. They recorded him yelling about killing Claudia and he even said where he'd taken her. We've got a team headed to that area right now. As soon as they find the body, it's over for him."

Meagan dug into her carton with a sigh. "I have to admit I like the idea of not seeing him for an extremely long time."

"Even better, he won't be seeing you. We can open the curtains again."

Meagan's eyes lit up at the man in the doorway. "Pops!"

"I was going to have to live till doomsday just to go get the mail from the mailbox for you. I sure wasn't letting you outside knowing some guy with binoculars could be out in our woods somewhere."

Kelsey arranged the balloons on the wheeled table near the bed. "It just gives me chills to think of him being out there all that time, staring. And following you." She shook her head. "And you were worried about Cole following you two or three times."

As if saying his name brought him to life, Cole Fleming appeared behind Meagan's grandfather in the hallway. Meagan's heart monitor betrayed her joy at seeing him. He'd only been gone a little over an hour. Pops clapped him on the shoulder. "Thanks for going after my girl."

"I wish I could have kept her out of here. If I'd only—"

"No you don't," Meagan said with a wave of her spoon. "We've already gone through that. No more regrets from anybody."

Cole looked over Pop's shoulder and grinned at her. "You're right. Let's have a birthday party instead."

"Is that why all these people are here?" If Steve turned a bit more, he'd look like a child who had been sent to the corner. "Did you invite them? They should have given Meagan a bigger room."

"He didn't need to invite us," Kelsey said, perching on the edge of Meagan's bed with one hip. "We're all here because we love Meagan." She laughed at the look on Steve's face. "Okay, well we don't *all* love her, but we're all glad she's doing so well. And goodness, if you were in the hospital on your birthday, wouldn't you want visitors?"

"Sure would," Meagan's grandfather said, clearing a path to the one chair in the room and falling into it with a huff. "Nothing worth watching on TV in these places."

Meagan looked him over. "You feeling okay, Pops?"

"Nothing wrong with me except I got bored half to death stuck in that hospital under guard when everybody knew I was healthy as an old horse can be. The nurses were starting to think I was in some kind of witness protection program. I told them I was former CIA, used to protect President Carter." He chuckled. "Got a few extra pudding cups out of a few of them before they figured me out."

Meagan's ribs ached from trying not to laugh. "Oh, Pops."

Her grandfather looked at Cole. "Well, son, don't just stand out in the hallway. Bring the food in!"

Cole angled through the door, balancing two large pizzas in one hand, flowers in another. Plastic Wal-Mart bags hung from each arm. Meagan smiled. Her right eye was swollen shut, her left leg was scraped raw, her bruised ribs complained with every breath, and the tips of her fingers were strangely numb. "I'll say one thing," she said as he set the flowers on her lap. "I've never had a more unforgettable birthday."

Thursday, January 8
6:19 p.m.

Kelsey stacked the used ice cream cartons into a pyramid over the empty pizza boxes. Steve tossed plastic spoons across the room, some of them making it into the trash can near the door. One went wayward and hit the entering nurse in the leg.

"Sorry," Steve mumbled.

"This is quite a party," the nurse said, picking up the spoon and the others littering the floor. "I'm glad you had a good time, but our patient needs some rest if she wants to get released this evening."

"This evening?" Meagan sat up, then grasped her ribs. "Ouch. Really?"

"Possibly." The nurse wrapped Meagan's arm with a blood-pressure cuff and mouthed a count. "But not if your numbers stay up like they are now. There are too many people in this room. Your noise is disturbing patients in adjacent rooms who need sleep." She half-smiled at Meagan. "I'm afraid your friends are just too much fun for our facility."

"Out, everybody," Meagan's grandfather said. "I want to get this girl home where she belongs."

Steve and Stephanie said their goodbyes. "I'd offer to take you home," Steve said to Cole, tossing his last spoon in the trash. "But you've destroyed three cars in the past two weeks, including mine. You're not getting within twelve feet of Stephanie's."

"Can't blame you there." Cole grinned. "But you've got to admit, none of them were my fault."

"Tell that to my insurance company."

Cole laughed. "You can get the FBI to call them."

"Speaking of the FBI..." Steve frowned. "There's something I need to tell you."

70

Thursday, January 8
6:22 p.m.

Kelsey and Brianna hugged Meagan one more time and carried the pizza boxes and cartons from the room. Stephanie slipped out after them to talk in the hallway, and the nurse followed, but Steve remained just inside. Pops lowered his chin to rest on his chest. He folded his hands over his belly. "I'll just take a cat nap while you fellows talk."

Meagan couldn't leave the room with the others and it would look pretty obvious if she up and faked a nap right then. She picked at the tape around her IV and then used the tip of her plastic spoon to poke at her numb fingertips.

"We can talk about whatever this is later, if you want," Cole said. Meagan noticed he still had one of the bags from the store draped over his arm. Unopened. She fought curiosity and pulled up her sheets, which had slid down to reveal too much of her unattractive hospital gown. "I brought Meagan's grandfather, so I'm going to stay to drive them both home if she gets released."

"Now works." Steve had his hands in his pockets until Stephanie returned to his side. He pulled his left hand out and put his arm around her. She hesitated, but then leaned against him and rested her palm against his heart. "Want me to tell them?" she asked.

"No. I'm not that much of a coward." He tugged on a strand of her hair, then spoke to Cole. "I wanted you to know I'm going to Washington next week. I've got the name of a guy at the Pentagon. I'm going to tell him what really happened. That I might have been the one to give away our envoy's position."

"But you aren't sure you did."

"I need to make it right." Steve pulled his wife closer and Meagan stopped pretending not to listen. "It's been eating me alive, Cole. I didn't realize how much. I want to be free of it, even if it means a court martial or worse."

Cole's eyes misted over. He put out his hand. "I'm proud of you." They shook hands. "Want me to come with you?"

Steve tossed a nod in Meagan's direction. "You have a good reason to stay. Keep an eye out for Stephanie while I'm gone, will you? Make sure her heating unit doesn't go out or whatever." He and Stephanie started out the door but he stopped to say, "But don't get near her car."

Cole laughed. "Will do." A heavy silence filled the room as Cole closed the door and only the three of them remained. Pops snored softly to the side. Self-conscious of her thin gown and thin sheet and black and blue face and scraped arms, Meagan looked everywhere but at Cole as he approached the side of her bed.

"I'm surprised you and Steve didn't need visits to the hospital yourselves," she said, focusing on her fingernails. Several were broken and they all needed a polish. They matched the rest of her. "And Quinn. Is he okay?"

"We're all fine. Somebody looked us over when we brought you in and gave us bandages and cream and stuff. All our cuts and bruises were superficial, thanks to you."

"I'm so glad you understood the note," she said. Her fingers clenched around the top of the sheet. If the nurse wanted her blood pressure to go down, Cole's car blowing up was the last memory she should be revisiting.

"I'm glad you wrote it." He looked around for a chair but her grandfather was in the only one, so he lowered himself to half-sit on the side of her bed. She shifted to give him more room. "I brought you something," he said. "A thank you present."

"I should be thanking you."

"A birthday present then. I didn't want to give it to you while everybody else was around." He lifted the bag from his arm and handed it to her. "Sorry it's not wrapped. I wanted to get back here before the pizza got cold."

Intrigued, she reached inside and felt something soft. "New bunny slippers?" she joked. When she pulled it out, she knew her face—the part that wasn't black and blue—went red within seconds. "You bought me pajamas?"

"They're all the same color, see?" He held up the different pieces. "The nightgown matches the pants, and the robe goes with them both." With a grin, he pulled a receipt out of his back pocket. "But you can have the receipt if they're the wrong size, or if you want to trade them out for a mis-matched set."

Even her ears were hot. What was she supposed to say?

Pops sat upright, lifted his head, and directed a glare at Cole. "Well, young man, I hope you have good intentions concerning my granddaughter. Buying her nightclothes is, in my opinion, equivalent to a proposal." Meagan wanted to dive under her flimsy sheet. Her grandfather dropped his gaze to the daisy-yellow cotton pants, long yellow t-shirt nightgown covered in bunnies, and yellow fleece robe, and chuckled. "Never mind. I'll get back to my pretend nap. Carry on." He lowered his head and ignored them both.

Cole grinned as Meagan held the fleece robe up to cover her face. "Thanks," she said behind it. "I think."

He laughed and she dared a glance at him just as her nurse opened the door and took brisk steps to her side. "What a cute nightgown," she gushed. "My daughter has one like that, but it has Tweety Birds on it."

Cole's smile was about to hit his ears. "How old is she?"

"Twelve."

His gaze never left Meagan's face. "Bet she looks cute in it."

Meagan ducked behind the robe again, but the nurse made her stick her arm out to check her blood pressure. "Hmm," she said. "Still high. I don't think they'd have let you go home even if all your blood tests had been normal."

"It's his fault," Meagan said, then glanced up. "Wait. You said they won't let me go?"

"Not tonight, I'm afraid. You've got some electrolytes that are up, probably due to the medication. They should be back to normal by the morning, but they want to keep you here one night just to make sure." She packed up her arsenal of equipment and patted Cole's shoulder on her way out. "It was nice of you to bring her something to wear tonight. Now you need to get going so she can get some rest."

Pops stood and stretched. "Sounds like I'll be finishing this nap at home." He patted her arm. "We'll be back for you in the morning, if this young man is willing to drive me over."

"I'm willing." Cole had pocketed the receipt and was pulling the tags off the pants. "Guess you're stuck with these whether you like them or not."

"I like them." She rubbed the soft fleece of the robe. "So I'll see you tomorrow?"

Pops made his way out of the room and Cole stood and leaned over her bed. "Tomorrow. And the next day. And if it's okay with you, every day after that for a long, long time."

Meagan's toes curled under the sheets. She couldn't stop her own smile from corresponding with his. He moved toward her, and just before his lips touched hers, she nodded and whispered, "It's okay with me."

ACKNOWLEDGMENTS

My thanks to Lou Ann Keisler for the enthusiastic response to *The Shadow* way back at the beginning. Your words, "I was terrified from the very first page. I couldn't put this book down! It has it all: two love stories, parallel missions, and justice—mixed with lunatic danger and a drug investigation. I loved *Shadow*!" were a big verbal cheerleader for me. And I loved knowing that the grandpa came through fun and loving, exactly as intended.

Though in heaven now, I have to thank my real-life grandpa, Joe Olachea, for being so much fun I had to make him a book character. Thanks, Grandpa, for all the quotes and made-up songs and wonderful memories! I'm glad you're beyond leg wrappings and sugar checks and all us women bossing you around. =)

To the Rahab's Rope team, my sincere thanks for your support and encouragement from the very beginning idea for this book. I love what you do and hope *The Shadow* will get some more people to know about you and get involved.

Emily Cohen, thanks for being excited about this book and helping me stay connected with information along the process. And thanks for that hair story that got this all started!

Thank you to all my fabulous beta readers. You are so much fun to send books to!

To my agent, Diana Flegal, thank you for your excitement about this book, for giving advice, making it better, pitching it to publishers, and believing it should get out there.

Brian, as always, you know why you're on here.

My thanks to Stephanie Alton and the Blythe Daniel publicity agency for helping get *The Shadow* to readers who would love it.

And lastly, to you readers, who enjoy my books, put reviews on Amazon, and send me encouraging notes. You don't know how much that means to this author when you tell me and others how much you liked what you read. You're the reason I keep writing!

SNEAK PEEK AT
THE RUNAWAY
BOOK TWO IN *THE RAHAB'S ROPE* TRILOGY

Hank grabbed a beer and turned on his computer. He propped his feet up on the table. "Just another day at the office," he said with a grin. The new guys in the business, the ones as young as Hank's Facebook, Instagram and Snapchat profiles claimed Hank was, didn't appreciate how much easier life was thanks to the internet.

Back in the day, he used to have to go to a new city and spend nights roaming the streets to find runaways. It cost money and time, and there was always the risk of being caught. He had never liked hunting outdoors, not even for animals. All that waiting, sometimes for nothing.

Now the hunt was less like a stake-out in a tree stand and more like throwing out a bunch of fishing lures and seeing who would bite. He logged in and looked over his spreadsheet. Last week he'd sent out a message to fifteen hundred girls in Gainesville, Georgia. This week he'd aim higher. Atlanta. It was already a playground for predators, but there were enough vulnerable girls to go around.

Just for fun, he typed up a new message:

I saw ur profile today and want to get to know you. You r beautiful and I am captivated by your smile. I live in a remote area and don't have many friends here. I love to meet people online. Would u write me back? Distance isn't a problem when fate it at work.

"Nice," he said into the empty room. He chugged down some beer and belched. Working the internet was ten times easier than the streets. He'd throw out this little piece of bait without even having to get dressed or brush his teeth. He was getting too old for young runaways to be drawn to him on sight, anyway. Funny how they looked at a guy their father's age as a potential danger, but a good-looking guy their own age as someone to trust.

He should go through the little message and look for errors, but why bother? Kids didn't care about things like that. A mistake or two made him sound more like the seventeen-year-old they would see on his profile picture.

His house smelled like BO. Or maybe it was just him. He'd need to take a shower before he went out to meet a girl he'd groomed in Roswell. She was running away next Tuesday. He'd send her a message and tell her to bring a friend.

By the time he finished typing, three new messages had arrived. He clicked on the first one and chuckled. Flirting with these girls, keeping it light while pushing just a little, was the fun part of the hunt for him. This girl from Gainesville, Bailey, had written back to tell him she was not fooled by his lonely talk and claimed he was probably sending messages to hundreds of girls. But still she'd written him. She hadn't been able to resist.

The ones like Bailey who got high on the risk were amusing, but his favorite where like the girl who had started a conversation with him after his last message to Gainesville. She was young and lonely and real needy. When he wrote, she responded quickly. She told him she was not supposed to be on the internet so their relationship had to stay a secret. He had confided some nonsense about his bad family background, and she'd told him about her father mistreating her and how she was in a special place to help her recover.

He thought that would be the end of it, but when she said she was due to get released in a week, and was afraid of facing life out there on her own, he knew he had hit the jackpot. Perfect. Once exploited, still exploitable.

I'll be there for you, he'd written. *I've got some money saved up. I'm going to come down thee and visit you. You won't be alone.*

She'd resisted at first. Said her brother wouldn't like it. He hadn't written back to that, and the waiting had worked. She wrote again, worried he was angry, afraid he had rejected her.

Yeah, those needy ones were like a drug to him. *I'm coming to Gainesville,* he typed into the computer. *I'll be meeting you soon, Sadie Fleming.*

Sign up for the author newsletter at
www.kimberlyrae.com
to keep updated on the latest releases.

Rahab's
Rope

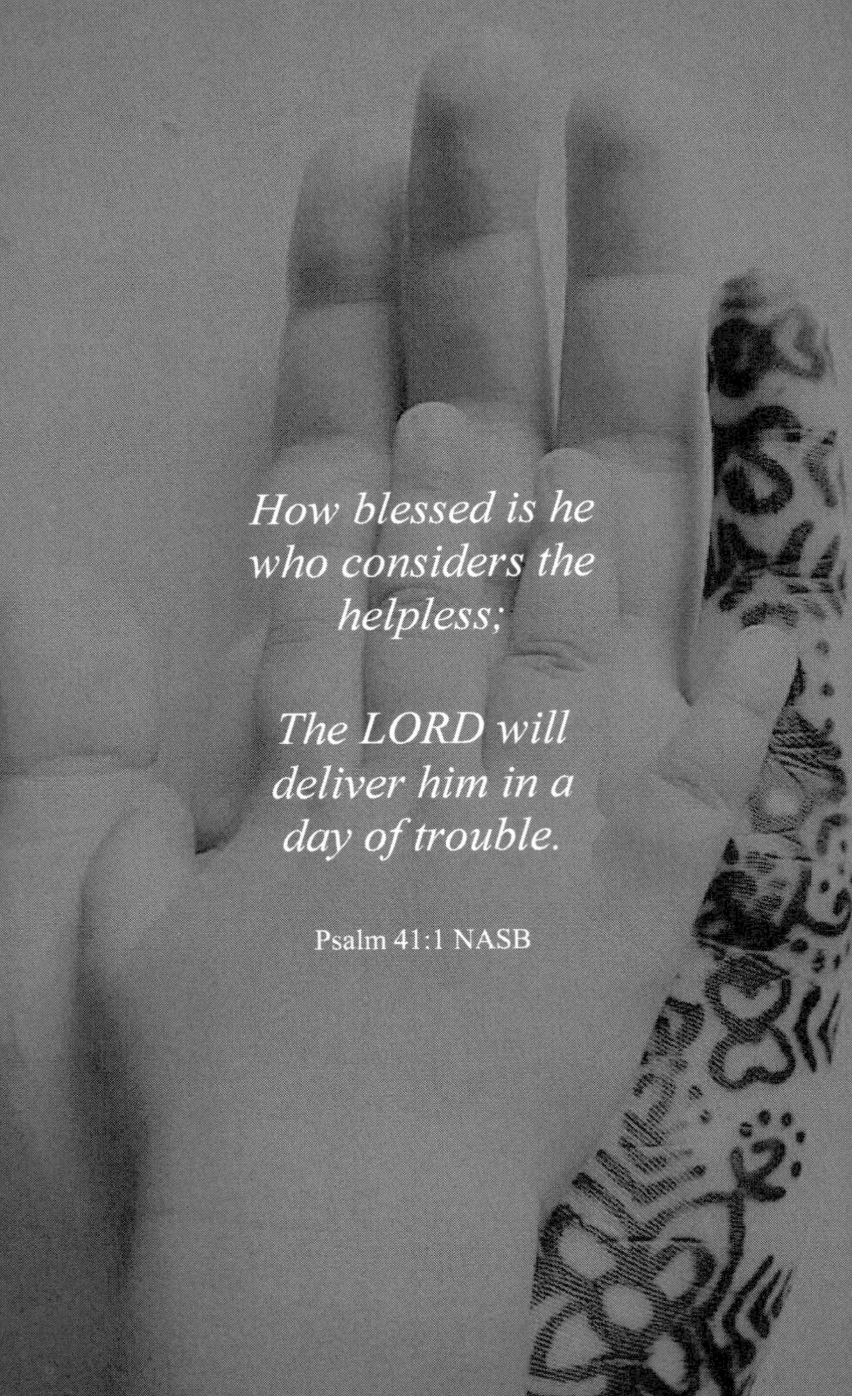
How blessed is he
who considers the
helpless;

The LORD will
deliver him in a
day of trouble.

Psalm 41:1 NASB

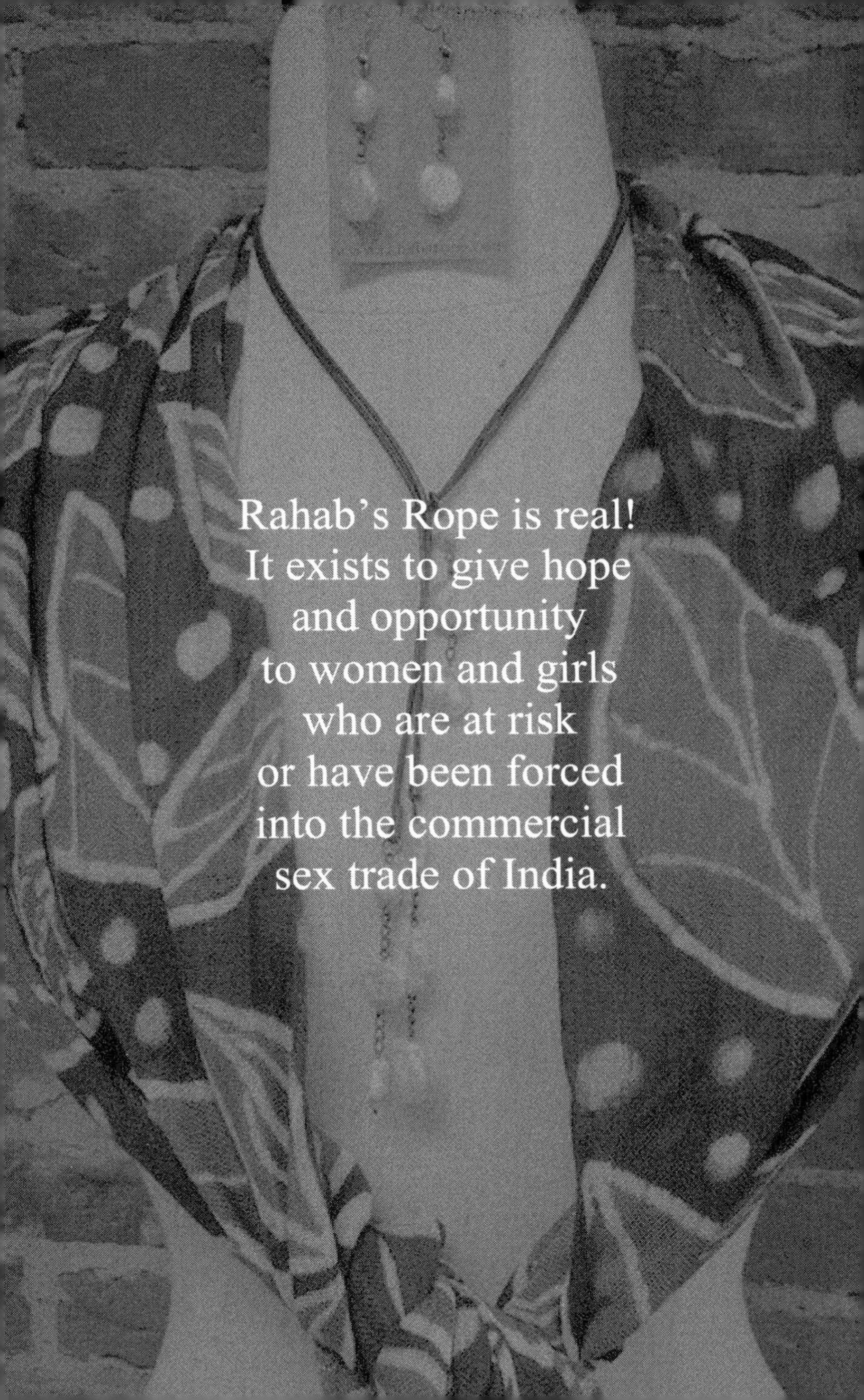
Rahab's Rope is real!
It exists to give hope
and opportunity
to women and girls
who are at risk
or have been forced
into the commercial
sex trade of India.

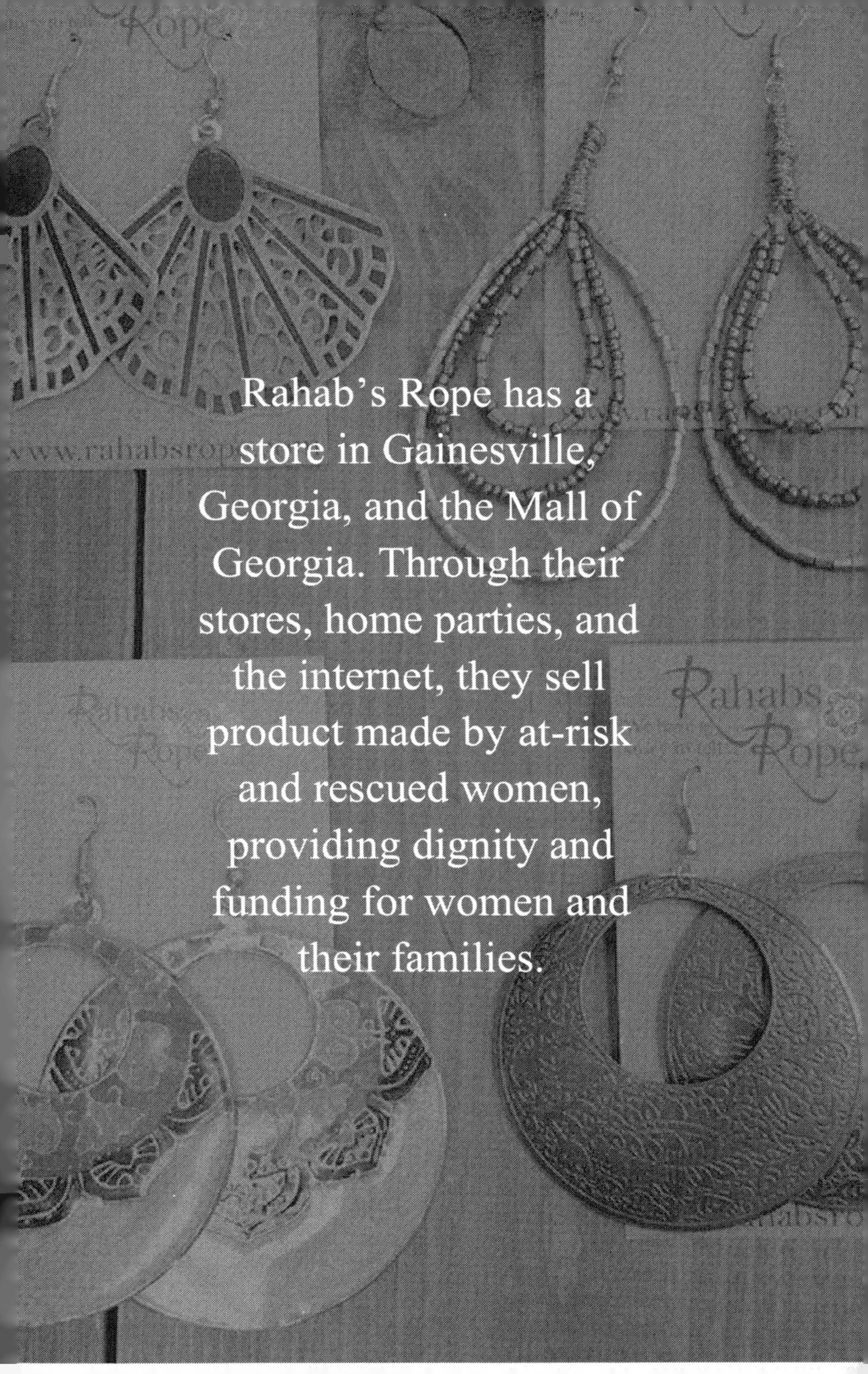

Rahab's Rope has a store in Gainesville, Georgia, and the Mall of Georgia. Through their stores, home parties, and the internet, they sell product made by at-risk and rescued women, providing dignity and funding for women and their families.

You can help!
Go to
www.rahabsrope.com
to shop in their online
store, find out about
overseas opportunities,
or click on
"Host Events"
to learn how you can
host your own
Rahab's Rope party!

Dear children,
let us not love with
words or speech
but with actions and in truth.
I John 3:18 (NIV)

This is the motto of Rahab's Rope-

"love in action"

I can tell you all day long that I care about you and will help you, but until I actually do something, how will you ever know?

Love is a word of action, and we must act for you to know we love you.

This action of love is instilled in our staff and carries over to our volunteers so that the people we serve will know, without any doubt, we care about them and that God cares about them.

We want them to see the truth about themselves and God because we know this Truth will set them free to experience God's lavish love.

-Vicki Moore
Founder, CEO

www.rahabsrope.com

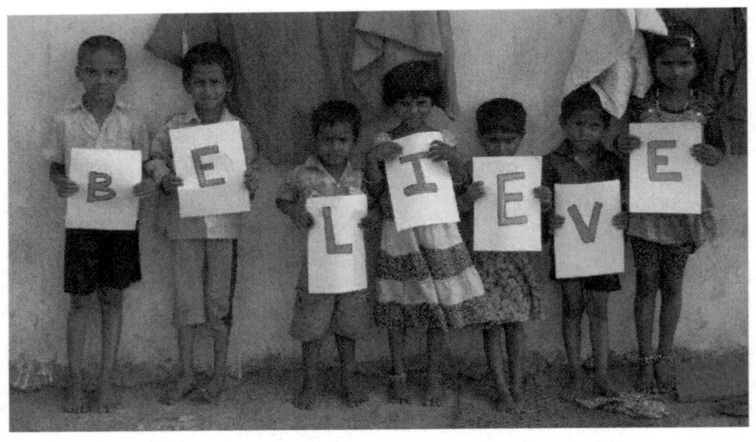

OTHER BOOKS BY KIMBERLY RAE

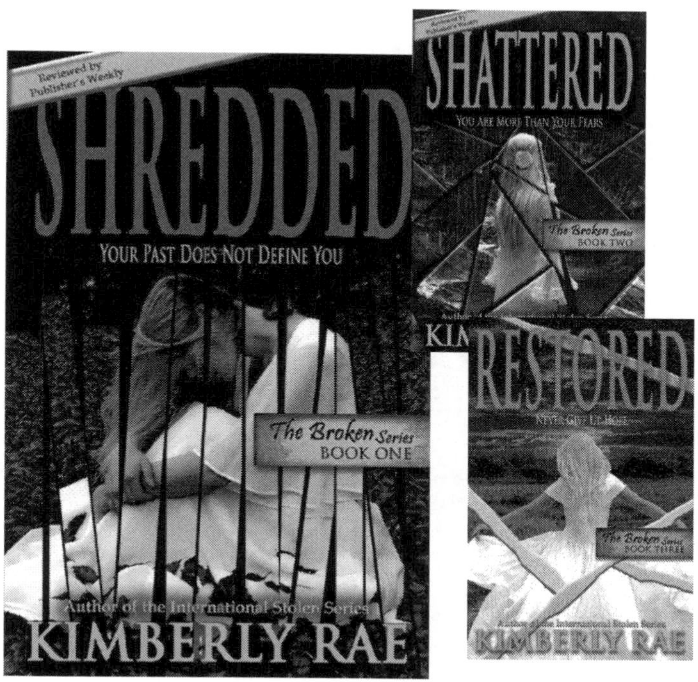

Jean has been called Blue Jean since childhood, but not because of her clothing. She wears nondescript colors and avoids people when she can. Her world is unhappy but predictable, until the new pastor and his handsome brother move into town. A chance encounter brings the town prostitute to church that Sunday, starting a chain reaction that will shake the church to its core.

Will Jean embrace the truth that will set her free, or will fear keep her captive forever?

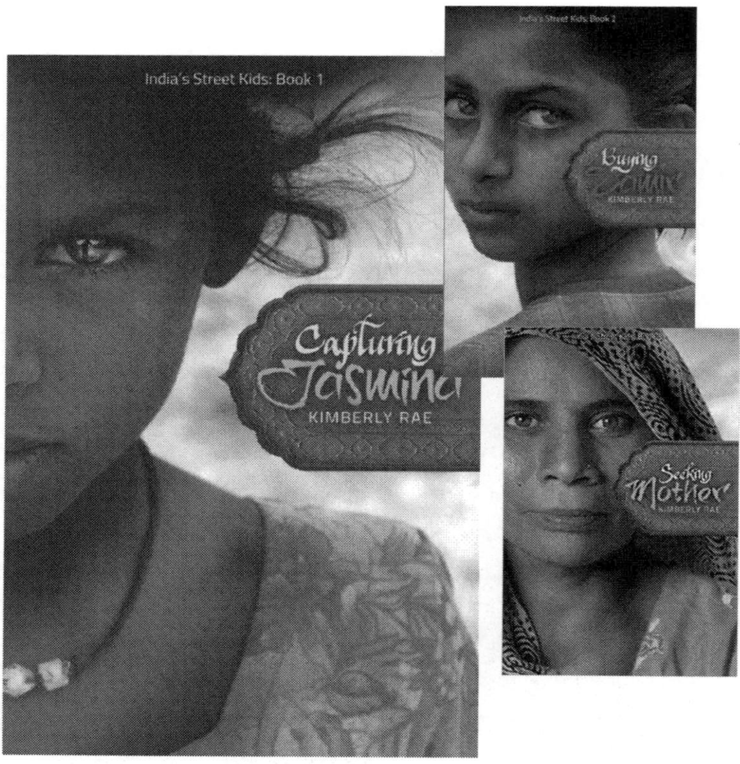

Jasmina and her brother, Samir, are sold by their father to a man promising them an education and good jobs.
They soon discover the man is providing an education, not in a school, but as a slave in his sweatshop garment factory. While Samir quickly submits to his new life of misery, Jasmina never stops planning an escape.
She comes to realize that escape doesn't always mean freedom.
(Series age-appropriate for ages 10-14)

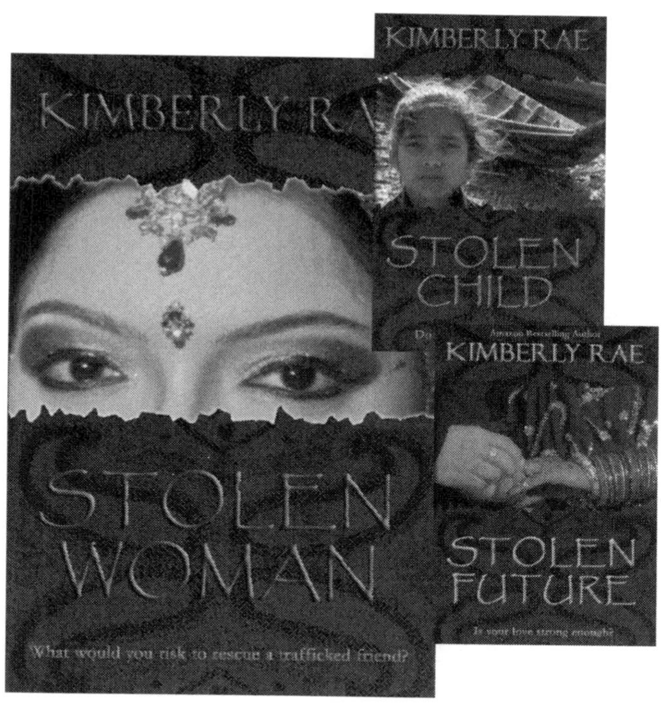

Human Trafficking...Asha knew nothing about it before meeting 16-year-old Rani, stolen from her home and forced into prostitution in Kolkata, India. Asha must help this girl escape, but Mark, a third-generation missionary, keeps warning her away from the red-light district and its workers. Will she ever discover why? And will they ever stop their intense arguments long enough to admit their even more intense feelings for one another?

When Asha sneaks out one last time in a desperate attempt to rescue her friend, someone follows her through the night. Is freedom possible? Or will she, too, become one of the stolen?

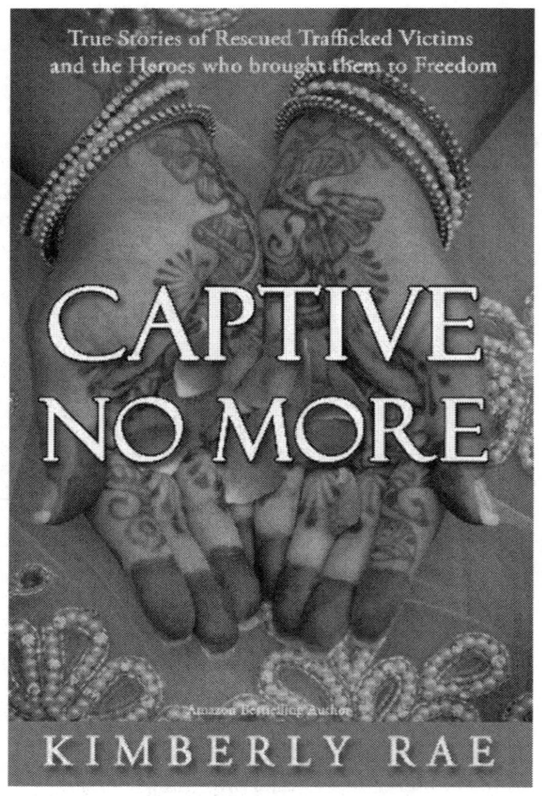

ORDER AUTOGRAPHED BOOKS AT
www.kimberlyrae.com

ABOUT THE AUTHOR

Award-winning author of over 20 books, Kimberly Rae has been published over 200 times and has work in 5 languages.

Rae lived in Bangladesh, Uganda, Kosovo, and Indonesia. She rafted the Nile River, hiked the hills at the base of Mount Everest, and stood on the equator in two continents, but Addison's disease now keeps her in the U.S. She currently writes from her home in Hudson, North Carolina, where she lives with her husband and two young children.

Rae's Stolen Series, suspense and romance novels on fighting human trafficking, are all Amazon bestsellers.

Find out more or order autographed books at
www.kimberlyrae.com.

Made in the USA
San Bernardino, CA
03 September 2017